The Apocalypse Crusade Day 4

War of the Undead

A Zombie Tale by Peter Meredith

Fictional works by Peter Meredith:

Forward

This is the story of the fourth day of the apocalypse as seen from the perspective of those who fought on the front lines of the Quarantine Zone and by those who were trapped within. Although there are easily ten-thousand stories from that time, few give us as full an understanding of the dire nature of the emergency as those depicted within these pages.

I have assembled a short list of the pertinent individuals mentioned within and they are as follows:

Dr. Thuy Lee—Lead researcher at the R & K Pharmaceuticals Walton facility. Using the innovative and inadequately tested Combination Cell Therapy, she discovered a cure for cancer, however her work was sabotaged resulting in the subsequent apocalypse. She is currently on the FBI's most-wanted list and stranded in the Quarantine Zone.

Ryan Deckard—One-time security chief at the Walton facility, now a desperate survivor trying to find a way to save Dr. Lee. Not only is he in love with her, he believes she is humanity's last hope.

Anna Holloway—As a front, Anna worked as a research assistant at the Walton facility. In truth, she was a corporate spy for a competing pharmaceutical company. She is in possession of a stolen vial of Com-cells and, after blackmailing her way out of the Quarantine Zone, she is on the run from the FBI in Baltimore, Maryland.

Lieutenant Eng of the People's Republic of China— Eng is a spy and saboteur. In his undercover role as a research assistant, he made changes to the Com-cells which had worldwide repercussions. Along with Anna, he is on the run from the FBI in Baltimore, Maryland

John Burke—A cancer patient who received only sterile water during the Com-cell trial. He believes that he is immune to the deadly effects of the Com-cells and is desperately trying to stay alive long enough to find his daughter.

Courtney Shaw—A state trooper dispatcher who oversaw the initial quarantine zone around Walton. She has used her guile to keep the disease from spreading.

PFC Max Fowler—Once a soldier in the 42nd Infantry Division, he is now simply one of many thousands struggling to survive on the wrong side of the line.

Marty Aleman—Chief of Staff of the President of the United States. He sees himself as a "king maker," and runs the country using the president as a figurehead.

Jaimee Lynn Burke—Aged eight, she is the daughter of John Burke and the first person to escape the quarantine zone. She is thought to be partially immune to the Com-cells. She has become a deadly, unfeeling, sweet little killer, living and feeding in Hartford, Connecticut.

General Mark Phillips—Commanding Officer of the newly created 7th Army. He is simultaneously fighting three wars: one against the zombies, a second against the Massachusetts National Guard, and lastly, against the President of the United States.

Chapter 1 The Fourth Day

1– Midnight—Shanghai, China

China's Communist Party called it "The single greatest engineering project in the history of mankind," and had proudly dubbed it the Grand Canal. However, the canal was neither a canal and nor was it grand. It was in fact nothing more than a very long ditch. It was true that where the ditch ran up to the Yangtze River, it had filled partially with river water and was a great muddy mess, but three miles of linear bog did not make it a canal.

Although not grand, it was impressive in its length and breadth, but, what was more impressive to most analysts, was the tenaciousness with which it had been built. In just seventy-two hours, a hundred and twelve mile long canyon had been hacked across the face of China.

Tens of millions of peasants had torn at the ground with whatever implements they could find. The lucky ones had shovels, but most used sticks or broken boards or even silverware. Ten-story apartment buildings, what the Party had named "Family share units" were demolished in hours. Wrecking balls were still swinging overhead when a flood of men, women and children swarmed in like ants to grab whatever they could carry.

During the three-day construction of the canal, thousands were injured and killed. The dead were carried off as if they were just another hunk of debris, while the wounded were expected to crawl out of the way, preferably someplace where their screams and moans wouldn't be heard. It was considered impolite to hang around while waiting to die.

The hive mentality of the Chinese served the party well. The Grand Canal was finished not an hour before the horde struck.

At first, the horde was not much of a horde. The millions of zombies didn't sweep across the land in one great wave as the nervous politicians, the frightened soldiers and the terrified peasants had expected. Instead, they came in dribs and drabs; a dozen here, a thousand there. And from across the hundred-yard wide ditch, the zombies didn't seem nearly as frightening as everyone thought they'd be.

For the most part, they looked like drunks in bloody rags. They would stagger and stumble through the piles of refuse and the mounds of dirt on the eastern side of the ditch before falling the seventy feet to the bottom. Some died from the fall, their heads splitting open like rotten coconuts, but most would only break a leg or an arm or a neck. Even the most injured of them would eventually start to crawl across to get at the waiting regiments. They didn't get far. To the delight of everyone, the amped-up soldiers riddled the zombies with bullets before they got close to the other side.

There was a great deal of cheering as if these minor victories were significant in any way.

General Okini, Vice Chairman of the Central Military Commission, was one of only a handful of people who knew better. The horde's true size, an estimated thirty-two million zombies, was a state secret that would fly in the face of the "official" count of three million. For reasons unknown to Okini, three million zombies was considered a palatable number and, supposedly, any more and the will of the people to fight would disintegrate.

For a time, the true horde, a vast sea of undead, was held back at the expense of crippling the nation's ability to defend itself from foreign threats. Every one of the three thousand aircraft in the People's Liberation Army Air Force had been flying around the clock for the last three days. Transport planes made endless runs, hauling every size of bomb in the inventory to the five airfields ringing the Grand Canal. The fighters and the bombers flew sortie after sortie, taking off so loaded down that they frequently scraped the trees at the end of the runways.

They would drop their payloads and fire their bullets into the advancing millions of undead and the carnage was unimaginable—headless bodies, pools and rivers of blood, brains splattered like old cottage cheese everywhere—and yet, Okini, who watched from his circling jet, grew more pensive with each passing hour.

More than half of his planes were obsolete holdovers from the seventies and eighties, and were piloted by men who had, for the last five years, flown the minimum number of hours to retain their flight status, and not a minute more. It showed in the fourteen crashes, the countless near collisions and the lack of precision when unguided weaponry was used.

What was shockingly worse than the piloting were the ordinance mishaps. A surprising number of bombs fell uselessly among the undead, having either been duds or left unarmed by ground crews who were both overworked and not properly trained for the sort of intensity demanded of them. It was embarrassing to Okini.

What enraged him, however was when a thousand-pound bomb fell from a forklift in a staging facility and exploded, setting off a chain reaction that sent a mushroom cloud half a mile into the air. The warehouse was vaporized, a hundred tons of ordinance lost, six planes put out of action and two runways damaged. There were also many deaths, but these did not concern Okini much. He screamed down the chain of command, uselessly venting his anger. No one had a second to spare for corrective action.

Although the Air Force was doing everything it could, airpower alone couldn't stop the horde, and on the fourth day of the apocalypse, the forward edge of the great horde of undead made its way through the rain of fire and metal. The dribs and drabs slowly built up so that tens of thousands would come in mass assaults, striking the ditch in dozens of different places at a time.

Okini attempted to break up the larger assaults with swarms of attack helicopters. Although the Z-10s and Z-19s were primarily antitank platforms, their nose-mounted 30mm autocannons turned the undead into mulch, but still the creatures surged into the ditch in terrifying numbers.

Opposing them were twenty-six million exhausted peasants, armed with an assortment of scrounged-up weapons, most of which were the same tools they'd used for digging. They were desperately afraid and even with the threat of immediate execution for running away hanging over their heads, Okini knew that they would break eventually. To reinforce them, he had managed to move the better part of the 12th and 21st Armies into position; twenty infantry divisions all told. On paper it was impressive sounding, and some in the politburo began making assumptions of victory.

Down on the ground, where the fear was palpable and the chaos unimaginable, there was nothing impressive about the soldiers. They fell into place on the line and frequently passed out from a brutal march that had few equals in all of history. Carrying seventy-pound loads, the soldiers had marched day and night from distances sometimes up to two hundred miles away.

Yes, Okini knew better than to talk about victory. Twenty divisions, minus tanks and APCs which had to be left behind because the roads were fused with endless traffic, amounted to about two-hundred thousand men and, as he had to spread them dangerously thin across the entire line, it was not a lot, especially when he held back a tenth of the number to be used as a fast-reacting reserve unit to shore up any weak point in the line.

Within six hours of initial contact, Okini was forced to send in his first reserve detachment at a nothing of a village called Xiawei. The ditch there had filled completely with wriggling bodies and stiffening corpses, and now the black-eyed fiends could walk across the bloody bridge.

Panic set in as the ammunition began to run out, and the soldiers and peasants came face to face with the undead for the first time. It was pure horror to see the zombies coming on relentlessly, bleeding from a dozen bullet holes or missing huge chunks of flesh. In no time, a rumor swept up and down the line that they were unkillable demons. Some people tried to run away and were shot down, but more often than not, those who reached their breaking point would simply cower uselessly as the creatures bore down upon them.

The battalion-sized reserve force that Okini sent arrived just in time and managed to stem the tide through a furious expenditure of ammunition, and the line held.

There was no time for congratulations. Twenty-six minutes later, Okini had to send in a second force at another spot, and then a third, and so on. Within three hours, there were so many points in his line that were on the verge of being overrun that he had used up the last of his reserves.

"I am no longer a general," he told his assistant, the moment he had sent in his last unit. "I am only a spectator, now."

What he saw made him physically sick. From a height of a thousand feet, the CRJ200 flew down the length of what had been an immense ditch and, from the safety of his private jet, he saw the true scope of what his people were facing. The numbers of undead, even after so many bombs had been dropped on them were still mind-boggling. Okini stared with his mouth hanging slack.

At the Yangtze, he ordered the pilot back along the ditch and he forced himself to look down and confront the inevitability of the situation. "Evacuate the peasants from here to Xeuhen," he ordered.

The order lacked substance and direction, and his assistant paused before relaying it down the chain of command. "Evacuate them to where, sir?"

"West," Okini said, simply.

"But there won't be enough men to fight," his assistant replied, skating right over the edge of insubordination.

For a moment, Okini felt a blinding fury that he had never known before. If there had been a screen door on the jet, he would have tossed his assistant out of it. The fury subsided as fast as it had come. "Give the order and then I'm going to need to speak to General Fenghe."

Okini's assistant, a young colonel with a flair for organization and precise attention to detail, wilted in his chair. "General Fenghe," he said, as if the name belonged to *Dizang* himself, the ruler of the ten hells. He swallowed and tried to come to grips with the order. "General Fenghe…Commanding General of the Strategic Rocket Force."

"Yes," Okini said, his eyes straying back to the window. "It's the only way."

The three DF-16 Dongfeng ballistic missiles with their nuclear payloads were launched sixty-three minutes later.

2–1:59 a.m.

Truong Mai woke slowly, cracking one crusted-over eye, but seeing nothing. Everything was dreadfully black. It was so black that under any other circumstances, Truong would have been frightened down to his core. He was too angry to be frightened. Though what he was angry about, he didn't know. He was just angry. Furiously angry. It was as if there was a fire inside his skull, burning along every neuron.

Groaning, he tried to sit up, only he could not. It felt as though a heavy blanket, one that weighed hundreds of pounds covered him from head to toe. "Tsao de…" His snarled curse was shoved back down his throat as dirt poured into his mouth. He didn't question the dirt or why he was under it. That part of his brain was ash.

A few days before, Truong had been a shoe salesman. He owned a musty little hole in the wall shop that smelled of leather and feet. It was so small that he couldn't afford to carry too much of a variety, and so he sold sandals and office shoes, both in only two colors, brown and black.

Officially, he'd been in the city of Xuancheng to visit one of his of cousins, which he did twice a month. Unofficially, he was there to purchase shoes at the city

11

morgues. Once the blood was washed off the shoes and they were newly shined, no one cared where they came from, or so Truong assumed. He never advertised where his supplier was located.

That was the old Truong. Somehow, that man had managed, through a combination of deception, determination and amazing luck, to stay just two steps ahead of the rampaging horde of undead streaming out of Shanghai. For three days, he had run from them. Nearing exhaustion, he had stumbled up to a low rise overlooking the newly dug Grand Canal and saw the army deployed across from him.

Truong's skinny legs quivered and his heart sank. Even though he hadn't been infected at that point, he knew they would never let him pass.

And so, caught between a horde of undead and the full might of the Chinese Army, he had done the only thing possible: he crawled into a cement pipe to hide. The walking corpses came soon after. Truong's only view was row after endless row of stumbling feet. Many were only bleeding stumps, yet he also saw many still wore their shoes and he wondered briefly at the fortune walking by. How much were all those shoes worth?

The bombers came next, and the ear-splitting explosions knocked all thought of shoes out of his head.

The heat and the smoke became too much to bear and Truong fainted. When he woke, it was to the sound of gunfire, torrents of gunfire that nothing could possibly live through. Still the zombies came. Hours went by and Truong grew terribly thirsty—thirsty enough to drink the foul, brackish water creeping down the pipe.

It tasted as if raw sewage had been mixed in with the water when it was, in reality, zombie blood he was drinking. Truong was finally infected and he was just starting to feel the madness closing in, when the first nuke went off and the world turned to soot and cinder.

The pipe in which he'd been hiding shivered into pieces when the shock of the explosion rolled across the earth, turning the mantle of the earth's crust fluid and causing the land to swell and crest like an ocean wave. The heat was beyond even his new zombie ability to withstand and once more he passed out.

Now, half an hour later, he pushed his hand up through the debris and furiously clawed his way out of his premature grave and into a land of flame. He didn't think it was possible, but seeing the afterglow of a nuclear bomb only made him angrier still. A scream tore from his throat. It was directed westward where everything was still beautiful and the land still green, and the people…the stupid, filthy peasants were still smiling and happy. Or so he guessed.

They had done this to him. *They* had bombed him and buried him and burned him. "And they'll pay," he seethed in a rasping voice. Truong started forward to where the Grand Canal lay. Unopposed, he crossed it, walking on the heaped and burning backs of the corpses. He then marched through the litter of dead soldiers. As he did, he stared—none of them had faces left.

When the nuke had gone off with the light of ten-thousand suns, a wall of fire, the *real* Great Wall of China, had washed over them and melted their features. Truong tried to laugh, however the air was poison and shriveled his lungs. He could no longer laugh or shout. He breathed as an asthmatic would, making a strident noise like a broken accordion.

Still, he plodded on through fire and heat and radiation. His flesh blistered and ran with black ooze. Whatever hair that hadn't burned away slid off his head like hot cheese. He was a horror to look upon, and if there had been anyone left alive, his appearance would have been enough to drive them insane.

But there wasn't anyone left alive, and there wasn't anything left alive, either. Even the birds had been flash-fried in midair.

Nothing lived, not even the zombies, except Truong that is and he was as black hearted and black-eyed as any of them had been. And he was hungry. He was maddeningly hungry. All he could think about besides the pain and the rage was his hunger as he set himself walking west into the heart of China, and unlike the millions of exhausted peasants who had been given an hour head start, Truong would never tire. He would walk for a year if that's what it took.

Hours later, the mindless beast that had once been Truong Mai had his first taste of clean human meat. It wouldn't be his last.

Chapter 2

Once more, Dr. Thuy Lee edged to the window and eased herself into a half-squat so she could see above the sill. It was difficult to make out anything. The dark night was intense, only shadows layered on shadow, painted against the ground; the trees were lines of the blackest ink. Still she stared, her eyes squinting, hoping against hope that those natural shadows were all she was going to see.

As she stared, she saw something move in the dark. It was man-shaped and walked slowly. *They* were still out there. The zombies.

She hated that term: zombie. It was immature and tasteless and led to the impression that there was something supernatural about the people who had been infected with the tainted Com-cells.

Thankfully, there wasn't anything supernatural about them, which was a good thing since they were hard enough to kill without bringing anything magical into the mix. Not that she wanted to kill them, really. If she had the opportunity, she would cure them if she could. It was a distinct possibility. As far as she could tell, what was causing the personality changes and the hyper-aggression was the prodigious and unrestrained replication of the Com-Cells along the neural pathways.

Despite this, there didn't seem to be any actual cellular damage to the infected persons. All of the lower functions of the involuntary nervous system: breathing, digestion, heart rate, etc, had not been affected, which suggested that once the Com-cells were removed, a person's brain would return to their previous mental state.

She hoped.

Of course, for her, utterly alone, completely defenseless and trapped in the Zone, it was all a rather moot point.

Thuy had been left behind. Ryan Deckard and Courtney Shaw had sailed away in a hot air balloon three hours before and now Thuy was at a loss of what to do, exactly. She was stuck in the Zone, possibly forever. This wasn't hyperbole either. She had tried every possible way to get out of the Zone and had failed time and again.

It seemed to her that staying put was somewhat logical. It had to be better than kicking around in the Zone as she had been for the last couple of days. If she left the meager safety of the school, she *might* find other people who were just as stuck as she was, but more than likely she would take off in her borrowed RAV4 and either run out of gas in the middle of nowhere, or she would blunder into one of the larger groups of infected persons. If the latter happened, she would be pulled out of the vehicle and eaten alive, and if the former happened then she would be in pretty much the exact same position as she was now, except she'd be without the possibility of transportation.

"Logically, staying put is the correct thing to do," she stated clearly as if speaking to a room full of students.

Although she proclaimed her motive for staying as "logical," there was a childish part of her that was wholly illogical. That part of her held out the foolish hope that Deckard would come back for her. When that part of her spoke, it came out in a mumbled, "He should have been here by now."

It had been three hours since she had watched him float away, dangling from the bottom of a hot air balloon and in that time, she had worked out the relatively simple math involved: with an average wind speed of three and half miles an hour, the balloon had crossed into Massachusetts airspace one hour and forty-five minutes ago, and that was more than enough time to hike back for her.

She pictured him striding along in that purposeful, long-legged way of his and thought: *Maybe he stopped to get more ammunition.* Was that wishful thinking on her part? She hoped not.

With a sigh, she slipped back down from the window and stared at the black wedges on her feet. She'd been wearing them for most of the last day. They had been useful as part of a "disguise" to get into Hartford, but since then they'd been killing her feet. With a groan, she pulled them off and saw the blisters that had formed. Two were running clear fluid; it looked like her feet were crying.

"Feels like it, too," she said, forcing herself to stand back up. "He might come, and then again, he might not. If he doesn't, I'm going to need different shoes."

In reality, Thuy needed a lot more than just new shoes to survive. She also needed a change of clothes, preferably something warmer and more rugged than the torn and stained blouse and slacks she had on. She would also need food, water, and shelter. "And somewhere to sleep." She was dog tired and the more she thought about sleep, the harder it was for her to stay awake.

"But first, I need a change of clothes." She wanted to be prepared before sleeping, "just in case."

Finding a change of clothes wasn't as difficult as she thought it would be, especially since everything was wide open.

The high school had been evacuated two days before in the middle of classes as the situation in Poughkeepsie had deteriorated rapidly. With cell phones ringing nonstop from worried parents, there had been an atmosphere of panic among the students and teachers, and the school drained of people in minutes.

Fear was so rampant that one teacher was almost run over as she tried to control the exodus from the parking lot in an orderly fashion.

For the teens, once they were behind the wheels of their cars, the passing authority of one cardigan-wearing teacher was utterly disregarded and with wild abandon, they drove across the front lawn of the school and down the sidewalks.

The teachers and admin personnel were infected by the growing panic as well, and followed so closely on the heels of the students that, in one instance, a bus driver had tried to leave before his bus was full. As much as the students wanted to get home, they wouldn't leave without their friends, neighbors and in many cases their siblings.

When the driver wouldn't wait, he was attacked by the students, who threw books and sharpened pencils at him, eventually forcing him off the bus. "Drive it yourself, you little shits," he snarled and stomped away.

Fifteen-year-old Coty Bill didn't hesitate and jumped in the driver's seat. He didn't have either a driver's license or a permit, but he'd been driving his daddy's tractor since he was twelve and didn't see all that much difference between the two machines.

The bus driver hadn't been the only one to leave in a hurry. The head custodian, a slovenly man who made fourteen dollars an hour, and who was maybe worth a third of that because he spent most of his time at the school "secretly" leering at the young girls, left even before Coty Bill. He locked the front doors behind the principal, walked directly through the school and was halfway to his aging Kia Sedona before he slowed and glanced back. It was part of his job to completely secure the school and there were six other exits that he hadn't checked.

"It'll be fine," he said to himself. It wasn't the first time he had forgotten to lock the place down, though this was the first time he did it sober.

It was his desire to get the hell out of there that allowed Thuy to get into the school at all. To her great relief, she had found a side door propped open by a rock.

Now the lack of locked doors helped her again in her search for new clothes. She ghosted through the dark halls on bare feet, slipping into the main offices without any problem at all.

And there, sitting in a big cardboard box labeled: Lost and Found, she discovered an entire heap of clothing. She picked up a shirt and her lip curled. The shirt was a rainbow of ugly stripes with a bubble caption that read: *Got me Some!*

"Got me some of what?" Thuy really didn't want to know and tossed it aside and poked through the box some more. Everything was so childish that Thuy gave her filthy blouse a second look. After a trip through the Hartford sewers, it was disgusting. With a sigh, she stripped and began trying to piece together an outfit in the dark. Thankfully, because of her height, just a few inches over five foot, and her trim form, she was able to fit into almost everything, although there was not that much to choose from.

Eventually, she found a blue top that had the word "Juicy" stretched tightly across her breasts, a pair of pink and silver sneakers, and blue jeans that were cut so uncomfortably low that she couldn't bend half way over without showing her underwear. "Kids today," she muttered and then went in search of a jacket or coat. She wasn't just cold, she also didn't like the idea of running across someone while wearing that shirt.

There were no coats in the lost and found, so she went room to room until she managed to find a man's sports coat hanging in a science lab. The coat really wasn't all that sporty in her opinion. It was checkered in brown and a slightly lighter shade of brown, had leather elbow patches, also brown, and it smelled of chalk, which for a woman who had spent most of her life in school, was reassuring.

She fell asleep in the principal's office on a leather couch, wrapped in that coat, and for a time she felt safe. It wasn't a zombie that woke her, it was the sound of someone thudding into lockers.

"Fuuuck, thas loud." The voice, a drunken muddle, had come from a man. A second later, came the unmistakable sound of a baseball bat being dropped. Thuy's sense of security left her in that second. There were no actual laws within the Zone. There was only survival of the fittest, and *everything* was up for grabs for someone strong enough to take it and Thuy wasn't strong enough to stop anyone from taking anything.

2- Walnutport, Pennsylvania

For the last two hours, the old man hadn't been
Lieutenant General Phillips, commanding officer of the
newly created 7th Army, he had been a soldier, and an
American, and a man defending his family, though his
family was far away and scattered like most military
families were.

He and the thin, thin line of soldiers and scraped up
civilians had made their stand along the Lehigh River, ten
miles west of the New Jersey border. It had been a crazy
mix of people who had fought in that deeply wooded river
valley. Alongside the Pennsylvania National Guard were
state patrolman and firemen, and there were also farmers
and insurance salesmen, realtors and hairstylists. Three
different fraternities had driven down from Penn State in a
rolling caravan, and twenty-six members of Boy Scout
Troop 41 out of Palmerton had biked twenty-three miles in
order to fight.

Phillips hadn't bothered to ask any of the Boy Scouts
if they had permission slips from their mothers. The
smaller boys ran ammo, while the older ones took up
their .243s and fired into the mass of undead just as the
adults were doing, while above all of them jets came like
clockwork lighting up the night with explosions and
napalm.

The line was long and dreadfully thin in places,
sometimes just a few men were all there was between the
deadly masses and the interior of the country, and for those
two hours as the third day of the apocalypse became the
fourth, the country had never been so close to utter
annihilation. But gradually more people, men as well as
women, came sliding down the line, filling in the thinner
areas until Phillips decided he could take a step back.

"Getting tired, old man?" Milo Musial asked. He had a
headache thumping that felt worse than a rotten tooth, and
it was making him nervous, because wasn't that how the

black-eyed plague began? A terrible headache, then inexplicable rage, and finally an unholy hunger for human flesh? Anxious about showing the least anger, he smiled up at the old man. It wasn't a fake smile; Milo was also a soldier now and a foxhole camaraderie had built between the two.

"Yes," Phillips answered, in total honesty. "But there'll be no rest for the wicked. Besides, I have some pull. I can get an M1A1 Abrams to replace me."

Milo glanced into the mass of dead creatures scattered in front of them before asking, "What's that? Is that a tank or something?" When Phillips nodded, Milo asked, "Can I drive it?"

Like a father who had no intention of following through, Phillips said, "We'll see, maybe. Take care, Milo."

Slowly, with the sounds of battle growing dim behind him, Phillips made his way towards the rear where everything was so muted that he stuck a finger in his ear and gave it a wiggle. It had been years since he had fired a gun without ear protection and now he was hearing the world as if his head was in an invisible fishbowl.

Even when he said to himself, "Where is everyone?" it sounded muffled. The command tent he had been using was deserted, forcing him to commandeer a Mercedes Benz that sat on the edge of the road leading into the town of Walnutport. Driving into town, he came across a leaderless mishmash of civilians and soldiers heading towards the sound of battle.

"Where's the C.P.?" Phillips asked.

A PFC jerked his thumb back the way he'd been walking. "At the Burger King, but don't expect to get a Whopper or nothing. As usual the officers are bogarting all the good stuff."

"You can whine once you've done something to deserve a Whopper," Philips snapped. His hearing was good enough to catch the bellyaching. "The front line is only a half-mile away. Double time it." The PFC didn't need to see the three stars on the general's collar to know he was mouthing off to the wrong guy.

He gave a quick, "Yes, sir," and jogged off, with his group following after.

Phillips drove the rest of the way into town, cursing the private because all he could think about was a damned hamburger. He was thankful to see that the restaurant was shut down or he would have had to ask for a super-sized #6 and bitch about the wasted manpower, at the same time.

The command post was practically empty. Phillip's two-hour old order to "man the line" had been obeyed to such an extent that there was a National Guard colonel, whom Phillips had never seen before, trying to direct the entire western flank of the 7th Army with only a skeleton crew of eight communications specialists. They were so busy and the situation so urgent that when Phillips entered the restaurant and a sergeant called the room to attention, only two others snapped to.

"At ease," Phillips said. "Back to work, please."

The colonel didn't bother to introduce himself. He held out a blocky sat-phone to Phillips and said, "It's General Heider. He's looking for a sit-rep."

"Hell, I'm looking for a sit-rep," Phillips said, with a snort. He took the phone and held it against his chest. "What's the line look like? Are we holding?"

"The Penn border is holding everywhere but Philadelphia. We thought that the city would hold longer than it did, but from what I gather, there are so many people fleeing that we can't get reinforcements in. Also, the entire right flank is up in the air because of what's happening in Jersey." He didn't need to explain the chaos of New Jersey. Practically overnight, civilization seemed to have died there. It was a madhouse. People weren't just fighting the zombies, they were killing each other left and right over food or weapons or shelter.

Phillips thanked the colonel and then grunted into the phone, "How are you General Heider?"

"Fucked," Heider replied. "The President is going to want some good news when he wakes up or the nukes will fly."

"So, you're saying I've got five hours to think up a lie? That shouldn't be too hard. Listen, sir, I've got to get a handle on things here. I'll call you right back." It was three hours before he could even think about calling Heider back and, even then, he didn't since he didn't have good news to give the president.

Despite the heroics of the individuals coming to the aid of their country, there just weren't enough of them and worse, the influx of volunteers was sporadic, coming in spurts so that there were too many men in one area and too few in another. Usually even the local commanders couldn't tell how many people they had on the line.

And this meant supplying them properly was nearly impossible. When the incredible variations in ammo type were factored in, things went right out the window. Allentown was nearly lost for want of .270 ammo. Four years previously the Savage Arms Company had run a promotion in Allentown for their .270 rifles and had sold hundreds. It seemed as if every other man was carrying a .270 and it wasn't long before they all began to run out of ammunition.

Many of the men had to turn their guns around and use them as clubs.

Phillips didn't think it was possible, but the coordination with the Air Force was even more chaotic. Without a central command on the Pennsylvania front, the Air Force was simply sending planes over the lines loaded for bear. If the pilots picked up a signal directing them to drop their payload at a given spot, they would. If not they would find the biggest mass of undead and drop what they had. For reasons unknown, certain areas hadn't seen a plane all night, while in others they saw too many. Everything from North Wales to Hatfield was nothing but a smoking crater.

The air situation was so out of control that when the first fleet of B52s rumbled overhead, everyone in the

23

Burger King went to the windows and stared up, knowing that one minor mistake with those bad boys would not only seal their fate but also that of the entire country.

"Colonel," Phillips said quickly. "Get me anyone from the Air Force. I don't care who, just someone."

Chapter 3

1– 3:22 a.m.
—Stockbridge, Massachusetts

Ryan Deckard came to realize that the people of Massachusetts simply weren't fucking around. They were protecting their borders with everything in their arsenal.

The stolen balloon cruised like a giant soap bubble two hundred feet off the ground, heading on an easterly course that would take them just south of the town of Stockbridge. Deckard's heart was in agony over leaving Thuy behind. He had hoped to land the balloon not far from the high school and go back for her, however, by the time he was able to shimmy up the very skinny anchor rope as it swung wildly over countless undead, he and Courtney Shaw were so high in the air that the zombies looked like nothing but moaning shadows.

"Get us back down," he had said, the second he dropped into the wicker basket. Just at the moment, he had no idea how high they were. Courtney was staring at the burner contraption in confusion while he was gazing at his hands. They were red and raw.

"I'm not sure how," Courtney answered. "These controls, well, they're not really controls exactly. I can turn this and that stops the gas." She turned the valve all the way to the right and the flame heating the air shut off. "But other than that, I don't think there's much we can do until the air cools enough…" Courtney suddenly looked over the side of the basket and her face went white. "We're still going up." She sounded afraid, as if the balloon would continue to go up forever.

Deckard had collapsed in the bottom of the basket and now he groaned his way to his feet. Like Courtney had, he squinted up at the controls, but couldn't tell what was what. This close to the border, he was nervous about using a flashlight, but he had to chance it. It seemed logical that there had to be a way of raising and lowering the balloon that was more efficient than simply turning the gas on and off.

He whisked the beam from his stubby Maglight all over the blower and the contraption that released the gas, however he didn't see anything that would help. "This is ridiculous," he said, tugging on the second valve. He knew already that it was the oxygen regulator and that it wouldn't do anything, and he was right. "You would think that it…"

"Make it go down!" Courtney suddenly gasped. She had sunk down into the basket, her fingers gripping the wicker. "Deckard, please, please, do something, just get us down."

"Are you afraid of heights…wait, never mind. It'll be okay, Courtney. I just have to figure out how to make a hole in the…"

"A hole!"

She looked as though she was about to barf. "Okay, not a hole," Deckard said, running his hand through his hair and gazing up again. He really didn't know what to do about her. She was perfectly safe, unlike Thuy. "I'll get us down, just stay right there and try not to think about it. I know, maybe you should just close your eyes and imagine yourself closer to the ground. It'll make you feel better."

"Yeah, yeah, I can do that. Just be careful." She scrunched her eyes down and Deckard turned back to the rational problem of putting a hole in the balloon so they could get back on the ground as fast as possible. They had been rising precipitously and now they were high enough into the atmosphere that the winds had picked up. From a gentle three miles an hour, they were now being pushed east at twelve.

Deckard couldn't tell how fast they were going but with the balloon canted to the side, he knew it wouldn't be long before they were over the edge of the Zone and into Massachusetts, and if they weren't careful they'd be halfway to the ocean before he got them down.

Once more he shone the light overhead and this time he saw a rope that had been caught up in the risers. It went straight to the top of the canopy, but passed through a ring and was attached to a dozen smaller ropes. It was called a parachute valve and Deckard saw that it could only have one function. He climbed up onto the edge of the basket and snagged the rope. With one pull, it slid back the panels at the top of the canopy. The sensation of dropping was immediate and Courtney let out a little screech.

"What are you doing up there?"

"Getting us down to the ground." He was about to step back down when the view stopped him. They were nearing the edge of the Quarantine Zone; a half mile away a battle was raging and he saw that, at their rate of descent, with the wind at their backs, they were going to land in full view of hundreds of soldiers and thousands of zombies. And that wasn't good.

Deck pulled harder on the parachute valve and the wind began whistling through the rigging as they dropped. "We're going to set down," he told Courtney. "It's going to be a little closer to the line than I wanted."

Courtney whimpered, still with her eyes shut. She felt as though she were coming unglued and didn't understand it. She had never been afraid of heights before, or at least this afraid. Then again, she had never been this high before either. The highest she had ever been was the three-meter high dive at the pool in Poughkeepsie, and that had been one time. It had turned her legs to jelly and from then on, she had subconsciously avoided anything to do with heights.

"Try not to worry," Deckard said, reaching over and turning the burner to low. "We'll touch down pretty softly. I'll hit the burners right before we land. It'll be the softest..." Something on the ground caught his attention. He saw what looked like four or five blinking lights which were quickly followed by new whistling sounds coming from the balloon.

They were being shot at!

His first impulse was to jump down into the basket and cower, only wicker wasn't any sort of cover. He was just as vulnerable standing on the edge of the basket with a hundred-foot fall awaiting him.

The balloon loomed. It was an immense target that would only get easier to hit, the closer to the ground they got and if they took too many more hits…he didn't want to think about that.

Immediately, he released the parachute valve and twisted the throttle wide open. A torrent of blue flame roared into the envelope, filling it once again and sending them skyward. But not fast enough. They were still being shot at and now pieces of wicker started blasting up, sending splinters everywhere.

"What are you doing?" Courtney cried, somehow associating Deckard's re-inflation of the balloon with the strange vibrations in the basket and the flying chunks of wicker. Then she saw holes start to appear in the canvas of the balloon. "Are they sh…hooting at us?"

"Looks that way," Deckard said and then calmly started to yank the ends of the knots that held the sandbags to the side of the basket. They seemed to fall for a long time before they thudded into the ground with the same sound a body would make, or so Courtney assumed.

Courtney was just about at her limit. The thought of falling was nerve-shattering, the idea of heights was nauseating, and the very real possibility of one of the bullets striking the propane tank and catching the wicker on fire was so absolutely terrifying that she jumped up and screamed, "Don't shoot! Oh, God, please stop!"

Her scream was filled with such fear that no one could hear it and not be moved. The blinking ceased. Courtney stood at the rail breathing heavily, afraid to move for fear of putting her foot through the basket. With so many holes in it, she had no faith in the integrity of the wicker. She had less faith in the canvas. Looking up, she saw in the light of the blue flame a couple of dozen holes.

"Oh, God," she whispered. "Stop, Deckard. That's enough. We could…we could pop."

Pop? The dark hid the rolling of Deckard eyes. "Sure, let's get this turned off. We wouldn't want to chance popping a balloon of this size." His real reason for turning off the flames was that it illuminated them, making them an even more obvious target. He glanced over the side and saw that they had climbed to about eight hundred feet.

With the wind picking up and pushing them eastward again, he thought that if no one shot at them for another half-minute or so, they stood a good chance of getting away. But then what? He had left Thuy behind. It made him ill thinking about her. As frightened as Courtney was, Thuy had to be more so. Being in the Zone was a grinding experience and as they floated over the line and Deckard looked down, he felt a weight come off of him.

They were over Massachusetts airspace now and he was free. For the first time in four days, he was free to go where he wanted, free to sleep deeply, and free to take a leak without having to look over his shoulder. He was free but not completely so. There was something about Thuy that drew his eyes back to the darkened land. He couldn't leave her back there. He knew that if he left her, it would eat away at him.

"Son of a bitch," he muttered, wishing he could be done with this entire business, but knowing that he couldn't.

"What is it?" Courtney asked. She still had a grip on the edge of the basket.

"Nothing I just…" He stopped as he saw that he wasn't quite as free as he had assumed. Although they were now a few hundred yards beyond the line and technically out of the Zone, they were being followed. A quarter mile off and far below were headlights moving slowly along a route parallel to theirs.

Quickly, he reached up and turned the burner to full once more. If they were going to be subject to the winds, it was better to run where they were fastest.

"Deck, what are you doing?" Courtney asked. "We can land now. Right? They can't do anything to us. We made it."

"I think they can do anything they want to us," he answered. "It's not like getting on base in baseball. We're not safe until no one's after us. But we should be okay. If we get high enough, they'll lose track of us in the dark."

Courtney could only nod, her eyes locked on the headlights as they tracked along with the balloon. At a thousand feet, the headlights began to look small. They were joined by two others and now a beam of light swept up. As if it were a laser beam, Courtney shrank down in the basket until only her eyes were level with the edge.

Next to the beam were more of the blinking lights. The twinkling came slow and regular, telling Deckard that someone had a hunting rifle trained on them. It was a long shot to make and getting longer with every passing second. The bullets must have missed and soon the headlights were on the move again, trying to get closer.

Deckard shut off the burner and crouched next to Courtney as they drifted in silence. The vehicles chasing them zigzagged around a few farms and then paused to use the searchlight again. It was an odd sensation watching the beam of light swinging back and forth. It reminded him of the black and white war movies he used to watch as a kid.

The light eventually found them, however they had drifted over a wide swath of forest where the vehicles couldn't follow.

Courtney let out a long breath and then peeked over the side. "I-I never knew I was this afraid of heights. Isn't that funny? I-I mean I never liked the idea of ladders but this, this is something else. Can we get lower, please?"

"No problem." Like a swashbuckler, he climbed up onto the edge of the airship and pulled on the parachute valve. He made sure to gently pull on it to keep her from freaking out. Once more the air started to whistle along the canvas. Underneath that noise was a rumble that began to build. It was horribly familiar and struck them with a sudden fear, Deckard stood on the edge of the basket and watched as a creature, much like a modern dragon, roared suddenly out of the night, heading right at them.

From its mouth came a gout of flame and then, before he knew whether or not he had been hit by the flying lead, it was a mile past him and turning on a gentle arc. It was an F15C Strike Eagle based out of Otis Air National Guard Base on Cape Cod and two quick bursts from its M61 Vulcan Gatling gun had torn ragged holes through the canvas.

Courtney began screaming, which matched the air screaming from the balloon as it plummeted to the earth. They needed all the lift they could get, so Deckard shut the parachute valve and turned the burner on full blast. It lit up the sky and still they fell. He was simultaneously afraid that they were falling too fast and, as the Eagle banked over the Zone and came roaring back, not fast enough.

There was no way they could withstand another burst from the Gatling gun, and there was no way they could stop it, either.

Almost casually, the pilot swung wide before straightening for its next strafing run. He was five hundred feet up and this was, technically, an air-to-air combat kill —the pilot was itching to pull the trigger. With such an immense and easy target, he had eyeballed his first shot. This time, he had a beautiful thermal image. It was a bright fin of light against a black background and when he fired twice more, it went up in a great gout of flame.

"Scratch one bogey," he drawled.

2—Taconic High School, New York

Thuy froze on the couch, not knowing what to do. A man was coming towards her and she had an instinctive fear of him that echoed back through eons of human existence. As the bat clanked on the tile, coming closer and closer, she found that her fear was so great she couldn't move. Her one hope was that he would just keep going.

There were a hundred doors in the building and yet he opened the door that read: *Principal Claudia Stevens*.

"Oh, the fucking big mama's office," he said, standing in the doorway. The room was more shadow than fact and

31

he didn't see Thuy lying just ten feet to his right, but she saw him. It was difficult to look past the wooden bat, but when she tore her eyes from it, she saw a man who had hit his peak years ago.

His brown hair was lank and thin, starting well back on his forehead. He had sallow skin, a gut that sagged over his belt and when he burped, she smelled rotten teeth and whiskey. At first, she thought he was wearing a green jumpsuit that was cinched around with a belt, however it wasn't a jumpsuit, but a green uniform and not the sort of green that a soldier would wear.

"Yes, Mrs. Stevens. No Mrs. Stevens. What the fuck kind of a name is Stevens for a girl, anyway? Stevens is a fucking boy's name." He went to the desk, plunked the bat down and sat down in the principal's chair. He thought for a moment about putting his feet up, however that seemed like too much work. He drummed dirty nails on the surface of the desk and sneered, "What kinda secrets you got Ol' Miss Claudia Stevens? You got some kiddie porn in here?" It was ugly wishful thinking on his part. He liked the girls young. He liked them small and weak. With a thrill in him, he went searching, opening drawers, rifling through them until he saw, with bitter disappointment, that they only contained files and notes on staff and students and budgets. It was all bullshit. Useless bullshit.

His name was Jerry Weir. He was the custodian who had left the school unlocked two days before. During most of those previous fifty-something hours he had either been drunk or high and the only reason he'd survived this long was that his mobile home sat on a parcel of land far out in the middle of nowhere.

But now he was out of weed and like most addicts, he couldn't function without a little something. Disappointed in the lack of kiddie porn, he was about to go to the locked filing cabinet against the wall where the most questionable confiscated items were kept.

He stopped when he saw Thuy. Given their surroundings and his limited world view, she looked to him like a scared and quite defenseless little girl. "Oh, hey," he said, his soft tone incongruous with the look on his face. He grinned like a fox eating a tendon off the bone. "You okay? All alone, huh? Don't be afraid, it's me, Mr. Weir. But, hey you can call me Jerry."

As he spoke, he came around the desk. Thuy sat up, quickly. She put out a hand, palm up. "And you may call me Doctor Lee," she said, her voice pitched high.

Jerry stopped abruptly. "Doctor? What, is that a joke? You aren't a doc…" He saw her hair was jet black and that her eyes were wide and her cheek bones were arching and, she was beautiful. "You're right, you're not a student here. The only Asian chick who goes here is that Cho girl."

Thuy was quiet for some time, not knowing exactly what to say. "Yes, I'm not a student," she said, sliding off the couch and easing away from Jerry, her hands out in front of her, wishing to God she had kept one of the empty guns.

He liked how she started shaking when he placed his hand on the barrel of the bat. It made him feel strange and strong. He'd had fantasies that started just like this. "If you're not a student, then what are you doing here? And why are you dressed like that? Are you trying to be sexy on purpose?"

She looked down at herself and saw that the word "Juicy" was showing. She pulled the jacket closed and backed toward the door, saying, "No, of course not."

"Really? You just happened to be here, laying on the couch, looking like that?" In Jerry's mind, it didn't seem possible that she was there by accident. He didn't want it to be possible. In the last few days, reality had been bent into a pretzel, and now this woman had been thrust into his life, all alone and helpless. She seemed like gift, and with his head swimming in alcohol and the fumes of the pot riding high in his system, all he could think about was touching her.

If he did, who would know? It wasn't like there were cops around. There was no one around. No one at all.

He reached out and touched the girl's lapel. When she flinched, it gave him a new thrill. "Don't be like that. It's fate that brung us here, together. Do you believe that? I mean, you're here, I'm here. We really are all alone. Allll alone." He traced the lapel again, touching her breast through the fabric. It wasn't just her tit he felt. Her heart was beating like mad.

Her fear was intoxicating. It brought something out of him; something animalistic, something hot but very, very wrong. It brought out something he had never contemplated before, because, before it had always been something illegal. Now, there were no laws and that just opened up all sorts of possibilities, didn't it?

Thuy was a tiny, bird-like thing compared to this slovenly brute, and she was under no illusions. She was at the extreme range of vulnerability and knew it. "I'll scream," she said.

Jerry smiled, showing off his unbrushed teeth. This new part of him, which, in truth wasn't new at all, wanted her to scream. If she screamed…if he could *make* her scream, didn't that mean he controlled her? Yes, obviously. He could make her scream if he wished. And he could make her cry and make her laugh at his jokes, and fetch his beer and suck his dick. And he could make her do it all with a smile.

That was evolution, wasn't it? Hadn't they been teaching survival of the fittest in this school since before he had come to work there? Wasn't that the rule in the animal kingdom; might makes right, and all that? And weren't we all just animals?

That's how Jerry heard it.

"Go ahead and scream. No one will hear you. It'll be like that 'tree falling in the forest' crap." He stepped closer so that his belly pushed into her, pinning her to the door with his filthy bulk. "If a girl screams and there's no one to hear it, did she really scream?"

She was deathly afraid and he could feel an involuntary scream brewing up. It only added to his lust and for the first time he came close to understanding what all those fucked-up feminists were always going on about —"rape was all about power," they said. They were wrong. Rape wasn't always about power, sometimes it was and sometimes it was just about some guy getting his rocks off.

In this case it was both. A happy accident Jerry decided as he slid his hand down Thuy's body.

"I'll scream," she repeated, with more conviction. "And someone will hear." His hand stopped on her flat stomach and for just a moment he was nervous. It was possible that she was there with others.

"Yeah, who?"

She turned to the window where the shadows moved. "Them."

With his new lust consuming him, he had forgotten about the zombies, though after the briefest consideration, he decided that they didn't matter. They weren't going to derail this train because there wasn't a chance in hell that she'd scream loud enough to attract them. "You wouldn't," he sneered. "They'll eat you little girl. They'll eat you right up. But I wouldn't hurt you like that. I would be good to you."

"Prove it," Thuy challenged, doing her best to keep her lips from quivering. "Prove that you'll be good. Take your hands off me."

Jerry scoffed at the idea and with a smarmy smile playing on his face, he slid his hands down to her crotch and gave her a squeeze. In response, Thuy screamed her head off.

Chapter 4

1– 3:36 a.m.
—Stockbridge, Massachusetts

Just as the clouds scudded in front of the moon, turning the dark night even darker, the F-15 lit up the balloon for the second time with its Vulcan. This time it had a heat signature. Deckard had the burner going full force, sending a gout of blue flame six feet into the shredded canopy. The pilot couldn't miss and he didn't.

Forty M53 rounds were targeted on the heat signature and half of them went right through the flame and flew out the other side doing absolutely zero damage. The other rounds struck mostly wicker, a few ropes and the burner itself, which exploded in a ball of fire, singeing the back of Deckard's arm as he lay atop Courtney.

Then the F-15 rocketed past, spinning the basket. Everything was a whirl of fire and smoke when Deckard looked up. The burner was blazing away four feet above him. The fire was chaotic, no longer directed into the canopy, which was beginning to sag like an old birthday balloon…a very old birthday balloon.

He didn't need to look over the side to see that they were falling fast, now. And that was the good news. They would crash before the F-15 could come back for another run.

On the flip side of this "good news" was that they were going in, burning like a torch. He saw their chances were crap, especially after he turned his head and saw that one of the rounds from the Vulcan had punched a hole in the basket. He could see quite clearly that they were heading right for the trees. From his position, they looked like a forest of dark spears.

Great. He was either going to be impaled on those spears or he would crash land in what was, essentially, a flying bonfire. The wicker and the canvas would catch on fire in a blink, not to mention the… "Shit! The propane!"

Next to his left leg were twenty gallons of propane in an aluminum tank. They were going to crash with a bomb sitting right next to them.

Courtney tried to wriggle away from it while at the same time, staying huddled away from the flame above them. *As if two feet would make any difference*, Deckard thought. He had to get the tank out of the basket. Logic suggested an easy solution: if he turned off the gas then the fire would go out.

Logic went out the window when he reached up to turn the knob, only to find that it had been shot away.

"Deckard!" Courtney cried. She had shifted toward the hole in the basket and had a perfect view of the trees rushing up.

"I got it!" he screamed. "Don't panic!" He didn't need her panic, he had plenty of his own. Frantically, he scraped at the strap holding the tank in place and, by a bit of fantastic luck, managed to get it free in seconds. Then it was just a matter of heaving it over the side of the basket without catching on fire himself.

It wasn't easy and the pain was harsh, but he got the tank over the side. Of course the tank was still hooked to the burning contraption and so instead of dropping away, the tank hung by the reinforced hose. The weight of it, combined with the fire eating at everything, pulled the burner down so that it rested on the side of the basket.

Burning ropes began to snap while the whicker danced with flame, turning one side of the gondola into a bonfire, a raging, falling from the sky, bonfire. Both Courtney and Deckard were screaming at the top of their lungs now and trying to get away from the flames, only there was nowhere to go except over the side.

It was the ultimate nightmare scenario for Courtney and yet, it only got worse. Desperately, Deckard started kicking the side of the basket, hoping to free the burner and the tank. On his fourth kick, the burning side of the basket fell away. It was an improvement of sorts. The gas-fed fire was gone, however the bottom of the basket was now in flames and within seconds the wicker began to lose all integrity, coming undone and falling into the trees that were now so close that Courtney only had time to grab Deckard before they hit.

There was a great crashing noise as branches, leaves and whicker went everywhere. Then came a sound like that of a hundred children screaming in unison as the canvas caught and tore.

Deckard had a grip on one of the risers and he held on for dear life, hoping that he wouldn't be run through by the endless number of branches that seemed to be aimed straight at his heart. He could only close his eyes and hold Courtney close and then—Bam! Bam! Bam! It felt as though they were being hit by a truck as they hit branch after branch as they fell through the canopy.

With a final bone-jarring thud, they hit the ground. When he opened his eyes again, he found himself lying beneath a burning tree.

It was an elm or an oak, or something like that. It was big and it was going up in flames faster than he would have guessed possible. Next to him, wrapped in a length of rope was Courtney. She stared up at the fire with a vapid expression on her face that suggested she'd had hit her head pretty good.

"How did we live?" she asked, in a whisper.

"I don't know," he replied and then groaned his way to a sitting position. He tried to get a bearing on their position relative to the points of the compass, but all he knew for certain was which way up and down were. He climbed to his feet and stuck out a hand.

Courtney didn't take it. "I think I just want to lie here for a while and, you know, just breathe."

"We can't. They're going to be after us pretty soon. We have to clear the area before they can figure out that we aren't dead in the top of one of these trees."

If Courtney had the strength, she would've cried. All she could manage was to squinch up her face for a moment and even that left her out of breath. Deckard had to practically lift her to her feet. Gazing around at the wreckage, he saw nothing useful. The M16 she had been carrying was gone, lost in the darkness.

It felt distinctly strange and unnerving to be traveling without a weapon, so much so that he had to keep himself from bending over and picking up a stick as they hurried out of the umbrella of light given off by the burning tree.

As they walked, Deckard oriented on the sound of gunfire and headed for it. Gunfire meant zombies and that meant the edge of the Zone. Beyond that was Thuy. They crossed through the forest for a few hundred yards and then found a north-south road. He approached it slowly, almost as if he were afraid to spook it.

Although he squatted low against a tree, Courtney stepped fearlessly and, in his opinion, foolishly, right out into the middle. "Which way?" she asked. She had her bearings back as well. "North to Canada or south to...well, I guess south really isn't a good option." She turned and stared back into the shadows through which they had just passed. "I say we go north and then if we want, we can go east."

"I'm going west," Deckard said, his voice low and firm.

Courtney's breath sucked in as she stared at him in fear. It lasted only a few heartbeats before the look turned to shame and her shoulders fell. "I-I can't go back. I can't. I hope you understand."

He understood. Courtney's flesh was torn and bruised, her eyes were circled in shadows, her clothing was in shreds, but what had suffered worse was the stuff inside of her. She had given everything she had to get out of the Zone, and he saw that she was done in.

Still, she wasn't a coward. "I'll help you get out. If you can get to Dr. Lee, I'll..." The sound of a car approaching sent them both scurrying like mice into the underbrush. Two matching black SUVs crept by. One had a searchlight attached to its side mirror and used it to sweep over the forest.

"Don't look," Deckard warned. "Just keep your nose in the dirt." Her shirt was white and to keep it from being seen, he lay over her; he could feel her shivering. "If they see us, don't move. I'll get them to chase me. But...okay, they're leaving." He rolled off her and allowed himself the small luxury of breathing a sigh of relief while he gazed up at the moon. It was a bright nickel high, high above them. "You were going to help? How?"

"I'll figure something out," she said, surprising him by sitting up first. "Try to find a police cruiser with a Motorola scanner. Tune in to 866.06250. My call sign will be Dispatch 6. If you hear me broadcasting, reply with Deck 1 and we'll go from there."

They stood and stared at each other, neither knowing what to say. They were outside the Zone, but neither was safe. With a final smile, the two parted; Courtney stopped after only a few steps. "Hey, Deck. Do you think she can fix this?"

There was no need to ask who Courtney was referring to. "If anyone can, she can."

2— J. Edgar Hoover Building, Washington DC

Everyone in the conference room, whether they were in black suits or black pantsuits, was ragged around the edges. Ties were loose, shirts were rumpled, eyes were red. The men sported five o'clock shadows and the women, their make-up wearing thin, had begun to look mannish.

There was one noticeable exception and that was Special Agent Katherine Pennock, who had been told to "keep looking like that." She didn't quite know what that meant, but as it had come from the Associate Executive Assistant Director for National Security, she had made sure to keep the lip gloss handy. While the Associate Executive Assistant Director for National Security was a ridiculous title, it was an extremely powerful position, two steps away from the Director of the FBI.

Katherine was in a room full of strangers. They were all FBI, but she was the only one who had been farmed in and not because she had special skill in tracking down domestic terrorists. She was there because the president liked young, hot blondes. Supposedly, it made him easier to manipulate.

It was embarrassing and degrading and, so far, she hadn't had the opportunity to manipulate anyone. In fact, she hadn't had the opportunity to do anything at all, except to make coffee and she had passed on that special opportunity.

Her expertise was in cyber-based crime, with an emphasis on child sexual exploitation. "And a minor in presidential stroking," she mumbled. She sat in the back of the room, well away from the coffee pot, and watched as the assignments were given out. An hour before, every agent in the room, except for Katherine, had been spread out all over D.C. prepared to swoop down on two of the terrorists.

But the terrorists were one step ahead and had forced their helicopter to set down in Baltimore and had disappeared into the wind with vials of zombie blood. Supposedly, there was a second group of terrorists somewhere on Long Island, but Katherine didn't think they'd be getting another note or another call. There was no honor among thieves and truly no evidence, beyond the word of cold-blooded murderers, that there were any more people out there carrying around vials of zombie blood.

The FBI couldn't take chances, however and now they were going to spread their already thin resources over a second major American city. Baltimore was now its own Quarantine Zone—and all the while, Katherine was just going to sit there, studiously avoiding the coffee maker.

The lights dimmed and the overhead projector kicked on displaying a map of the city of Baltimore. An agent with short-cropped dark hair began speaking in a no-nonsense monotone, "You will need to familiarize yourselves with the city. Maps will be provided. Roadblocks are in red. As you can see, the Baltimore office had concentrated on the roads heading south. That is the prime directive, keeping these terrorists from getting to the capital. We will be coordinating with local law enforcement and what is left of the Maryland National Guard. Don't expect too much from them. For the most part…"

Katherine tuned him out. She wasn't going to Baltimore so why bother memorizing useless details? Instead, she went back to her own investigation. For the last day and a half as she had waited to speak to the president she had been free to do as she pleased just as long as she didn't leave the J. Edgar Hoover Building. What pleased her was doing her job. In this case she only wanted to find out who had let the disease loose and who had escaped from Long Island. In other words, she wanted to break the case wide open.

Cracking her Mac Pro, she gazed once more at a copy of the letter that had been sent:

To Whom it may concern,

Because the military has not been able to control the spread of the "zombie virus," my comrades and I do not believe we are safe on Long Island. By chance we have access to "zombie" blood and have used it to create a dozen infected persons. Each of these persons is being held in separate homes behind locked doors, but as you know, doors and locks will only hold against them for so long, meaning you are on a time crunch to respond.

Our demands are simple, we would like to have safe passage arranged for the ten of us. You will provide two helicopters for our use. The first will convey a small group of us to Washington D.C. where we will be freed at a destination of our choosing. Once the first group is safe and outside of government control and surveillance, the second will follow.

Yes, each of us will have the virus on our persons and yes, we will make zombies within the capital. None of this is open to negotiations. Once we are safe, the location of each zombie will be released.

We do not wish to spread the disease any further than it has been. Our only goal is survival. Our safety and the lives of twenty million people are in your hands. If you

*agree to our demands broadcast the words: Lord
Abraham's Revival on ISR channel 12 in the following
locations: Garden City, Brentwood, West Hampton, and
Riverhead. We will reply with Morning Glory Blinders and
instructions for the first pick up. It is advisable for you to
hurry.*

    Yours,
    Professor X

Her eyes scanned it once, rereading the letter for the
hundredth time, searching for meaning behind the
meaning. As always, certain words jumped out at her:
zombie virus, comrade, by chance, Lord Abraham's
Revival, Morning Glory Blinders and Professor X. These
were marked in red.

Deep within the building was an analysis team pouring
over the letter, agonizing over every word. She was sure
they had a hundred different theories cooking. Katherine
was working on her own. The letter had been written by a
woman. A smart woman who had put quotes around the
word *zombie* and the *zombie virus*. That meant she was
dismissive of the term. Was she dismissive because she
knew the true origin of the apocalypse?

"Dr. Lee, perhaps? Maybe…maybe."

Katherine clicked on another folder, this one dedicated
to Dr. Thuy Lee. Thuy Heather Lee: age thirty-seven;
Vietnamese/American. She had been born in Saigon in the
closing days of the Vietnam War and smuggled out of the
country in a cardboard box by her mother when Saigon
fell.

With another click, Katherine opened up the very thin
file on Dr. Lee's mother. Heather Lee—real name, Hue Le.
She changed her name in '75 when she emigrated to the
U.S by way of the Philippines. Other than twenty-eight
poorly filled out IRS forms, there wasn't anything else on
her besides a death certificate. Heather Lee had died of
breast cancer in 2003. She had just turned fifty.

43

"Hmm," Katherine said and then closed out the file so that Dr. Lee's was once again front and center. Katherine went back to reading about a woman who had lived what seemed to be a happy American life. Thuy had ridden academic scholarships to a Bachelor's degree in chemistry from Yale University and a Doctorate in Molecular Microbiology and Immunology from Johns Hopkins. Among her many credits, she had published thirteen papers, all of which had lengthy titles and might as well have been written in Greek for all Katherine could make out of them.

It was a given that there was another team going through each of these papers, line by line, looking for anything un-American.

Although Dr. Lee was number one on the FBI's Ten Most Wanted List, Katherine didn't think they would find much of anything in her research papers. Only in the movies did people write secret messages into papers that were subject to strenuous peer review. If there were messages they would be out in the open.

Katherine's lips pursed as she flipped back and forth from the handwritten letter to some of Dr. Lee's work. "Not her," she decided. Dr. Lee was far too precise to only capitalize two of the five words in the greeting. The sort of meticulous verbiage and attention to detail found in her papers was ingrained. She closed the folder and opened a second and then a third until she had seven open, each a thin file on the female doctors associated with the Com-cell project.

Anna Holloway, a lowly research assistant, one of dozens, wasn't among them. Katherine paid more attention to the foreign born researchers and when she finished with the women, she went right to Shuang Eng's folder. Her gut told her that he was involved up to his squinty eyes. China had let him come to the US with so little fuss that it was suspicious.

Had he been the second person on the Apache? The description of the two had been exceedingly vague: one had a female voice and the other male.

"And there was the term *comrade*." It just jumped off the page and yet the prevailing theory was that this was the work of two American soldiers, which did make sense and was the most likely scenario. The kidnapping of a soldier right from the lines could not have been easy except by another soldier.

That was the most likely scenario, especially since Dr. Lee was last reported to be in Hartford, Connecticut, a city that had been overrun only a few hours before the soldier on Long Island had been kidnapped. In Katherine's mind it would have been nearly impossible to travel through so much zombie-infested land in such a short timeframe.

Of Eng there had been no reports whatsoever. As far as anyone knew, he had died in the R&K facility along with practically everyone else on the first day. But, once more, her gut told her otherwise. Chinese agents were notoriously tough and well trained. If Eng had something to do with the outbreak, he would have made plans for escape—"If so, why hadn't he flown the coop in the beginning?" Katherine leaned away from the laptop and stared up at the projected map without seeing any of its lines. "Did it all go to shit faster than he expected? It sure exploded in China and that probably wasn't on the cards. So, if Eng is our guy, who was the woman? A nobody? One of the scientists?"

As the overhead lights went on and the other agents began to head for the exits, Katherine went back to the letter and started reading it once again. The woman who had written the letter used the words *held, hold, lock* and *locked*, and then used *safe* twice, *safety* and *release* once each. In Katherine's eight years of experience, it wasn't suggestive of a code, however it could be inferred to mean the woman had been held against her will.

"And a combination of fear of the zombies and Stockholm Syndrome would account for the murders and the blood vials. Okay, I have a possible motive for her actions, at least, but I don't have a name. I should call…"

"Agent Pennock?"

She jerked and looked up to see the agent who had been handing out assignments. He looked her over once and gave her a curt nod of satisfaction. "I was told to have you wait here. Keep your phone handy."

He was already out the door before she could leap up, asking, "Do we have the analysis on the letter yet? Any prints?"

"No, it was clean; a dead end. And, at the moment, it's none of your concern. Just be ready when the Director needs you."

Only when he was out of the room did she dare to roll her eyes. "Maybe I should get a freaking mini-skirt," she grumbled as she went back to her laptop. She didn't sit. She was tired of sitting. She was tired of doing nothing. "It's Eng," she stated. There were dozens of possible suspects from the Walton facility alone, but she went with her gut.

"So, if I'm a Chinese national, where would I go? What's in Baltimore? Any connections? Any family?" Feeling the churn of excitement within her at the prospect of the hunt, she leaned over her laptop and started searching. First Facebook, then Instagram, then on down the list of social websites. There was nothing. Eng was a ghost. His banking statements weren't much better. He was a creature of very dull habits: grocery store once a week, McDonalds three times a week, the gas station every eight days.

Eng was the essence of dull, which made her all the more suspicious. She dug deeper, ignoring the bounds of legality and still there was nothing—he had no friends, no family; his phone records were virtually nonexistent and his email was the height of banality. It was almost as if he had been living his life expecting or perhaps knowing that he was being spied on. It was how spies lived.

The excitement in her grew. Normally, she would have gone to her immediate supervisor with her suspicions and her findings, only he was fast asleep three hundred miles away in Charlotte, North Carolina.

Katherine went to the hallway and paused at the doorway, afraid to take a step out, afraid to disobey a direct order. Stern-faced agents hurried past. A few would nod, even fewer would smile. She caught the eye of one who had not only smiled but had given her body a quick peek.

"Excuse me. Hi, do you know who is looking into the researchers from the Walton Facility?" For the FBI, there was only one case, so the question wasn't completely out of the blue.

"Ummm, there's an analysis team on the fourth floor, I think."

Her heart sunk. The fourth floor was out of reach. She couldn't wander up there pretending to have gotten lost looking for a bathroom. "Do you happen to know…" She paused as the agent in front of her became distracted for a moment with something behind Katherine. It had only been a quick look on his part, but she knew exactly what he had seen: a woman. Katherine turned as well and her breath caught in her throat. This woman was strikingly beautiful.

Her hair was a Nordic blonde, her eyes the color of blue denim, and she was young, even younger than Katherine. "Are you an agent?" Katherine asked.

Perhaps because of the odd look on Katherine's face, the woman answered with a guarded, "Yes, I'm with the Cincinnati office. We just got in and I'm…"

"Excellent. I'm going to need you to debrief the President."

"The President of the United States?"

"The one and only. You'll be getting a call from the Director on this phone. Don't worry, he'll inform you of your duties as liaison to the White House." Katherine saw the confusion and the suspicion in the woman's eyes. "I know this is a little strange," Katherine said, "but the Director wanted the prettiest agent we have, possibly because there could be some camera time. He's looking for someone beautiful and smart. You are smart, correct?"

The blonde blinked at the question. "Yes, I have a Master's from…"

"That's great. Look, this is going to be a great opportunity for you so don't screw it up. Keep the phone handy and don't leave this room. They'll be sending a car for you very soon. If it's a limo, just roll with it and pretend it's not your first time."

"I've been in limos before."

Katherine gave her a smile. "Not like this you haven't. Good luck." She then swept out of the room, heading for the fourth floor. Even if everything she had said turned out to be true, she didn't care. She didn't want to be an FBI spokesperson; she didn't want to be on television. She had joined the FBI to catch bad guys and to right wrongs. That wasn't going to happen when she was sipping tea with the President and pretending not to notice his eyes roving all over her.

She was at the elevators in seconds and quickly found that even at four in the morning, the fourth floor was a place of mayhem. "Who's looking into the Walton scientists?" she asked, popping her head into the first office she came to. There were seven people clicking like mad on keyboards.

"End of the hall on the right," one of them said without looking up. She thanked him and he grunted.

"Is this Walton?" she asked, when she came to end of the hall. The room was divided, eleven cubicles for eleven analysts. Each of the cubicles was so overly stacked with files that it looked as though the analysts had built little forts out of the reams. None of them answered and none looked up. Katherine was about to repeat herself a second time but then saw the handwritten signs on the sides of the cubicles: *Patients, Security, Family, Hospital Staff,*

Security, Cleaning Crew, Research A, Research B, R&K, R&K BoD.

She went to the cubicle marked Research B and paused, waiting for a mousey looking woman to glance up from her computer. She was doing the thankless and very tedious job of cataloguing data from a full work-up. Under this sort of scrutiny, any single mention of a person's name was captured, organized, and filed. Even the dullest, most stay-at-home person, such as Eng, would have thousands of data points and each had to be taken into consideration.

"Hi, I'm Special Agent Pennock. What do you have on an assistant researcher named Eng?" she finally asked when the analyst wouldn't look up.

"Other than him being dead, not much," she said, her fingers going at her keyboard without let up.

She had warts on her fingers. Not big ones but many small ones. Katherine tried not to stare, but she was drawn to them. "Do we have a body? Or an eyewitness to his death?"

"It's assumed."

Katherine struggled to keep a pleasant smile on her face. "And you base this on what?"

Finally, the warty fingers ceased their clicking dance across the keyboard. The analyst placed her hand on one of the stacks of folders. "Do you see these files? Do you? I have another thirty stacks that are just as high. My job is to put this stack of information into the computer so that someone else can condense it further, and then someone else can turn it into a pithy little report for all to see."

"Wrong. That's not your job," Katherine replied, matching her stare for stare. "Your job is to catch bad guys, just like me. And you can help me by giving me anything you have on Eng, starting with any information on his death."

The mousey analyst steepled her fingers beneath her chin. Katherine tried not to react seeing all those warts sitting so close to the woman's face. "Wow," the woman said. "You act like I don't know my own job. Do you think that just because you have a gun and the word 'special' in your title that you are, in fact, special? You're not. There are over thirty thous…"

Katherine cut her off. "So, you have time to give me a speech, but not enough time to show me the raw data on Eng? Maybe I was wrong, maybe you are just a typist."

The two stared at each other in a frosty silence until the woman shrugged and dug through one of the stacks, pulling from it a small file. "Knock yourself out, but only four people got out of the facility. Lee, Deckard, Glowitz, and Singleton. Everyone else got eaten or turned."

"That may not be true," someone in the next cubicle said. "Didn't you see the note on Wilson and Burke in the Meeks report?"

"No, they weren't mine," the mousey analyst said, giving Katherine a very neutral glance that suggested she couldn't be held responsible for every line of every report. "I have Research B. Just the junior research assistants."

"Who's got a copy of that report," Katherine demanded. A minute later, a stapled report was passed over the top of the cubicle wall. She snatched it and immediately started reading. It was a preliminary report concerning the capture, quarantining, and initial interview of six people who had escaped from the Walton facility. It was barely a page long and at the bottom was an almost throwaway line: *Two others who escaped the Zone were added to the quarantine tent; Dr. Lee in particular seems to have some animosity toward them, which will undoubtedly help during my next interviews.*

"It's Eng, I'm sure of it," Katherine whispered.

The analyst heard and, not quite understanding, shook her head. "My money is on Anna Holloway. She was getting a little something extra from a competing research company. As far as I can tell from the money being moved, it was low level espionage stuff, but it's not that far of a leap to actual sabotage."

"Is she alive? Are you getting any banking hits, any credit card transactions? Phone calls?"

"Nope. There's nothing on any of them and that area where Meeks had been was overrun within minutes of him sending his prelim. Dr. Lee was the only known survivor. She might have made it to Hartford, but even if she did, she didn't make it out again. I'm pretty sure they're all dead."

Katherine didn't believe it. If three stage-four cancer victims and an overweight, over-the-hill doctor could make it out of Walton, then Anna and Eng, who were both young and strong, could have as well. Especially if one was a spy and another a saboteur. People like that, people who were ruthless enough to infect total strangers, would have found a way to survive.

"I'm going to need a copy of these files," Katherine told the mousey analyst, holding up the dossier on Anna Holloway and Shuang Eng.

Chapter 5

1– 4:12 a.m.
—Taconic Hills Central High School, New York

Trapped in a school that was surrounded by hundreds of zombies and pinned against a door by a hulking, half-drunk wannabe rapist, Thuy did the only thing she could, she drew in a deep breath and screamed at the top of her lungs. At five-foot four inches tall and a hundred and five pounds, the scream was practically her only defense. It was so loud that it bounced around the walls of the principal's office and sent a *zing* along the glass surface of her fancy diploma. The scream echoed down the corridors of the empty school, penetrated the windows and raced out into the night where the zombies waited.

The undead creatures turned their black eyes towards the school. They knew only hunger and hatred, and with a communal roar they came on.

Jerry Weir slammed a beefy, tobacco-smelling hand across Thuy's mouth, cutting off the scream. He wasn't gentle. Thuy's lips were crushed against her teeth as the back of her head hit the door with enough force that a thousand points of lights shot across her vision.

"Shhh!" he hissed, cranking his head around to stare at the windows. Outside the principal's office was a bank of rhododendrons; their long, shiny leaves began to shimmy and shake as the creatures pushed into them. "Fuck! Look what you did. Come on."

He reached past her for the door knob. She almost fell when the door opened, but he caught her by the back of the ugly sport coat and propelled her through the admin area. He stopped in the main hall as glass started to break behind them. They were coming in through the windows, uncaring that shards of glass were tearing their flesh to ribbons.

"My bat," he said. "I forgot it." Jerry was just drunk enough to think that the bat was a big deal, but not drunk enough to want to go back for it. "You get it," he said, pushing Thuy back towards the office. "You're the one who called them. 'Sides, we'll need it to get through all them." He pointed towards the front doors to where a small mob was closing on the school.

Thuy wanted to argue against the sheer stupidity of both suggestions, however this was a fine excuse to get away from this fat janitor. She darted back to the principal's office just as the first zombie fell through the glass and landed in a black-blooded mess on the carpet. Another followed a second later.

When she paused, Jerry pointed. "It's right there, you dumb bitch."

As much as she liked the idea of watching Jerry die swinging the bat around, she wasn't about to die alongside him. She climbed up onto Principal Stevens' desk and from there leapt to the top of her filing cabinet, knocking over a plant that was so green she assumed, incorrectly to be fake. Its black soil mingled with the black blood of the first zombie which was beginning to stand. It gazed up at her just as she pulled down one of the acoustic tiles that made up the ceiling. The tile landed on the zombie's face and broke in half. With the dust adding to its already blurred vision, it took a moment to realize that Thuy was a human and in that moment, she climbed up into the cramped space between the faux ceiling and the real one.

Below her, more zombies congregated, staring upwards, their near-useless brains unable to grasp the simple concept of climbing. Around her was near complete darkness. It made the prospect of moving in any direction frightening. One false move and she would fall through the tiles and they would be on her in a flash.

She did have a five-inch wide safe space which ran along the top of the wall that divided the principal's office from a counselor's office next door. Thuy started crawling along it, moving like a frightened cat so that at least she was out of sight of the zombies.

It didn't take them long to lose interest in staring up at an empty hole in the ceiling. When they did, they saw

Jerry foolishly standing out in the middle of the school's atrium. He was basically surrounded. "Fuck!" he cried, when he saw them heading for him.

Up in the ceiling, she could hear the slap of his running feet followed by a door slamming. He must have closed it right in their faces because only a fraction of a second went by before the door was attacked with such savagery that Thuy knew it wouldn't last more than a minute or two—and then would come the awful screams.

She wasn't looking forward to hearing those, and yet, she was looking forward to the diversion they would cause. She'd be able to slip away. But where would she go? Where in the Zone was there a safe…

Thuy jerked as the ceiling tiles forty feet in front of her suddenly fell in and Jerry poked his head up into the space. He turned this way and that, looking for her, but with the darkness she was basically invisible. Of course, he had a remedy. Hanging from a carabiner on his belt loop was a four-inch long flashlight. In a second, he had it out and she was caught like a rat in its hole.

"Stupid bitch," he said as way of greeting. Sticking the flashlight into his mouth he struggled to climb up as well. The light, though focused away from her, was enough for Thuy to see the thin line where the tiles met and she crawled along it as fast as she could. At the beginning of the fifth tile, she began tapping in front of her, afraid of falling through the tiles when she reached the hallway and the wall beneath her ended.

It didn't take long to reach the hallway and when she tapped the tiles they bounced. Very carefully, she turned a rickety corner and then waited for Jerry Weir as he crawled towards her.

He was huffing and puffing, struggling to keep from falling, but still managed to spit out, "You're gonna pay, bitch. Oh, you're gonna pay."

"You'll have to catch me," Thuy answered. "And I know for a fact that you are too slow and, judging from your attire and your speech patterns, not all that smart, either."

"You want the horns dontcha? You mess with this bull and you get the horns sweetie. That's right. I don't…" Jerry had been crawling towards her, and just as she hoped, he ran out of wall. One of his filthy hands went right through the ceiling tile and, as she watched, he nearly plunged through completely. First the one hand went and then the other, and then his left leg sunk up to his thigh. He screamed and flailed, breaking the tiles all around him, but somehow he didn't fall.

Breathing like the bull he professed to be, he righted himself, staring across at her. Between them was the hall, a gulf filled with the undead. "You did that on purpose," he accused.

"And you were going to rape me, so I guess we're even."

"Oh, no, we're not even. You'll get yours. I know this school inside and out. Who do you think has to replace all these fucking tiles? Huh? Me. All those fucking nitwit kids throwing pencils and shit up here. I know where the walls are. I know where it's safe."

Thuy knew where it was safe as well: in her RAV4. She began working her way along the bisecting wall. She knew the hallway ran for a good sixty feet before it branched. When it did, Jerry would be cutoff. There would be an even larger gulf between them. All she had to do was remain on her very narrow perch.

She was sure that because of her size she would have a great advantage over the lumbering custodian. He sweated and cursed, working his way along a parallel course and, at first, she drew ahead. But with one careless hand placement, she fell through the tiles in a great storm of white dust.

The room she landed in was where English was taught to incoming freshmen. There were no filing cabinets in this room to assist her in making a quick escape up into the ceiling. And she definitely needed a quick escape. Both doors to the classroom were wide open and out in the hallway were a whole slew of zombies.

As fast as she could, she ran to the nearest door and slammed it in the face of an onrushing beast, what had once been a bank teller, but was now a monster out of a nightmare, missing most of its face. The ex-teller, its frilly blur blouse torn and dirty, threw itself into the door, rocking it on its hinges. The door wouldn't hold long.

Thuy didn't have time to worry. She darted to the further door. This one was clear and she saw she could run into the hallway if she wished—it would be a quick death if she did. There were enough zombies in the hall to tear her into pieces in seconds. She slammed that door as well. There was nothing she could do about the windows. More of the beasts were at the glass, pounding on it and breaking them.

"Oh boy," she whispered, turning her back on them as they scraped through the jagged holes, leaving curls of diseased flesh behind.

She was too short to just use the teacher's desk, so she grabbed one of the student desks. They were much more solid and heavier than she remembered from her time in school. Her adrenaline was pumping and she managed to heave one desk on top of the other. Feeling younger than her thirty-seven years, she climbed up onto the two desks and popped out the tile above her with little ceremony. She leapt for the edge of the wall and clawed up into the ceiling just as the first zombie got to the desk. It tried to emulate her but ended up falling on its face.

Thuy wasn't watching. She was concentrating on where to put her hands and knees. A slip now would doom her. It was a moment before she realized that she couldn't see the custodian or his light, which meant she really couldn't see much of anything. "Follow the line," she whispered, feeling in front of her for the junction of the tiles.

This worked for a while and she passed two more classrooms before an insidious thought struck her: *Where was the custodian?* She hadn't heard a crash or any screams. Did that mean he had climbed down and was now running around to meet her on the other side of the building? The idea freaked her out to such an extent that she stopped crawling and lifted up the edge of the tile in front of her so she could see where she was.

Below her was a darkened classroom. Its doors were shut and beyond the windows was only empty lawn running down a green slope. Fear caused her to throw caution to the wind. As quietly as she could, she pulled back the tile completely and climbed down the wall, her sneakered feet bumping softly. The zombies in the hall were making such a racket smashing doors and growling that they didn't hear.

They didn't hear the window squeak open, either. It didn't open all the way. It only canted about eight inches back—just enough for Thuy's slim form to shimmy through. Then she was alone in the night. Well, mostly alone. Fifty feet to her right, there were creatures still trying to get into the classroom that she had fallen into a few minutes before. To her left, in the direction she needed to go were three shadowy figures slowly turning towards her.

Acting as though they were merely hoodlums she would find on a street corner, she tucked her hands in the pockets of her sport coat, dropped her chin and walked straight away from the building. Although she kept her face pointed forward, she was busy looking out of the corner of her eyes. The creatures followed, angling towards her. They were all lame, limping like they had just been run over by a truck. That was the good news. The bad news was that one of them was small; a child.

In many ways, the small ones were far more terrifying than the big ones, even the huge ones that were whole and "healthy." The healthy ones were fast and grotesquely strong. The children, though not exactly smart, were cunning and dangerous. Unless they were in a blood rage, the big ones listened to the children and did what they said, and right then, the child zombie was pointing for one of the big ones to go right for Thuy.

To the other, the child said, "Stay!" It was a boy with a piping voice. His shirt was open, as was the flesh of his abdomen, which reminded Thuy of a torn vest. What was left of his intestines looked like thick grey spaghetti. He had cut Thuy off from where she had parked her RAV4, and was trying to send her north where there was nothing but miles of farm and forest. If she went in that direction, they would hound her down and eat her alive.

Even lame, the zombies would never stop and never tire. Thuy's only chance was to string them out and then dart through, but she couldn't string them out for very long. The child had called to the others and there were some who were physically whole enough to run. Thuy could sprint and in a short sprint, she was faster.

She ran full out, heading north for thirty-five meters and then abruptly changed course aiming for a gap between the zombies blocking her way to the car. There was no doubt that it would be close as the child converged more quickly than she had expected. He was on her like a cheetah on a gazelle. His ragged, horrible claws closed on her with shocking strength and his momentum spun her around.

He had a grip on her sport coat and wasn't going to let go for anything, but with a twitch of her thin shoulders, she shrugged it off and he went flying. She turned on the jets, running faster than she had since she was a kid.

With a twenty-meter head start, she rounded the corner of the building and saw her RAV4. She also saw, parked right next to it a beat-to-shit KIA Sedona and there was the drunken custodian trying to fumble the keys to it out of his pocket. Further on was another wave of zombies bearing down on him. He was panicking, making a whining noise in his throat as he struggled for the keys.

Her keys were also in her pocket, however since she had left the doors open, she'd be safe in seconds. Jumping in, she lifted her hips, dug her hand into her pocket and fished them out, just as the custodian dropped his on the pavement. He screamed, "Fuck, oh, shit!"

Sucks to be you, Thuy thought and jammed the keys into the ignition. Just as she turned the engine over, the custodian opened the passenger door to the RAV4 and jumped in next to her.

"Drive! Drive!" he cried.

She drove, backing frantically out onto the main road with dozens of zombies chasing. A minute later, she began to turn west, but he grabbed the steering wheel. "Go south," he said. "You're going home with me."

2—Baltimore, Maryland

Charlie Martin was a long way from his beloved twenty-acre spread down in Denver City, Texas. He had never liked the bustle of the big city—Denver City had more cows than people—and if he could have gotten his fifth-wheel out of Baltimore, he would have just been the happiest man alive.

But he was stuck, pretty much like everyone else in Maryland. Virginia, West Virginia and Pennsylvania had shut their borders. No one in and no one out. He could go to Delaware, but why would he want to?

Still, he had it better than most. Although the army had come by and had cleared traffic from all the main highways, he was safe and cozy in a honking big Northwood Arctic Fox. It was thirty-eight feet long and with the slides out, eighteen feet wide. It was bigger than his first apartment. Leticia, his wife of so many years it wasn't worth counting any longer, called it their "go anywhere house."

It was well stocked with enough food to last them a month. Where it lacked was in true protection. The doors were terribly flimsy. Any child with a crow bar could pop right in for a quick hello or to snatch the thirty-inch flat screen. Charlie had seven guns at home back in Denver City. He had his Remington "Turkey Thumper," his 30-30 deer rifle, his Smith & Wesson .44, his sawed-off twelve gauge, his .22 rifle for heckling the crows with, a 30.06 just in case a moose ever wandered into Texas, and finally, a vintage 1911 colt .45 which he was plum afraid to shoot for fear of the thing blowing up in his face.

In his "go anywhere house" the only weapons he had were a rolling pin and a set of steak knives that Leticia had bought off the TV. Then again, he was a friendly, easygoing Texan and tended to think that a smile, a tip of the sweat-stained cap, and a beer was enough to settle almost every difference known to mankind.

Even when traffic had snarled for a full day and he hadn't been able to budge more than a few miles in all that time, he hadn't been swept up in the road rage that had overcome everyone else. He had put on some Waylon & Willie and sang along with every song.

Charlie loved his Arctic Fox, but there was one major drawbacks to it, and to all RVs in fact, and that was the limited grey and black water waste storage. Black water was what went down the toilet and a black water overflow was something ol' Charlie wanted to avoid at all costs. It was why he was out at four-thirty in the morning looking for a dumpster to piss against.

With the army clearing the roads, he had found a parking spot for the thirty-eight feet of RV and the eighteen foot GMC Silverado that towed it around in the parking lot of a burned-out grocery store. It had been nothing but a smoking crater when he showed up. As sketchy as the neighborhood was, he knew that no one would be coming back. Why would they? There was nothing here that anyone would want, not any more.

Even with the area deserted, Charlie didn't like the idea of draining the lizard right out in the open. He unzipped and ran a yellow stream against the building, leaning back and breathing in the smell of ash and wet air. He was just thinking that a storm was coming in from the west, when he heard a voice say: "Excuse me?"

Charlie jumped and almost zipped up his goods. "Oh, hey little lady. Y'all don't wanna go sneakin' up on a fella when he's doin' his business."

She was a pretty young thing. Blonde, but frazzled and rough around the edges. She had bruises around her neck, more around her wrists and mangled fingers on her left hand. "I'm sorry, you're right," she said, in her Yankee accent. "It's just scary out here and I'm all alone."

A man's jacket hid her figure, but Charlie could tell she was too thin. Leticia would want to fatten her up.

"All alone? That's no way to be, not with all this, whadyacallit goin' on. I wonder if I even believe it. Monsters? It sounds like hooey. You know like the *War of the Worlds* and all that."

"The people are real," she said, looking around at the dark with big eyes. "They're real and they've all turned crazy and mean." She shivered and Charlie knew he had to help her. Even if he didn't want to, Leticia was a fine Christian woman; she would never turn away someone so helpless.

Charlie gave her a warm smile. "It's gonna be alright. Y'all can stay with us for a whiles, if you wish. We got plenty of all sorts of food and stuff. What's y'all's name, sweetheart?"

"Um, Ginny. I wouldn't be putting you out or anything, right?"

He put an arm around her and steered her toward the fifth wheel. "Oh no, don't be silly, child. We have a pull-out bed and more room than we know what to do with."

At the door, she said, "Thanks, it's very kind of you." When she opened the door, she took a sharp breath. It was one of wonder and not of fear.

Charlie laughed. "It's pretty nice, ain't it? Leticia wanted it all gold-plated and leather-coated, and all that hoo-ha. Hey, step in a little, will ya? That's it. See, I think that's y'all's problem. You're too trustin'. For all you know I could be like one of them serial killer types."

"Are you?"

He laughed, his Texas-tanned face breaking into a wide grin. "No way. And neither is the missus. She might put y'all in a food coma, but that's about it. Oh, hey, here she is." Leticia came out from a back room. She was tired and old and wrinkled, and was strictly angular as though beneath her nightgown she had copper pipes for bones. She had a bit of a lurch in her step. "Look what I found wandering around out in the dark," Charlie said. "I thought you might be able to help her out."

"Of course," Leticia said, coming forward. "Look at you, dear. It looks like someone put you through the blessed ringer. It's just a shame when people…" Leticia's mouth came open when Anna Holloway produced her Beretta. "W-What are you doing?"

Before answering, Anna reached over and flicked the light that hung on the side of the RV on and off. "It's just the two of you, correct?" she asked. When they only stared at each other in shock, she added, "I just don't want anyone to get hurt. Do you have any grandkids or anything back there?"

Both started shaking their heads, the extra flesh on their necks swinging gently along. Eng came in seconds later, gun drawn, his dark eyes roving back and forth. "Face the TV," Eng ordered, speaking curtly. "Hands up." Anna kept her gun pointed at them as Eng frisked Charlie and Leticia. They were clean. "Sit," Eng said, pointing to the two leather chairs.

He then went through the RV, opening drawers and looking under mattresses, making noises of approval over all the cans of food. Next, he checked the Silverado, noting the half tank of gas with only a grunt. The CB scanner, a little black box with seven knobs, got a pat and a smile.

"What are you going to do with us?" Charlie asked, when Eng returned.

"Chances are we're going to save your life," Anna said, dropping down onto the couch, glad to finally have a chance to rest. She sighed long and deep, stretching her legs out. "Those monsters you were talking about are very real and they can't be stopped. We've seen them rip right through the 82nd Airborne and the 42nd Infantry Division and every pansy-ass National Guard unit from here to Connecticut. Our only chance is to get as far away from them as possible."

Leticia raised a hand. It was blue-knuckled and spotted with age. "But no one's allowed to travel. The roads are closed and they won't let no one past the check points."

Anna knew that better than these two old geezers. They had ordered the chopper down in the middle of Baltimore, thinking that they were far enough away from the fighting that things would be calmer. They had hoped the local officials would be facilitating an evacuation and that they could just slip away with the rest. They had been wrong. The people of Maryland were bottled up, trapped as an army of undead poured south. They would all die in the next couple of days.

"We have to try," Anna told Leticia. "If we wait until it's too late, we won't live long enough to regret it."

Charlie's face was twisted in anger and confusion. "I don't get it. Y'all saying 'we this' and 'we that' but y'all keep pointin' them guns our way. Are we supposed to be on the same team in this? I-I don't know about that. The news people say they's shootin' people at these checkpoints. I think we'll have to pass, sorry. Me and the missus do wish you well, however."

Eng laughed, his gun never wavering. "You aren't getting a choice."

"No," Anna said. "No, hold on. They have a choice. You see, we're going to try to get past the check points by claiming an emergency. Now, I can shoot the missus in the belly or she can fake a heart attack. Which will it be?"

Charlie and Leticia looked at each other in horror. Charlie started to stammer, "But…but we aren't the… the…"

Eng advanced on the pair, his gun pointed at Leticia's midsection. "Choose or I will choose for you."

The China-man wasn't playing around, Charlie saw. He had the darkest, most evil eyes Charlie had ever seen and the thought of his Leticia in any pain was enough to cause him to fold. "Don't hurt her. We'll…we'll do what you want."

Anna beamed. "Excellent! Now, I'll play your concerned daughter. He will play my husband; call him Scott. And you two will try to look just like you look now, scared. It'll be perfect."

Chapter 6

1– 5:36 a.m.
—The Massachusetts Border

As everyone knew, the boys from Massachusetts had turned unexpectedly hard. It had been over two hundred years since Bunker Hill and the siege of Boston, and in that time Massachusetts had become associated with high taxes, the Boston Red Sox and the scandal-plagued Kennedys.

They were known for their high-brow Harvard elites, the complete whiteness of Cape Cod and the crusty upper-crust hanging around Martha's Vineyard. But they weren't all soft. Through their veins ran a pugnaciousness that few outside of Southie ever displayed on a day to day basis. For better or for worse, that fighting spirit was out now for all to see.

The refugees fleeing Connecticut had run into it first hand and now the border between the two states was littered with corpses. The zombies had experienced it as well. A terrific two-day battle had been raging along the Konkapot River in the south-west corner of the state and despite the frightening numbers arrayed against the men and women dug into the hills on the northern side of the river, they had held their own.

Not only was it their stubborn refusal to give up an inch of land that helped them maintain their lines it was also the simple fact that the rules of engagement set down by the President had been utterly ignored by everyone right from the very start. Uncaring what the airheads in Washington thought, the soldiers and the citizen warriors had used everything in their arsenal: tanks, APCs, machine guns, napalm, and bombers. So many artillery rounds had been fired that it sometimes felt that night had been turned into day and the earth was crumbling all around them.

And yet, that battle was nothing compared to the full-on war being waged along a twenty-mile front from

Putnam, Connecticut to Providence, Rhode Island. On the Massachusetts side were tens of thousands of Bostonians backed up by National Guard units including the 101st Field Artillery Regiment and the 181st Infantry Regiment, the oldest combat regiment in the army.

On the other side of the border, General Milt Platnik commanded what he called the Army of Southern New England. It consisted mainly of the 101st Airborne Division, the shattered remains of the Connecticut National Guard, a handful of MP and engineering companies from Rhode Island and about a hundred thousand civilians carrying every sort of weapon imaginable.

Over the last twenty hours, Platnik had shown amazing skill in saving his Army from destruction. His western flank had been under constant attack from millions of zombies and he was forced into an endless retreat as the beasts came in waves, threatening to envelope his command over and over again. His men were constantly on the edge of panic, and yet he never wavered once. With cool deliberation, he shifted his units back and forth, never allowing them to get beyond their tactical depth and always keeping a line of retreat open.

But he could not fall back forever, especially when his left flank crossed into Rhode Island. His men were well in hand, however the masses of refugees fleeing in all directions made resupply, communications and maneuvering exceedingly difficult. Platnik made his mark by overcoming all of this, and had he been able to slip into Massachusetts, his army could only have strengthened the border.

Instead, the people of Massachusetts pointed their guns at his men and told them to: "Go fuck yourselves." Platnik got on the phone with his counterpart across the state line and the two solved nothing by shouting at each other. Then he got on the phone with General Phillips, who squinted at his map and cursed.

"What about going south towards the ocean?" Phillips asked. "Can you shift towards Bristol? I bet you can hold out there for some time."

Platnik had seen this "opportunity" hours before. Bristol sat on a peninsula with a two-mile wide neck. There would be no room for anything but a slugging match and if his men couldn't hold, he would be forced to retreat to Aquidneck Island along a two-lane bridge that would be packed end to end with refugees.

The crossing would be hell and when he got to the other side, what would he do then? Including the civilians, there'd be over three million people on an island seven miles long and three at its widest. They'd run out of fresh water in two days and out of food in one. And where would they all live? He could cram maybe a quarter of a million people into the current houses and the rest would have to sleep in the dirt until "something" could be done. That something could be weeks if not months away.

When he explained this to Phillips, the commander of the 7th Army said, "I'll talk to the President." It was a tense hour before Phillips called back, asking in what was basically a conspiratorial whisper, "Can you punch through the border?"

"Why? What's going on?"

"The governor of the fucked-up state of Massachusetts just told the President to kiss his ass. He's not letting anyone in no matter what. The President wants to teach them a lesson. Normally, he's an idiot but I don't see any other way to save all those people."

Platnik pulled the phone away and stared at in disbelief. Phillips was talking about starting a civil war in the middle of an apocalypse. Slowly, he brought the phone back to his face and said, "They're very heavy in artillery and armor. I'm going to need air superiority, bomber support and my Apaches. But…but are we really going to do this? We'll be killing our own people."

Phillips made a choking sound and then said, still in his whisper, "I'll call you back." Forty minutes later, dozens of telephone pole-sized Tomahawk cruise missiles streaking overhead marked the beginning of the Second American Civil War. The Tomahawks were followed across the border by a squad of F/A-18E/F Super Hornets carrying HARM packages and acting as "Wild Weasels."

The cruise missiles went for the airports. Each missile contained a hundred and sixty-six submunitions that rained down on the runways, cratering them, making them useless. The mission of the Wild Weasels was to knock out radar and they were very effective. With a ninety-mile range on their AGM-88s, the Weasels launched their missiles within seconds of crossing into Massachusetts airspace and then turned for home on afterburner, blue shock diamonds glowing in their wake.

Home for the F/A-18E/F Super Hornets was USS Harry S Truman, a Nimitz class super carrier operating a hundred miles off the Atlantic Seaboard.

With two successive attacks coming from the east, it should have been no surprise that the next would come from another direction. From the south, a flight of F-22 stealth fighters ghosted through the night, looking for targets, their pilots furious at the people of Massachusetts and ready to vent their anger on the first blip to show up on their passive weapons guidance systems.

It wasn't long before three Massachusetts Air National Guard F-15s were obliterated, and from then on, the United States owned the sky. B2s and B1s roared into the predawn light, raining bombs all along the state line, knocking out tanks and turning batteries of artillery into little more than piles of rubble and bloody bone.

If Platnik had the time for more "softening up" the attack that followed would have been something of a cakewalk. As it was, the zombies were pressing too closely from the south plus the panicking refugees were making the battle unbearable.

He planned to make the civil war a quick one. He would attack from two directions, straight up the middle at a town called Webster and at the same time he would use practically the last of his fuel reserves dropping an air assault force behind the lines—the way he envisioned it, they could be in Worcester in an hour, splitting the state directly in half and allowing the refugees room to run to safety.

At a quarter of six, General Platnik began the ground attack on Webster with a hodgepodge of units which had been pulled from every section of the line that wasn't neck deep in the undead. Five minutes later, the first units of the airborne assault took off.

With the heat of the downwash rushing over him, Sergeant Troy Ross climbed into the UH-60 Blackhawk and all he could feel was relief. The zombies had been a running horror that no amount of training could have prepared him for. But this was different. He would be facing real people and although he thought it was the most fucked up thing in the world that he would be fighting his own countrymen, at least he could understand them.

They would bleed, they would cry and they would die. This was the sort of war that he had trained for. In a way, it was natural.

"Push in! Push in!" one of the crewman yelled over the thrumming of the twin General Electric turboshaft engines. "We're going in heavy. It'll be a quick trip, so get cozy. Cheek to cheek, damn it!" Their destination was the town of Auburn. They were going to land smack dab at the junction of I-90 and I-395, a few miles south of Worcester. They would hold until relieved, which they had been told would be two hours at the most.

Ross knew that when the army said two hours it normally meant six, however in this case, he didn't think so. The situation was getting desperate. The Navy and the Air Force had given the Mass-boys a good drubbing and he guessed that they would take to their heels as soon as the assault began. Just in case, there were civilians waiting in the forest; they constituted the next wave in the air assault. Ross could see them smoking their cigarettes and checking their guns. To tell them apart from the Mass-boys, they had white triangles taped to their backs and silver duct tape banded around their arms. Even from a distance, they seemed afraid.

Afraid or not, they were better than nothing.

"Let's get fired up, Bulldogs!" someone yelled, as the last of the soldiers were crammed aboard and the engines really started to throttle up. There was a general growling of the men and a few echoes of "Bulldogs!"

Ross only swallowed and tried to look tough. He had started to get the shakes, which for him was normal, just like it was normal for his stomach to turn a flip when the Blackhawk elevatored straight up into the air. They didn't go far along the vertical plane, which meant they'd be flying nap of the earth at a hundred and sixty miles an hour.

He swallowed again, knowing his stomach was in for a tough time. Sure enough, they picked up a head of speed, shooting over a lake and dropping down so that the water was whipped up by their passing. Ross looked down, thinking that if he reached out with his M4 he could have grazed the surface.

Then they bounced up as if they had hit an invisible ramp, flying over a line of trees and then dropping down again. Now there were hills rising up on either side of them. He could see people looking down at them! A second bounce over more trees and someone yelled, "Now that's hedge-hopping!"

More water below them and to the east the sky was turning pink. "Shit," Ross cursed. "Come on, let's get there already." He wasn't the only one eyeing the coming dawn with trepidation. In the dark, the Blackhawks were amazingly hard to see. Sure, they could be heard, but whoever had painted these birds knew their business. In the daylight, it was a whole other story. They stood out like big fat targets.

The pilot must have felt the same way because Ross was suddenly rocked back by a burst of acceleration. The choppers were no longer worrying so much about hugging the earth; they were racing the coming of the sun.

The Blackhawk beat the light by seconds. They were cutting along the land at an angle to the highway and so Ross saw their LZ for the first time just as the bird pitched upwards slightly and decelerated so quickly it was as if the Blackhawk had an airbrake. Then they thumped to the ground.

Ross was out in a flash, the wash so hot it was almost blistering. Around him, the highway was a strange combination of light and dark. He could see the pavement and the dividing wall just fine, but everything else was only slowly morphing from shadow to fact. That meant he'd be morphing into a target in seconds. He ran in a hunch, his full battle rattle bouncing and shifting all over his body, his lungs billowing despite the short sprint because that's the way it always was. Every time he came off a Blackhawk, he was keyed up and pumping adrenaline, ready to fight.

Making it to the short cement wall, he paused to look back at his squad. They were huddled in a line like a bunch of bullet magnets. "Spread out, damn it!" he bellowed, grabbing PFC Jake Monnens by the shoulder and thrusting him away. His hand was still on Jake's arm when there was a heavy thud. Ross could feel the thud run through his fingers.

Then Monnens was falling back, his legs unbuckling, a look of shock on his face. Ross felt his own face gripped by the same look and it was only when Monnens hit the ground that he snapped out of his shock. "Incoming! We're taking fire!" His adrenaline was a force within him; with one hand, he fired down the highway in the general direction of the shooter and with the other, he pulled two-hundred pounds of grunt closer to the dividing wall.

"You okay, Monnens?" Ross asked, again working in an ambidextrous manner: M4 trained outward with his right hand, while his left swept over the soldier's chest. He felt the hole in the kevlar before he felt the blood welling up. Monnens began to gurgle. "Fuck!" Ross cried. "Medic! I need a medic over…"

He stopped as he saw a twinkling of light from the roof of an adjacent building. "Two o'clock! I got incoming fire at our two o'clock!" Ignoring the blood on his fingers, he brought up his M4 and fired in three bursts before yelling, "Miller get that SAW rocking on that rooftop!"

Ross fired again. He could have sworn that he had only pulled the trigger a couple of times but as his M4 was empty, it had to have been more. He reached for a spare mag and that was when he realized that Miller wasn't working his SAW. Looking back, he saw his light machine gunner slumped on the side of the highway, unmoving. And he wasn't the only one.

Tiggly and Ryan were flat out on their backs, staring at the brightening sky with empty eyes. Private Gibson was in a ball clutching his stomach and DeBerg was only recognizable by his red hair; he no longer had a face. There were bodies scattered everywhere. Further away, the Blackhawks were big crows slowly retreating while closer, chips of cements were kicking up all around him.

They had landed in an ambush and no one was getting out alive.

2-Ryan Deckard

It turned out that sneaking either into or out of the Zone was basically impossible, at least on the Massachusetts side. Whoever was running the defensive line knew what they were doing. Generally, the line zagged away from the heavier forested area, but when it couldn't be helped, the trees had been chopped down to build stockade walls, with the result that there were wide open fields of fire.

They even had drones flying over the lines so that the commanding officer of each section knew precisely what was happening and where. After two hours of hunting for a way across the line, Deckard finally gave up on the idea of sneaking. There was a chance they would shoot him without asking a single question. Just then, Deckard was too tired to care. He had been going at it for too long and he was starting to get frazzled.

He felt like walking right up to the soldiers on the line and asking to be let through, only there would be questions and there was still the possibility of immediate execution. With a long, weary sigh, he moved to a quiet point in the line and went looking for someone in charge.

It wasn't difficult. The sound of laughter and the good-natured ribbing common to soldiers drew him to a clearing where he found thirty or so men and women. Some were racked out, snoring away, some were eating, some were talking and some were gazing off into space with a haunted look in the depths of their eyes.

Deckard guessed that if he came back two hours from then, he'd still find them staring.

"Excuse me," he said, walking past one of the staring men and toward the lively part of the group. They were a motley bunch: young and old, male and female, soldiers and civilians. They were unified in one respect, however. He could see suspicion written on their faces.

"What happened to you?" a middle-aged man asked. He looked as though he belonged in slippers in front of a fire, not out in the woods with a deer rifle across his knees.

"What didn't happen to me?" Deckard replied, with a soft laugh. He had survived fires and falls, disease and gun battles, and zombies of course. Thousands and thousands of zombies. "Are you in charge?"

Another man, young with piercing eyes, scratched at a shock of thick brown hair on his head. "The woman in charge is right down that trail," he said, getting to his feet.

"I don't need an escort."

The man's name was Malachi DeMott and he certainly didn't like the look of this person in front of him. They had been told to keep an eye out for anything suspicious and this guy was as scruffy and ripped up as anyone Malachi had ever met. Even in a world with zombies, no one looked like this guy. "Maybe you don't think you need an escort, but I think maybe you do. You got a gun?"

Deckard lifted his arms. His shirt and pants weren't just torn but singed as well. There was no place to hide a gun.

Malachi gave him a closer look and even gave him a sniff. "We heard a rumor that someone tried to escape the Zone in a balloon, like one of them hot air ones. They said it got shot down."

Deckard only stared at the young man, not saying anything.

"Would you happen to know anything about that?" Malachi asked, his finger slipping into the trigger guard. "I ask because you smell like one of them gas fires. You know like the ones people use for barbecues? They use them for balloons too, I bet." He started nodding to himself as if coming to some realization. "Maybe you should put your hands up in the air."

Slowly, Deckard lifted his hands to shoulder height. "Sure, but I wouldn't shoot if I were you, especially if you think I was in the Zone. Blood spray could infect everyone around here. Is that what you want?" The people in the clearing were suddenly all ears. They sat up, looking nervous.

The young man was a cool customer and only lifted a shoulder. "I could kill you further out in the forest, away from everyone."

"Where the birds would get at my body and then fly here or there infecting everything? I think it would be best if you just let me talk to whoever's in charge. It'll be safer for everyone."

The two were silent, appraising each other. Another man, this one older with a paunch and wrinkles in a net around his eyes, eased away from the clearing, moving in a half-circle, looking ready to bolt out of there if Deckard so much as twitched. "I could get her for you, Malachi."

Malachi shook his head and then pointed Deckard on toward the trail with the tip of his rifle. He didn't follow close behind; he gave Deckard a good ten-foot lead, plenty of room to shoot and probably not get infected. The two followed a well-worn path that led through the forest to a grouping of pop-up tents, all of which were nylon and surprisingly brightly colored.

These were store-bought tents and around them, for the most part, were civilians, the twenty-first century equivalent of the Minute Men. Centered around one of the larger, family-sized tents was a hum of conversation. It sounded to Deckard as if there were ten conversations going on at once. It would be the communications tent and next to it, more than likely, would be the C.O.'s tent.

Both tents were flung open and in the C.O.s tent was Rebecca Vance, a woman who looked far older than her twenty-six years. Two days without sleep, no make-up, and the weight of responsibility crushing down could do that to a person. She was a warrant officer in the Massachusetts National Guard with only six months under her belt. Before the zombies, she had been a JAG officer, a military lawyer.

A warrant officer was still an officer of sorts and was rank enough to give her command of a section and she had done well enough to earn the respect of the soldiers and civilians fighting for her. She was currently eating part of an MRE that she had saved from the day before; their food situation was nearly as dire as their ammo problems.

"Stop right there, mister," Malachi said to Deckard. He then called to Rebecca from thirty feet away. "Excuse me, ma'am? I think you might want to see this."

She turned and gazed at Deckard, and all the while she chewed her food like a bunny might, her teeth going up and down like thirty-two little white jigsaws. Just watching her made Deckard's stomach growl.

He didn't bother waiting for the questions to come. "I came out of the Zone in a hot air balloon a few hours ago." She didn't look surprised. She looked too tired to react as she would have done just four days before.

"And you want me to shoot you in the head?" Rebecca asked. There was no attempt at humor or bluster in the question. She had asked it honestly.

"No, thank you. What I need is to get back into the Zone." This perked her up, but not so much that she was going to stop eating. She grunted for him to go on. No one made such a bald statement without explanation. "There is a scientist that we were trying to help escape from the Zone, but she got cut off and we were forced to leave her behind. It was a mistake. She is vital to finding a cure and, for the sake of humanity, I have to go back for her."

Rebecca continued her bunny-like mastications, saying only, "That's nice."

Astonished Deckard and Malachi shared a look before he turned back to Rebecca. "Nice? That's...that's all you have to say? I just told you that the cure for this plague is right on the other side of your lines and all you say is: that's nice?"

"Actually, what you said is: *She is vital to finding a cure*. That's not the same thing as having a cure, is it?" When Deckard could only splutter, Rebecca followed up by saying, "If you had the cure, you would have led with that. Not that I would have believed you. Unless you have some proof; do you have any?" His eyes narrowing was his only answer and she said, "Of course you don't. So, is she cute?"

"Very."

She grinned at this and the years seemed to fall away. "Love is a very powerful motivator. It also makes us do the stupidest things. You have my permission to go into the Zone if you wish, however, I can't let you come back, no matter how cute she is."

It was the most Deckard could have hoped for, though he had to try for a little more. "I understand, thank you. Just one other thing, do you have an extra gun?" Rebecca shook her head and took another bite, the years sliding back on once again.

"We don't have a lot in the way of ammo or guns," Malachi said, as he escorted Deckard to a quiet section of the line where the land had been folded into a series of steep, rugged hills.

They paused on the top of the last hill. "I'd shake your hand," Malachi said, and then shrugged. Deckard settled for a friendly wave before plunging down the slope. In seconds, he was at the bottom. He took the next hill at an angle and when he reached the crest, he crouched next to a tree. There were zombies in the ravine sixty feet below.

The sight of them drained him in a way he wasn't expecting, and for a moment, he looked back across to the ridge line where Malachi and a few others were watching. Just then they weren't citizens or soldiers, they were just people and he was one of them…except he wasn't. He was an outcast, a voluntary one this time. There was no going back.

But he didn't want to go back, at least not just then and not alone. After a long breath, he ran down the hill, heading to a copse of trees where the zombies were fewest in number. It was still early morning and the sun had yet to penetrate into the ravine where the shadows were puddled and he was among the beasts before they knew it.

Then he was past them and chugging uphill with a hundred or so hot after him. He didn't bother looking back. His concentration was fully on his feet as he ran, putting miles between him and the line. The zombies fell further and further back, but there were always more of them, constantly coming out of the woods or from behind barns, or just loitering like perpetual vagabonds.

Deckard ran on and on, the soft hiking boots he had picked out the day before in Garnet Corner were easy on his feet and with all the holes in his shirt and jeans keeping him cool, the jog was a piece of cake. He was still running easily when the high school came into view. Only then did his chest tighten.

The football field was empty as he had expected, but so too was the school. There was no sign of Thuy anywhere.

Chapter 7

1– 6:21 a.m.
—The Taconic Valley, New York

Thuy drove the RAV4, noting landmarks, watching signs, counting mile markers. She hated that they were going southeast. They were going deeper into the Zone and with every minute that passed, the edges of it were growing: east into Rhode Island, south into Jersey and Philadelphia, and west, as the Pennsylvania National Guard slowly retreated to the Susquehanna River, where thousands of civilians were preparing defenses in depth.

Only in the north had the zombies been stopped completely. The lines hadn't budged more than an inch in the last thirty hours.

"Kinda quiet out here," Jerry said, sitting back and tipping a bottle of Fireball to his lips. As it was cinnamon flavored, he thought it mimicked the smell of having just brushed his teeth. It did not. "I like it. It's nice and peaceful."

It was an odd thing to say as they passed groups of zombies shambling about in packs of two or three or fifty while, scattered here and there were decaying corpses and cars with smashed-in windows. Above them was the constant rumble and roar of jets. In Thuy's mind, this was the opposite of peaceful. It was her version of hell.

"I guess I'm not seeing what's peaceful about any of this," Thuy said.

He tipped back the Fireball, enjoying the warmth in his gut and the heat in his loins. "I don't know, I guess I just like it. You know it being just the two of us out here. Kinda feels like we're the last two people on earth."

The thought sent a shiver down her back. Had she been in this same situation a month before, she would have aimed the RAV4 straight for a tree and taken her chances with a head-on collision. She couldn't do that when her world was infested with zombies. The first rule of zombies was that there were always more of them around than it seemed.

"Where exactly are we going, Mister…"

"To my house and it's Jerry. Just Jerry. Mister Weir is what the kids call me." That wasn't true. They didn't call him anything. For the most part, when he went about the school with his bucket and mop, he was a total nonentity. Eight hundred kids a day swept right on past without looking him in the eye or even acknowledging him in any way. If there was a spill, or if he was parked in front of a locker and he had to be addressed, it was always the same: *Hey*, as in "Hey, Mrs. Stephens needs you to unclog a toilet," or, "Hey, can you move your mop bucket? The smell is nauseating, God."

When he thought about it, Jerry was glad all those kids were dead. "Yeah," he whispered, taking another slug. As he brought the bottle back to rest on his gut, he saw a sign with an arrow: *The Greens*. He sneered. The Greens was the name of a posh country club where all the high-box bitches pranced about in their short tennis skirts and never worked a day in their lives. Just the thought of them nearly upset the fine mellow the Fireball was giving him, but then he had a better thought: how many of them high-box bitches and their richy-rich husbands were now dead? And how many of them mansions were just sitting empty ready for a new occupant to take over?

He glanced over at Thuy, leering as he did. She was probably one of them high-box bitches. In fact… "You said you was one them doctors, didn't you?"

"I have a Ph.D, yes."

She would fit right in. She probably had *two* mansions. That's how it was with doctors. They charged a man a million dollars just to save his life and you gotta pay it because what else can you do? Are you just gonna die? No, and that's why they are all rich and why he wasn't nothing but a janitor cleaning up the diarrhea speckles out of the boys' stalls every living-fucking day.

A cruel laugh escaped him. He'd been about to have her turn back for The Greens, but he had a better idea. It had been never since he had cleaned his own toilet. It looked as though a water buffalo with a case of the runs had been using that toilet for the last twenty years. And holy fuck, did it stink. What would this high-box bitch think of that toilet?

He'd fuck her. He'd fuck her brains out and then he'd make her clean that toilet. "She's gonna need a chisel," he said and then cackled.

Thuy looked at him out of the corner of her eye. That cackle was a mean thing. It didn't bode well. She began to get a *worse* feeling in her stomach. Her stomach had been squirrelly ever since Jerry's thumping bat had woken her in the dark.

"Turn here," he said, pointing at a crumbling run of asphalt that had probably been laid out thirty years before and hadn't been resurfaced or even touched since. There were potholes and frequently the shoulder was bumped up by roots that were on the verge of erupting. Around them was scrub forest strung up with barbed wire that had rusting *No Trespassing* signs placed every hundred yards or so.

She began to regret having put on her seat belt. In those first few seconds with the zombies bashing her windows and Jerry screaming at her to drive, putting on the seatbelt had been the only automatic thing she had been able to accomplish. Everything else had come slowly to her as if she had never seen a steering wheel before.

Slowly, she dropped her hand down to the latch release button, but then Jerry shifted his bulk in the seat and she pulled it back.

"You gonna like my place," he said, breathing his sickly-sweet whiskey breath on her. "It has a very lived-in feel. You'll feel like you're at home. Turn here."

She actually planned on running the second they drove up to whatever crappy little house they came to. She expected it to be bad, but the mobile home was a shithole. It sat leaned back on its foundation so that there was a gap of about a foot between the front door and the "stairs" which were nothing but three concrete blocks he had glued together with a pint of Elmer's glue he had lifted from the school.

Around the mobile home was an obstacle course of rusting junk. There were two cars that hadn't had tires since the 1990s, a stack of bedsprings four high, a dozen bicycles that were in good condition—these had also been liberated from the school—any bike that had remained overnight, was in Jerry's book automatically communal property. Finally, there was a bathtub, a seven-foot tall pyramid of filled to bursting trash bags that he kept meaning to take to the dump, a kitchen sink and about a thousand aluminum cans.

Part of the home itself was black from a grease fire. Just looking at it made Thuy's skin crawl and before the car was even stopped, she had her seatbelt unbuckled and her door open. There was no way she was going into that place and if she did, she didn't think she'd get out again.

She was half out of the RAV4 before Jerry woke up to what was happening. Quicker than Thuy thought possible for such a slob, he reached out a long arm and just managed to grab the back of her low-riding jeans. He had a great view of her pink panties and the glorious golden tan across the top of her ass. It mesmerized him and he had the beginnings of a chub growing as Thuy started screaming and flailing.

It was like landing the biggest, sexiest bass ever. Big as she was, she was light, light, light, and he reeled her right back into the RAV4. When he had a hold of her silken black hair in his dirty paws, he spoke into her ear, "Don't be like that, baby."

The struggle went out of her. "I-I'm sorry. I j-just thought I saw a zombie. It was right over there. We should maybe go…" She was cut off as he yanked her back into the RAV4, dragged her over the console and then out the other side, knocking over his bottle of Fireball in the process. It hit the driveway and shattered. Jerry's eyes flashed with fury and he yanked her to her feet by her hair.

She had to stifle a scream. He was about to explode in violence; she could feel the hate thrumming through him and just then a scream could set him off. "I'm sorry," she said, again, forcing her voice to remain calm despite him still having his hand bunched in her hair. If she tried to run away now, she'd lose half her scalp. "It'll be okay. We can get more. Alcohol is everywhere now and it's free. We can just take it. As much as you want."

Jerry's anger disappeared in a snap. "We? You, uh, you like to drink? Huh? I got some gin inside. And some other stuff. Like some Midouri Sour, you know shit like that." He had all sorts of weird mixes that he had confiscated from the kids over the years. They just sat in his cupboards, aging poorly. He never got into those sorts of concoctions but, at the same time, he couldn't bring himself to throw away anything alcoholic.

He pulled his hand out of her hair, but didn't let her go. As if they were boyfriend and girlfriend, he slung an arm around her shoulder and copped a feel of her right breast. "I'll fix you up with something good. You'll be able to relax and have fun." This idea appealed to him. When they had been in the school, he had liked the thought of hurting her, of dominating her. Now that she was at his home, he wanted her to be as into the coming fuck-session as much as he was.

Of course, when they were done, she'd still clean his toilet. That was for dead certain.

He led her to the door, the one door in or out, and he leaned past her to open it, like a gentleman would. She stiffened and her breathing started to pick up, still she managed to say, "Thank you so much," without her voice cracking.

Inside was a cave. It stank of urine, cheap pot, and rotting garbage. The smell made her woozy and weak. Jerry effortlessly guided her to the kitchen, where he reached into the brimming sink and found two mugs, both with the Taconic Titan emblazoned on the front and some sort of grey liquid swimming around in the bottom. As a nod to the evils of bacteria, he turned them upside down for a moment so that the fluid ran out.

"This is the good stuff," he said, producing a bottle of Beefeater Gin. "You'll get plenty spun on this stuff as small as you are." As if to reassure himself that she was indeed small, he ran a hand down her shoulder and arm. He then encircled her wrist with his pinky and thumb. "Man, like a kid's wrist."

As he marveled over it, Thuy gazed around at the inside of the mobile home. It was squalor and filth on a third-world level. Roaches crept brazenly around the dishes in the sink, while flies hummed over a grey drum of a trashcan that was overflowing onto the floor. There were stains and cigarette burns everywhere, walls and ceilings included.

She was beginning to feel something wanting to come up from the back of her throat when Jerry let her hand go and started filling the cups.

"Whoa," she said, with what she hoped was a smile on her face and not a complete look of disgust. "I'm little, remember. You don't want me puking, right?" She was only guessing that he would care. The carpet wouldn't be appreciably worse off if she hurled all over it.

"Yeah, I wouldn't want that, I guess." Hers was half-filled while his ran to the top. "Cheers." He lifted his mug and pushed hers towards her. She took a sip and tried her best not to make a scene, but she had never been a big drinker and straight gin from a dirty mug was enough to send her into a coughing fit.

Instead of getting mad, Jerry laughed and slammed an open hand down on the formica counter over and over again. "What a lightweight! Hell, this is the good stuff. I got some real hooch that'll knock you on your ass. Try again."

Her only hope was that he would get drunk faster than she did. With his head start, it was a possibility. Before she raised her mug, she said, "Show me how it's done."

"Sure thing," he said, and drank off half his mug off. "Your turn and you better not waste any. Like I said, this is the good stuff."

The good stuff had a small raft of green-grey mold floating on top. She fished it out and tried to grin at him. The grin was all grimace and his face darkened at the sight of it. "Cheers," she said and took a large sip. *It's just medicine. It's just medicine,* she tried to tell herself. It tasted like gasoline and she coughed and spluttered.

This time Jerry was not amused. "It's just never like it is in the movies. In the movies, a little, skinny thing like you can always drink big guys under the table. And you always got skinny bitches like you knocking out full grown men with a single punch. That shit never happens. You don't believe me?"

He had turned menacing again and Thuy shrank back, holding the mug, hoping it would keep him from hitting her. "I-I believe you."

"Go ahead and take a poke at me. Go ahead. Punch me right in the face. Knock me out if you can." Jerry presented the side of his face, his jaw jutting. She knew better than to try. Even if he let her hit him, it would accomplish nothing but angering him more.

"I think you're right," she told him, making a show of sipping from her mug. "Those sorts of movies are stupid." She almost added: *And women are stupid, too*, which was clearly what he thought. It was his manner of thinking, but he wouldn't be fooled into thinking it was hers. "I actually like, uh, romantic movies, if you know what I mean."

He straightened, his face still twisted by anger. "Of course, I know what romantic movies are. Everyone knows what the hell they are."

"No, I mean *romantic* movies. You know, erotic movies. Do you have anything like that here? It gets a person in the mood." This was another lie. Her hope was that in his eagerness, he would duck into a back room to search for a stash of porn and then she would run. He didn't, however.

The angry look disappeared to be replaced by a leer. "Oh yeah? You like that? What else you like? You like to be tied up? I betcha do."

Thuy thought that she had been afraid before, but it was nothing compared to the fear racing through her now. "T-Tied? I'm not into that sort of thing. I was hoping that you had…"

"I don't really care what you were hoping," Jerry said, bringing one hand into her hair again and yanking her head back. "I saw that movie *Fifty Shades of Grey* that all the teachers were whispering and giggling about. According to that movie, all you women want is for a man to *make* you do things that you wouldn't otherwise consider, like being tied up or whipped. You ever been whipped?"

Thuy was trembling so uncontrollably now that she couldn't form words and nor could she stop Jerry as he propelled her towards the back of the mobile home to a bedroom. It hardly seemed possible to Thuy that the bed with its never been washed sheets was the foulest thing in the mobile home. "Kneel," he commanded.

She knelt.

2- I-395 Just South of Auburn, Massachusetts

As Dr. Thuy Lee panted in fear, watching Jerry Weir pull the leather belt from around his waist, Sergeant Troy Ross found himself pinned down next to the cement median separating the north and south lanes of I-395. He seemed to be in some sort of magic bubble where the bullets zipping past just couldn't seem to reach him, though everyone else around him was dying.

His safe spot wouldn't last. All it would take was someone to shift a few feet in one direction or another and then he would be as dead as PFC Jake Monnens, who was sprawled and unmoving an arm's length away.

Ross was in a state of shock. The woods across from him were roaring with gunfire, while very little was being returned. Two hundred troops landed in the space of a minute. It had seemed to be a picture-perfect insertion. Now, three minutes later, most of them were dead. The air assault operation had been perfect; the ambush even more so.

Hoping that the grass was greener on the other side of the waist-high median, Ross heaved himself over and squatted down, pointing his M4 out. Almost immediately, bullets reached out to take his life. They were like darting fireflies which meant someone was working a machine-gun and they were aiming for him. For the briefest moment, Ross missed the zombies. At least they had to come within arm's reach to kill him.

Then he forgot everything as his training took over. Before he knew it, his M4 was at his shoulder and he was aiming through the scope—there was the gunner partially hidden behind the black M240 and the fire spitting from it. With the tracer rounds zipping past him, Ross felt as though he were stuck in a video game as he started returning fire in short bursts.

He had always been a dead-eye shot and the gunner went down in a second. Another man wearing blue jeans and a leather jacket with the Patriots emblem stitched on it tried to take his place. Ross shot him as well. Then, like an automaton, he twisted his trunk slightly and took aim at others. He fired with precision until his M4 ran dry.

By the time he reloaded, a matter of seconds only, someone new had manned the M240 and out of the corner of his eye, he saw its 7.62mm rounds chewing up the cement divider to his right. Chips and splinters and dust were going everywhere, especially in his direction. There was no time for counter fire. Ross dove forward, flattening himself as the rounds streaked overhead. He didn't remain in place. That was the quickest way to get killed.

Low crawling with his face in the grass, he made his way into a shallow drainage ditch that ran between the lanes. It was just deep enough for him to raise his head a few inches without it getting shot off.

A few others had made it into the ditch as well. Some had crawled like Sergeant Ross and some had rolled there, lifeless and leaking blood into the brackish water at the bottom of the gulley. "What the fuck?" Ross screamed at the others further down the line. It wasn't a question, it was a statement and its meaning was twofold: *We're all going to die!* and *Holy fuck, we're going to die!*

A few of the handful of men left whimpered in reply, one answered, "I don't know! Fuck!"

Another man, lying still with his head cocked at an ugly angle, seemed to be throwing his voice without moving his lips. Ross heard, "Say again Raid-One. We're not picking you up. Say again. You have Opfor where?"

Ross crawled to the soldier, knowing he'd find him dead. He was after the radio the man carried. Grabbing it, he shouted into the mic, "We've landed in a hot LZ! Say again, the LZ is hot as fuck! We got bad guys east and west of us. They were waiting on us."

A few seconds went by with Ross waiting expectantly. Finally, the radio crackled to life. "We now have real-time visuals, Raid-One. Pop smoke." Although Ross was decked head to toe in his battle rattle: helmet, tactical vest, ruck, and all the rest, he didn't have a smoke grenade. Quickly he searched the body of the dead comm guy and found a grenade with a green marking. He tossed it onto the highway to his front.

"I see green," the voice on the other end of the radio said.

"Affirmative. What sort of inbound action can we expect?"

Another pause, then, "A squad of Apaches; ETA one minute. Hold on, Raid-One. Wait, we have a second identifier. Green smoke to the west of the first. We're going to need you to authenticate. Pop smoke again."

Ross lifted up a few inches and saw the smoke. He also saw a platoon-sized body of men moving at a diagonal to the highway. "Get your asses up!" he yelled to the few cowering soldiers who were left alive. "We got bad guys at our ten o'clock trying to flank us. Up! Up! Up!" He led by example, firing a full magazine into the enemy.

When he ducked back down, he wasn't done yelling. "I am not going to pop more smoke, you dumb shit! You dropped us on the damned highway five minutes ago and we're still there. Clearly, the bad guys have the same comm equipment we have, so if I pop yellow smoke they will, too."

"Affirmative Raid-One. We have your position marked as…" Ross didn't hear the rest. A flight of Apaches seemed to have appeared out of nowhere. They fired off a salvo of Hydra-70 rockets and although none of the Apaches seemed to be focused on the ditch, Ross wasn't taking any chances. He hunkered down, squinting, as the birds came in low and slow, wanting to maximize the damage done by adding their nose-mounted 30mm chain guns to the carnage.

It seemed like nothing could live through that much destructive firepower, however, just then missiles began to streak upwards. The enemy had Stinger antiaircraft launchers—a lot of them. The Apaches were hit from every side and despite their tough hides, not one escaped and now the air was filled with spinning blades of death that struck friend and foe alike.

"Stingers!" Ross was screaming into the radio. "They've got Stingers all over the fucking place! At least twenty, and they're situated all around us."

Two hundred miles away, General Phillips commanding officer of the 7th Army, was listening to the battle as if he were sitting in his doctor's office being told that he had cancer. "Shit," he whispered. "They have Stingers. They have Sting…what the fuck? Of course, they have Stingers. They are us."

He glanced up at his map. It aged him every time he did so. The President would be woken from his fucking beauty sleep at any moment and he would want good news. And they all knew that if he didn't get it, he would do something stupid. If there was one thing that could be counted on in all this God-forsaken mess was that the old man was always up for a bit of idiocy.

And there wasn't much in the way of good news. The line was, for the most part, holding. But it was thin. Oh God, was it thin. In some places it was as thin as the skin of a soap bubble. Any little pressure and it would pop, and then all hell would break out, starting with nukes.

Phillips couldn't tell the president that he had lost, in the space of a day, not only the 82nd Airborne Division, but the 101st as well. That was the sort of thing that could get Boston nuked. And Philadelphia. And half of Pennsylvania.

They needed that breakthrough. They needed it desperately. Combining his force with the hard-nosed crowd in Massachusetts was the only way they would be able to hold the northeast. Then Phillips would be free to concentrate on holding the western and southern sectors of the Zone. It was the only path to victory that he could see.

He picked up the phone and dialed in General Platnik. "Send in the next wave."

"No, the LZ is too hot. It's going to need to be softened up first. I'm calling in some fast movers, but they were all configured for air superiority. It'll take some time."

"Send them in the next fucking wave, Platnik, and if you say 'no' to me again, I'll send you in as well."

"Then go ahead and send me," Platnik said, easily. "They have our comm frequencies and can hear everything we say. If we go in, it'll be suicide. Do you know how many men we lost on that last assault? The drones show a hundred and fifty-four bodies and that doesn't include the losses among the Apache pilots. So no, I won't be sending in the next wave, unless that consists of just me. Should I get a chopper spooled up?"

Platnik's tone was infuriating and so was his limited tactical and strategic viewpoint. "Get them all spooled up, damnit. If they have access to your communications then, for fuck's sake, tell them the LZ is being moved."

The commanding officer of the 101st groaned at failing to see the obvious. "Shit, right. Sorry." He hung up.

Phillips gazed down at the phone and then back up at the big map. He was overdue in giving his boss, General Heider, his report. "He's going to have to wait a little longer."

Chapter 8

1– 7:03 a.m.
—Fort Meade, Maryland

At about the same time the President was woken up by a gentle knock on his door by his Chief of Staff, Marty Aleman, who had a servant with him carrying a tray of tea and coffee cakes, Special Agent Katherine Pennock was pulling into the parking lot at Fort Meade.

Among other agencies within the facility, it was the home of the Headquarters of the United States Cyber Command. Forty hours earlier when it was decided that cyber attacks were the absolute least of anyone's concerns, the Governor of Maryland had breezed in with a phalanx of officials and had commandeered the building, its personnel and all of its equipment. There had been a general outcry, but the governor had the backing of Marty Aleman, who wanted an extra layer of defense between him and the zombies. Since Marty spoke for the President even when the President was sleeping, it was a done deal.

From then on, the assets of Cyber Command had been used exclusively to monitor and control every street, avenue, bridge, river and sewer pipe along the northern portion of the Maryland State line as well as the entire eastern coastline. It was a tremendous undertaking involving thousands of police officers, state troopers, soldiers and civilians, hundreds of linked radios, six repositioned satellites, fifty unmanned drones and whatever boats they could steal from the naval reserve and the Coast Guard.

After the city of Baltimore was placed on complete lockdown, it was added to the Command's scope of responsibility, but since they were tapped out, Marty snapped his fingers and sent in the FBI and five companies of federalized Virginian guardsmen.

The Virginians were spread thin, untrained for what was being asked of them, and unfamiliar with the city;

Katherine figured that there had to be holes. She also figured that Eng or Anna would try to find those holes and exploit them.

The building that held Cyber Command was one of the most imposing buildings she had ever seen. Twenty stories of cold, black glass. It was the sort of government building that when you looked at it you just knew "they" were doing something illegal inside: wiretapping, unauthorized surveillance…torture, maybe.

Once inside, Katherine had the opposite feeling. It was bedlam. People went in every direction, many with lost looks on their faces; there were shouted arguments going on in unseen offices; and the security arrangements, once an impressive obstacle course of guards and full body scanners and secret codes, were now empty. Katherine bypassed the unmanned scanners and proceeded to a reception desk where eight women were taking who knew how many simultaneous calls.

Even though nobody asked, she held up her FBI I.D. card. One of the women pointed to a sign which read: FBI 16th floor. There were a dozen signs just like it.

Katherine shook her head and waited until the woman, a harried fifty-something with layered bags under her eyes, finished her phone call. "16th floor," she said right away. "The elevators are just to your right."

"No, hold on," Katherine said. "I want to talk to whoever's in charge of this operation. I'm supposed to be briefing the President pretty soon." This came out smoothly, since as far as she knew it was still the truth.

The woman chuckled and shook her head. "The FBI is in charge of the FBI. Cyber Command is in charge of Cyber Command. The NSA is in charge of the NSA. You get it?"

"No, I don't," Katherine replied, feeling that lost look everyone seemed to be wearing start to creep onto her face. "This is supposed to be a joint operation. Who's in overall command? And what happened to security?"

The woman leaned over the desk and Katherine leaned in close to her. "It's a cluster-fuck," the woman said. "I don't normally use words like that, but in this case, it's true. This Baltimore business has thrown everyone for a loop and I can't really tell you who's in charge of anything. No one knows. Not even the military. The Virginians won't listen to the Marylanders. And the regular army won't listen to the national guardsman. And all the spook alphabet agencies won't listen to anyone." She leaned even closer and whispered, "There have been actual fist-fights, can you believe it?"

Katherine didn't want to believe it, not with so much at stake. "And the security?"

"Someone came through and took them to man the lines, but if I was a wagering woman I'd say more than half took off. There are roadblocks two miles away. Two miles." She looked ill at the very idea.

Katherine leaned back to look at the different signs. With her specialty being cyber crime, she decided to go straight to Cyber Command. She certainly didn't want to talk to anyone in the FBI not since she was sort of AWOL. She thanked the woman, who was already taking another two calls and went to the third floor.

Everything here was humming along with far greater efficiency. For the most part the people who worked here were soldiers, used to taking orders. These were their offices and their equipment. It was their mission that was now completely different.

Katherine wandered among offices trying to find anyone who was willing to talk, but everyone was too busy to talk to an FBI agent. A captain walked by while she was going in circles. He was in his mid-forties, but hard as a rock. He glared as she explained why she was there. His name tag read *John Questore* and he was obviously unimpressed by her. "*You* are going to debrief the President on Cyber Command?"

"I work for the cyber criminal unit in the FBI," she explained. When he only lifted a skeptical eyebrow, she added, "What can I say, he likes them young and blonde. It's stupid and embarrassing, but what can you do?"

Questore grunted. "I heard that about him. It's embarrassing to have a lecherous hound in the White House. I didn't vote for him. And why on earth would he have a fed debrief him on our activities? This is a military operation and that should…"

She held up a hand. "Sir, I'm on a time crunch. I need information on the domestic terrorists. Do you have anything at all on them?"

He shook his head. "I was hoping you feds knew. So far, the only thing the FBI is willing to release is that we are looking for a man and a woman. Is that all you really have?" Reluctantly, Katherine nodded. He looked pained at the admission. "Then I don't know what to say. There are close to a million people within the city and with descriptions like 'man and a woman' it's like looking for a needle in a haystack."

"I agree, but I still need to report something. Can I see what your people are doing?"

Captain Questore waved an arm. "*Me casa es su casa.* Just say nice things about us to that useless, horny fuck in the White House."

Katherine gave him a grin. "If he looks up from my tits, I will." The captain laughed and then disappeared, giving her the freedom to range where she wanted. She went through the corridors, ducking her head into every office. In one she picked up a clipboard and pen thinking it would make her look "official."

"What are you working on?" she asked each person she met. Invariably they would give her a *who the hell are you* sort of look and so she learned to cut them off quick. "We have a ton of redundancy. Captain Questore wanted me to make a list."

For the most part, they were monitoring the events occurring along the Maryland border and sending reports up the chain of command. These events consisted mostly of armed clashes with fleeing civilians coming south out of Pennsylvania. There were also problems with people coming out of Delaware. No one knew what to do about that.

There wasn't enough manpower to fully contain the city of Baltimore and shut down the hundred mile border with Delaware. Katherine found herself staring at the map and thinking that they were being fools. They had no evidence whatsoever to believe that Eng and Anna or whoever it was who had made the zombies on Long Island would make more.

It seemed highly unlikely and yet the orders had come from the President, a man whose leadership and mental state were questionable. For just a moment, she considered racing back to FBI headquarters and dismissing that other blonde. She'd then meet the President and tell him to give up on Baltimore and concentrate on the Pennsylvania border. "But would he listen?" She doubted it. From the Director on down, the scuttle-butt was that the President was losing it. He was chasing shadows.

In this instance, the shadows were real. Katherine just had to find them.

She went to the newly formed Baltimore team and talked to each member, pretending to write on her clipboard. This led her to a large room partitioned off in little cubes, each with a desk and two or three monitors. There were twenty men and one woman working there. It was the same sort of setup Katherine spent most of her days in and the same sort of male to female ratio.

She went up to the lone woman, looking for a little solidarity. The woman was a lieutenant commander named Dawn Brockett and she had started the night with her hair pulled back in a severe bun. It was now a loose, floppy thing with stray curls escaping everywhere.

Dawn was studying infrared images of the city; she didn't look up from her keyboard as she answered Katherine's question, "I'm doing a comparison of the southeast quadrant of the city. Since midnight there have been six recon passes; one by a military satellite and the rest by UAVs. The circles are changes from the first and second passes. The squares are changes from the second to the third, and so on."

Katherine came to lean over the woman's shoulder and was tickled by one of her errant curls. The screens were fantastically convoluted with circles and squares and triangles and figure eights all over the place. Katherine knew there really wasn't any other way to collect data on such short notice.

"Do you have these same pics in the visible spectrum?" Katherine asked.

"Yeah, but why would you want it?" The question was legitimate. There had been rolling blackouts for the last two days, but as of midnight the Eastern Interconnection, what people called the east coast power grid, had been shut down completely before it could fail in a catastrophic manner.

Only buildings with generators such as the one they were in had power. Outside, everything was very dark. It had been strange driving through such darkness. Katherine had felt distinctly alone, as if the entire population of the world had quietly left when she wasn't looking.

A picture of the darkness would have limited value, but on a hunch, Katherine directed the lieutenant commander to bring it up. Dawn began to splutter, but Katherine lied, "Captain Questore has given me access to everything. If you have a problem, bring it up with him."

The lie worked and even though Katherine felt like a gambler letting her winnings ride and ride, she shooed Dawn over and sat in her still warm seat.

"See? Useless," Dawn said, once the "picture" was on the screens. She was right. Other than the headlights of a few vehicles, almost everything was pure black. If people had candles or flashlights in their homes, they were hidden behind dark curtains or layers of wood. Since they couldn't flee, people had fortified their homes as best as they could.

Snapshots of car headlights were also of very limited value. They gave her the position and the direction of a handful of cars. It was impossible for her to know if car A in the first picture was any of the cars captured in the next picture, which was taken forty-five minutes later.

"What is this lit-up building?" Katherine asked, pointing.

Dawn squinted at the screen. "Police station and that one is a hospital."

Mentioning a hospital sent a queer thrill through Katherine. This entire mess had started in a hospital. "Which one? What's it called?" she asked chasing a new hunch.

"That one? Uh, University of Maryland Med Center."

Katherine clicked through the images to see if any of the cars were pointing its way. None were, however on the second to last picture a tiny pinprick of light in the corner of the frame caught her eye. "What's that? Can I enlarge this?" The program was similar to Google Earth and she was able to center and zoom in. But only so far. "What is that? Is that a mobile home?"

"Yes, I think so. Let's see if it comes up on infrared." Dawn reached across Katherine and clicked so they could see if the mobile home was giving off a heat signature. "Yup, right there. It's low, probably a propane heater." She clicked through each of the shots and then when she got to the last, the heat signature had disappeared.

"Blow that up!" Katherine ordered and scooted out of the chair. Dawn took over and went to full zoom mode, going through all twelve shots of infrared and visible light.

"See that? The one picture with the light? You can see a truck hitched in front. Now look at the infrared views. You can see it just as a smudge near the front, except on the last. Someone moved that truck between shot five and six."

Katherine felt excitement brewing in her gut. "When was the last pass and how do I get to this place?"

"It was a quarter of five this morning and I guess you just drive." That really wasn't what Katherine had meant. She knew how to get there. She just needed to know how she would get back.

2-Baltimore, Maryland

Getting through the first roadblock would have been impossible without Anna's acting skills and Eng's deathly cold stare. Charlie had driven the Silverado just down the block from where a group of soldiers had strung rolls of concertina wire across the street. When he slowed the truck, Eng stuck his Beretta up under Leticia's throat and pressed it hard until she started crying.

"Hey, *Scott*, what are you doing?" Anna asked.

"I need them to know that I will not hesitate to blow her brains out if they try to signal those soldiers in any way. You hear that, Charlie? I will kill her and then I will shoot the soldiers. And it will be your fault. So don't be a fucking hero."

This got the two senior citizens properly frightened. They were both shaking and pale, however it was Anna who stole the show.

Seventy yards from the roadblock, someone with a bullhorn stopped them and demanded that they turn back. "Turn off your lights, but keep going a little further," Anna said. "Slowly, slowly, slowly…"

"Stop or we will open fire!"

Charlie stopped. His fear was so obvious that it couldn't have been faked. Anna was ramped up, but not precisely afraid. She had been through too much to be afraid of a few nitwit, part-time soldiers. Instead of going to the very closest roadblock, they had used the CB to tune into the frequency they were using and had steered clear of the first two crossing points because they had officious sounding policemen with the soldiers. Police officers were naturally suspicious and generally hard-hearted from having had to deal with human scum for so long.

"Have grandma hold her breath until I get back, it'll make her panting more believable." Anna let her own breath out and then opened the truck's door. She climbed out, pausing to point in at the cab.

The bullhorn blared, "Get back in your vehicle and turn around."

"I can't! It's my mom." She started lurching forward with her hands up. "She's having a heart attack! We need help. Do you have a medic or something like that?"

"Stop or we will shoot. Miss, I said stop. We will open fire!"

"Go ahead!" Anna shrieked, and at the same moment tore open the green blouse she was wearing Her bra looked stark white in the beams of light. "I'm unarmed, but my mom is having a heart attack and the hospitals are overflowing. They said she wouldn't be seen for hours and she doesn't have that long. Please, take a look at her."

She was only twenty feet away, near enough to see the looks of confusion on the faces of the guardsmen. She was close to sealing the deal. Dropping to her knees, she begged, "Please, she never hurt anyone."

"None of us are medics," a sergeant said. "I don't think there's anything we could do for her."

Anna pointed at the early morning skyline to a building rising just beyond I-695, the Baltimore Beltway. "That's Roosevelt Memorial Hospital. It's just two blocks. You can follow us if you want, but please just let us through."

"I don't know, miss."

She got up, clutching her shirt around her bosom and came forward, right to the wire. "Please take a look at her and you'll know we're not lying."

"Aw fuck," the sergeant said. "Let me see her."

Leticia was so scared she was practically wetting herself. She hadn't been able to hold her breath for the entire time that Anna was gone; she could only gulp in air like she was trying to eat it. She looked truly pathetic, but that didn't stop Eng from glaring right up until Anna and the soldier arrived.

"What can you do for her?" he asked, using his best American accent. "I think she's dying."

"I-I don't know, um…" The sergeant didn't know at all what to do. His instructions were to let no one through, under no circumstances. And yet his LT hadn't mentioned someone having a heart attack. "I guess I could have one of my guys follow you."

Anna faked tears and hugged the man while Charlie was so relieved he actually felt like puking. In minutes, the rolls of wires were pulled back and the Silverado had a military escort to the hospital, which was shockingly busy. Fear was in the air and it brought the paranoids and the hypochondriacs out of the woodwork. On top of the crazies there was a greater than average accident rate due to darkness. All of this was aggravated by the immense stress everyone was under and it was no wonder there were patients lying in the halls.

There were also cars parked bumper to bumper all around the Emergency room. "What do we do?" Leticia asked, afraid that the two maniacs would blame her for this.

"Just keep acting sick," Anna said. "Lay back down. Charlie take a left. Start looking for a parking spot. Go slow." The Humvee followed, but after five minutes the sergeant got nervous about being gone too long from his post and flashed his lights.

Anna ran back but before she could say anything, the sergeant said, "We got to go. Will you be alright?" She said she was good and even grabbed his arm in a very friendly way as she smiled.

"Man, that is one fine piece of ass," he murmured, watching intently as she hurried back to the truck. The private sitting in the passenger seat growled appreciably. "Yeah, she is all that, but we got to forget her, got it? It'll be our ass on the line if anyone finds out that we let someone through, got it? No one came through."

When Anna got to the truck, she grinned, "We can ghost now."

3-The Taconic Valley, New York

"Take off your shirt," Jerry said, his voice low and hungry. He had taken his belt off and was now running it through his hands. Thuy had her chin set straight forward, but her eyes were canted. She couldn't look at anything but the belt.

"Y-You w-won't need the b-b-belt," she said, her lower jaw jabbering up and down.

Thuy sucked in her breath as Jerry brought the belt up and around. When it hit her back, the pain was fierce, a strange combination of fire and ice except that it was not any fire or ice she had ever felt before. It was agony, and after that one breath, she couldn't seem to suck in another.

Jerry was saying something only just then she couldn't hear anything but a rushing in her head and the sound of her teeth grinding together. She was squirming on the ground when she caught sight of the belt lifted a second time. "No." She tried to scream the word; it came out as a whisper. The belt came down as she flung up an arm and turned her head.

This time the belt struck her on the forearm and across the top of her back. Because she had managed to block part of the blow, the pain was far less. She was able to breathe, which meant she could talk. "Okay, I'll take it off. I'll take it off."

"Slowly, slowly," he said, grinning. He seemed to like that her hands were shaking. They were shaking so badly that slow was all she could handle. "Good. Very good." He had the belt ready.

Thuy did not find anything sexy about taking off a t-shirt even if it did have the word *Juicy* on it. Once it was off, she had no idea what to do next. That this horrid man was going to rape her was, it seemed, inevitable. She shuddered, and tried her best to think of a way out, but he was so big and the belt hurt so much that she realized there was nothing she could do to stop him. Her thoughts skittered to what would happen after…Would he kill her then?

She held the shirt against her chest and waited to be told what to do next. As she waited, she forced her eyes away from the belt and scanned the trash scattered all over the floor, hoping against hope that she would see a gun or a butcher's knife or something she could use against him.

"Drop the shirt," he said.

Thuy let out a shaky breath and dropped the shirt. It landed, covering the toes of her borrowed sneakers. She couldn't look up, now.

"Now unbutton your pants, slowly."

Her hands were on the first button when she heard something. For the last few days there had been a constant rumble in the sky above the Zone as planes flew back and forth. This sound was a rumble of a different nature. It was a car.

"I said unbutton your…" Jerry stopped, his head cocked. Thuy had a great view of him as washed-out sunlight from a cracked window framed him in a square. Jerry was unpalatable in the dark; in the light, he seemed to be part ogre. She was still staring when he suddenly leapt on her, slapping a hand over her mouth.

The two of them, an unlikely pair who could only have been brought together by the most unlikely series of events froze, listening as the car came closer. It was driving on a course that would take it south, unless it turned. For a second, Thuy felt a tiny spurt of hope, but the car didn't turn. It just kept going.

When it passed without stopping, hope left Thuy completely. She knew this man would use her, break her bones, wreck her face, and then kill her. Instinctively, she knew he was an outcast who had lived with rejection for years while hate was filling his entire being. Now, she realized, he had an opportunity to unleash it all on her and get some sort of revenge on the world--without consequences.

As the sound of the car diminished, Thuy was suddenly aware that his grip on her had relaxed and she thrust away from him.

"Hey…" he started to say, but she spun and unleashed a straight right square into his jaw. Pain flared in her hand. It felt as though she had broken a bone, but she ignored it as she drove her left fist into his gut which had the consistency of a slab of beef.

Thuy had hit him as hard as she could and Jerry sucked in a sharp breath and then laughed. "That's more like it!" he cried.

This was why she was without hope. Her right hand ached and her left wrist throbbed; she had hurt herself more than she had hurt him. She wasn't built to fight, but she could run. She turned, meaning to run and had she been in the open she would have gotten away, however the mobile home was narrow and cluttered. He was right behind her as she got to the one door and as she grabbed the knob and heaved the door back, he put one hand on it and slammed it closed.

She tried to run towards the living room, but he gave her a light shove, sending her flying. Jerry laughed as she scrambled around the folding card table and tried to keep it between them. He slapped it aside, his eyes gleaming. He was enjoying himself. He was getting jazzed. For him, this was foreplay.

"Yes," he whispered. "And to think I was afraid you'd just lie there and take it like a Chinese fuck-doll."

"I'm Vietnamese, asshole," she said, glaring.

"Oh? Then it's time for some payback."

Chapter 9

1– 8:16 a.m.
—The Taconic Valley, New York

Ryan Deckard jogged past the football field with the sun climbing on his left. The school was ahead of him, sitting quietly as if waiting, as if it had been expecting him. If Thuy had decided to wait for him, it would be in there.

He slowed, moving past a dinged-up Sedona. Glancing in, he saw that it was trashed, filled with old McDonald's bags, empty liquor bottles and a thousand cigarette butts. A rust-bucket like this was the last vehicle he would want, or so he told himself, but then his right foot kicked something that jangled.

On the ground was a set of keys, with a heavy emphasis on the plural. There had to be thirty keys on the ring. Stopping, he picked them up and singled out the longest; it was stamped: KIA. This was a lucky break of sorts. What would have been luckier was if the RAV4 had been in view.

"She's gone," he said, and let out a long sigh. "She met up with the guy who drove this piece of crap and took off." In his mind, he had a picture of Jerry Weir and other than an imaginary mullet and leather jacket, he wasn't far off.

"But she would have left a note." He was sure of that, only he didn't know where. Back at the football field would have been the most likely, only there hadn't been one and she wouldn't have hidden it. Glancing at the school made him think twice about going in. It was eerily quiet. Still, it was the most promising spot and he figured that he would find a hastily scrawled note at the front desk or maybe taped to the front doors.

Walking past the Sedona, he went to the side door of the school and found it open. *Another lucky break*, he thought, but then paused. Two blackbirds stared down at him from a tree; they had blood on their talons. Although they did nothing but stare, it gave him the willies and he wanted to pick up a rock and whip it at them. It was an urge he resisted. The morning was too still to be broken by him. Someone or something else would have to do it.

The school was dim but not dark, and as quiet as the morning. He could see almost to where the hall bisected another at an angle. It made sense to jog down there, hang the left which would undoubtedly lead to the main section of the school, find the note and get the hell out of there—but something warned him to be cautious.

Going on cat's feet, he slipped down the hall, making almost zero noise. Thirty steps in, something metallic echoed in the school. It might have been a locker closing or a drawer of a filing cabinet thumping shut. Deckard ducked into the nearest classroom and paused, listening. For half a minute, he waited but when nothing else happened, he kept going, making it to the intersecting hall, where he glanced in both directions.

To the right, the hall was empty and clean, the doors all shut. To the left, the hall was littered along the edges, but by what he couldn't tell. Wishing he had some sort of weapon, he crept to the left, walking somewhat hunched over, fully expecting the worst. A sheen of sweat on his forehead had nothing to do with the temperature of the morning, which was cool; he was simply afraid, something he found strange. He was almost never afraid and here he was afraid of what? The dark? The fact that he was alone? He didn't know and he didn't like it.

The mess in the hall turned out to be broken ceiling tiles. Looking up he saw that there were cracked and holed tiles on both sides of the hallway. Perplexed, he glanced into one of rooms and saw more of a mess. An entire panel was missing and there was white dust on the floor beneath the hole.

No zombie had taken down the tile. A person might, but why would they want to? The oddity of the missing tile only unsettled him further, but he shook off the desire to run away and pressed on. At the front desk, he found himself in the geographic center of the building. What he didn't find was a note.

"Son of a…" The curse froze on his lips as he caught sight of an open cardboard box behind the front desk. There were piles of clothes around it and to the side was a torn white blouse, a pair of black slacks in a crumple and a pair of dirty high-heeled shoes. They had been Thuy's.

"Okay, she changed into something a bit more appropriate for a zombie invasion. Good. But where did she go?" To the left of the receptionist's desk was a short hall and an open door. There was more ceiling dust here, another missing tile and broken glass. It was the principal's office. A baseball bat sat on the desk. Deckard gladly picked it up. He hefted it as he looked around, trying to piece together what might have happened by the presence of the bat, the holes in the ceiling and the window, and the dust on the filing cabinet.

"She found a bat, maybe down by the field. Came here. Got changed, but zombies came and she climbed up into the ceiling. She made her way outside and found there was someone there. Someone with a KIA. They joined forces and left…without leaving a note. Probably because there wasn't time."

This all seemed very likely, except for the bat. It was pitted like a kid's bat, but it was sticky with what might have been steering fluid, and it smelled like…well, he didn't know what the smell was, but it was unpleasant.

On a hunch, he pulled the chair from behind the desk and stepped up on it to peer into the crawl space. Right away he saw a matching hole in the ceiling across from him. "What the hell? Two holes?" That meant the person with the bat had been in the school with Thuy. With the dull light gleaming up through the holes, Deckard could see the trail left by the two of them as they had progressed across the tops of the walls.

As he was staring, he saw a quick shadow from one of the holes. It was as if someone or something had walked beneath the hole and had momentarily blocked the light. Then there was another shadow, this one slightly closer.

Whatever it was, it was getting closer, moving down the hall. Now, there were more shadows and the sound of moans.

"Shit," Deckard whispered. They were zombies. He dropped down and hurried to the door, shutting it as quietly as he could and turning the lock. The door was far from heavy duty. It would take them only minutes to get in, but that's if they heard him…or smelled him. Zombies had a surprisingly good sense of smell. He crossed to the couch, pulled up two of the cushions and laid them in front of the door as he considered his options.

They were very limited: Sit there and hope they went away or go out the broken window. The window, its jagged edges black with zombie blood was a last resort. It would be too loud and there was a chance that…

An ugly face suddenly emerged from the shrubs peering in at him. Perhaps because he was standing still, Deckard wasn't seen at first. It wasn't until a second zombie joined the first that they saw him. At the same time, the door's handle began to twist back and forth. "Fuck," Deckard whispered. *They* didn't normally use the doorknobs. This meant that there was a "thinking" zombie in the hall. It was either a child or a zombie on an overdose-level of pain meds, and this meant that Deckard had wandered into a trap.

Since luck had abandoned him, he had to rely on speed to save him. Quick as a monkey he was up on the chair, then the cabinet and then into the rafters. Balancing on the top of the wall was much harder than it appeared, and it was killer on the knees. Still, crawling was the only way to go.

He had passed two classrooms before the office he had left was breeched and the beasts poured in. *Suckers*, he thought as he scurried.

Another classroom passed below him and as he came up to the next, the tile behind him unexpectedly burst upward, breaking into pieces. He glanced back thinking he would see a zombie, instead he saw a gleaming brass eagle the size of his hand. It was set on a pole and beneath it was a white-dusted American flag.

It disappeared and then came blasting up again almost directly behind him, scraping the wall as it came through. Deckard wobbled, but managed to hold on. He was on a T section of the walls. If he went right, he'd trap himself. Going back was useless and going forward was suicide. With no good option, he stayed in place. Thirty seconds later the tiles in front of him began to explode.

"Where are you?" a high-pitched guttural voice asked. Deckard was sure if a jackal could speak, it would sound like this child-thing. He could just see the creature, a bloody-faced boy, below him. Thankfully, he was staring up into the next hole. "You can't hide," it said in its high-dog-like voice. "It's not allowed. It's not allowed at breakfast. No playing at breakfast."

The kid was right. There'd be no hiding for long and when Deckard was found he'd be treed like a cat. The boy would use the pole to knock him down and if that didn't work, he would, no doubt, use fire or throw rocks, and one way or another he'd get to Deckard.

Another man might have frozen in fear, but Deckard had already survived too much to be killed by this little thing. He dropped down out of the ceiling, bringing three tiles down with him in a great plume of billowing dust. His sudden appearance shocked the zombies. Although the hall was crowded with them, there were only two in the room: the child-thing and a small adult that had been so chewed up that it looked as though it had been run over by a lawnmower and Deckard couldn't tell if it had been a man or a woman back when it had been truly alive.

Regardless of its sex, it was dangerous just being within proximity to it. Before it could fully recover, Deckard picked up a desk and used it as a battering ram to drive the beast out into the hall. He shut the door behind it and turned, just as the child attacked, trying to spear him with the eagle-headed flagpole.

Deckard snatched the pole right out of its hands and then jabbed the blunt end into the child's stomach.

Although the creature was half-demon, it had the flesh of a child and Deckard had the strength of a linebacker. The pole drove through the thing's soft skin and came out its back. It didn't even blink.

It stood there grinning as black blood dripped down Old Glory. Deckard thrust the eagle away and picked up another desk, fifty pounds of metal and wood. He brought it crashing down on the demon-child, breaking the arm it flung up, snapping its clavicle in two, and taking off half its face. With the first desk contaminated with diseased blood, Deckard picked up a second desk-chair and finished the job by caving in the child's head.

Feeling a moment of disgust, mixed with strange compassion for the child, he said, "Shit," which was an apology of sorts. It was all he had time for. He had to get out of there before the door came down. He used a clean chair to bash in one of the windows and then he was out in the sunshine and running for the KIA as zombies flocked in from every direction.

He was quicker and made it to the minivan, which stank of weed and old, congealed milk. He inserted the key he had picked up from the driveway and backed away from the school. Which was worse, he wondered, as he cranked down a window, owning a car that smelled like this or stealing one that smelled like this. "Of course, maybe whoever had this hadn't stolen it."

With a wild hope, Deckard opened the glove compartment and, after letting two empty whiskey bottles fall away, he dug through the piles of paper for the vehicle's registration. "Jerry Weir, 211 Maiers Road. Where the hell is that?" Just as he was saying this, he saw a gas station ahead with a sign that read *Xtra Mart*. He grinned, knowing the little gas station would have a map. He was on Thuy's scent and his heart was filled with the idea of seeing her.

Maiers Road was three miles away and Deckard pushed the Sedona for all she was worth—it wasn't worth much and it rode choppy, spewing blue smoke out the back whenever it changed gears.

Jerry Weir heard the mis-firing engine and knew it immediately. It was why he had frozen with his hand over Thuy's mouth, his breath pent up in his chest. It seemed like the Ghost of Christmas Past was coming for him. Guilt robbed him of strength, and if Thuy had fought him then, he wouldn't have been able to stop her from running out of the mobile home.

But then the minivan slipped on by and, too late, Thuy had fought back, uselessly.

Deckard knew nothing about any of this. He drove on by, missing his turn into the overgrown drive. It wasn't until he saw the next mailbox that read *412 Maiers RD— Troutman*, that he realized he had missed the Weir residence. He turned the rusted Sedona around with growing excitement, thinking that Thuy was safe up in one these farmhouses.

"Probably napping. Oh man, I sure could use a nap myself. Or an actual real night's sleep." He found the turn off and right away started to get a sick feeling in his gut as he saw the RAV4 and the ugly mess in the yard. He knew what sort of low-rent trash he would be dealing with and he knew that if the people in the mobile home had guns, he would be in a world of hurt. But that didn't stop him or even slow him down.

Inside the mobile home, Jerry grabbed the half-naked Chinese chick and dragged her back to the kitchen, where he fished around in the drawers for a knife. At first, he found a steak knife, but as Deckard got out of the car and came crunching over broken glass to the canted stoop there was a strange menace in the air and Jerry knew that a steak knife wouldn't do the job. He found a seven-inch boning knife that looked sharper than it really was and stuck it up under the woman's throat and waited.

When the knock came it came softly and for a moment Jerry felt a touch of hope as he pictured a woman on the other side of the door. The second knock was louder and shook the door on its frame, killing that hope.

"Tell him to go away," Jerry whispered in her ear. "Tell him I have a gun and I'll shoot you if he tries to come in."

Thuy didn't know who this was but she said a silent prayer, begging for it to be Deckard. If it was him, he was Thuy's only chance and she wasn't about to send him away. She cleared her throat, forcing herself to remain calm. "Deckard? Is that you?"

"Yeah," he growled through the door. "What the fuck is going on?"

As Thuy sagged in relief, Jerry cried, "I have a gun! So, get your ass back in the car and get out of here if you know what's good for you."

For the last few hours, Thuy had been living in a state of fear that rivaled her fear of the zombies, but now as she felt Jerry's confusion, her courage perked up. "He's only got a knife," she said. "You'll be able-glaug…" Jerry had pulled the blade tight against the skin of her throat.

"I'll kill her!" Jerry yelled. "I swear I'll slit her throat if you…"

Deckard didn't wait. He could hear the uncertainty in the man's voice. It was pathetic. He opened the cheap door and strode in. To his right was a dinky kitchen with a two-burner stove and a refrigerator that came up to his shoulder. Leaning against it was a slob of a man holding Thuy by her silken black hair with one hand. In the other was a long knife that had sparkles of rust along its edge. It was tucked up under her chin.

"I'll slit her from ear to ear," Jerry said, sneering. "What do you think about that?" Jerry couldn't help the sneer. The man didn't have a gun. He didn't even have a knife. The fear Jerry had been feeling left him. It was replaced by embarrassment and a sharp headache that was beginning to come over him like an express train. It was a fucked up hangover that stemmed from drinking too much crappy whiskey and even crappier gin.

It made him mean.

"Then slit her throat," Deckard said. "Go ahead. That way there'll be nothing between you and me. I just have to warn you that if you hurt her, I'll take that stupid knife right out of your hands and I'll use it to take your eyes. Then I'll call some zombies I saw wandering around out by the road and watch while they eat you."

"Yeah right," Jerry said, growing in confidence. "I got all the aces dipshit. I got a knife and you got nothing. I got the girl and all you got are empty threats, and you better believe me, I'll slit her wide open, because unlike you I don't give a rat's ass about her. Now get the fuck out. You can have what's left over when I'm through with her."

Deckard didn't budge. "You won't slit her throat because if you do, you and I are going to come to blows. And let's say you win, what do you have? Two dead bodies stinking up your kitchen. And if you lose, well you're just dead. So, do the smart thing and let the girl go and we'll forget about this little incident."

The knife didn't budge. "Fuck you," Jerry said, but with less emphasis. Thuy could feel the cold edge of the knife against her throat going back and forth, see-sawing in conjunction with his indecision. She closed her eyes and waited, hoping that he would just let her go.

But he wasn't that kind of guy and this wasn't that sort of world anymore. In his head, everyone was dead and that meant everything left was up for grabs and that included chicks. Holding the knife close, he shoved her down to her knees and forced her face into the greasy door of the oven, all the while he watched Deckard. "Stay there, bitch. I'll just be a moment."

Deckard shook his head, not really wanting to fight. He was tired, deeply tired. After four days of action and just snatches of sleep here and there, he knew his reactions were slow; he knew he could lose. He had hoped to bluff his way out of this with his calm demeanor, but Jerry had his pig-sticker and a nasty attitude.

"Fine," Deckard said, and rolled his head on his shoulders, trying to loosen up as Jerry got into an awkward crouch.

There were three basic attacks with a knife: the overhead stab, the slash along a horizontal plane, and the straight forward thrust. Jerry ruled out the overhead attack because of the low ceiling, and the slashing attack, which was useless because the knife wasn't all that sharp. That left the basic thrust.

The point was deadly sharp and it came at Deckard hard and fast with Jerry's enraged face behind it. Deckard jumped back, reaching with his right hand for whatever he could grab as a weapon or a defensive tool. His hand found Thuy's mug full of gin and he threw it. It hit Jerry in the chest, doing little damage, but it did cause him to blanch long enough for Deckard to grab the second mug. He threw that too. It missed completely exploding with a rain of gin and mug shards. Jerry flinched back, but now stabbed out at Deckard, the tip of the blade missing him by a fraction of an inch.

The blade was so close that it snagged in his shirt for just a brief moment. It was a wasted opportunity.

Deckard had trained for this, but never under these narrow, obstruction filled conditions, with not just his life on the line, but also the life of the women he loved, as well. Jerry had left the knife hanging uselessly in the air, his arm extended for a fraction of a second too long, but Deckard was out of position, slightly unbalanced, his left foot on a stack of empty tv dinner trays that slid beneath him.

Jerry, thinking that he had to press the attack, tried to stab again. He pulled the blade back, readying it for another thrust and giving Deckard a half second to recover. He grabbed the only weapon in sight: the gin bottle, and held it like a short club. The two paused. Jerry stared at the bottle, understanding coming slowly that its presence might have changed the balance of things slightly, but he wasn't sure by how much.

For Deckard, it was obvious. Neither the knife nor the bottle had any use defensively and he saw that whoever attacked first would have the advantage. Unexpectedly, he hurled the bottle at Jerry, who flinched as Deckard knew he would. The bottle clipped off Jerry's shoulder and exploded against the wall. Although he hadn't hit Jerry squarely, that flinch was enough for Deckard, who leapt forward, landing a terrific kick to Jerry's round gut.

Whereas Thuy was tiny and unused to the rigors of combat, Deckard was well practiced and was now feeling his form and getting into his rhythm. The kick struck with the force of a sledgehammer and it knocked the air out of Jerry. Another man might have tried to grapple for the knife. Deckard ignored it and shot a straight left at Jerry's face, following it with a straight right and then a looping left and another right.

He hit with every punch. Jerry could only blink at the speed and ferocity of the punches. The first stunned him. The second made his knees buckle. The third turned his eyes up in his head and the fourth sent him toppling to the ground, unconscious.

Deckard stood over him, ignoring his training, which told him to drop down and pummel him into a bloody hunk of barely breathing meat. It wasn't necessary. Jerry was beaten. With a new sigh, he helped Thuy up and was surprised that despite nearly being raped, and still bearing the red welts where Jerry had whipped her, she didn't cling to him.

That would come later. First, she had to take care of Jerry. Within the Zone there weren't laws and thus there weren't courts or civilization as anyone would recognize it. But there was common sense and she was going to exercise it.

"You are a danger every bit as much as the zombies," she said, going to one knee and picking up the knife.

"Thuy, what are you doing?" Deckard asked.

She looked up, the tip of the knife poised on Jerry's pulsing carotid artery. "I'm executing Jerry Weir."

2—The White House, Washington DC

Marty Aleman watched as the president came down the stairs to the Rose Garden. "And stop," he whispered into his microphone. "Touch one of the roses. There you go. Linger on it for just a moment. And sigh. Good. Perfect. Now turn to the podium."

The president went to the podium and although the Seal of the Presidency was emblazoned across the front, it didn't feel the same. His trusted teleprompters had been removed and he felt naked without them. They had always guided him. They had always told him exactly what to say.

But this was a press conference. A real one. For the last three years, he had conducted plenty of press conferences, however those had always been "orchestrated." Marty salted the press corps with pre-arranged questions. Usually they were softballs that the President could swat out of the park, but for the tougher ones, he turned to his teleprompters.

Supposedly, they couldn't do that today, and the President was sullen and on the verge of a tantrum because of it. He struggled to smile down at the gathered reporters. "I suppose you have some questions," he said.

Marty groaned and made fists out of his manicured hands. "Smile, smile. There you go. Remember, you are the President. Now, take Joan's question."

"Joan, how about we start with you?" the President said, somehow managing to sound fatherly.

She stood, her blonde mane, normally so perfect, was flat and the dark circles under her eyes were obvious. She was finally looking her age. "Yes, Mister President, General Heider's briefing was a little too brief. He didn't give us any more information than he did last night. He just repeated himself. Can you tell us, are we in danger here in the capital? Did Philadelphia fall?"

"Emphatically no," Marty said. "Tell her that. Good, good. Now, tell her about the 42nd." The President nodded, making Marty wish that he really did have strings working this idiot's moving parts as everyone joked.

"We are in no danger, Joan. We in the White House are on top of this situation, though it is very fluid. Thanks to our friends in the Navy, we were able to extract large elements of the 42nd Infantry Division from Long Island and are using them to shore up the line in Philadelphia."

This was a minor truth laced heavily with a terrible lie. The 42nd had been shattered. Of the eleven thousand soldiers it had started with three days before, they were down to just over two thousand exhausted men. Everyone in the Pentagon knew that Philadelphia could fall at any moment and if it did, Wilmington would be next and then Baltimore and that was only twenty miles away.

"We're fine," the President concluded, relaxing a little. "David, did you have a question?"

"Yes, there seems to be some sort of upswell of citizens taking up arms. Is that safe? All the experts seem to think that untrained civilians running around the country armed to the hilt could be dangerous. If we look at what happened in Rwanda and the Congo, we can see that maybe this would be a good time for moderation, perhaps even a scaling back of the second Amendment."

The President's smile froze and he turned slowly towards Marty. This sort of question was why Marty hated a free press that thought it was free. It was the stupidest question he had heard in years and if the President had any backbone he would have laughed in the man's face. Mankind might have sprouted in Africa, but civilization had long ago abandoned that continent. The Rwandans and the Congolese were not Americans and had it not been for American citizens coming to the rescue of the army, the black-eyed plague would have hit Ohio by now.

But the President wasn't the sort of man who could articulate that sort of thing.

"Tell him that is a question for another time," Marty said, dancing around the issue, careful not to make enemies when none needed to be made. "Pick Raj from USA Today. He just gave me a wink."

True to his training, the President did what he was told and Raj stood to ask, "Can you tell us what is happening in Massachusetts? Governor Clarren claimed in his own news conference that he's being attacked by US Army forces."

"Ah yes, good question," the President said, stalling, waiting on Marty.

"Tell him it's actually the opposite of what is really happening." Marty paused to allow the President a chance to repeat this and then went on, "We were trying to relocate refugees, *harmless* refugees, when we were attacked by them." Another pause and then, "It's a tragic situation, but one that we are taking steps to fix. The refugees should be getting through to safer locations any time now and once they do we should have the northeast pretty well battened down."

Three hundred miles north, Sergeant Ross would have laughed if he had heard the answer the President gave. The refugees hadn't budged, while he had progressed only about fifty yards into the tree line and was fighting for his life against a counterattack that was being pressed home as if he were fighting veterans instead of the "untrained civilians running around the country," as that douchebag from ABC had put it.

General Platnik's ruse of broadcasting a separate LZ had worked long enough for Ross to gather the twenty-six remaining troops of the first assault into the thinnest perimeter. They had fought like the Bulldogs they were until the second assault force landed. They had pushed into the tree line and towards the closer buildings, only to be hurtled back as the Mass-boys turned on their heels and raced back.

The fight was stiff and the call of "Medic!" rang out on both sides. Ross found a niche between two downed trees where he could shoot and move, rolling from one firing point to the next. He fired single shots only, but was still burning through ammo at a scary rate. With the enemy sometimes only yards away, there was no way to disengage and no one but the medics had the balls to run ammo.

Ross had just slapped in his last magazine when a huge grey monster roared almost directly overhead. The F-15 was so low that Ross felt the skin on the back of his neck burn from the heat of the twin engines as he was diving beneath the logs.

115

And then the CBU-87's started spinning in the jet's wake, releasing its submunitions. It had been dropped so low that only half the bomblets were jettisoned before the CBU streaked into the ground in a tremendous fireball. The explosion felt like it turned Ross's brains to mush and as he lifted his head, he had to wonder if he was seeing things.

What was left of the forest in front of him was on fire as far as he could see. There were people in the flames. Some were charred corpses and some were crawling with their heads on fire.

Chapter 10

Even with her badge and credentials, it wasn't easy for Special Agent Katherine Pennock to get into the Baltimore Zone. She had to resort to lying and throwing around the President's name as if they were best friends and, of course, she had to recite the tiring line: "He likes 'em young and blonde. It's embarrassing, but it is what it is." For some reason, that seemed to work like a charm.

Once she was in the Baltimore Zone, no one gave a crap about the President or what he liked. Things were fast becoming tense as the line holding southern Philadelphia slowly caved in and the sound of the artillery seemed to be getting closer and closer. She was still within shouting distance of the checkpoint that she had passed through when the Exxon-Mobile Storage complex across the river from the Philadelphia International Airport was hit by an errant shell.

Even from forty-five miles away, it felt like an earthquake. Her driver, a nervous Virginian with a single eyebrow that stretched almost completely across the low bulge of his forehead, shared a look with Katherine. Then they both turned to stare northeast, where a smudge on the horizon quickly grew as the fire in the complex sent flames and smoke miles into the sky.

The Virginian then looked back at the checkpoint as if to say: *There's still time to*.

"We're going on," she told him and then checked the map. "Stay on this road until it becomes Caton Ave. Then after a while it gets kind of wiggly and you'll want to somehow veer left."

The Virginian didn't want to veer in any direction except for back to his own state. He had heard bad things about Baltimore even before the shit had hit the fan and now a thousand eyes were glaring down at his Humvee.

With the coming of the sun, people had thrown back their curtains and weren't too happy with what they saw: mostly empty streets. The only traffic were military vehicles either speeding north crammed with men or military vehicles trundling slowly by with loudspeakers attached to their roofs.

Since dawn, these came around once an hour spouting the following: "Stay indoors! The city is in a state of lockdown under the lawful orders of the President. Do not attempt to flee. Await further instructions."

The one plus to all of this was the open streets. The Virginian wanted no part of the city or the mission and he hauled ass down Canton, illegally went up a one-way street and then screeched to a stop at the next major intersection.

Katherine struggled to keep her bearings. "You don't want to be lost in this city," she said.

No, he did not. With the power out and the dark buildings and all the angry faces, it didn't even feel like America.

"Take a left here and then your third right," she told him. In a surprisingly short time she found the burned-out store and the lone, forgotten RV. Katherine pulled her Glock 22. "Watch my back," she told the Virginian as she slipped out of the Humvee, angling towards the big camper, her gun sighted on the back window.

It had an empty feeling, so when she knocked on the door, it wasn't a shock that no one answered. The one door was unlocked and she crept in with her gun poised, fully expecting to find a few corpses, but the place was empty. While the Virginian crouched behind his Hummer with his M16 pointed out, she went through the camper from one end to another.

She found out who the owners were: Charles and Leticia Martin from Denver City, Texas. She got the info on the Silverado, its VIN and tag number, and she saw that all the food had been taken. What she didn't find was a single clue that anyone else had been there. Under normal circumstances, she would have impounded the fifth-wheel and gone through it with a fine-tooth comb.

Under these circumstances, she had to hope that no one would come by and steal the entire thing.

"Okay we have some good news," she told the Virginian. "The couple who owns this left sometime before dawn and they have not come back."

"How's that good news? They could be anywhere."

Katherine walked around the Hummer, saying, "Yes, but most likely they're outside the Zone." This perked the Virginian up and he jumped in the car like an over-eager dog being offered a ride. "Let's go to the nearest roadblock."

He drove straight to the beltway and found the first checkpoint. He was so keen to get out of the zone that he nearly got shot when six soldiers leveled their rifles at him. "What the fuck, you numbskulls? It's me, Bill Bramlett from Bravo Company."

"Oh sorry, Bramlett. Who's the chick?"

Katherine rolled her eyes and advanced with her FBI credentials and badge on display. "Special Agent Katherine Pennock. Have you seen these two people?" She held up a pair of 8 x 11 pictures of Anna and Eng, and then the smaller pictures of Charlie and Leticia that she had taken from the RV's refrigerator. The soldiers on the other side of the wire craned their necks forward and all shook their heads.

"Thank you," she said and headed back to the Humvee. Bramlett began to splutter questions, clearly thinking that he would be allowed to cross back into the safe area. "Not yet," she said. "We need to find where they crossed."

Defeated and glum, he dragged ass back to the Humvee, and when he drove to the next roadblock he wasn't nearly as excited as he had been. The next roadblock was the same as the first and Bramlett looked like a lost puppy when he drove to the next. Here the reaction to the pictures was completely different.

Now, one of the main reasons Katherine had decided to join the bureau was that she could tell in a flash when someone was talking out of their ass, and these six soldiers were lying. Bramlett, who hadn't caught the lie, mumbled in his Virginian drawl and started heading back to the Humvee. Katherine didn't budge. One of the men's eyes had gone wide at the sight of the pictures and another had glanced at the sergeant with a question forming on his lips.

"Hold on, Bramlett," she said. She waited with an eyebrow cocked, staring coldly from one soldier to the next until things got uncomfortable. That discomfort was another admission of guilt. It wouldn't hold up in court, but she didn't need it to. She turned for the Humvee and heard more than one sigh of relief. When she returned with her laptop she heard curses. "Do any of you know the penalty for lying to a federal investigator?"

The sergeant set his face. "We ain't lying."

"That wasn't the question. The penalty for lying to a federal investigator is up to five years in prison and a $250,000 fine…per offense. Now, who knows what the penalty is when your lie helps a wanted fugitive to escape arrest? I'm talking about aiding and abetting the people who are guilty of mass murder on a scale that dwarfs what Hitler did. Anyone care to venture a guess? No? They'll put you in the chair for that and that's if they don't line you up against a wall, first."

Some of the soldiers went pale and some shuffled their feet, but they all looked at the sergeant who took a step back. "M-Maybe I should take a look at those pictures a little closer," he said in a hoarse whisper, holding out a hand. He pretended to study them closer. "I think I was mistaken before. We did see these people. The old lady was having a heart attack and we let them through to go to that hospital. And that's the truth." The others nodded and Katherine didn't doubt it for a second.

"And all four got through?" she asked. The six nodded in unison. Her stomach sank a little. "When?"

"Just a little before sunrise. They were in a truck with a big bed. It was white. We brought them to the hospital. I swear that's all we did. We thought that the old lady was having a heart attack."

Katherine waved him to silence. "Let us through," she demanded, curtly. As she ran back to the Humvee, she reached for her cell but then saw that it wasn't getting any service. "Shit! Do any of you have a sat-phone?" They only had a radio. She cursed again and could only hope that she would get lucky and that someone at the hospital would have a working phone.

They did, but it wasn't lucky. She called the FBI office in DC and was shuttled up the chain of command as each person either didn't believe her or couldn't verify who she was or was too busy to even listen. These were the excuses they made, but she knew that chasing rumors and taking chances were, for the most part, career killers. If they didn't pan out, and they rarely did, someone would be blamed.

Eventually, her call was kicked upwards far enough that her name was recognized by the one person she didn't really want to talk to: the Associate Executive Assistant Director for National Security, John Alexander. "Is this the Katherine Pennock who was supposed to brief the got-damned President of the United States?"

"I technically found a replacement, one that seemed far better suited for the task since she…"

"And is this the same got-damned Katherine Pennock who is now absent without leave and is currently conducting an illegal investigation *within* the got-damned perimeter of the of the Baltimore-Zone?"

Katherine took a deep breath before answering in the hope of maintaining a calm voice. "I prefer to think of it as 'extra legal' since…"

"I don't give a flying fuck what you think is legal or extra-fucking legal. You are running around using authority that was never granted to you. Do you know how much trouble you're in? You'll be lucky if you just get booted from the bureau. There's talk of bringing you up on charges. Hell, my boss, the Executive Assistant Director, had to pull agents away from their assignments just to track you the fuck down."

So much for remaining calm. "I'll make it easy for them to find me," she said, her voice as cold as his was hot. "I've tracked Anna Holloway and Shuang Eng to the Roosevelt Hospital. That's *outside* the Zone in case you were wondering."

The Associate Executive Assistant Director for National Security drew in a breath but was slow to release it. "Got-damn. When?"

"Approximately two and half hours ago and they had access to a truck."

"But you tracked them to a hospital? We got to shut that place down. Tell me they aren't busy."

The place wasn't just packed with patients, it was overflowing and when she told him, he went on a rant that included a handful of "Got-damns" and other far more colorful language. Katherine couldn't get a word in and before she knew it, he had hung up, but not before saying, "Secure the scene and wait for me."

"Got-damn," she whispered. "How am I supposed to secure an entire hospital with just one soldier?"

2—Hudson, New York

They needed a police car. "Where are the cops when you need them?" Deckard said, yawning.

Thuy yawned right after, her eyes dripping tears. She didn't say anything and hadn't said much since she had slid the deboning knife between Jerry Weir's ribs. It had pierced his heart. She had stood, wiped away her prints from the knife, and then dropped it on his lifeless body. In silence, she had recovered the ridiculous "Juicy" shirt, put it on and begun searching the place.

She gathered food and water, which made sense. The booze didn't. She found four full bottles and sixteen partial bottles. Mostly it was whiskey but there was also some gin and vodka. Passive-faced she began pouring the alcohol around. "You never know," was all she said when she lit a match from a half-empty book.

The mobile home went up like a torch. Although destroying evidence was a waste of time in a land without a single cop left alive, Deckard understood what she was doing. Thuy had committed murder and the fire would put it behind her, at least legally. Getting over it mentally and emotionally was another thing altogether and from his experience, time was the only medicine.

After covering up a murder, they ironically went in search of a police car. They needed a scanner to contact Courtney Shaw.

It was a strange world driving through the middle of the Zone. With millions of infected people spreading out from the epicenter, the land seemed empty and yet there was an ominous, ever present feeling of being watched. Deckard couldn't tell whether it was lone survivors staring out from their hiding spots, or zombies too torn up to walk, that were watching them, but they were definitely being watched as they drove the mostly empty roads.

When they came to the first roadblock, Deckard slowed the RAV4. There were four state trooper cruisers lined up across the road. Two of them had been set on fire. They were blackened husks, their emergency lights melted into blobs on their roofs. The cruiser at the far-right end of the row had all its windows broken, including the front windshield which was starred to the point of being undrivable.

The cruiser on the left only had the two passenger side windows broken into, but otherwise seemed perfectly fine. Deckard pulled up next to it and was about to get out when he felt Thuy's hand on his arm. "Don't," she said, indicating the cruiser door with a lift of her chin. It was covered in what looked like black grease.

"Com-cells, crap," he said. He drove around the line of cars and kept heading west, pulling into the town of Hudson ten minutes later. Again, the quiet was strange and unnerving. Even the birds were quiet. They sat on telephone wires, silent and judging.

123

"We'll need masks and gloves," Thuy said, her first sentence in an hour. "We should also consider gathering cleaning agents."

And guns, Deckard thought.

Other than the fifty or sixty corpses rotting in the sun, it was a pretty little town situated right on the Hudson River. Looting had been minimal, so they were able to find quite a bit in the way of supplies, except for guns and ammo.

They did find a police car with nearly a full tank of gas. The officer who had driven it was on the sidewalk a few feet away. He had his arms torn off. "Judging by the arterial spray, he was still alive when it happened," Thuy remarked. She was trying to be cool and scientific, yet her face seemed stuck with a crooked smile plastered on it.

"Let's not worry how it happened. I'll just check him for the keys." Now it was Deckard's turn to wear the crooked smile as he felt the man's pockets. He half-wished he would come up empty. Hot-wiring a car took time, but at least you didn't have to touch a diseased corpse.

The keys were in the cop's pocket, and after swallowing his gorge, Deckard fished them out. "Hold on," Thuy said, bringing out a can of disinfectant and giving the keys and Deckard's gloved hand a thorough spraying. "You should be good. We just have to…oh, his gun." A black Taurus was lying in the gutter a few feet away. She gave it a healthy spraying and then checked the magazine. "Only two bullets left," she said, sighing in disappointment. "Darn it."

"Darn it? Maybe you should cool your jets, missy. You're starting to sound like a sailor on leave." The joke fell flat. Thuy was so done in that she actually apologized. "No, it was a joke," he told her. "Come on, let's get out of here. This place is ugly." The town, almost untouched by the apocalypse, was quaint, but the bodies just soured the whole effect.

He hustled her into the cruiser, turned the thing around and never looked back. While he drove, she worked the police scanner, tuning into frequency 866.06250 as

Courtney had told him to do. "Dispatch 6, can you hear me?" Thuy asked, holding the microphone in both hands as if she were praying to some electronic god. "Dispatch 6, this is Deck 1, over."

She repeated this for an hour as they drove into the rising sun. She repeated it until they saw zombies ahead of them, surging like a hating, hungry wave, pounding into the border between New York and Massachusetts where men and women stood their ground and fought back.

"Dispatch, please come in," Thuy begged, as she watched the explosions and the gunfire and the black bodies coming apart, as the wave got closer and closer. There was no response from Courtney. "What do we do?" Thuy finally asked when her voice began to fail.

Deckard thought for a moment. "We wait to see who wins this battle. If the zombies win, they'll fan out looking for clean blood. We might be able to slip through. We'll find Courtney and head north to Canada. If our side wins…we'll think of something else."

He parked the car two miles from the border, where they had excellent view of the battle and yet neither watched. They leaned into each other, smiled once and fell asleep, too exhausted to keep awake.

Twenty-two miles away, Courtney Shaw was fast asleep as well. When she and Deckard went their separate ways, she had marched for two hours in a straight line, going east, trying to put as much space between her and the crash site as she could.

She walked with her head cranked around, with the crazy fear that at any moment a truck with a bunch of toothless Harvard hillbillies would suddenly appear and chase her down.

When she was stumbling with exhaustion and couldn't go on, she found a very recently abandoned home off a lonely strip of road. There was still-warm coffee in the pot and cold milk in the refrigerator. She drank the milk, greedily and then helped herself to four fried eggs and toast.

With a full belly, the demand for sleep came on her like a freight train, but she couldn't let Deckard and Thuy down, so she drank the coffee black and went up to the second-floor bathroom, which was decorated with cat figurines, cat wall paper and cat towels, and went about cleaning her many scratches and lacerations. Then she bathed in warmish water before poking about the house in an effort to make herself as presentable as possible.

Courtney looked at herself in the mirror over the sink and didn't much like what she saw. She decided to make herself look as presentable as possible if only for her own satisfaction. She felt couldn't she go much further looking as though she had just been shot out of the sky by an F-15, or had been chased for hundreds of miles through the Zone by zombies, or had fought an all-night battle on a lonesome hill in western Connecticut.

It took a lot of makeup for her to appear anything close to her old self, and even then, the effect would fade if she let her face sag from exhaustion. She would have to force a fake smile onto her face if she ran into someone.

There were no cars in the driveway or garage, so she "borrowed" a bicycle and pedaled east a few miles before coming up on another house. Afraid of being shot for breaking and entering, she knocked for five minutes. She tried the door—it was locked, as were all the doors. The windows were locked as well, but she picked up a round do-it-yourself key in the form of a rock and let herself in through a back window.

The house was divided by gender. The ground floor of the ranch style home, obviously belonged to a female with crocheted doilies, pinkish-mauve furniture, lots of throw pillows and family pictures. The basement was the male's territory with an oversized television, a small fridge filled with beer, and a musty, nose-wrinkling smell. Courtney searched for a gun, but only found a few shotgun shells in the master bed room closet.

It wasn't a wasted stop, however. In the garage she discovered someone's baby, snuggled under a tarp: a vintage '57 Corvette. "Oh man," she said, reverently touching the immaculately shinny red paint. "I can't take this…it'd be like a sin, not just to God, either."

Taking a bike or a Jeep was sort of expected in an emergency, but this? A Corvette was just not an apocalyptic vehicle, but she had no other true option. Courtney found the keys, heaved up the garage door and got behind the wheel. With the interior so perfect, she had no doubt when she turned the key in the ignition that it would start right up, and it did. It purred like the biggest, happiest lion in the world and, with an odd guilty/euphoric feeling, she backed out into the street and once more headed east.

On an open stretch of road on Route 23, she goosed the gas pedal and the fuel injected, 265 cubic inch V8 sent her rocketing forward, laughter in her throat, her worries and exhaustion, at least for that second, gone. When she glanced down at the speedometer, she saw she was zooming at over a hundred miles an hour.

"It's not mine," she whispered, backing off the gas pedal until she was coasting along at a respectable fifty. Now that she had gotten that out of her system, she went in search of a radio. It didn't take long even though this was the emptiest part of the state. She followed the sound of shooting southeast until she came to the battle for Springfield.

The night before, after fighting nonstop for hours alone and unaided, the 82nd had finally failed in their mission of containing the undead city of Hartford. Out of it had burst millions of feral creatures, sending the last remnants of the division scattering in all directions. Some had gone north along the Connecticut River and had died in a short but violent fight with the Massachusetts National Guard, who were not just dug in, they were dialed in, well supplied and eager to defend their state, their homes and their families.

That eagerness slowly faded when hundreds of thousands of monsters had come out of the dark and made for them next. Although the eagerness faded quickly, their determination held. They fought hard and in the last fourteen hours, they had only fallen back to I-57, two miles from the border. Because the battle against the 101st, forty miles to the east was sapping their reserves, a second fall back point was being readied along the Westfield River, a mile further back.

Courtney, who knew nothing about the extent of that fight, felt strangely like an imposter as she tooled up to a city park in the shiny Corvette and watched as several filthy, exhausted women dug up the infield of a baseball diamond, filling sandbag after sandbag, taking the "sand" part of the word literally. They looked up at her, each glaring. Courtney was wearing a simple sweater of yellow over jeans that didn't exactly fit; in her mind, she looked ridiculous. It made her wonder what sort of reception they would have given Thuy, who managed to make everything she wore both elegant and sexy.

"Hi there," she said, pleasantly, with a little wave as she got out of the car.

"Hi yourself," one of the women replied, with the harsh bray of a New Englander. "Grab a shovel and get to digging."

Courtney tried to ignore the woman's tone and forced the smile to remain. "Actually, I'm looking for a police station."

Another woman chimed in, "Actually you're looking for a hardware store, so you can get a fuckin' shovel and start diggin' like the rest of us."

The smile on Courtney's face slipped into a grimace; she didn't have the energy to deal with the likes of this sort of woman, who seemed like the kind of person who held down a barstool six nights a week, telling anyone who would listen how they should live their lives. "Thanks anyway," Courtney said and turned back for the Corvette.

"There's one over on Montgomery," a third woman told Courtney. Under the dirt and sweat Courtney could tell she was a young woman barely out of her teens. "Go back on Main and hang a left."

"Thanks," Courtney said and then jogged back to the Corvette. She didn't have time for the whining she was sure had begun behind her. To drown it out, she rumbled the Corvette to life and roared it in the direction suggested by the younger woman. She found the station easily. It was dark, empty and locked. There wasn't a patrol car in sight —there was no one in sight, so she used a piece of cement to break in the front door.

Although her reason for being there was to get a scanner, she felt naked without a gun, so her first order of business was to search for a weapon. The obvious place to begin was the station's armory, only it was locked tight and no hunk of cement was going to break down the reinforced steel door.

Still, she had options. From experience, she knew that many officers carried secondary weapons, while some even carried special "drop" weapons in case of accidental shootings. Going through the desks one by one she found two guns: a .38 and a squatty, little S&W P9. She took both. The .38 went into her back pocket and the P9, what everyone called "The Shield" though she didn't know why, went into her front right.

She then went in search of a portable scanner and had plenty to choose from. "Now let's save the day," she said and left the building. She took the Corvette back the way she had come, broadcasting as she went—but she was too early; Thuy and Deckard were just then setting Jerry Weir's mobile home on fire. Still she didn't know that and she broadcast: "Deck 1, this is Dispatch 6, over," until she was blue in the face.

The Corvette was so fast that she had zipped back to the western border where the fighting was crazy and still she hadn't heard from them. Just like they would, twenty minutes later, she parked on a hill to increase the range of her scanner, and then just sat there, her eyes growing heavier and heavier.

"I have to stay awake," she whispered, a second before she slumped over and began to snore.

129

"Dispatch 6, this is Deck 1, over," the radio squelched, but she didn't hear it. She was too far gone.

3—Beiping, China

The arguments had lasted for hours. Sometimes a member of China's Politburo argued both sides of the same issue in the same long-winded, run-on sentence. It was all very useless and annoying to General Okini since they were arguing about whether to take half measures or token, face-saving measures.

While the bickering continued, Okini sat in his chair, studying the footage from the reconnaissance planes. Some of the pictures were perfect while others had odd rainbow blobs obscuring parts of the image. It was the radiation from the bombs.

Since the Chinese did not have the same technological capabilities as western countries, their recon planes had to fly much lower to get the same resolution. Six pilots were already puking blood from radiation poisoning. They'd be dead soon and Okini would have to send others to replace them. That was the way of things in China. People were expendable, planes were valuable, and information was priceless.

He picked up his secure phone, dialed a number and spoke as soon as it was answered, "Send up the next two." They were now tracking five of *them,* creatures that had somehow lived through the nuclear blasts. There were battles still raging all up and down the line, but all he cared about was the village of Xeuhen.

One of the nuclear warheads had detonated right over the village and, impossible as it was, two miles away, one of the creatures had crawled out of the fire and now it was struggling west. The creature was none other than Truong Mai, but just then he was no longer Truong Mai.

Truong Mai wasn't even a memory in the creature's miserable head.

"Two miles from the blast point," Okini said, comparing the pictures. "That's the closest one." He then went to the large map of China that hung in the chamber and imagined the Grand Canal as it ran from the Yangtze River in the north to the Qiantang River in the south. It was a hundred and twelve miles long.

"We'll need to secure both rivers." The southern border along the Qiantang was short, barely forty-five miles, however the northern run was over a hundred and thirty. "Damn! We don't have enough warheads." Over the last ten years, China had been scaling back its nuclear arsenal and now they only had two-hundred and forty warheads. General Okini considered it an outrage.

"Do you have something to add to this debate, Vice Chairman?" one of the minor members asked. He was part of the Finance Chairman's faction. It had been a powerful faction, one that held considerable sway when the life of the country wasn't on the line. Things had changed very quickly and suddenly Finance was grasping.

"No, I don't. A debate is the last thing any of us should be involved with. I'll be ready when you're done bickering."

This unsettled the other twenty-four members of the Politburo. They glared, they whispered, they pretended not to have heard. "We aren't bickering," someone growled. "We are exploring ideas."

"Yes, just as washer-women do," Okini replied, standing. "Your 'debate' has centered around the use of a second release of nuclear arms. Some say six warheads and some say ten. Some say none. I say our only choice is to use all of them."

Some of the members laughed and some looked confused, while some waved their hands dismissively. None sided with him. Okini didn't care. Each member could access the overhead projector but only when a senior member gave permission. Okini didn't ask. He showed them a picture of the small figure of Truang Mai as seen from above. "This man crawled out of the rubble two miles south of the village Xeuhen. He is infected and he is heading west."

Within the factions, the members glanced at each other, looking for someone other than themselves to offer a solution. Some muttered. Okini let them go on, standing there placidly, hoping that they would understand the full ramifications of the picture.

One of the General Secretary's toadies asked, "How do we know he is infected? That is an assumption. I'm sure anyone who survived a nuclear blast would look like that. And where else would he head, but west."

"So frequently the answer to the question is within the question," Okini said. "We know that he is infected *because* he survived a nuclear blast. And we also know he is infected, not because he is heading west, but because he is *heading* anywhere at all. He has walked straight through a zone of radiation that would have killed a normal man."

"Then we have lost," said the Secretary of the Central Commission for Discipline Inspection. "If our greatest weapons cannot stop them, we have lost."

Okini stared at the man for so long that the secretary dropped his chin in embarrassment. Then Okini said, "We will lose only when we first lose the will to fight. I have not lost that will. Those of you who have lost the will, please stand up, so that I may denounce you." No one dared to stand.

"And do you have a plan, General Okini?" the General Secretary asked.

"I do, but before I suggest it, I would like you to use the power of your position to limit debate on it to one hour. If we wait longer than that then no plan will work and we will indeed have lost."

The General Secretary's face remained flat and blank; he would have made a frightening poker player. He had a very good guess what Okini's plan entailed and could have offered it himself, but he played a far-reaching game. Okini was worried about what the next day would hold, while the General Secretary, with a true Chinese mentality, worried about ten years from then and a hundred years. He had to consider where his name would lie in the history books.

Of course, he also had to wonder if there would even be history books in ten years if he didn't act.

"I so stipulate," the General Secretary said. "Please inform us of your plan."

An hour later, it was decided by a near unanimous vote that they would unleash the county's full nuclear might on their own soil.

Chapter 11

With his face screwed up in a look of disbelief, Sergeant Troy Ross watched the last of the assault force being flown in by Blackhawks. There were civilians among the camouflaged troops. They had deer rifles as weapons and although they wore blue jeans and yellow slickers or black leather jackets, they had painted their faces green. They looked ridiculous.

"What the fuck?" he whispered.

Next to him was an infantry captain, the highest ranking man left alive. "They must really be scraping the bottom of the barrel," he said.

"What the hell are we supposed to do with them?" Ross asked. There were now five hundred air assault troops sitting on the junction of I-395 and the Massachusetts Turnpike. Their presence was bottling everything up for the Mass-boys, who were really in a shit position. Their supply lines had just tripled in length.

"We'll intersperse them with Delta and Echo companies," the captain said, making sure not to look Ross in the face. "They'll hold the flanks while Alpha, Bravo and Charlie forge the link-up with the main body pressing north."

Ross tried not to let his disappointment show. He had been given command of Alpha Company, which in his opinion wasn't really a company at all. It was made up of the survivors of the initial assault. It was a patchwork company.

Half of his men were hiders who hadn't fired a single shot during the dawn battle. The other half, men like Ross, had put it *all* on the line. They had dug deep to find the last scraping of courage, and sometimes, when you went that deep you found yourself hitting the bottom where there was nothing left. You were empty. A number of his men had that look. The look basically said: *I've done my part, now it's someone else's turn.*

This was why the captain wouldn't look at him as he said, "Our initial objective is Federal Hill Road. Bravo and Charlie will move along the west side of the highway and you'll take Alpha along the east. We move out in ten." The captain clapped Ross on the shoulder as he walked away.

When the officer was out of earshot, Ross closed his eyes and whispered, "Fuuuck," in a long groan. Alpha company was in trouble. The fighting had been so tough that he had an E-5 named Henley leading one of his four platoons, and three overwhelmed E-4s leading the others.

Ross went to each and told them what was happening. He didn't like the looks in their eyes and some of these men were veterans who had fought in Iraq. Next, he gathered up his hundred-man company and gave them a look over. Perhaps worse than the thousand-yard stares were the few men who had sharp creases in their still clean uniforms. These soldiers he named "hiders." He gathered up ten of these and went to the company commander of Echo Company and demanded a trade from the E-6 running the show.

"I need some snipers," he explained to the sergeant, who was more than willing to give up some of his civilians in exchange for real soldiers. Ross went to where the civilians were standing in throng, many of them chain-smoking and looking ready to piss themselves. "You boys here to fight?" he demanded of the group.

One of them answered with just the right amount of surliness, "What else would we be doing here?"

That's one, Ross thought to himself. "You, come stand over here and if you have any friends have them come too." The man had two brothers, three cousins and six friends. They were an ill-tempered lot, and it was a shame that Ross had to leave two of the younger men behind.

In a fight, he liked his men mean and ready to scrap. He just wished he had more time to prepare them for battle.

135

With two squads of veterans leading the way, the company marched south and as they went, Ross gave the civilians a lightning quick lesson in tactics. He then split them up among the platoons. It wasn't a minute later that the first shot rang out.

From the start, the battle was complete chaos. As company commander, Ross had to lead his troops without getting killed in the process, something that didn't seem likely as he was targeted over and over again. Pretty much whenever he bellowed orders he could expect to get at least five guns shooting his way.

After a few minutes of near misses where the misses, were getting ever nearer, he took to crawling through the underbrush with what sounded like angry bees whipping by as he yelled to his men. There could be no doubt that he looked like an idiot, but he was alive and fighting the enemy and that was what counted.

His 1st and 2nd platoons were deeply engaged, but his 3rd platoon was hunkered down fifty yards back and the 4th was even further back. He screamed himself hoarse to get them up and moving, but just as he managed to get the 3rd platoon into position on the line, he changed his mind, thinking that a real commander would try to flank the enemy instead of sending men straight into a meat grinder.

As quietly as he could, he shifted the 3rd platoon to the east. Almost immediately, it ran into an enemy force that was trying to flank them!

The platoon found itself slugging it out toe to toe in a heavy forest where the cover was so dense that people were yards apart but still couldn't seem to hit anything but branches and tree trunks. Afraid that he was losing whatever limited control over the battle he had, Ross crawled right into the thick of it. It seemed to be raining bark and snowing leaves, and there were thousands of those angry bees zipping by. He kept crawling, trying to find the edge of this new flank and before he knew it he found himself staring across a field. Although thick, the forest was not very deep or wide. Ross was on the sharp edge of it and saw that it bordered a farm.

Right away he turned around and started hustling back to where he had left his 4th Platoon, hoping that if he acted first, he'd be able to send the platoon around the farm to get in behind his enemies.

It might have worked, but the 4th started taking fire before they were halfway across the field and got stopped along an irrigation ditch. Soon enemy soldiers swung out wide, as well, only to find themselves huddled seventy yards away in their own ditch. To Ross, this part of the fight looked like a throwback to World War 1. It was trench warfare with a deadly no man's land between that was being blasted by every caliber of bullet known to man.

So far, Ross's twenty minutes as company commander seemed to be a disaster. Alpha Company was stretched along a dangerously thin line and Ross could only hope that the Mass-boys were spread just as thin.

There really was just one way to find out and that was to attack…again. He felt as if he had to, as if there was some sort of time limit to all of this. And, in a way, he was right. A storm of undead was brewing in Connecticut. It was as mindless as any natural storm and for the last few hours it had spun, slowly progressing into Rhode Island, and now it was moving north where millions of refugees were being protected by a force too weak to stop it.

Sergeant Ross didn't know this as a fact; it was in the air, however. That same air was being tortured by the sound of so many guns going off at once that Ross had to shake his head so he could think straight. He had to attack, but where? An attack across the open fields of the farm was insane on the face of it, while the fight in the thick forest was too fierce.

The only place that seemed quiet was in the middle of the battle where they'd had made first contact with the enemy. It was as good a place as any. Stripping three squads from the 4th platoon that were uselessly cowering in the ditch, and one each from the first and second platoons, he designated this new force as the 5th platoon and led it straight through the center.

"Here's the plan," he said, quietly to the nervous group of men, "You're going to follow me and you're not going to stop unless I stop." It was a terrible plan but with no time, he couldn't think of another.

The land was lightly treed, sloping down toward the unseen enemy, and Ross decided that getting in close was his best, and perhaps only, hope. With the 5th behind him, spreading in an inverted V, he sprinted out of the thin cover and ran straight into a line of civilians who, only a week before, had been students in Cambridge.

Ross charged into a crackle of rifle fire and the thunder of shotguns.

The man next to Ross went down, catching a 12-gauge blast to the face from a distance of twenty feet. Before Ross could shoot, someone else had exacted revenge and the shotgun-wielding man went to his knees as his internal organs became external. The mess was sickening, but there was no time to think. Ross only knew he had to shoot, and shoot, and keep shooting because he was pretty certain he had blundered straight into what had to be the entire Massachusetts army.

He fired and fired and almost couldn't miss because there were so many targets. That's how he had to think about the people he was shooting. To keep sane, he said to himself: *Just knock down the targets. Just like at the range, just knock down the targets*. Except he had never been to a firing range where the targets fired back. It seemed like there were a hundred guns pointed at him from every direction. White hot 30-30 rounds blazed within inches of his face and 5.56mm rounds hissed by from behind. He was going to die. It would be impossible not to.

2—Three miles south of Woonsocket, Rhode Island

The three million refugees who had fled eastern New York and Connecticut were cowering just south of the city of Webster. Unarmed, unfed and with little but the clothes on their backs, they awaited the outcome of the battle between the 101st and the Massachusetts National Guard.

Save for a thin shell of soldiers, they were defenseless against the hordes of undead pressing up from the south.

General Platnik turned the mission of saving them over to a colonel named Blaine Declan. Declan's job was to bait the main host of zombies away from the refugees and to do this he only had a few hundred soldiers, a smattering of police and a thousand or so armed citizens to square off against the millions of undead. It was a suicide mission and there was no pretending otherwise.

Seemingly without fear, Declan and his little force caused such a ruckus as to bring the entire enchilada down upon him. Then, using his men sparingly and skillfully, he retreated into Rhode Island and like a great spear, the numberless army of undead came after, aimed straight for the heart of the little state: Providence, a city of nearly two million people.

Now, Declan had a new refugee problem and instead of running, he was forced to fight against overwhelming odds. He drove his weary men without let up, forcing them to make stand after stand always behind some barrier, whether natural or man-made, he didn't care. All that mattered was stopping the horde long enough to allow the people of Providence to find a place of safety.

The only way to do that was to sacrifice his men, making each life count to its fullest. They didn't die in a single grand battle, they died slowly, valiantly resisting at every river crossing, at every stream, every highway. When their numbers began to dwindle too much, Colonel Declan dusted off a stratagem from antiquity: the redoubt. These were basically small battlefield fortifications that had to be conquered one by one.

With no central control, the army of undead would converge on each so that the soldiers would look out on a veritable sea of corpses. The outcome of each of these minor battles was never in question—and there was never any escape. The men fought to the last, making not just every death count but every minute as well.

Declan himself could have escaped by helicopter, but he chose to stay with his last thirty men. They made their stand in a three-story, brick farm house and for an hour they beat back wave after wave, but the numbers proved too great. When one wall of the house was torn down, it precipitated the final stand which ended soon after in a bloody orgy of feasting.

Declan's delaying tactics had allowed the refugees from Providence to flee, but they quickly found they had nowhere to go. Many before them had made their way to the thirty islands within Narragansett Bay, however by ten that morning the islands were no longer a haven. They were overcrowded and the people on them had turned savage to outsiders. Bridges had been thrown down and armed groups patrolled the shores, driving everyone away, even those that had swam out through the choppy waters.

The rest of the refugees had only one place to possibly go and that was to Massachusetts, however, the border was still being held tight. In the hope that something would give, a large portion of the population of Rhode Island went northwest towards Webster where Sergeant Ross and a good chunk of the 101st were duking it out, trying to pry a hole in the border through which they could all escape.

Almost none went east towards Fall River. Even if they could get through the border, where would they go from there? Cape Cod? Even among the people of Massachusetts, it was generally agreed that the Cape was a trap waiting to happen and was already mostly abandoned.

At least a million people went straight north to Woonsocket on the Mass border. There were a couple hundred soldiers among them, sixty or seventy police officers and a *few* armed citizens. Before the apocalypse, Rhode Island had the fourth lowest gun ownership per capita in the Union, barely twelve percent of the people owned guns. The vast majority of these had already died alongside Colonel Declan. Most of the rest had used their guns to gain access to the islands, where people with guns had been given precedence over everyone else, including women and children.

Thus, it was a mob of a million beggars who hurried north to Woonsocket and the Massachusetts border where they came to a deep moat behind which was an earthen mole twenty feet high and fifty miles long. The mob went down on their hands and knees, tears in their eyes and begged to be allowed to cross. Their pleas fell on deaf ears. The national guardsman on the other side of the built-up line knew that there was only one sure way to keep their own families safe and their lands from being overrun.

As hard at it was, they refused them entry and more than a few warning shots were fired. In a desperate attempt to protect their children, people held them out, pleading with the soldiers to take them. Sometimes they got too close to the ditch, which resulted in screams and guns fired into the ground at their feet or in the air over their heads.

No one knew what to do, especially as the zombies drew closer and closer. In a mindless panic, the mob began to flow back and forth towards the border and then away again. Those at the edges who could hear the monsters coming ran away.

Others wanted to follow, but then the screams of those being eaten alive echoed in the forests or along the empty streets of the nearby towns. The mob shrank inwards and began a collective moan that was perhaps the most eerie thing to happen in the past four days. A huge number of people moaning sounded like a wind of terror. It was horrible and maddening to hear, and in some places the men on the northern side of the border relented and let some children in.

When the rumor of this circulated, there was a surge toward the border that resulted in hundreds of people being trampled to death. Warning shots seemed to be useless. Someone panicked and let loose with an M240 machine gun. In seconds, the entire border was alive with fire and when the smoke cleared, ten thousand bodies were stretched out.

It was then that the inevitable seemed to strike the collective conscious of the mob.

People began filing south, picking up any weapon they could find. It was predominantly men with families, but there were single men in the mix and some women.

Gloria Snodgrass didn't have children, but she was an aunt seven times over and a great-aunt twice over. She had waitressed at an IHOP for too many years, as her varicose veins and grey hair attested. She had been planning to retire in four months. She went with the others, her heart pounding, her tongue coming out to lick her dry lips, ceaselessly. When she bent over to pick up a hefty branch, she became lightheaded. Still, she didn't pause.

There were no orders given; they weren't organized into regiments and no one knew precisely what was going to happen when the zombies came. They only knew that they would fight and they would die and maybe they would buy some time for the rest.

When the first of the zombies came into view, filtering through the forest, there didn't seem that many and some of the men tried to screw up their courage by screaming at them—but the beasts just kept coming. There was no end to them.

"Stand your ground!" someone yelled, as a few of the men began to back away. This was the only order given. The fight began a minute later. Gloria was four ranks back and it was twenty minutes before the people in front of her were killed, torn apart by the fiendish teeth. When it was her turn, she didn't flinch. With a battle cry that sounded more like a cry of despair, she waded in, swinging the branch and connecting with a grey, diseased head.

"That's one!" she yelled. Three million to go.

3—Roosevelt Memorial Hospital, Baltimore

Katherine Pennock had been tasked with "securing" a modern hospital complex where, on a normal day, three-thousand people would be working, healing, or dying. On the fourth day of the apocalypse, there were over five thousand people there and she and her Virginian driver,

Private Second Class Bill Bramlett, were on their own to fulfill that task.

"And that's why God gave us the satellite phone," she said and dialed the number to Cyber Command. "Captain Questore, please," she said to the receptionist who had answered the phone. "This is a Priority One call from the office of the Director of the FBI." It was…sort of.

When Questore came on the line, his anger was obvious. "This is Captain Questore. I'm a busy man, what do you want?"

"Oh, hey, Captain, it's me Special Agent Katherine Pennock."

He snorted like a bull about to charge. "Well, well, well, isn't this a treat? Katherine Pennock, Special Agent in charge of lying her ass off. You know I didn't need to be so nice the last time we met, right? But you told me you were going to brief the President. That wasn't true, was it?"

"No. I had to…"

"No, it wasn't true. I give you access to my building and to my people and what do I find out? You're throwing my name around left and right."

"Sorry about that but I needed…"

He cut her off. "I don't really care what you need. What I need is not to have some assistant to the assistant to the Director of the FBI all up in my shit, threatening me with jail time."

Katherine felt her stomach drop. "They threatened you because of me? That's not fair. What did you tell him?"

"What did I tell him?" Questore suddenly laughed. "I told him he could go fuck off. I told him that if he couldn't keep track of his agents that was on him, not me."

"Oh," Katherine said, wondering what sort of balls this guy had. Big brass ones by the sounds of it. But he wasn't the only one. "I need a favor," she said and then paused as he laughed into the phone. He laughed so hard that she could imagine the tears coming out of his eyes. "I found Anna Holloway and Shuang Eng," she said, hoping this would shock him into sobriety.

143

He snorted, again. "Why do I doubt it?"

"Okay, I didn't find them, but I found where they escaped from the Zone that *you* were supposed to be keeping secure." She could tell he was listening now with more attention. "I have six eyewitnesses. They were manning a road block a mile from where Anna and Eng hijacked a truck. These soldiers took one look at their pictures and nearly crapped themselves."

Questore was silent for a few moments as he soaked all this information in. "And what do you want from me?"

"I need soldiers, at least a hundred of them, to lock down Roosevelt Memorial Hospital. I also need an APB out on Charlie and Leticia Martin of Denver City, Texas. They are driving a 2015 Silverado, license plates: mike, tango, tango 634."

She could hear a pencil scraping like mad and then he asked, "You want an APB out on the truck, does that mean you don't think they're in the hospital?"

"It's unlikely. If I had just escaped the Zone, I'd want to put it miles behind me. And at the same time, they are both scientists who know their way around a hospital. They might have set Roosevelt up as a giant time bomb."

"Except it'll explode zombies," he said and then sighed. "Alright, I'll move some people around."

Captain Questore had a hundred men at the hospital within eighteen minutes. The FBI had sixty agents there within twenty. The two sides immediately started to bicker. Katherine had expected exactly that and had to physically haul men around until she had them all in place.

By then the hospital was in a state of escalating panic. With the entrances guarded, people tried to slip out of windows and shimmy down drains. The soldiers had set up a perimeter outside and although they appeared very menacing with their camo, their armored vests and their guns, they were tested. Two people were shot in the legs before the rest subsided.

While that was happening outside, Katherine and the FBI were going through the hospital floor by floor, room by room. There was no sign of Anna or Eng and thankfully no sign that any zombies had been made.

They were just finishing up when a helicopter landed on the roof and Katherine was told that she was wanted. With a sinking feeling, she mounted the stairs, fearing the worst. When she got to the top, her fears were justified. There was John Alexander sitting in the back of an Army Blackhawk. Even though he wore mirrored sunglasses, she could tell he was glaring at her.

Ducking under the whirling blades, she went to the side door and had to shout over the engine. "Yes, sir? You wanted me?"

"We need you to debrief the got-damned President, like you were supposed to. The Chinese just launched a major nuclear strike on their own soil and now the Director is afraid the got-damned President is about to do the same. It's going to be your job to talk him out of it."

"Me?"

"Yeah, you. Remember, he likes his debriefers pretty? It also helps if you know what you're talking about. That other blonde agent didn't do much but flirt. We need you to focus the President away from the idea of using nukes, especially in Baltimore. We found Eng and Anna's prints all over that camper. They were the ones who escaped from Long Island last night, just like you thought. And now they've escaped Baltimore to boot. You need to drill that into his got-damned head. So, put on some makeup and doll yourself up on the way because we're meeting him as soon as we land."

Katherine nodded slowly. She was in shock and slightly sickened to think that the fate of millions was in her hands.

Chapter 12

1– 11:41 a.m.
—Washington D.C.

Marty Aleman sat in front of a window in the library as rain beat silently against the three-inch thick glass. It was bullet proof and thus the rain was silent. As he waited on the coming helicopter, he sipped Mylanta. The president was being dangerously unmanageable and Marty's stomach was in an uproar.

Up to an hour before, the President had sat in the Situation Room, brooding over the maps. He had begun to fancy himself as some sort of Napoleon, an emperor/god who could have won the war twice already. It was easy when he was able to dismiss the facts of the situation as blithely as he did.

He gave no consequence to basic realities such as logistics, infrastructure, or even human nature.

Marty had sent him off for his nap, early. Marty could have used one as well, but he was waiting on call. He had made calls everywhere to practically every one of consequence, but, alarmingly, he wasn't getting calls back.

The cascading military debacles of the last few days were beginning to take a toll on the President's image as a decisive leader. That image had always been more of a mirage than a reality. It had been foisted on the American people by a fawning press who had been happily spoon-fed a sticky pablum of information and lies by Marty. He'd been doing it since before the election.

He didn't regret it. He was too tired for regrets. Besides, regrets were for people who lived in the past. A yawn was stretching his face into a caricature of itself when a Blackhawk came into view; it was flying very low, moving fast.

His phone finally rang, but it was only the secret service giving him a heads up on what he already knew: the FBI was coming back for another confab. Supposedly, there had been a breakthrough, but he feared that it would be just another useless meeting. What he desperately needed was a call from General Phillips telling him that they had finally cracked the Massachusetts border. Or better yet, a call from that treasonous Boston fuck saying that he had relented and was willing to open his border, at least temporarily.

He needed that call, badly. Half of the other governors were testing the limits of the constitution. Pennsylvania, Maryland, West Virginia, and Vermont had all thumbed their noses at the President and closed their borders the day before. Now it was Virginia, North Carolina, and Ohio. It was really making the war effort a tremendous headache.

If any more states followed suit, Marty was going to pack his bags and head for Tahiti because the President had not been shy talking about a nuclear option, including using one in Baltimore of all places.

"A couple of warheads will tidy that mess right up," he had said, sending a cold shiver right down Marty's back.

"So fucked up," Marty mumbled, gulping down the last of the Mylanta and heading for the stairs as the helicopter flared and landed on the White House lawn. He met the three-person FBI team right after they cleared security and groaned at the sight of the new blonde. The last one they had brought had been useless, or rather what she had to say was useless. They had been looking to cover up failure with a pretty face.

Marty didn't need a repeat performance. He needed answers to keep Armageddon from being added to an apocalypse. Holding up his hands, he looked the Director of the FBI right in the eye and said, "Sorry Dave, the President is in a meeting and we have more lined up around the corner and halfway down the block. I hate to be this blunt, but give me good news or go away."

The Director's eyes narrowed. He wasn't used to anyone talking to him like this; not even the President's puppeteer. "Okay, Marty. We found out who blackmailed their way off of Long Island last night. Shuang Eng and

Anna Holloway. They were two research assistants from R&K. They landed in Baltimore last night as you know, but escaped just before sunrise."

"And your proof?"

"Their fingerprints on a camper within the Balt-Zone and six eyewitnesses from soldiers who accidentally helped them to escape."

Marty stared at the Director. "Soldiers helped them to escape? Why is that so fucking believable?" He didn't expect an answer to the question, but the woman stepped forward.

"Hi there, my name is Special Agent Katherine Pennock. I'm the lead investigator on this aspect of the case." She didn't know who the lead was on any part of the case, but this was a career-making situation and if anyone could make the claim of lead investigator, it was her. She had put her ass on the line and the gamble had paid off and now it was time to rake in the chips. "The two perps took an older couple hostage and probably threatened them. The soldiers thought that the woman was having a heart attack. They acted out of compassion."

Marty gave her a long look, liking what he saw. She had short blonde hair, a pert nose, and long, slim legs; just the sort of woman the President liked, but she also had intelligent blue eyes and confidence. It made him think that this woman might actually be what she claimed to be, unlike so many others.

"We don't pay them for compassion," Marty said, after the pause. "They aren't trained for it. Damn it. Okay, I want you to brief the President, Pennock. I know you might be nervous, don't be. He's just a man. You'll see."

Marty signaled for a uniformed officer. "Please send for the President. We'll be in the Situation Room."

As confident as Katherine appeared, her insides were shaking as they marched through the White House. She couldn't stop thinking: *Holy shit! I'm in the White House! I'm in the White House!*

They entered a cramped elevator where everything was gleaming brass and the carpet under her feet was so thick that her heels sunk. The ride was so smooth and quiet that she was still waiting for it to move when the doors opened again and Marty escorted them to a rectangle of a room that held a long table, dozens of chairs, eight television monitors and one snoring general. It was General Heider, leaned back in a chair with his feet up in another, and his head thrown back, his mouth open, showing a mouth full of discolored teeth and a white-coated tongue.

Had it not been for his snoring, Katherine might have mistaken him for a corpse.

"Excuse me, Heider," Marty said. "We're going to need the room. I'm sure we can get you a bed upstairs."

Heider opened bleary red eyes and, perhaps out of habit, he stood. He wore a crumpled green suit that was decorated with little multicolored rectangles. His grey hair was roostered, jutting in the middle. "What? No, not with His Royal Shit-breath acting the way he is. Who are these…oh, Director. How's it going? You get the people who did this, yet?"

"Almost," the Director said, putting out a hand.

The two men shook hands and chatted with the Associate Executive Assistant Director for National Security, John Alexander hovering, trying to look as if he belonged there with the big boys. Katherine knew she didn't belong…at least not yet. When she caught Anna and Eng and ended this particular threat, then she would be fast-tracked. She would be a name. She'd be famous within the bureau and perhaps out of it as well.

She was still picturing the glory of it all when the President came in. He looked just like he did on television, all except his eyes. His eyes gleamed with a strange fever.

Everyone came to attention when he entered, even Katherine though she didn't know if this was proper protocol or not. The President didn't seem to notice. "There's news?" he asked. "You get the fuckers who did this, David?"

The Director of the FBI, David Blaise nodded. "We're hot on them. Here, let me introduce Special Agent

Katherine Pennock. She'll fill you in with what's going on."

The gleam in the President's eyes turned cold. "Didn't we go through this earlier? You parading some young thing in front of me so that you can influence me one way or another? That's not going to work anymore. This situation is real. There are real lives at stake. This isn't about legislative shenanigans or backroom deals. If you got something to say then tell me right to my face. Leave the floozy out of it."

This took the Director by surprise. It took Heider and Marty by surprise as well. Over the last couple of days, the President had been getting crankier and crankier as he was forced to adjust his habits and his way of thinking to this new paradigm in which things were actually expected of him beyond smiling at the cameras and giving speeches.

Even more than usual, he had been feeling lost and, as always, he had looked to Marty to save him. Then, a few hours before, as he looked at the maps in the Situation Room, he had come to an odd and startling conclusion: *We are losing.*

How? he asked himself. Hadn't he done exactly what Marty had told him to do? Marty had said do this and say that and, dutifully, the President had done exactly that and had said precisely this, and so far it hadn't worked. Marty's advice and the advice of everyone around him had proven to be demonstrably shitty.

It was then that the President had decided to be his own man. The situation they found themselves in called for a leader and wasn't he the leader of the free world? That's what all the news people said and they were usually better informed than Marty.

There was something the President understood and that was the real leader of the free world should not be swayed by a pretty face.

Katherine wasn't just a pretty face, however. Lines etched themselves around her eyes as thunder clouds formed on her brow. "Excuse me, sir," she said, her voice very loud in the small room. "I am no floozy. I am a special agent with the Federal Bureau of Investigation, and as such you will treat me with respect."

He turned on her, his anger building. Marty tried to intervene, "Look, sir, the FBI has an obligation to report directly…"

"I know what their obligations are, Marty!" he snapped. Looking back at the young agent, his demeanor softened. "Please, do your duty. Have you caught the bastards who did this?"

"Almost," Katherine said and then went on to explain her hunch about Anna and Eng and how she had hunted them to the edge of the Baltimore Quarantine Zone.

The President listened, nodding gently. When she was done, he shrugged. "That's it? They could be anywhere. Hell, they could still be in Baltimore for all you know."

He had blame in his eyes, as if it was Katherine's fault that Anna and Eng weren't standing on a corner holding signs that read "Domestic Terrorist!" She stared at the President in shock. "No," she eventually said. "You're wrong. They're not in Baltimore. Their motivations are obvious. They are looking to escape."

"How do you know?" the President asked, and then pointed at the largest of the monitors which showed almost the entire northeast covered in red. "They could be trying to destroy the entire nation!"

"If that were true, could they accomplish that by staying in Baltimore?" she asked.

He began nodding some more, shaking a finger in Katherine's face. "You're right. They're coming here. They're coming to the capital and we need to stop them. David, pull your agents out of Baltimore. Heider, get those national guardsmen moving south, right this second. And what about the 3rd ID?"

General Heider, Chairman of the Joint Chiefs of Staff, had been rubbing his temples where a migraine was starting to take hold. "What about them?"

"Why can't they get here faster?" the President demanded.

"Because they can't," he replied, wearily. "As I've explained, it's a big operation moving an infantry division eight hundred miles. I mean, if you want to do it properly, that is. I think after what happened with the 82nd and the 101st we've learned a valuable lesson about the need for planning."

The President glared. "I know for a fact that the 3rd ID has tanks. They can drive them."

Heider closed his eyes, which helped with the migraine. After a moment, he said, "You'll ruin their operational range that way. And besides, North Carolina has closed its borders. Virginia, too, in case you didn't get the memo."

"What about the Navy? We can just load them up and sail them north. This isn't difficult, Heider."

"You're right, it's not. But it would take at least a week to get the right materials and the right ships together to make that happen. Of course, if I did that we wouldn't have enough ships to patrol the coastal portions of the Zone."

"Not enough ships?" the President asked. "Every year since I've been in office you've demanded over a trillion dollars in spending and now you tell me that there aren't enough ships?"

Heider went right on rubbing his temples as if he were looking to hit bone soon. "Actually, I wanted more than that, but you shot me down. It wouldn't have mattered anyway. Are you forgetting where all that money went? You wanted a 'green' navy and you wanted fairness in housing for our 'beloved' military and you wanted diversity training and anger management classes and a hundred other bullshit plans that did nothing but sap our strength and waste money."

The President went red in the face. "Enough! Heider, get the 3rd ID here by tomorrow. I don't care how you do it, but do it." He turned to Marty. "Get the Mass border open today. Assassinate that traitor, Clarren if you have to. Blow up his house, I don't care. Get the border open, now!

Or you'll force *me* to do it and you know you don't want that."

He meant nukes. The threat hung in the room like a poisonous cloud.

Katherine was still trying to come to grips with the image of a nuclear war on American soil when the President turned to the FBI Director. It was his turn and Katherine shrank back, not wanting to get between the two men. She had been so focused on getting Anna and Eng that she had misjudged what was happening outside her little world very badly. Deep in her heart, she had thought that "things" would get better. She had thought that the military would stop the zombies and that, in time, the USA would get back to the way it had been before. Yes, she had been nervous about the talk of nukes, but hadn't really thought it would come to that. She wasn't nearly so sure about that now.

"David, find the people who did this," the President said, speaking quietly. "You will have whatever resources you need, including from a legal standpoint. From now until those terrorists are captured, there is no law when it comes to the FBI, do you understand? If you have to torture people then torture people. If you have to imprison them, then do that, too. If you have to execute suspects… well, the greater good compels you."

The President gestured to the door. They were being dismissed. All of them. Katherine, Marty Aleman, General Heider, the Director of the FBI and the Assistant Director for National Security went into the elevator in a stunned silence and, when they reached the main floor, they went their separate ways without speaking.

It wasn't until they reached the waiting Blackhawk that the Assistant Director whispered to Katherine, "Find them. Find them quickly."

2—Brunswick, Maryland

The four of them had tried to pass into Pennsylvania at three different places and West Virginia at four. They had been turned away, time and again, despite Anna Holloway's acting skills. "I'm a wasted talent," she said, returning to the truck, pretending to help Leticia along. "I could have won an Oscar for that last performance."

Eng, who thought of actors, even in China, to be overpaid pussies, only shrugged. He had the frail woman's other arm. He gave it a hard squeeze, his nails biting into her flesh. "I don't think this one has her heart in it. I think we should shoot her. It would make her acting more realistic."

Leticia began to whimper and Charlie started to shake his head. "Please don't," he begged. "She'll do better. Or…or I could do it. I can be the one faking a heart attack."

"I say we give them one more try," Anna said.

"And I say we shoot one of them in the stomach," Eng replied. "I guess we could meet somewhere in the middle. I could shoot the woman in the leg."

Anna didn't see how that would be better than a faked heart attack. Leg wounds could sit for days before becoming critical. And yet, they were running out of fuel, and worse, running out of time. The longer they meandered around the relatively small state of Maryland, the more likely they would run into an over-curious state trooper.

"One more try," she insisted. When all of this had started, it had been about money. She had never thought that it would end in murder and even though that ship had long since sailed, she still wasn't comfortable with shootings and blood and all the rest.

Eng looked at her with his dead eyes and then shrugged. "One try, Grandmother," he said to Leticia, "and then I will shoot your husband in the stomach. Consider that during your next performance."

Leticia tried her best. She moaned and groaned and shook and even cried when the dozen people at the next crossing discussed the matter. She had cried more when they told the four of them to try to cross in Morgantown where the "head honchos" were.

The threat of her Charlie getting shot left her too weak to walk, so she had to be carried. "It'll be okay," Charlie told her over and over. "The Lord is with us. He won't let anything happen."

Eng had smiled at this. The way he smiled was as if he had learned how by reading an instruction manual. "Maybe we try one more time." He drove, heading away from Morgantown, earning him a look from Anna. "The further away we get from danger, the less pressing are the injuries and the more likely we are to be passed on to someone higher up the chain of command."

He was right. With each stop, the deliberations among the citizens and the citizen-soldiers had been shorter, the urgency less pronounced, and the suspicion in their eyes much greater.

Anna checked the map. "How about Virginia? I think we should rule out Pennsylvania, and we've tried West Virginia. Maybe Virginians will be nicer."

"Sure," Eng said. He smiled again and Anna had to fight the shiver that wanted to twerk her shoulders. He was going to shoot Charlie but like a farmer about to slit a lamb's throat, he didn't want spook his victim. It queered up the flavor of the meat.

They took a little two-lane nothing of a road and passed through Brownsville, the very epitome of small town America. It looked oddly pristine and when Anna rolled down the window, the quiet was nostalgic, not eerie. Cows lowed in the pasture, and birds chirped, and in the forest, squirrels made a ruckus, chasing each other about.

There was even an old farmer sitting on the back of a tractor as it snorted its way through a field, setting down perfectly churned rows of dirt. A hand with heavy calluses and dirty nails was raised and Eng smiled his lizard-smile back, but from a distance it looked like a normal one. There weren't many farmers working their fields and the streets were, for the most part, empty, but there were a few shops still open.

Once Brownsville was behind them, they traveled along forest roads, heading southeast until the jets could once more be seen roaring their way through the skies. Once she saw the first one, Anna felt the urgency come back. She didn't think the FBI was on to them and if she had, she would have shot Charlie two hours before. Still, there was that feeling, the overpowering need to escape.

When they saw the sign for Brunswick, Eng calmly perched an elbow over the console and asked, "Are you two ready for one more go?" They both nodded, anxiously. "Good. Look out there. These are your people. These are Americans. They'll believe you."

Dutifully, they had both turned to look at the town and Eng took advantage of their distraction to shoot Charlie in the gut.

The gunshot was piercingly loud; a knitting needle in the eardrums. Leticia's screams were an old echo from another time compared to the sound. Anna found herself working her jaw around, trying to clear her ears as if she had just got off a plane. When she looked back she saw Charlie, pale and trembling, trying to staunch the flow of blood that was coming out of him like a fountain.

"It don't hurt," he said, in a whisper. Leticia didn't believe him and neither did Anna. It looked horrible. And the mess! The amount of blood he was losing was shocking. It just kept coming and coming, bubbling up through his fingers.

Leticia, unable to help the man she loved, seemed to grow stronger at this outrage. Her eyes bulged, but they were bone dry. "You killed him," she accused Eng.

"Not yet," he answered, the cold, mechanical smile back on his face. "Not yet, so get smart."

Anna pulled her eyes from the bloody mess long enough to see that Leticia was no longer functioning like the whipped dog she had been. She looked ready to bite and scratch. She looked ready to do almost anything, including making a scene and ruining everything.

"Hey," Anna said, trying to sound as normal as she could. "If you want him to live, then act like you love him. You look angry, not sad."

"I am mad," the old woman hissed, those eyes bulging so far out that Anna feared that if she sneezed they might go rolling around on the floorboards.

Anna put out both hands. "Yes, you should be mad, but you should also be worried about Charlie. Do you want him to live, or what?" Leticia looked like she wanted to claw Anna's eyes out, but her worry for her husband was a close second and when she glanced his way, the fight went out of her. She became small and weak again, overcome with grief.

When Eng saw this, he settled in behind the wheel of the truck saying, "We'll say that someone tried…no *someones*; there were four of them. They tried to hijack the truck. They shot poor Charlie and we were just able get away. We tried the hospitals on this side of the border, but all the doctors were tasked with working with the army. Leticia will be filled with sorrow and Charlie will be stoic as he awaits necessary care."

"Sounds good, but let me do the talking," Anna said. "You sound a little stilted. It's that smile. Stop it. There's nothing to smile about. It's…it's just wrong."

He didn't take offense. "My smile should not factor into this equation. What counts is how you look and how Leticia looks. These will be the deciding factors that give us victory."

Now it was Anna's turn to mold her smile into something believable. There wasn't going to be any victory. There would be survival or death and even if they managed to get away, what then? A life forever on the run?

It began to rain as they entered the north end of the town. Ahead of them was a main street with the usual assortment of diners and gas stations, banks and salons. Cutting through the middle of the town was the western run of the Potomac River. On one side was Maryland and on the other, Virginia.

157

The speed limit was a sluggish twenty-five, and Eng kept the truck pegged right at it, the smile back in place as they passed a few lost-looking souls. They looked like beings trapped in purgatory, standing with a view of heaven but unable to cross the river of fire separating the two.

As they headed for the first roadblock, a bedraggled woman with a wet mop of brown hair on her head and pleading hands, stepped right in front of the Silverado. Eng slammed on the breaks, skidding on the asphalt until he was inches away from her.

The woman looked at Eng with dull eyes and there was a strange moment when no one seemed to know what to do next. The rain came in spurts; it sounded like children were throwing handfuls of peas onto the roof. The wind surged, blowing a plastic bag across the front of the truck, and still the woman just stood there as if caught in mid-thought.

Eng looked back to warn Leticia against saying or doing anything foolish but then he paused. Anna seemed like the only person capable of action. She shooed the drenched woman away with a wave of her hand.

"Eng, come on…" Anna nearly froze as well when she saw what Eng was looking at. Charlie was dead. He was slumped onto his wife's lap. His mouth open wide, his cheeks stretched and already looking waxy and yellow. His eyes were open and staring right into Eng's face.

"You killed him," Leticia said, flatly.

The 9mm bullet from Eng's Beretta had been aimed perfectly. Charlie had enough of a layer of fat that a bullet shouldn't have been able to do more than rip up some intestines, a bit of muscle and not much else, but fate had intervened. The bullet had taken a weird spinning turn and cut an almost perfect diagonal swath through Charlie, heading for the abdominal aorta and smashed the shit out of it.

"You killed him," Leticia said, again. "And now you're gonna kill me."

"We won't have to if…" Anna began, only just then the old woman reached for the door handle.

Eng was fast. Like an old west gunfighter, he pulled his gun and shot her in the back of the head. Her hand on the door handle spasmed, releasing the catch and out she spilled, falling dead in the middle of the street.

Chapter 13

1– 11:41 a.m.
—Auburn, Massachusetts

Full of piss and vinegar, Jason Bernard and three of his oldest friends had piled into his fourteen-year-old Mustang and driven down from Boston the day before to do their part. It had been an almost spiritual calling, a compulsion etched into his genes which had been egged on by foolish boasts and a strange need to prove himself. Feeling like a man for the first time in his young life, Jason had explained to his teary-eyed mother, "It's just somethin' I gotta do, Ma."

Her begging for him to stay had only cemented his desire to leave. Squaring his jaw, he had kissed her once on the cheek and breezed out of the house, stepping loudly, importantly.

The machismo was still running strong when he had locked up the Mustang on a side street in Webster and pocketed the keys. Jason could have fought a hundred men right then. The lust for battle was running through him like an electric current, making him feel alive and powerful.

As he, and what felt like thousands of others, marched towards the sounds of guns crashing and men yelling, and in some instances screaming like women, he gradually began to feel anxiety and perhaps a little fear, but the battle lust was so entwined with his fear that he could barely tell the fear from the electricity. That was a good thing. If they had been separated, he probably wouldn't have stepped one foot out of that old Mustang because there in the sky were jets streaking back and forth, and black helicopters wup-wup-wupping about full of menace and deadly venom in the form of blazing lead. And all around him were rippling explosions that sounded like ceaseless thunder if thunder came from a clear blue sky.

Then he was under the cover of the woods and his fear began to amp up. It made him hesitate but, like it was a red brick, he gulped it down and went with his friends deeper into the forest toward a war that he had no business being in.

He was just sixteen and had shot his daddy's rifle twenty-three times over the course of two camping trips. Jason mistakenly thought that he was a pretty good marksman. After all, those soda cans he had sent spinning hadn't been all that big and at forty yards, they had looked smaller still. He knew that if he had a clear shot at a stationary target, he was pretty sure that he could kill the crap out of it.

But there wasn't anything clear except those jets and helicopters, and what was more, the fight hadn't been stationary at all. The enemy had shifted to the right and then before things could settle down, they shifted to the right some more. "They're just probing us!" a burly sort of man yelled over the hellacious sound of the firefight. He was big-bellied and big-bearded, and had a cheek full of chaw. When he yelled or even just spoke, brown spittle would fly. He looked like a tough kind of man, a mean kind of man, someone that Jason would have been more than a little nervous about approaching a week before.

Despite his toughness and his brown tobacco spittle, he seemed scared and that had Jason's fear ramping up so that it began to eclipse whatever battle lust he'd been feeling. A man next to him threw up in the dead leaves, coming up white and shaking, a long string of greenish-brown drool hanging from the corner of one lip.

This display seemed like a permission slip for Jason's fear to come completely out of hiding and he was just about shitting his pants as the battle rolled down at him.

And he wasn't the only one with a puckered sphincter. All the men and boys who had been tramping towards the gunfire stopped and waited. More and more of them were shaking and cringing, less and less were boasting as they had been. The battle seemed to Jason to be like a terrifying creature that roared and shook the ground and moved in an undulating way more or less like a living wave, washing here and there, chewing up men and breathing out flame

161

and smoke. Birds and small animals fled from it, and instinctively he wanted to flee as well.

With all his quaking heart Jason wanted to run, but he held his ground, perhaps because everyone else held theirs, but it was a close thing. His feet were so light that he had to concentrate on keeping them planted, because if he wasn't careful, he thought that they would, all on their own, do what came naturally and propel him as fast as they could out of there, just another squirrel or sparrow.

No one else ran, so he stayed, hunkered down next to a tree, pointing his gun out at other trees, listening to that monster come closer and closer, thinking that when it was finally his turn to fight, he wouldn't be fighting other men, he'd be fighting this beast that had been unleashed on them.

But by a miracle, the fight shifted far to the right. Relieved, Jason lifted himself up from the tree, and peered along a firebreak and saw that there were guys strung out for as far as he could see. Some were shooting and some were just squatted down as if bushes were bulletproof or that their flannel shirts weren't as obvious as they were. But no one was running. *Perhaps we're even winning*, he thought.

He was still standing there a perfect target, thinking that by some miracle he had escaped the horrible fire and thunder beast when something smacked into the tree next to his head, sending bark flying into his face.

Had he been at home, he would have thought that someone had thrown a rock at him. Only he wasn't at home. His body reacted faster than his torpid mind—his knees buckled and he dropped even before he realized that someone was shooting at him.

And it wasn't just some *one.* Guns were going off by the hundreds, enveloping his little acre of the forest in such a deafening fury of sound that the air pulsed with each gunshot. His heart seized in his chest, however the rest of him reacted, once again without much work on the part of his brain. He popped up almost as fast as he went down, and like magic, his daddy's spare rifle was on his shoulder and the scope was at his eye.

What he saw down that scope was a blur of green and brown that refused to come into focus. Only when he pulled his head back did he see that he'd been aiming at a bush fourteen feet away. The bush seemed to be coming apart under a withering fire and beyond it, maybe fifty yards or so, was a man in camouflage, an M4 in his hands. Jason fired without aiming and the shot went high. With fumbling hands, he jacked back on the bolt, but he was unpracticed and fear had made his fingers numb. What should have been a fluid motion was herky-jerky and instead of flying out, the spent cartridge "stove-piped," meaning it got hung up in the chamber and just sat, half in and half out of the gun, gumming up the works.

"Oh, God!" he cried, uselessly pushing and pulling on the bolt, certain that at any second a bullet would hit him square in the face or tear out his throat or puncture his heart or rip into his soft belly. His skin tingled with the horrible anticipation of it as he struggled the cartridge out. When it finally dropped into the leaves at his feet, he quickly pushed the bolt forward again, sending a new round into the chamber.

Now, he could fight again, however by then, his mind was no longer processing fear rationally. Pure panic had its talons in his heart, and when he looked up again it seemed to the frightened boy as though the entire 101st Airborne Division was practically in his lap.

Unlike him, these were real men, real soldiers, wearing real uniforms and firing real guns. Their guns weren't anything like the crappy deer rifle he was clutching, either. They were a sinister black in color and when they fired, they shot not just bullets, but flame as well. And they never missed. There were screams erupting in the forest. The screams cut through the tremendous din of battle and burrowed their way right into Jason's soul.

No part of him wanted to stay and fight, but even if he wanted to, his feet were already moving without his permission. He was running before he knew it, sprinting

163

blindly through the forest, leaping over bodies and dodging trees, plowing through the underbrush and the hanging vines. Seconds into his mad flight, the strap of his rifle got hung up on a twig and, quite unexpectedly, there was what seemed to be an explosion in his right hand.

His finger had been curled around the trigger of his rifle and at that first jolt, he had squeezed his hand, sending a bullet blazing out. By purest luck, he didn't shoot himself. The bullet, a wild card in the middle of a wild battle, passed under the nose of a pompous, self-appointed captain who had been cowering behind a tree and zipped unseen and unheard through the melee, hitting a tree half a football field away.

Jason had no idea what had happened. He actually thought that his rifle had been hit by a bullet and had the insane idea that his rifle was somehow attracting gunfire. He let out a scream and flung it away from himself. Now, he could run even faster; and he did. With the mad eyes of an escapee from an insane asylum, he hauled ass south for a quarter of a mile to where the world was quieter, more rational. He slowed to a jog, his heart calming, his mind clearing, but then he heard shooting ahead of him and he realized that he hadn't escaped danger completely. To the south was the border and beyond that were more soldiers, and beyond them were millions of zombies.

"Son of a bitch," he whispered, realizing he was caught between a rock and another, heavier and harder rock. He took a hard left, heading east, heading toward Boston and home. He ran for his Ma, and behind him the others wheeled east like a flight of swallows.

Jason had been the first to run and that one weak link had caused the entire chain to snap. In seconds, he was joined by a dozen men, then a hundred, then a thousand others.

Behind them, Sergeant Ross of the 101st, came huffing and puffing to a stop, leaning against a tree. The sweat dripping down into his eyes went ignored as he watched the Massachusetts boys running away. It was shocking how many of them there were. Somehow, his little company had managed to dislodge a battalion-sized element—a thousand men. A wave of goosebumps broke out across his flesh.

Never all that articulate, Ross could only whisper, "Holy shit," as he stared with a feeling of stunned amazement. How he had lived, he didn't know. "Not even a scratch," he said, out loud in amazement. Just to make sure, he ran a hand over his chest and arms.

A soldier next to him was wide-eyed and looked as though he had been hit on the head with a rock. Ross was sure he looked the same way. The two simultaneously grinned at each other and, for that brief second, they were happy. They had lived! Impossibly, they had lived. But the smiles faded as they heard the moans and the cries of "medic" behind them. They had lived, but there was no saying they would live much longer.

"Hold here," Ross told the soldier and turned away to gather up what was left of his company.

The line had been broken; the bubble holding in the air assault element had popped. That was the good news. The bad news was that the other part of General Platnik's two-pronged attack had failed miserably. The drive north had sputtered right from the start and he hadn't been able to budge the Massachusetts National Guard even a foot from their trenches. Even with air power on his side, the fight had eaten up precious supplies and most of his reserve forces so that now that he had a breakthrough he was limited in his ability to exploit it.

Red in the face, Platnik cursed over his maps. Sergeant Ross and the others might have survived, but they were still trapped behind enemy lines, while the rest of the 101st was trapped between two armies; one living, one undead. General Platnik knew he could still win if he could just act quickly and decisively, and if he could get just one more miracle.

"God, if you're listening, I need fuel, please, please," Platnik begged with a glance to the sky.

He only had a trickle of fuel left for his Blackhawks, and if he didn't get any more, the air assault force that had just won a great victory would be stranded and open to counterattack. "And if they fail, I will have used up the last of my reserves for nothing and we will all die," Platnik whispered.

For long seconds the command tent was silent except for Platnik's mutterings. He was like a physicist at a poker table, systematically going over every known variable. General Platnik knew precisely how much ammo his men had. He also knew that his counterpart in Massachusetts was throwing everything he had into the fight, and that with every passing minute, more national guardsmen and militiamen and even teenage boys were hurrying south to hem in his assault force. He also knew that a massacre was happening twenty miles away in Woonsocket where millions of zombies were feasting on the civilians trapped there. He had seen the satellite photos and they had been enough to turn even his stomach.

Platnik knew what the situation was. He knew that everything was against him: he didn't have enough soldiers, enough fuel, and enough ammo. It didn't matter. He had to break the deadlock around Webster even if it cost him every troop under his command. "Send in the reserves, now!" was his order.

It was a gamble with millions of lives hanging on the outcome. If he lost, there would be nothing to stop a second massacre.

As Sergeant Ross poked about through the dead, looking for spare ammo, Blackhawks by the dozens, each overflowing with men and boys, started to land along the highway. At first, he cheered along with the rest of the survivors of the fight, but after not quite a thousand soldiers and civilians had been hastily dropped in the middle of enemy territory, many of them with not much more than a handful of ammo, the flights ceased as did the cheering.

The 101st was out of fuel.

Sergeant Ross's company of a hundred men was down to twenty-three rattled souls when the order came to move south where the battle had been raging for hours, they were very slow to get up. They were heading for the meat grinder. They all knew it. But they didn't have a choice.

2—Alford, Massachusetts

Slumped over in the front seat of the vintage Corvette, Courtney Shaw had been making an intermittent noise, a sound that was a cross between a cat's purr and a chainsaw being used to cut up a block of cement. It was a snore that would have shocked and appalled her.

It had gone on and on for hours and probably would have gone on until evening had she not been awakened by something, but she didn't know what. She sat up and gazed out the front window seeing trees and a black topped road that wasn't at all familiar, while a quarter of a mile behind her a C-17 Globemaster transport plane burned.

The C-17 was one of seven which had been shot down while attempting to resupply the soldiers who were fighting to preserve the border against the hordes of undead. It had gone up like a bomb when it hit the ground, but Courtney had been so thoroughly exhausted and deep in sleep that she had no idea what had woken her.

Her first thought was to reach over for the police scanner. "Thuy, are you out there?" she asked. It was a terrible breach in protocol as well as in operational security, but she just wanted her part in all of this to be over. She wanted to find Thuy and Deckard, somehow talk them past the border and then get the hell out of there. Possibly to Canada, but more likely Alaska.

Only Thuy didn't answer. Courtney tried again, this time doing it correctly: "Deck 1, this is Dispatch 6, over." Again, no answer. In vain she repeated the phrase three more times before giving up—temporarily.

"Are they out of range, or am I?" It was a legitimate question. She was still waking up and really didn't know where she was. Not only that, her brain felt slow and woolen, as if there was an old sock stuffed between her ears instead of good old grey matter. She gazed about until something caught her attention out of the corner of her eye.

It was only then that she saw the burning wreckage of the C-17 stretched out over an area greater than a football field. "Holy cow," she whispered, wondering what had happened that could have brought down one of those huge birds. The crash was captivating in a gruesome sort of way and she had to tear her eyes away.

The keys to the Corvette were in the ignition and she was still so out of it that it was a surprise to her to find them there. She pulled the 'vette around to see if anyone had lived through the crash. It didn't seem possible, but as a state trooper dispatcher, she knew that stranger things had happened. In this case, there wasn't any sign of people or people parts there was just a noxious, oily smoke that blanketed everything and seemed to cling to the inside of her nose.

For a good minute she gazed dully at the flames before she thought to leave. "Gotta pull it together," she whispered, and once more turned the Corvette around. She knew which way the border was by the sound of explosions and the distant rising smoke. As she drove, she started in again, broadcasting, "Deck 1, this is Dispatch 6, over."

There was no answer and she was beginning to think there wouldn't be one, unless she could boost the signal, which she wouldn't be able to do with the power out. "The military's got power," she said. "And they probably have radio relays, too." An idea was beginning to blossom.

"I'll be the Governor's scientific liaison and I need to inspect the thingy. I mean the…uh…crap! That's not going to be believable at all." She needed an excuse to get to the communications equipment that the communications people would believe. It had to be urgent but not verifiable.

The miles zipped by under her tires, and before she could come close to any sort of plan, she was close enough to the border to smell the spent gunpowder and the rotting flesh of the zombies. These combined odors hung in the air like an invisible veil, making her want to gag. She slowed the Corvette, her gorge rising in the back of her throat.

On her right, next to a pasture of clover, was a burned-out tank. It was black, scorched right down to its treads. The turret was popped off and was sitting more than thirty feet away, turned upside down. A helmet sat in the middle of the road and as Courtney went around it, she saw that there was a head still in it which had only the stump of a neck left. The stump itself had a shaft of vertebrae that was black with dried blood and swarming flies.

It looked like the sort of potted plant one would find in hell, and Courtney stared at it for so long that she almost drove off the road and into an elm that had sprung up decades before and had sat, unmolested, on the edge of the road for all that time.

"This can't be happening!" she cried, hauling the wheel around, her breath coming fast and high up in her throat. She missed the tree by inches.

The image of the helmet and the stump was horrible, but there were more of these types of scenes to come as she got closer to the fighting. A Stryker sat on its side with two corpses pinned partially beneath, the faces of the people, both women, were twisted forever in agony. Further on there was a charred pile of what looked like just arms and legs. Courtney had to stare hard to see a few torsos and another bodiless head in among everything else.

Then she came to a number of strange, green-painted, metal-beaked multi-axil vehicles, and of course these were burnt and twisted as well, but what really caught her eye were the destroyed radar dishes and the radio uplinks and the boosting equipment. "What the hell?" she exclaimed in a haunted whisper as she realized what had done all this damage.

"They're fighting each other. Shit." It made her sick to think that brother was fighting brother when there were enemies at the gates.

She moved closer to the burned-out equipment and didn't need to see the sign that read, "Comm Unit, 345th"

169

to know that the US military was targeting the Massachusetts command and control apparatus with a heavy emphasis on communications.

Even though the machinery was destroyed, she felt suddenly vulnerable and glanced up at the skyline above the trees, thinking that the jets could be coming back to make sure the job of blowing everything up was completed. Perhaps, she thought, flying by at Mach-2, these vehicles didn't look this bad. Maybe they even looked serviceable.

Her only consolation was that the idling 'vette, with it shiny red paint, didn't look like anything but a fancy sports car. She was all set to relax, as far as being bombed was concerned, when she realized that, although a person would recognize the car, a computer chip in the brain of a Tomahawk missile wouldn't know or care that the Corvette was a classic.

For all she knew, a submarine eight hundred miles away could have launched an entire salvo of missiles at her already, and at any second they would come zooming in out of the clear blue. In a flash, it would be her head lying in the middle of the road, and it would be her stump of a neck and her jutting, glistening red run of vertebrae poking up.

"Oh, shit," she whispered. Clearly, she needed a new plan, but just at that moment, what she needed more was to get the hell away from those vehicles. Courtney tore her eyes from the skyline and started to turn the Corvette around yet again. She was in the middle of a frantic K-turn when she saw a Humvee far down at the end of the road.

To her frightened mind, it had an air of menace to it and she quickly completed her turn, all the while watching the Humvee come closer and closer, not knowing which side it belonged to. She got the 'vette pointed back the way she had come and when she stomped the gas, the Corvette accelerated as only Corvettes could. In five seconds, she was doing eighty with both hands gripping the steering wheel. The forest road hadn't been designed with that sort of speed in mind and she took hair-raising turns with screeching tires and hit little hills where it felt that she was airborne for a second or two.

By the time she looked into the rearview mirror, the Humvee was nowhere in sight and she realized it hadn't been following her at all and nor was she being tracked by cruise missiles or Harrier jump jets, if those were really a thing. She was alone, which, when she thought about it, wasn't all that comforting, either.

"Deck 1, this is Dispatch 6, over," she said, for the fortieth time since waking up, and then held her breath, hoping that Deckard or Thuy would reply. When they didn't, she sighed, on the verge of giving up. So far, she had survived mainly by being lucky. She had managed to find the right people in the right set of circumstances to get her to this point: somewhat safe within the Massachusetts border.

"So, what do I do?" she asked her bushy-haired reflection in the rearview mirror. "Do I leave it to them to get out on their own? Or do I stay and muddle through?" She had no clue what to do and a part of her wished that Dr. Lee was still with her. Right from the start, with people turning into zombies all around her, Thuy had always seemed so composed, and a part of Courtney wished she could be that way, too. "Maybe the question should be, what would Dr. Lee do?"

Courtney's lips pursed and little lines creased her forehead as she thought and thought and thought until minutes went by and she realized that she had no idea how a genius saw the world or how they were able to think the way they did, or even what they thought about. She assumed they spent the day pondering tremendous, world-altering concepts, while Courtney, who had never considered herself anything but average, usually spent her free time thinking about how she needed to get her gutters cleaned out, or what was going to be on TV that night, or if she was going to her mother's house on Sunday night even though all her mom ever did was badger Courtney about who she was dating and when she would get married.

171

Thankfully, her mother was safe in Vermont with her sister. It was one less thing for Courtney to worry about.

"Maybe the better question is what would Dr. Lee think that I would do?" That was easier. "Thuy would expect me to help get her and Deck out of the Zone, like I promised. But how?" That was the question and as she thought about it, she watched a plane rip across the sky just a few hundred feet over head. It shook the Corvette on its springs.

The one thing she wasn't going to do was get near any communications equipment. Those jets were probably hunting anything emitting a radio frequency above a certain strength. Nervously, she shifted her gaze down to the scanner. Were they hunting her? Had they heard her broadcasts?

Almost on cue a second grey jet roared by, half a mile away

Her hands itched to reach over and turn the radio off even though she knew that just sitting there it wasn't emitting any signal whatsoever. It was probably safe to broadcast as long as she changed positions frequently. But did she have the guts to do it over and over again with the jets overhead?

"No." It would be suicide. No, what she had to do was end the fighting as fast as possible, and then save Thuy and Deckard.

Chapter 14
1– 12:36 p.m.
—Warfursburg Road, Maryland

As Thuy and Deckard slept and Courtney sprinted east as fast the Corvette would go, Katherine Pennock was setting down in a Military Blackhawk, smack in the middle of Warfursburg Road, a hundred yards south of the border separating Pennsylvania and Maryland.

"Keep her running," she yelled to the pilot.

The pilot, Warrant Officer Joe Swan nodded, but rolled his eyes behind his aviator sunglasses. She wasn't the only one who had things to do and missions to accomplish. It had been bad enough that he'd been tasked with one taxi ride to the White House, but now he was supposed to be at this chick's beck and call? He wasn't a limo driver for goodness sakes, and it really chaffed his ass to be sitting there while others were out bringing down zombies by the score or lighting up those stupid Massachusetts morons who thought they could mess with the real army. He was just dying to load up a dozen Hellfire missiles and go against their tanks and teach them a lesson in manners and obedience.

Unfortunately, all the weaponry he had was a single port-side door gun and even that had nearly been pulled off the bird by one of the armory punks. The punk, who only held the rank of specialist, had already taken his starboard M240 and most of his ammo and had the balls to say, "According to this, you're just on taxi duty."

"We're hunting domestic terrorists who are presumed armed and dangerous," Swan had snapped. "The gun is staying." He had to resist the desire to throw himself over the gun. In the end, he signed for one M240 and only a hundred rounds of ammo. It wasn't an auspicious start, made worse by the fact that his co-pilot was pulled to take part in operations in Massachusetts.

Swan was still grumbling when they landed down the road from the border. "We should be taking this bird north," he said to his two-person crew who also shared his desire for actual combat when there was a war to fight. "We should be kicking ass like we're trained to. Didn't those Massachusetts pinkos say the Pledge of Allegiance when they were growing up like everyone else?"

Katherine walked away from the helicopter pretty much clueless as to what Swan was thinking. Her mind was spinning on a different mission. It was simple: hunt down Anna Holloway and Shuang Eng, and save America. With this whack-job of a President, you couldn't do one without the other.

She had a few good clues to go on: a white Silverado with Texas plates, an old and very average white couple, an Asian man who looked anywhere between twenty-two and forty-two, and a young, pretty blonde.

But what would happen if Anna colored her hair, or they ditched the truck, and killed the old couple? What if Anna and Eng went their separate ways and both released their viruses in different parts of the state? That was pretty much the nightmare scenario and there was no way to know what the President would do. If she had one true fear, it was that of the President using nukes on American soil.

The threat from the zombies was very real and frightening, that was a given. However, the possibility of the civil war expanding to other states and possibly tearing the country apart was more sad than scary to Katherine.

But if the President tried to solve the problem with nukes, there was no knowing how far he would take it. If one zombie showed up in Chicago, would that be enough to irradiate all of Illinois? What if one showed up in Ottawa? Would he declare war on Canada?

Katherine was still worrying over a North American war when a voice snapped, "Stop. Go back the way you came. Pennsylvania is closed."

The roadblock was an improvised affair with cinderblocks, tree branches, a few garbage cans and three cars—two Honda Civics and a grocery-getter that Katherine couldn't name. She already had her badge out and now she raised it up. "I just need to talk. I'm with the FBI."

"The FBI, the Federal butt-fuckers in charge," someone joked and although it was a weak joke, the seven men and two women at the roadblock laughed uproariously.

Another elbowed his friend and said, "Are you with the Federal Bureau of investigating my junk? If so, you can come on over to the good side." More laughter. Katherine just waited until it was out of their system.

"Hey, hey, I got one," one man cried. He was very round, probably as round as he was tall, and despite the coolness of the day and the threatening rain clouds hanging over them, he was sweating. There was even a sheen in the bags beneath his eyes. He started laughing even before he could say, "The fucking butt investigators! Oh, that's a good one."

No one else laughed. "That's dumb," one of the younger men in the group said. "You killed it, Jeff."

"Nuh-uh, no I didn't."

"Don't worry," Katherine told him. "It was pretty much dead to begin with. I'm Special Agent Katherine Pennock. I need to know if anyone has tried to get through this road block. Specifically…"

Jeff interrupted with a snide, "Only like a million people, special agent in charge of investigating my special butt."

Katherine acted like she hadn't heard him. "Specifically, a caucasian couple, man and wife in their seventies, an Asian man, thirty-ish and slender. And lastly, a pretty, blonde woman about five foot six inches tall and a hundred and ten pounds." They started looking back and forth to each other, all except sweaty Jeff, who was thinking of some new and even funnier joke. He was stuck on the F and the I since B had to stand for butt. That was certainly logic as far as he understood the word.

"I have pictures," she said, reaching into the black leather handbag she carried across her shoulder. She took only one step before she froze.

175

At least two members of the little squad had brought their weapons up. They both had plenty of grey in their hair and looked like they were a couple who had been picking out window treatments the week before. Just then, it looked as though they were more than willing to fire those guns and wouldn't bat an eye if Katherine died in the street.

"No one has passed through," the woman said, "and no one will, not even you."

"I didn't ask if anyone passed through, I asked if they had tried," Katherine said. "These two," She held up the pictures of Anna and Eng, "are responsible for all of this. They are carrying vials of the plague with them. Look at their faces." She wasn't asking. They looked, leaning over the hoods of the two Civics and the grocery getter.

The woman shook her head; her husband looked indecisive, and Jeff blew a raspberry and dismissed the pictures with a wave. She thrust the pictures toward the rest and received only negative responses. "What about just him?" she asked, holding up just Eng's picture.

"The fucking bureau of Chinamen investigations," Jeff said, trying again to get someone to laugh. No one did.

"Let's see the young woman again," one of the others asked. "There was a girl who tried to get through with her mom, but, but, no that's not her."

One crossing down, five hundred to go, Katherine thought. And that was if they hadn't crossed on foot through some field or forest. These were being guarded as well, but she guessed that there were ravines or thick forest or endless curtains of Kudzu that a determined person could slip through. Of course, they'd have to steal a car once they were on the other side of the border but that was another danger and another point of contact.

She thanked the little group, walked a little way off to a storm bent elm that offered some shade and took a map from her purse. It was already folded and creased, open to a panel which showed a section of the northern Maryland border that sat to the northwest of Baltimore. It had been her first choice because it was close enough to get to quickly, but not so close that it was obvious. It was just a guess.

"Did they try further away?" she asked herself. "Or closer? A bigger crossing point? A smaller? One with more women?" She was certain that they had crossed, or were in the process of trying to cross into another state. But where? There were so many different factors that could have swayed the fugitives.

She had chosen the Pennsylvania border because she figured it would be easier to cross as the state was currently embroiled in a life and death struggle, but judging by the reaction she had received she had been wrong about that.

She worried over the map as precious minutes went by. Each passed like it was part of a countdown and at the end was the President's finger looming over a red button. Five minutes passed in indecision before she pulled out her sat-phone and dialed Cyber Command.

"Lieutenant Commander Brockett?"

Dawn sounded less like a naval commander and more like a harried mother trying to do three things as once. "This is she. Who is this? Special Agent Hancock?"

"It's Pennock. Do you have anything for me?" Katherine wondered if she sounded like she was begging, because it sure as hell felt as though she was. "I know it's only been fifty-seven minutes, but I…"

"When I hear anything, you'll be the first to know," Dawn said, inadvertently reinforcing the picture Katherine had of her as a mother, with her hair sticking up in all directions and that night's roast thawing in the sink.

Before Katherine could say a word, Dawn had cut the connection, leaving Katherine staring at her phone. "I deserved that," she said. "These things take time." She knew that. She knew that leads developed slowly, they didn't hatch, fully formed in minutes or even hours. Calls had to made, people had to be talked to, areas and incidents had to be investigated. Only she didn't have time.

"I don't have a lot of time," she corrected herself, and then turned and ran for the Blackhawk, twirling her hand in short circles above her head, giving the crew chief, Mark Rowden, the universal signal for "get the bird ready."

She didn't have her helmet completely on her head, before she was yelling, "Take her up to three hundred feet and shift west." Katherine hoped that from three hundred feet she would be able to get a feel for what Eng and Anna had seen. It just looked like trees and forest to Katherine.

They flew for a quarter of an hour before she had the pilot set down at another roadblock. She chose it because there were only three people standing guard behind a huge tree that someone had butchered with an axe.

The pictures went unrecognized and Katherine sent the bird aloft once more. Ten miles later, she had Snow set down again, thinking that this shouldn't be as hard as it was. If they had crossed, it probably hadn't happened on the first try. If she could just find one spot where they had tried and failed, she could really narrow her search—on the flip side, if she could find where they had crossed, she would be on them so fast they wouldn't know what hit them.

Two more attempts were a waste of fuel, or so Swan hinted strongly, giving her a running count of either their current fuel levels or their range in miles or in minutes. "Just set us down!" she had yelled, losing her temper.

Rowden gave the junior member of the team, PFC Jennifer Jackson, a knowing glance that Katherine read as: *Who does this bitch think she is?*

She ignored all of them and concentrated on the next roadblock. From any perspective, this crossing was the same as all the rest: half a dozen locals holding their deer rifles or their shotguns in sweaty hands, looking at Katherine in a dubious manner.

Over the course of the flight, with the near hurricane force wind that washed over her every time she climbed in and out of the chopper, she had been losing the crispness that the FBI was known for. In short, she looked like a complete mess. Her blonde mane, once the envy of her friends, was a frizzy bush with what appeared to be several self-styled bird's nests spun into the mix.

Had it not been for the Blackhawk and her badge sitting on the waist of her black slacks, the locals would have either laughed her off or sent her packing to the nearest looney bin. They looked at the pictures she presented and, at first, all of them shook their heads. One woman, older and looking a little tired and washed out as though she were finding life a little too much of a hassle lately, stopped Katherine just as she was about to turn away.

"Was that the little group what had the lady with the heart condition?"

Katherine answered faster than the others, "Yes! That was her. She was faking a heart attack, right?"

"I don't much know about her faking anything," the woman answered. "I just know what I saw. She was about ready to up and die right where you are standing. We sent her on to Morgantown. They got a fine hospital, 'cept they couldn't save my mother, but I can allow that wasn't their fault."

"But that group didn't have an Asian guy," one of the men said.

"There was someone driving that truck, Chet. I didn't get good look at him but there was someone in the driver's seat, I know it."

Katherine's heart jumped. She hadn't even mentioned the truck yet. "Which way did they go…right, the hospital, forget that. Which way did they come from?" Everyone in that little group pointed to the left. They pointed east.

She yelled, "Thank you!" over her shoulder as she ran back to the helicopter. In her excitement, she had forgotten to ask when they had been there, but that was immaterial. They weren't going to a hospital, especially one still within the border of Maryland. Chances were they would try to cross again further west and she wanted to be there when they did.

"The fuel…" Swan started to say.

"I don't care about the fuel! They were here. Get us up." She marked the spot on her map as they shot upward. Three miles later, they dipped again, and again found a spot where the fugitives had tried and failed to cross. Now Joe Swan was hot into the chase as well, and he didn't even give her time to strap in before he lifted off.

They struck out twice more, got lucky twice and then went on a dry streak that had them turning back east. By then, they had crossed the entire state and could see West Virginia as a hazy green run of hills. After forty minutes of going up and down without finding anything, Katherine was getting tired and sloppy. "Do we go back to the last place and try closer?" she asked the pilot.

"I don't think so. Their pattern suggests they were putting a few miles between tries. What about south to Virginia? Maybe they went south this time. It's not that far." She agreed and Swan ran the Blackhawk south into a rainstorm that spattered on the windshield and turned the cabin cold. Rowden handed over his jacket and pretended not to be affected by the spray.

Katherine watched out the window, feeling lost, feeling unsure and a little nervous. They didn't have but a few more tries at this before they really would run out of gas. A town was coming up and she saw that it straddled the border. She didn't like it as a crossing point and neither did the pilot. They rushed past it until PFC Jackson looked down and saw a crowd of people waving at them. They were waving and pointing.

"What the hell are they pointing at?" Swan asked. From his side of the chopper he couldn't see anything. "What's over there?" he asked the crew chief.

Rowden tried to see through the rain and the gloom. "I don't see nothing. The rain is pretty…wait, what is that?"

Katherine hadn't really been listening to the conversation. They'd been waved to from one end of Maryland to another, but when Rowden said, "I think it's a body," she jumped out of her chair.

Even from three hundred feet, the blood was a stark red against the white dress and pale flesh of Leticia Martin.

3—Brunswick, Maryland

"That was a mistake," Anna said, her eyes coolly appraising Eng. "You didn't need to kill her. Yes, I know she would have talked, but who would have believed her? She would've looked like, I don't know, some old biddy off her rocker. Now, they have a body and how quick do you think it'll be before someone comes after us?"

Eng knew she was right and yet, he hated being corrected by a woman and he especially hated being corrected by *this* woman. She had grown more and more insufferable as the day progressed, and where before she had proved her usefulness in helping them to get across the border, now she was a liability.

He no longer needed her because he already had a way across the border. All around them were fields and forest. He could cross anywhere he pleased. A plan began to develop: they would go on for another mile or two, he would shoot her, dump the body and then peel out, making sure to leave tracks. Next, he would find a good spot to turn around and double back. When he could safely ditch the truck, he would then take to foot. Once on the other side of the border, he would get a new vehicle and head west. To California maybe.

"I lost my temper," he said. "It won't happen again."

Her look was the same as if she had sniffed sour milk, but she said nothing. The mile went by quickly, and surreptitiously, he eased his right hand off the wheel and laid it next to the console just inches from the grip of the Beretta which he had stuffed, barrel down, into the gap next to his seat. Now he just needed a spot where the road was open. He didn't want anyone to miss the bait.

Ahead was the perfect spot, farms on either side, a nice view of the faraway hills. It would be a good place to die. When he started to slow, Anna immediately began to suspect something, however her gun was in her jacket which had slid down to the right, next to the door, while his was inches from his hand.

"Eng…" she began to say, but then something strange started happening around them, making her blink. There were barley fields on either side of the road and they began to bend as if pressed downwards from above. "What the hell is going on?"

He saw the circular pattern in the barley, and he knew they were just about fucked. There was a helicopter above them. They had to get under cover of the forest if they had any chance. He stomped down on the gas so hard that Anna was thrust back in her chair; the sudden acceleration seemed to be pulling her eyelids back. She took a breath to scream out a question, only just then a tremendous shadow dropped out of the rain ahead of them.

It was a military helicopter and there was a man with a machine gun pointed at them. Anna felt an immediate shock of electricity and then her muscles all sagged at once. They were caught. This was an unkillable machine; it was useless to do anything but stop and hope they didn't get killed on the spot.

Eng had other ideas. Without slowing, he turned the Silverado sharply left, bashing through a rusted wire fence and speeding into the barley. At the same time, the helicopter seemed to hop into the air, disappearing from sight, which Anna knew couldn't be a good thing. She was sure she was screaming to Eng, but with the truck's engine racing and the helicopter making a noise like an alien beast and the rain coming down in buckets, she couldn't hear anything, especially not the gentle hum of Eng's window coming down.

It was the sudden influx of cold air that caught her attention; there was only one reason to lower a window in a situation like this. "Eng, no!" This time she screamed loud enough to be heard, but Eng wasn't listening. His Beretta was in his hand and pointing out the window, just as the Blackhawk dropped into view.

The helicopter was a tremendous, solid hunk of metal. A machine that defied gravity by hovering in the air, ten feet off the ground. The world around it was only a blur of flying grey rain, spinning blades and the shimmer of heat from the engines. When it started to shoot its lone gun, the fire was mesmerizing. Anna stared as the side of the machine suddenly erupted in flame and golden sparks started zipping at them.

She couldn't move as the first ten of these sparks stitched holes in the side of the Silverado just at the level of their seats. They hit, going from back to front. Bam! Bam! Bam! The truck shuddered as each 7.62mm round smacked home. Then the zipping golden sparks were missing, raking the barley, sending up little chuffs of dun-colored stems and fine leaves.

Eng had his Beretta out and seemed to be taking forever to aim. He still hadn't pulled the trigger when the gunner on the Blackhawk corrected himself and brought the zipping, glowing rounds back to bear, now on a slightly higher plane. The first dozen or so hit the hood, but just barely. Like stones thrown across the surface of a pond, they skipped right off the top, leaving grey streaks in the paint, but otherwise doing no harm.

The gunner didn't seem to care. He kept on firing, walking the bullets right across the hood and toward the windshield. Anna's reaction when the glass started flying wasn't even to cringe. Her mouth came open and her eyes went as wide as they could go. She had a fleeting thought that she was going to get glass in her mouth, but still she didn't close it. All she could do was sit there and await the bullet that would end her life.

Eng finally fired three quick shots that all sunk home, hitting the door gunner squarely in the chest. Eng then turned slightly, aiming into the crew compartment and had the pleasure of seeing people scramble for cover. There was one target in white that just stood out, begging to be shot. He centered the pistol and fired at Special Agent Katherine Pennock.

Chapter 15

Warrant Officer, Joe Swan pilot of the Blackhawk, had always flown with instinctual precision. He saw Eng and his pistol, the barrel sparking. A second later, he felt the vibrations from the M240 cease. Fear spiked in Snow's gut, not for himself but for Crew Chief Mark Rowden, who had been working the gun in the window right behind him. They had been best friends for the last two years and it didn't take a genius to know that something very bad had happened.

Before anyone could even think to blink, Snow shifted the cyclic to the right and pressed the right yaw pedal, causing the bird to turn and pitch slightly over at the same time, so that the armored undercarriage of the bird was presented to the terrorist.

Katherine Pennock was thrown off her feet, just as Eng fired, aiming for her white blouse. The bullet rippled the fabric as it blasted by and Katherine felt the heat of it, thinking that it was like someone had pulled up a fiery zipper next to her flesh.

She tried to stand, however in the front of the bird, Swan increased the throttle which added to the steepness of the angle of the deck and before she knew it, she was tumbling out of the aircraft.

The last crew member, and the youngest, a PFC named Jennifer Jackson, who had been surfing the rain-slicked deck without effort, dove for Katherine, catching her by the wrist. For a brief second, Katherine dangled by one hand from the helicopter, her feet swinging in the open air, her heart in her throat. Jennifer's position was only slightly less perilous. She had one foot hooked on a temp seat and the rest of her weight was pulling her face-first off the edge of the bird.

"Hold on!" she screamed, over the roar of the engine. Too much was against Jackson to keep a grip on the agent. Although she had two hands on Katherine's one, the acceleration of the Blackhawk coupled with the rain slicking everything up sent Katherine sliding right out of her grip.

The agent fell, though luckily, they weren't far from the ground, which was a marshy, muddy mess from the downpour so she wasn't hurt when she landed. She wasn't even stunned. Katherine hit feet first but her momentum sent her sprawling backwards into the mud with a splash. Around her was a barley field, grown to nearly four feet in height.

From the ground, all she could see was the barley and the helicopter lifting away, leaving her very alone. With a thrill of fear starting to get a firm grip on her, she rolled to her left side so she could pull her Glock 22. The weapon helped to ease her fear.

"This is Special Agent Katherine Pennock of the FBI!" she yelled through the barley, doing her best to sound tough and competent and not as if she was only one young, frightened woman who had just fallen out of a helicopter like an idiot. "Throw down your weapons and no one will get hurt."

"Throw down your weapon," Eng countered, sliding out of the truck and gesturing for Anna do so as well, "and we won't hurt you. You're the one who is outgunned." He wasn't wrong. The Blackhawk had pulled out of sight behind the trees.

Katherine pushed herself up into a kneeling firing position, her gun out, the barrel shaking along with her hands; she didn't notice. "That's where you're wrong. I've already called in back-up. In no time, this entire area will be blanketed by a Special Forces team we have tasked for this very mission."

"I'm very certain that is a lie," Eng said. "Your voice is shaking. You are afraid. Why would you be afraid if you have these so called special forces coming to your rescue?" His voice had shifted to the right, while at the same time there was swish of grass from the left. They were flanking her; a frightening prospect, made all the worse because he was correct; she was lying. There wasn't a Special Forces team within three hundred miles. They were all up north. Everyone was up north.

There probably wasn't a single police officer or state trooper anywhere close to them either. The governor had called everyone he could north to the border near Philadelphia. The best she could hope for was some old-timey deputy dawg or an elected constable who kept his only bullet in his shirt pocket and drove his own Plymouth station wagon with a bubble on top as the town's only police cruiser.

"It's no lie," she lied. "I-I called them myself when I saw the Martin's Silverado." The movement on her left stopped immediately, while at the same time, there was a sharp intake of breath from the right. Katherine could almost guess what they were thinking: *If the FBI knew about Charlie Martin's Silverado, what else did they know?*

"Didn't you two know that you are on the FBI's Most Wanted list?" she asked. "Yep, number one and two: Shuang Eng and Anna Holloway."

For a second, the barley field was silent save for the rain pattering down as the ramifications of what she had said sank in. Generally, there was no way to judge how people would react when they were told they were on the FBI's Most Wanted list. Katherine guessed that Eng and Anna would choose a violent response.

Eng fired his gun first, spraying 9mm slugs through the barley. Anna fired next, aiming with far better precision than Katherine would have guessed. Thankfully, Katherine had dived back into the mud and hunkered down as bullets whipped above her. When there was a pause, she fired in Eng's direction, but only twice. She couldn't waste bullets, not when she only had three magazines of fifteen rounds a piece.

Anna fired again. Her ability to aim through hearing alone was frighteningly precise. Two bullets sped into the mud right in front of Katherine's face. The agent could only duck her head as a third whipped through the screwed-up bird's nest of hair on her head. She looked up as she heard a squishy, splashing sound as the two fugitives ran. One of them was firing over their shoulder as they ran. She could tell because the bullets zinged in all directions.

Ignoring these bullets, Katherine jumped up and chased after Anna and Eng, keeping low, letting the spring-planted barley hide her as she ran on a parallel course. They were heading for a lone outbuilding, a small barn with a silo attached. It was the kind of building that would be a hard nut to crack if the FBI wanted to take Anna and Eng alive—which Katherine did. They had to be taken alive in order to find out if there were still missing zombies on Long Island, locked up in basements or garages. Even more importantly, there was also the question of where were the vials the two fugitives were carrying when they boarded the chopper the night before.

Had they made more zombies? Did they have the vials on them? Could the vials break open in the middle of a fire fight? Would Anna or Eng coat themselves with the zombie blood before they gave up? This last idea put a damper on Katherine's enthusiasm and she slowed, cursing under her breath. She had no protective gear, not even latex gloves. It seemed ridiculous, but she could get infected from a sneeze.

"I-I will just have to be careful," she said, steeling herself and forcing her feet to go on. It wasn't just her feet that were struggling to behave; she couldn't seem to be able to get her breathing under control, either. She was gulping down air and no matter how deeply and rapidly she breathed, she couldn't seem to get enough oxygen. This was her first shootout, the first time she was using her weapon in a real situation. She was supposed to have her training to fall back on, only she was a little lost since she must have missed the day they taught how to fall out of a helicopter into a bio-hazardous environment, and take on two terrorists without backup.

To go along with the dog pant she was affecting, her heart was racing at over a hundred beats per minute as she detoured far to the right so she could come up to the outbuilding without being spotted. She went for the silo, which was a windowless, jutting, tube.

When she made it, she put her back to it and now all she had to choose was to go left or right around it. This seemed simple enough, but with two people hell-bent on killing her, it was harder to choose than she could have believed.

She inched around to the back of the building, the Glock poised, ready to fire, her breathing still completely out of control. There was a wide set of double doors that were partially open in the center of the building. The structure itself was aluminum and resembled more of a pre-built warehouse than a real barn. The tempo of the rain picked up, coming down harder and harder, making more of a thrumming ruckus that drowned everything out.

Katherine was moving towards those doors, thinking that if she could lock it, she'd be able to trap them, only just then the door began sliding back. She froze as out of the door came a black pistol and then a head. Short black hair; it was Eng, whom Katherine foolishly considered far more dangerous than Anna.

Finally reacting like a true FBI agent, Katherine stepped forward and touched the back of Eng's head. "Drop the weapon," she said, just loud enough to be heard above the din.

Eng flinched; hesitated; then took a deep breath. These were not the reactions of someone about to drop their weapon. Katherine slide-stepped back a foot. She was in her element now and her training began to take over. "Don't even try it," she said. "You aren't fast enough. I'll put a hole in your head before you can blink. Now, drop the gun."

He turned the barrel to point up, but didn't drop it. "You won't kill me. I know where the bodies are buried and I know when they'll dig themselves up. It won't be long, so be careful, Special Agent."

"Drop. The. Gun." Katherine ordered through clenched teeth. "I only need one of you alive. It could be you, Eng, or it could be her."

Slowly, he raised his hands, the gun still in his right. He then began to turn. Somehow, he was able to ignore the Glock pointed at his eye; he was a cool customer, but he had lost. "You don't think I'll shoot you in the face?" Katherine asked, a small smile on her lips. "After everything you've done, I'll happily do it. You have three seconds before I pull the trigger. One, two, thr…"

He stopped her count by letting the gun tumble from his fingers. It splashed into the mud at his feet. "Satisfied?"

"Yes," she answered, curtly. "Now, face the wall; hands behind your head and get on your knees."

He smiled and was so smug about it that she wanted to thump him with the butt end of her Glock. She should have known that the smile meant something more than him being a dick. Through the thrum of the rain, she heard a metallic click behind her head.

It was Anna or so Katherine guessed. "It's your turn to drop your gun," Anna said. "Nice and easy and no one will get hurt."

Now it was Katherine's turn to smile. "No," she replied around the smile, a strange feeling of calm coming over her. "You, ma'am are a liar. You will kill me but not before you use me. Perhaps it'll be as a hostage; perhaps you'll turn me into one of *them*, but one way or another you will use me for your own selfish desires, and in the process, you'll endanger the world. So, no, I won't put down the gun. If you shoot me, by reflex, I'll shoot Eng and you wouldn't want that."

Anna snorted laughter. "Actually, I do want you to shoot him. In fact, I'd prefer if you shot him first, that way you won't miss. I'll wait."

By the look on Eng's face, Katherine could tell Anna wasn't lying. "You really want me to shoot him?" This was so far from expectations that Katherine chanced a glance at Anna. She had never seen such cold, flat eyes in her life.

189

"Yes, I do. Now would be good, before he opens his mouth and spins his lies." Eng had indeed opened his mouth. Anna shifted the gun towards him. "This is your fault," she hissed at him, the cold look replaced by fury. "All of this. He was the one who sabotaged the Com-cells. He raped me and he…he made those zombies in Long Island. He did it all. I just went along to get out. You have no idea what it's like in the zone. It's hell. It's life and death in there."

"And now you are pointing a gun at a federal officer," Katherine said. The gun had slid back to point at her. "If you wish to be taken seriously, you're going to need to drop your gun, too."

Eng snorted. "She has all the innocence of a serpent. You'll see. I would bet good cash that she doesn't drop her weapon."

Katherine glanced back at Anna and saw that the gun was still pointed at her head. Anna wasn't going to drop it. "And I guess that puts us at an impasse."

"There's no impasse," Anna said. "Pull the trigger or I will."

2—The Quarantine Zone, New York

It was the smell that woke Thuy. It was rancid and ugly. It was the smell of death and along with it came the crunch of gravel and a chorus of low moans. There were zombies nearby. Carefully, nervously, she cracked an eye, but saw nothing; the windows were fogged over and only indistinct shadows shown through.

The shadows were in the shape of people, only they weren't people at all. Thuy was finally starting to get that. They weren't "infected persons" as she had insisted for so long. They were zombie monsters that she had helped to create.

And now they were at her window.

She and Deckard were in a patrol car; he was slumped, his neck crooked so far to the side that it was a little unsettling. It looked as though he had broken it in his sleep. *He's going to have a heck of a crick when he wakes up*, she thought. She had aches of her own—her left shoulder, her back, both knees, and so on.

Thuy was fit, but also thirty-seven. She was no spring chicken and what might have gone ignored twenty years ago now made her cringe and groan as she sat up. It felt like a win just to do that. She hadn't had many wins in the last few days and so she took it.

"Yay me," she muttered, scratching the grit out of her eyes and looking around at the interior of the car. The radio was hissing softly, a continuous fuzzy sound. As she was still in the process of waking up, she found herself staring at it and at first the static was calming. It was a steady, white noise that had a stupefying effect that made her eyelids heavy and her brain sluggish. The noise was practically engrossing and she tuned out the moans and the shadows beyond the windows.

Right at that moment, falling back to sleep seemed like a legitimate plan. After all, wasn't the cure for exhaustion, sleep? "Yes, sir it is." This line of reasoning seemed extremely logical and very quickly her eyes were closing once again.

They popped open when something thumped into the side of the police cruiser. *It's only another zombie*, she thought and then wondered how she could be so calm about being so close to a creature that would eat her face if it could only work a door handle or if it realized that there was just a quarter inch of glass separating them.

That woke her up for good. It also got her feeling paranoid. Had they locked the doors? Of course, they had. Compulsively, she had triple checked them, hitting the *Unlock All* and then the *Lock All* buttons three times in a row.

Now, her right hand strayed to the door and she was about to go through the quick routine again when she stopped herself.

The buttons made a *clunking* noise that could be heard outside the car. In fact, it *would* be heard and then they'd be attacked once again. By how many? Would it only be a mere handful of zombies this time, pounding on the glass or scratching the paint off the doors as their black nails bent back, or were there a hundred of them out there ready to tear the doors off the cruiser and haul the two of them out into the afternoon sun where they could feast. It was impossible to tell without cracking the windows and that was the last thing she wanted to do just then.

Thuy settled for wiping away a bit of the condensation from the glass with the fleshy part of her balled fist. "Oh no," she said, under her breath. She thought she had been quiet, however Deckard had heard.

"How many?" he asked, pushing himself up, grimacing and rubbing his neck.

"Thirty or so. It's hard to tell. Do you want some Tylenol for your neck? I know I can sure use…" She jumped in her chair as the glass next to her thudded. Thuy turned to see a zombie's face smearing black gunk across the window as it tried to stare in at them. Their eyesight was generally so poor that she only gave the creature a thirty percent chance of picking her out.

Moving would only draw its attention, so she forced herself to remain still despite the urgent desire in her to scream to Deckard to get them out of there.

Through the marred glass, the beast stared for nearly half a minute before it tried to bite Thuy through the window. Smashing into the glass knocked out one of its front teeth and splintered another, but the glass held—for the moment. The monster lifted what Thuy thought was a fist, but it was only a raggedy stump of gnawed wrist.

Deckard was already reaching for the keys to the ignition when the stump hit the glass, striking it at an angle which deflected the majority of the force down. A shard of bone that was still attached at one end to the zombie, stabbed down between the glass and the frame of the door and got stuck. Thuy stared, not knowing what to do while

Deckard started the cruiser with one hand and wiped furiously at the fogged-over windshield with the other.

This gave him a head-sized, cloudy view in front where he saw a much larger number of zombies than the thirty Thuy had mentioned. There were thousands all heading east in long lines. The closer ones heard the car's engine and turned toward them.

"I can't see!" Deckard cried, sticking the car in gear and spurting it forward. "Find the defrost."

There seemed to be a lot more dials and whatnot associated with a police cruiser than in a normal car, but Thuy was able to scan through them rapidly despite the car bouncing along. She got both the front and rear defrost going just as they left the road and flew down a steep hill, hitting hidden stumps and moss-covered logs and zombies, lots and lots of zombies.

It was rough ride and what lay at the bottom of the hill Thuy didn't know because the window was still covered. She just knew that if they hit something big or got stuck in a bog, they'd be in big trouble. From what she could see, Thuy could tell they were in the middle of one the larger hordes. Unbidden, she glanced away from the grey windshield and towards the pistol they had found back in Hudson.

Had it been just an accident that the Taurus PT92 just happened to have two bullets left? Or was it fate telling them that their time was nearly up? Thuy was a scientist and didn't believe in fate, she believed in the Law of Probabilities, which was based in Probability Theory—a way of relating conditional and marginal probabilities to determine the outcome of certain events.

She felt safe when mathematics were involved. It gave her the illusion of control and yet she had an irrational desire to throw the Taurus out the window; as if she could change the fate that she didn't believe in by modifying one element of it. Of course, she couldn't throw the gun out the window because there was still a zombie attached by the wrist to her door.

"Deck," she called to him and then jerked her head when he glanced over. "It's stuck."

He grunted and with the fog clearing, he lined the side of the cruiser up on a tree and with all the fanfare of scraping a turd from his shoe, he knocked the zombie away.

Now, Thuy could see just fine and wished she could go back to driving with blinders on. They were still bouncing and dodging their way through what felt like the entire zombie army. They weren't even on a road. In front of them were two ruts, which suggested that someone had driven through the area.

Had it been anyone else behind the wheel, she would have told them…no, she would have ordered them to turn around. But, she trusted Deckard. In the last four days, he had come through time and again, demonstrating that he was much more than he seemed.

"Do you have a destination in mind?" she asked, clicking on her seatbelt and bracing her legs against the inevitability of a crash.

"We're near where I crossed back into the Zone." He frowned at the steering wheel as the cruiser hit a dip and a knob popped off the dash. "There weren't this many zombies before. I'm worried that the line didn't hold."

Thuy frowned as well, not quite understanding. "I would think that would be advantageous to us. We should be able to slip through while they reform."

"They were nice people," Deckard explained.

"Oh, sorry." She knew that one of her greatest failings was in her inability to see the humanity in humans. She tended to see people as beginning and ending with what they did for a living: phlebotomists were people who drew blood, firemen put out fires, and soldiers fought battles. Sometimes they lived, sometimes they died, but only rarely did she remember that they were real people with real families.

"I'm sure they're fine," Deckard said, but didn't sound convincing. He pointed ahead of them. "I think the line was over that hill." The twin ruts ran up to the bottom of the hill and then skirted to the right, running along its base. After a mile or so and about ten thousand zombies, he swore under his breath and said, "This isn't taking us anywhere. Hold on."

There was only a bar over the door to hold onto and it wasn't all that convenient, though she supposed that nothing about the cruiser had been designed to mount such steep hills. Deckard went right at the hill, going straight up it with Thuy holding onto the one bar and thinking that there would certainly be a cliff on the other side, or that from above they would see that the little rutted path actually cut through a much shallower slope if they had only driven a little further. And this was assuming they made it to the top at all.

The hill grew so steep that she felt the front of the cruiser wanting to tip backwards. Whenever it got too bad, Deckard simply fed the beastly machine more gas, as if speed was the answer to everything.

Up and up they went and Thuy foolishly looked back for barely a second before she slammed her eyelids down, gritted her teeth, and gripped the bar until her knuckles were so white she suspected that they would split through her skin at any second.

Then they were on top of the hill and for some reason, Thuy found herself out of breath and sweating. Deckard was stoic, staring out at the further hill.

The defensive line had been shattered by successive waves of zombies. In front of them they could see the corpses of thousands that had been chopped down by every weapon known to man. Thousands more were pushing up and over the hill, disappearing into the forest beyond.

"Damn," he whispered. Thuy was about to offer what condolences she could, but just then he took his foot off the brake and sent them hurtling down the far side of the hill. She reacted much as a cat would if it were in this situation. Her nails clawed the upholstery and her sneakered feet were splayed on the dash. She had never ridden a rollercoaster in her life but assumed it would be just like this: horrible.

Gravity sucked them down at an astounding pace, which made the trip down very fast. Before she could catch her breath or collect herself, they were plowing through the corpses that littered the bottom of the ravine between the two hills and now she was glad for Deckard's apparently reckless driving. They needed all the momentum they could get just to make it through what seemed like a stagnant river of corpses.

The ravine was so foul that she actually looked forward to the run up the next hill which was blessedly small and less steep.

Deckard drove along the top of the hill where there was another mass of bodies strung out just inside the tree line. He found a landmark and then turned east until they came to a tent that lay on its side. "Oh man," he whispered. There were great tears in the fabric, and there were splashes of fly-covered blood everywhere, but only a few corpses, which were bullet ridden and torn to pieces.

Only a single "living" zombie was standing near the tent. The rest were either struggling around the hills or, having already mounted them, were heading east where the rattle of gunfire could be heard. The lone zombie turned dull, black eyes on the cruiser as it pushed down from the crest of the hill through the thin forest. Deckard only had the two bullets in the Taurus, so he used the cruiser as a weapon and ran the beast down, pinning it beneath the front tires. He then opened the door and gave it a glance. It looked to him, with its feeble gesturing, like a dying cockroach. It would keep, he supposed.

"Hold on," Thuy said, sliding over and grabbing his arm. "Put on your mask and gloves before you go out there."

She thought it was crazy to leave the safety of the car, but he wasn't gone for half a minute before she opened her own door. The outside of the car was covered in sprays of black blood which was disgusting as well as dangerous. She grabbed a can of disinfectant, which she used with such abandon that she had to duck back in for a second one.

As she worked, Deckard went to the tent and, despite his latex-covered hands, he used a stick to pull back the torn fabric. Inside were two boxes of MREs, a radio, three cots and a hundred and twelve rounds of 5.56 ammo. He took the bullets and the food and stowed them in the cruiser. All around the forest floor were spent shell casings but very few corpses of any sort. He didn't like it.

Deckard wanted to explore more, however there were a few dozen zombies making their way through the forest towards them and he had to shoo Thuy back inside the cruiser. He paused before moving on, picturing the fight as it likely went down. "The line fell unexpectedly," he told her. "The horde crested the hill in one big wave. It couldn't have been more than an hour after I came through."

"How can you tell?"

"The lack of bodies," he told her. "If any of the soldiers were injured, they would have turned after a few hours and if the zombies were hurt, they healed and walked away. That way." He pointed east.

There was a trail through the forest, one made by the passage of hundreds of feet. Deckard decided to follow the trail. Every hundred yards or so they would come across piles of bodies and they weren't always zombie bodies. He slowed to look at these, but only stopped when he saw an M4 sticking out from beneath one of the corpses.

This was why he had come in this direction. Deckard stopped the cruiser, took one quick look around and got out holding a fresh can of disinfectant.

Thuy got out as well, she had to urinate so badly her lower abdomen was swollen and she worried that if she waited any longer, she would pop. She couldn't remember the last time she had used the bathroom. "I have to…you know," she said to him.

Deckard had just knelt and was reaching for the rifle's strap. "Sure, but stay close. I won't look, I promise."

She knew that he wouldn't; still she wasn't one for camping and wasn't quite sure of the mechanics or what the entire procedure of urinating in the woods entailed. Did she take her pants off? Or did she leave them on because she was in an environment where a fast get-away could be in order? If she left them on, she was quite sure she would make an embarrassing mess.

A skirt was starting to sound pretty good at that moment. "Uh, Deck? Do you, uh, happen to know the, uh, how to, uh…never mind. Sorry." She had a deep enough tan that she didn't turn pink when she got embarrassed and for that, at least, she was thankful.

"Pants off," she decided. And that meant she would be going a little deeper into the woods. Thirty yards off she spied a run of bushes which seemed very appropriate for the moment. Since she couldn't have cared less about botany or biology, beyond microbiology of course, she had no idea of what sort they were.

They were leafy and green and hopefully not poisonous. They blocked Deckard from view and she had her pants halfway down before she noticed the corpses. There were seven or eight and she assumed that because of the headless state of two of them and the fantastic amount of blood, that they were very dead, but then she noticed that one of the corpses was staring at her.

At first, she thought that it had simply died with its eyes open, but then the eyes blinked. Thuy's body did a spazzy, reflexive jump. The same sort of jump a person makes when they walk into a cobweb in the dark. She might have also let out a yelp, but wasn't sure.

The body attached to the head was covered in blood, both old red blood and black blood. "You smell good," it said in a low, gravelly voice. "You smell like a treat."

Face to face with a zombie, her pants almost to her ankles, Thuy knew she wouldn't smell good for much longer; her bladder was screaming to let go.

Chapter 16

1– 2:08 p.m.
—Brunswick, Maryland

"Shoot him, now," Anna Holloway said, rain dripping down her chin. "It's the only way you're going to live through this."

"Dropping your gun is the only way that *you* are going to live through this," Katherine Pennock shot back.

Anna groaned in exasperation. "Will you please stop? I need a hostage, one that will listen to me and obey my commands. What I don't need is a wanna-be secret agent who thinks she's all that. Now, shoot him and you'll live beyond the next five minutes."

Katherine tensed, her muscles bunching, ready to spring. She wasn't going to shoot Eng. Anna's insistence that she kill her unarmed partner smacked of a set up. She saw how it would go down: if she killed Eng, then Anna would kill her and if she was ever caught, she could claim that Katherine had been out of control, killing both the guilty and innocent.

Either way, Katherine would end up dead. "I don't think so," she said, lowering her gun. "You'll have to do your own dirty work." She went so far as to drop the pistol and regretted it the moment she did. Without it, she felt naked.

"What? Do you think that as a woman I'll be too caught up in my emotions to pull the trigger?" Anna asked, a smirk on her face. "Let me show you how a real woman protects herself." She took one step to her left, her shoulder touching the thrumming aluminum wall as she aimed her pistol at Eng. His only chance was if lightning would suddenly shoot down from the storm above them and fry Anna.

The trigger was halfway back when a new sound could be heard over the rain beating on the roof. It was the Blackhawk dropping down from the clouds. Jennifer

Jackson had dragged Rowden's body out of the way and now she squatted behind the M240, determined not to die as he had. She wasn't going to give the bad guys a second to blink—or so she thought.

What she hadn't expected to see was the FBI woman with a gun pointed at her head. She was standing directly between the two bad guys and as much as Jennifer wanted to let the M240 rip, she hesitated, just as Rowden had.

Katherine did not hesitate. She wasn't a wanna-be anything. She was an FBI special agent, a rank that she had worked her ass to get. The Blackhawk dropped into a hover, ten feet off the ground, its blades ripping through the rain, sending the drops hurtling sideways with stinging force.

When Anna blinked against it, Katherine made her move, spinning with her right arm out. Her forearm hit Anna's wrist, smashing it against the side of the building. The gun went off, the bullet drilling through the siding. Katherine ignored it; she was already following up with her next strike: a stunning left hook to Anna's cheek, which landed a half-second after the first.

Anna's eyes went wide as the force of the blow sent her head into the wall. It made a comically hollow sound. Now, Katherine went for the gun, one hand on the barrel, the other on Anna's wrist. Against another woman, the struggle would have been a second from being over, however Anna was a feral creature, fast, shockingly strong and determined to live.

The two grappled for the pistol just as Jennifer Jackson let loose with the M240. She couldn't chance hitting Katherine, but Eng was an entirely different story. The Chinese agent had jumped back and was just ducking into the building. "Oh, no you don't!" Jennifer cried and fired a five-second burst, stitching holes through the walls, missing him by the barest margin.

She started in with another burst when Swan yelled into his mic, "Careful! That's all the ammo we have." She glanced at the hopper and was shocked to see they probably didn't have more than twenty rounds left. If it ran out, they only had their pistols. They'd have to dismount and fight hand to hand. As brave as she was, Jennifer really didn't want to do that.

With so little ammo and without a proper target, the machine gun was basically useless, so Swan shot the helicopter up and leap-frogged it over the barn coming down just as Eng was about to make a break from the far side of the building. He scampered back inside as Jennifer shot a handful of 7.62mm rounds from the M240. With the rain and the wind tipping the Blackhawk back and forth as if it were perched on a see-saw, the M240 wasn't the easiest gun to aim and the rounds passed harmlessly by— they were down to twelve rounds.

Katherine had no idea what was happening with Eng and the Blackhawk. She had a grip on the gun with both hands, while Anna had one on the gun and the other snared in Katherine's hair.

Anna was yanking the hair with all her strength, turning Katherine's head far to the side. Katherine was in such an awkward, twisted position that she could tell she was going to fall at any second, so she preemptively threw herself in the direction of the twist, adding momentum to the fall. The two hit the ground with Anna on top of her, but only for a brief second, then they were rolling in the mud.

Now, it was the FBI agent who came up on top. Katherine let go of the gun with her left hand, threw her forearm across Anna's neck and pressed down with all her weight, crushing the woman's larynx, causing her pretty, blue eyes to bulge and her face to go red. Anna was seconds from blacking out. She let go of her Katherine's hair and tried to claw at her face. Katherine only pressed down all the harder.

"Drop the gun!" she screamed into Anna's ear. "Drop it, now or I swear to God I will pry that gun out of your cold, dead fingers!"

She meant it and Anna knew she meant it. The pain in her throat was becoming too much, and Anna opened her hand letting the gun fall from her fingers. Katherine didn't let up on the pressure until she had secured the Beretta. She then slid off Anna, who lay there choking.

"Roll over," Katherine ordered. When Anna only continued to cough and splutter, Katherine jabbed the gun into the side of her head and repeated, "Roll the fuck over." Anna stopped her dramatic coughing and complied. "Don't move, stay face down. I will shoot you in the back if you try to run. Whatever laws you think are protecting you have been revoked by the President. Do you understand?"

Although Anna nodded with all the sincerity she could fake, she was actually only a quarter of a second from hopping up and booking it out of there. She hadn't given up just yet and all she needed was a simple distraction and she would be gone, because she completely believed Katherine. Civil protections had probably gone out the window, while torture and summary executions were, more than likely, the "in" thing.

She watched as Katherine scrambled to where the other two guns were lying in the mud. They went into the waistband of her filthy slacks. "Eng!" she called. "Give up. You are surrounded." The Special Agent then turned to Anna and snapped, "Get up. Clasp your hands in front of you, interlocking your fingers, and get over here." Katherine wasn't in the mood for backtalk and was seriously toying with the idea of putting a bullet in Anna's leg on the grounds that it would make her more compliant and keep her from attempting to run.

Also, she didn't like the blonde bitch.

As though she was a whipped dog, Anna complied, pushing the "Oh, woe is me," act nearly too far. When she got to Katherine, the agent forced her into the aluminum wall face first, smearing mud on it. She then grabbed a thick hunk of Anna's hair at the base of her skull, and jabbed the gun into her back, digging into her vertebrae.

"Be cool," Anna said. "I'm complying. I'm being good."

"Shut up," Katherine hissed as she pulled Anna away from the wall and towards the open door, using her as a human shield. "Eng, don't be stupid. You can still get out of this alive. We both know that the Blackhawk is equipped with a radio. It'll be only a few minutes before there are a hundred more agents here."

The two women were at the door now. It was dark inside the barn and smelled of oiled machinery and moldering barley. It was a sickly combination. "Eng, I only need one of you alive," Katherine said, her voice sounding flat and dull under the heavy thrum coming from the rain.

"I have a vial of zombie blood!" Eng yelled, from off to the right. "I'll break it open and contaminate every one of us if you don't leave right this moment."

"Ooh scary," Katherine said. "Do you really think we hadn't thought about that? The Air Force is probably going to napalm a square mile around us already. If you break a vial, they'll just do it with us still here. Do you like the sound of that?" This was no lie. The Assistant Director for National Security had made the suggestion on the chopper ride from the White House to Cyber Command where, supposedly, he was about to throw the entire weight of the FBI behind the hunt for Anna and Eng.

Katherine hadn't waited around to find out what that looked like. They had limited computer access, one chopper, a few dozen vehicles and only satellite phones as communication, the FBI was a shadow of its former self. It's why she had jumped at the chance to take the Blackhawk.

Eng was quiet, thinking hard. Anna didn't need to think hard. Duplicity came second nature to her. "Like you said, you don't really need him. You need me. I know how to make a cure for the Com-cells."

"That's a lie!" Eng shouted. "She was nothing but a research assistant. All she knew how to do was take notes and flirt with the *real* doctors."

There was a cure? Excitement flared in Katherine, but like a shark at a poker table with a bunch of fish, she kept her face neutral. "Come out, Eng," she said, her tone softer. She had won half the battle. She had captured Anna and Eng when no one else could have, now she had to turn their capture into something more than an exercise in retribution.

He came out of the shadows holding a vial in one fist. Katherine aimed the Beretta at him. "Lay it down," she commanded. When he put it on the ground, she pushed Anna into the building and had them both lay face down. As she frisked them, discovering another vial in Anna's possession, she said, "Tell me about this cure."

2— Western Massachusetts

The zombie wore the uniform of a national guardsman. The blouse and pants had been the usual mottled green, now it was mostly black, covered in Com-cells and zombie blood. The uniform was torn as well. The tears were far from precise. They had been made by teeth, many, many teeth.

So many teeth that it was a bit of a surprise to Thuy that the zombie was in fact a zombie and not just another of the rotting corpses littering the forest. What was more of a surprise was that the zombie had been a woman.

She was missing chunks of her face, large mouthfuls of her chest and arms, and most of her left hand, but that didn't make her any less dangerous. Perhaps it made her more so. In life, the woman had been a fighter. The bodies of the "real" zombies surrounding her could attest to that. She had somehow killed seven of them before succumbing to the disease.

"You smell so sweet," she said, her black eyes, wet and shining, glittering like a beetle's. "Let me have some of your blood. Just a taste. It'll make me…the same again. I want to be like before. I need it."

Even though she had been fed upon so atrociously, the zombie was able to stand. She held a knife in her good right hand. It was the length of her forearm and black with blood.

Thuy wanted to back away, in fact, she wanted to run away, but the jeans she had taken from the lost and found back in Taconic High were around her ankles. She would never be able to yank then up in time.

She only had one other option, one which had worked for her before—she could urinate on herself. The undead seemed to find that as distasteful as the living and she had an entire bladder's worth of urine on tap.

There was one problem: if she lived, she would have to face Deckard, smelling like piss. The idea was revolting.

All her life she had heard people using the phrase: *I'd rather die than be caught wearing that or looking like this.* Thuy had assumed this was hyperbole, but just then it was no exaggeration. She couldn't bring herself to pee on herself.

She couldn't run and she wouldn't befoul herself and so she had to find a different way to get out of the situation. She told the zombie woman, "You wouldn't want me, I-I'm sick. I'm infected like you, but I sprayed myself with perfume. It was…" She tried to think of a perfume that had some sort of human scent, but since that wasn't even a thing she drew a blank. "It…it's that grandma smell," she said, reaching for her jeans with one hand, steadying herself with the other. "You know the one?"

The soldier shook her head. "I know your smell. I know your outside smell. What do you smell like on the inside?"

"Stop!" Thuy said, raising her voice and putting out her free hand. The other was yanking at her jeans, which seemed stuck on something and wouldn't come up. "Y-you just need to stop. This isn't you, uh Ms…What's your name? Your name tag is sort of covered."

"My name?" The question seemed to stymie the soldier, who looked down at her camouflaged blouse. When she did, Thuy grabbed for her pants and pulled them up. Now she could run, but before she could, Deckard pushed through the foliage. He held an M4 in his hands; it smelled of disinfectant.

"Her name is Vance. Rebecca Vance," he said.

The soldier started nodding. "That's right. That's me. Or it was. I feel different now. I feel hungry and…and angry. And my head hurts. I took all the pain pills I could find, but my head still hurts."

"I bet," Deckard replied. "We'll make it better, but first can you tell me what happened? The line was pretty stable."

A nasty look crossed her disfigured face. "It was them." She pointed up at the clouds. "It was those Air Force fucks. They destroyed all the radio things and we couldn't talk to anyone, and motherfucker, if I could get my hands on one of them, I'd…"

"Rebecca!" Deckard snapped. "Stay with me. Is there another line? Do you know if one was set up?"

She glared hard at him, but then her beetle-like eyes glanced at the gun in his hands and her glare became a pout. "Yeah, there was another line. There's always another fucking line. But I didn't make it." She turned and looked back toward the downed tent. "I tripped. I-I fucking tripped and something snapped in my leg and then *they* came and I fucking fought them and I fucking killed them!"

Rebecca held up the knife, proudly. "I gutted them and I stabbed and stabbed, but that didn't stop them, so I hacked off their heads while they ate me. It hurt, but I won. I fucking won."

"You did," Deckard said, his voice sad. "You won. You should be proud." He lifted the M4 and shot her between the eyes. When she toppled back, he sighed and eyed Thuy. "Are you going to pee, or what? We can't stay for long."

Even though he turned away, it wasn't easy for Thuy to squat down near the body of Rebecca Vance who had black blood dribbling out of her head. She was turned in such a way that, like the other heads, she seemed to be staring at Thuy. "Sorry," she whispered. It seemed impolite to use the bathroom so close to the dead, but it was coming, no matter what.

A minute later she sat in the cruiser with Deckard, who was pensive as he drove east. The sound of fighting was picking up, as were the numbers of undead that were flocking across the Massachusetts border. "I don't know what I want to see when we get there," he said. "Is it bad to want to see the line overrun?"

"Yes," Thuy answered.

He nodded and rubbed a hand across the scruff on his chin. "It is wrong, I know it, but I'm tired. I'm tired of all of this. That lady back there? She was nice when she didn't have to be." He was quiet again until the sound of gunfire became very loud. They were on the same stretch of blacktop that Courtney had taken earlier that day. There was forest on either side, and there were zombies that outnumbered the trees. They would glance at the cruiser as it rumbled by. The ones with whole legs would chase after for a time before they forgot exactly why they were running.

It was only three miles before they came to the next line. Thousands of civilians, who didn't own guns, had taken up shovels to do their part. They had built up a huge mound on the eastern side of the Housatonic River. Bridges were destroyed and shallow areas were filled with rolls of concertina wire.

Even without the hundreds of thousands of zombies, there was no getting through. "Now what?" Deckard asked.

Thuy only shrugged, feeling the weight of despair and defeat. Then her eyes fell on the radio and for a few minutes hope surged as she turned it on and called, "Dispatch 6, please come in Dispatch 6," on every channel. There was never an answer save for endless static. Not only was Courtney not broadcasting, no one was. The US military had wreaked so much havoc and destruction that no one within the Massachusetts border was talking to anyone else.

It was a situation that couldn't last much longer and Deckard wondered whether going east really was the best plan. In an attempt to save millions of refugees, the military was destroying the one bastion left in the northeast. It seemed obvious to him that when the border finally fell, it wouldn't be just refugees streaming across, it would be the zombies as well.

Chapter 17

1– 3:17 p.m.
—Worcester, Massachusetts

Things could not get any hairier for Courtney Shaw. She was in a bright red Corvette racing through a green forest—a perfect target for the bombs that were falling all over the place. And there were missiles flying about. Some shot up from the ground in silver streaks, others were launched from the jets roaring overhead, and others just appeared out of the thin blue air.

These last were the scariest. Who knew where they were coming from or who was controlling them? Courtney had a sinking feeling in her gut that they were the "fire and forget" variety, which meant that she was driving through what was, essentially, a gigantic game of Russian roulette.

A missile could get her at any moment, however there were times when she felt extra vulnerable. Whenever she came to an intact bridge, her stomach would go queasy and her palms would grow so sweaty that she barely trusted her own steering, especially since she always gunned the 'vette across at top speed, her face screwed up, knowing that this was it, this was when the missile would get her.

It seemed like a reasonable thought since half the bridges in the southern part of the state had been targeted. There were so many downed bridges that she had been forced far to the north. With each detour, her fear ramped up. Time was getting away from her. Without communications, a central leadership, and the ability to resupply themselves, the Massachusetts National Guard could only hold out for so long and she knew that if she wasn't careful, she'd find herself once more trapped in a quarantine zone.

The stupid civil war had to end quickly, and it had to end with a Massachusetts loss, something that the stiff-necked Bostonians had so far resisted with more determination than common sense.

Courtney was on her way to change that. After her detour, she raced south on a nothing of a little road that was of such minor consequence that it seemed to have been overlooked by everyone. There wasn't even local traffic on it and whenever she came to a stop sign, she would blare her horn and race through. Its name went from Wachusett Street to Chapel Street and then to Holden Street without any obvious reason. Then it t-boned Grove Street and disappeared.

"Left or right?" Courtney wondered, trying to decide which way to turn. Everything would have been easier if there was a sign that read: *Army Headquarters This Way!* She was in the northern fringe of Worcester and it was only a guess that there would be a commander of some sort nearby. The fighting to the south of the city, what had begun with an air assault attack on Auburn, had turned into a battle of tremendous importance, if not size. Neither side could afford to send in nearly as many fighters as they wished they could. Both were being so hard pressed by the zombies surrounding them that the struggle for the border was a clash between companies of men instead of regiments or divisions.

Still, there would be some sort of command center nearby. "It could be underground," she mused. It made sense since the US Air Force could take it out with a single bomb—she assumed they had bombs of every size and strength.

She was about to make a turn to the right, mostly because the map suggested that the city flared in that direction, and she had a picture in her mind of an underground bunker smack dab in the middle of Worcester. But she didn't take the right, at least not then. Next to the cherry-red Corvette, paper and trash suddenly began to kick up and fly in circles.

There was only one reason for this focused spin of air and she torqued her head upwards at the window to see. Just off center of the front of the 'vette and fifty feet above it was a black helicopter. It wasn't a Blackhawk, it was an Apache—a gunship. The helicopter could have destroyed the car in three different ways and it could have done it in a blink.

Courtney froze behind the wheel. The Apache appeared to her less like a machine built by the hand of man and more like a giant metal insect. She had never seen anything so terrifyingly alien in all her life.

Two incongruous urges gripped her. The first was to flee, screaming, pushing the Corvette to its top speed. The second urge was to hide, only the Corvette was too flashy to disappear and, despite the oversized engine, too slow to escape. Of course, to try either would only draw attention to herself, but to try neither and just sit there seemed to be the height of stupidity.

"What would Thuy do?" The question just popped out of her mouth and strangely, it focused Courtney and an idea struck her: knowing Thuy, she would try to flee and hide at the same time. "Just be like her. Be cool." She took the right, waving to the pilot as she turned. "Keep smiling, keep smiling, keep…" The Apache turned in midair, the multitude of rockets hanging from its stubby wings pointed at her.

"Shit." The feeling coursing through her was vaguely familiar. It was similar to how she had felt as a teenager when a cop would pull out of whatever hiding spot they had burrowed themselves into and creep up behind her. This provoked the same feeling but about a million times worse.

Courtney was freaking out. She had no idea what to do. Her brain had hit vapor-lock and she just kept driving, making sure to stay beneath the posted speed limit. She found it of utmost importance to keep her hands at ten and two, and by golly, she used her turn signals, nearly giving herself a stroke worrying when exactly she should click them on.

When she looked up again, the Apache was no longer hanging on her right as it had been. It had disappeared. She didn't trust it and for another few minutes, she drove with all the precision she could manage. When she saw a sign for the Hadwen Arboretum, she took a left. She didn't know what an arboretum was, she only knew that there were about a zillion trees there and she figured she could hide from the helicopter beneath them.

Stopping the Corvette and then turning off the engine wasn't enough. Courtney got out of the car, or to be more precise, she snuck out, looking fearfully up at the ceiling of leaves and branches high above her. The sound of jets was a constant background grumble but of the Apache, she could hear nothing. Had it been a secret stealth chopper? Was it up there on "whisper" mode? She didn't know if that was a real thing outside of science fiction, but she wasn't going to take chances.

"I'll give it five minutes," she said, getting back into the Corvette. Out of habit, she checked her look in the mirror and did a double take. She was covered in a sheen of sweat and her normally bushy brown hair was lank. Beneath the sweat, she was pale and a twitch was jumping under her left eye. A quick survey showed that she had wet rings under her arms and around the collar of her shirt. Even the crack of her ass felt distinctly damp. Her hands were shaking.

"Get a hold of yourself, it was just a helicopter." It wasn't a secret that she had been afraid a great deal of the time over the last few days, but it was supposed to be different now. She was supposed to be on the safe side of the lines for once, and the idea that death could reach out and get her, even here, had done a number on her subconscious. Her heart was still going like a rabbit's.

Courtney didn't need to ask what Thuy would do in this situation because it would never happen. Thuy had always looked so collected, so cool, even with fire and zombies and bullets going everywhere that Courtney just knew Thuy would have been unfazed by the Apache death machine.

"But I'm not her," Courtney whispered and felt herself hit a wall, one in which giving up was a viable option. She pictured herself going north in the Corvette—it was a fine car to run away in. "But, then what?"

The quick answer: *I'll need a warmer coat*, had her shaking her head. "No, that won't work."

Courtney reasoned that if the border fell, Boston would fall, and if Boston fell then the entire northeast would be lost. The whole area would be overrun by further millions and millions of zombies. In fact, she realized, if Boston fell, the result would be an absolutely unstoppable army of zombies; astronomical in number. Canada would be no refuge.

Without any hesitation, Courtney climbed back into the Corvette. The time for whining and self-doubt was over. She drove out of the arboretum without looking back and only once glanced upwards. If the Apache was still there and wanted to kill her, it would be able to do so. She started to sing an old song her grandmother used to sing; *Que Sera Sera*—What will be, will be. It made her feel almost cheerful.

She needed to find the headquarters of the Massachusetts National Guard, but first she had to transform herself from the pathetic, sweaty creature that stared out from the mirror. The day before, Thuy had made the transformation from urine-smelling refugee to "Assistant to the Governor" with a simple change of clothes. Courtney didn't think her transformation would be so easy. Thankfully, Worcester had its fair share of high end boutiques and salons, usually in very close proximity to one another and all it took to gain entrance was the tire iron from the trunk of the 'vette.

The streets were deserted and there was no one to hear the breaking glass.

Finding a sharp lady's suit was a snap. Unlike Thuy who wore a size that somehow ranged into negative numbers, Courtney was a respectable size four and never had a problem finding outfits in her size. Shoes were found two doors down: conservative black pumps to go with the black pant suit and white blouse she had chosen. She then crossed the street to a salon, tapped on the door for thirty seconds, before bashing her way in.

"Hair first," she muttered, dragging a mirror to the large front window in order to capture all the light she could. Not that it mattered all that much. She didn't have time for anything fancy. She wet down the untamed bush and then grunted and pulled it into a bun which was so tight it felt spring-loaded. One sneeze and it would explode in a brown mess.

Finally, she did more than just cover up the stress and exhaustion sagging her skin, she painted on an entirely new face. It had been her luck in life that she had always been pretty enough to go with a minimalist, "natural" look when applying makeup. Just then she went heavy on everything.

It felt like she was priming a car before painting it as she went with two coats of foundation. She then darkened and thickened her eyebrows, next she nearly put out an eye as she went scandalously heavy on the mascara. Finally, she lacquered her lips a fine and glistening, deep red.

"Ugh," she said, when she looked herself up and down in a floor to ceiling mirror. Although she had "prettied" herself up, conforming to the current standards of beauty, she didn't particularly care for the transformation she had wrought. She didn't look like herself. "But that's the point, I guess," she said, and then marched through the broken door and back out to the Corvette. "I'm no longer Courtney Shaw, one time state trooper dispatcher. I'm Eva…uh, Mansetti, assistant to the governor, here on important business."

Now, all she had to do was find the head honcho and convince him that the governor was giving up.

"Should be easy," she joked. "All I have to do is follow the sound of the guns." She raced straight south toward Auburn, where the 101st's landing zone was being counterattacked by men in hunting camo, and women wearing ratty jeans and old long sleeve shirts—their "gardening" clothes.

No one stopped Courtney and she was able to drive right up to the battle and, if she'd had a death wish, she could have driven right into it. She stopped two hundred yards away on a little rise. In the shiny, red Corvette, she was the perfect target but, perhaps because the car was so oddly out of place, no one took a shot at it, not even the F-16 that suddenly appeared out of nowhere.

The pilot had a bombing run set up and was ready to take out the building that housed the EZ Pass Massachusetts Service Center, where some rebels were causing a ruckus. He didn't think anyone would miss the service center or the fees and penalties it collected. "I've been wanting to bomb one of those toll plazas, but this'll do," he said to himself.

With the AA defenses as stiff as they were, he had all of two seconds to engage his target, but then his eyes fell on the red Corvette and lingered on it as his mind tried to reconcile the presence of such a car on the edge of battle. A second went by, as did his chance to drop on the service center. He turned for the Corvette with no intention of blowing it up; he was only curious.

From Courtney's perspective, she saw a deadly sharp jet bearing right at her and for a moment, her new persona wilted and when it rocketed past, shaking the 'vette, she found herself shaking as well. She whipped the car around in a flash and raced out of there, her head going back and forth. She needed to find the command post asap.

What she found instead was a wounded boy of about fifteen. Courtney turned and pulled up next to him as he limped along a side road. "You okay?" she asked. "You need a ride?"

His eyes weren't right. They were wide and dry. He didn't blink as he looked at Courtney and the 'vette. "I don't know," he said.

"Get in," she said, hopping out and assisting the boy around the long nose of the car. "What's your name?"

There was a long pause before he answered, "Jason Bernard. I got shot. And there were bombs." His unblinking eyes looked down at his right leg, which had left a red smear on the leather seat. "I didn't run this time…and there were bombs," he said again.

"I bet," Courtney said. "Say, do you know where the command…never mind. Do you know where the med tent is? Did they tell you to go someplace to have your leg checked?"

He pointed straight forward. Afraid that any jostling would hurt him, Courtney gently goosed the Corvette on. The road bent north and came to the parking lot of a bowling alley. There were a few Humvees and trucks in the lot, but there wasn't room for much more. In the center of the lot, someone had laid out white sheets in the form of a giant cross.

Outside the bowling alley doors were fifteen or sixteen soldiers and civilians. Some were bleeding and some were just bloody. Courtney addressed one of the latter ones. "I have a wounded boy here. It's his leg. It looks bad."

The bloody ones were medics and two hurried to the Corvette, lifted Jason out and laid him down on the asphalt among shards of old beer bottles and the butts of cigarettes. Not two feet away from the boy's head was what might have been vomit or someone's spilled casserole. Working quickly, they cut away his pants and exposed a skinny leg. There was a fist-sized hunk of his thigh missing and although it bled continuously in what looked like a red waterfall, the medics didn't seem overly concerned.

"There were bombs," Jason whispered.

"Oh yeah?" one of the medics asked. "Did those bombs get you anywhere else?"

Before he could answer, Courtney said, "I need to find the command tent. It's urgent. I'm with the governor."

One of the medics jerked his thumb over his shoulder. "They're inside. Go to the left past the shoe rental. They're in the bar."

Courtney thanked him as she jumped up, heading for the door. She paused with her hand on the pull handle. "Do you happen to know his name? The general in charge, that is?"

The two medics looked at each other, their faces screwed into "thinking" looks. One finally said, "It's

Axelrod, I think. He's the bald one. I mean it looks like he spent time shining that fuck…sorry, ma'am, I mean that *freaking* dome of his."

Once more she turned to the door handle, but the other medic stopped her. "Can you tell us what's going on? No one knows anything. Are we winning?"

The true answer was that both sides were losing simply by fighting, but it wasn't something she could say to the people in the fight. "We're reaching a compromise that will benefit both sides and make us stronger. So, yeah, we're winning." They smiled at this and once more she turned to the door. This time she stopped herself.

"Do either of you guys know the governor's name?" They shared another look, this time mingling suspicion in with their confusion. "It's for polling purposes," Courtney added quickly. "Normally, I'm with, uh, public relations and we are always looking to find out what the governor's name recognition numbers are."

One of the medics looked disgusted over the idea that the governor was worrying about name recognition in the middle of a zombie apocalypse. Thankfully the other came out of his confusion with an answer. "Is it Clarren?"

Courtney didn't have any idea. The second medic nodded to the answer but still didn't look happy at the question. "Okay thanks," Courtney said and then pointed at the injured boy. "You guys are doing a great job and the governor thanks you as well."

Leaving them to attend Jason, she breezed into the bowling alley. She had never been to this bowling alley, but she could have made her way around it blindfolded. For eight years as a teenager, she had belonged to a Thursday night league, and from her experience, bowling alleys were all the same.

Only, this one was different.

There were soldiers everywhere. Hundreds and hundreds, all rushing around or working furiously or lying in pools of blood. The bowling alley was both a command center and a hospital. Even Courtney knew that was against the rules of warfare.

217

She turned towards the bar and nearly ran into a surgeon who was moving from patient to patient. His blue gown was no longer blue. It was glistening red and she did her best to dodge out of his way. A man who had just stepped from the bar smirked. There was a heavy dose of contempt in the smirk. Courtney understood. Here they were fighting a war to keep their land free of the zombie plague and she was worried about her outfit. He had a right to his contempt and a part of her wanted to explain that she wasn't really like that.

A smarter part of her told her to shut the hell up. She had spent time to look the part of a privileged, prima donna, it only made sense to act like one as well. "Do you see something funny?" she asked the soldier—officer, really. He wore the gold cluster of a major on his camouflaged shirt.

"I see something ridiculous," he shot back.

She riled in hot anger, but she forced her response to be cool. "If you are talking about a bunch of useless junior officers kissing a general's ass, I see it, too." He glared and she felt the sweat in the crack of her ass, again. *It's okay*, she told herself. *That was a perfect response*. She had dealt with enough of Governor Stimpson's toadies to know they sounded just like that: in awe of their own imagined and inflated importance in the world.

Ignoring his glare, she said, "I need to speak to General Axelrod. I'm with the governor's office."

"I'll see if he's available," the major said.

When he ducked back into the bar, Courtney practically fell against the wall, her legs wobbling and the sweaty feeling creeping up from her ass was now all the way down her back. This was a dangerous game she was playing. If they found out who she was and what she was trying to do, it wasn't out of the realm of possibility that they would take her out to the parking lot, force her to her knees next to the vomit and the yet to be triaged soldiers, and shoot her in the back of the head.

From their point of view they were on a spiritual and physical crusade to maintain the purity of their people, and she flew in the face of that. She was as much of an enemy as the soldiers in the 101st, and the pilots who bombed them relentlessly, and the zombies who never stopped.

Courtney was still trying to gather herself together when the major popped his head back out. "It'll be a half hour or so," he said, with an insincere smile.

This wasn't her first time around the block. She knew that a half hour could mean forty-five minutes or sixty, or even a hundred and sixty minutes. What it most certainly did not mean was thirty minutes.

"No," she told him, hoping that her voice wasn't quivering. "That w-will not do. I-I need to see the general, now. This is by order of the Governor."

"You have your orders and I have mine."

There wasn't a real door that led into the bar. Someone had tacked a sheet over it and now the major disappeared behind it. "Son of a bitch," she hissed. It was just a sheet, but she had to screw her courage up to the breaking point before she could pull it back and step into the room. The major hadn't gone far inside, a bare inch or two, and he was much more of an impediment than the sheet was.

Courtney was small and when he twisted to the right to snarl, "You can't come…" she slid to her left and strode quickly into the room. They had turned the bar area into a dozen work stations. The tables, with their old water rings and the gum stuck beneath, were now heaped with maps and piles of paper.

Although the room was dim, she saw that for the most part it was an all-boys' club. The only two women there, besides Courtney had been relegated to a far corner table. Both were writing on yellow notepads, while around them was a low hum of voices. There were seven or eight conversations going on at once, but they all ceased and everyone looked up when the major grabbed Courtney by the back of her jacket and spun her around and started to manhandle her back to the sheeted door opening.

"I'm with the Governor's office!" Courtney yelled. "I have a message for General Axelrod!"

"Wait!" Major General Mark Axelrod snapped, staring so hard at the officer that Courtney could hear him gulp. A second later, he let go. This was supposed to be her cue to give her message, but Courtney was somewhat mesmerized by the general and his dark eyes. There was a strength of personality behind them that was far beyond the average. "Well? Out with it."

"It's supposed to be for your ears only."

"Fuck that," Axelrod stated. "Spit it out or get out."

Courtney took a deep breath, but with those eyes drilling into her, and an entire room full of high-ranking officers staring at her, she felt like a fawn surrounded by a pack of wolves. "W-We're s-surrendering."

The room exploded in an uproar. It was such a violent reaction that Courtney took a step back, nudging into the major. He had a stunned look on his face as though he couldn't decide whether to be happy or not. The general was definitely not happy.

"What the fuck is this!" he cried. "Get me the governor on the phone." A sat-phone was brought to the general and Courtney could only gape as a lieutenant began dialing the number. For some reason, the idea that the general and the governor were still in communication wasn't something Courtney had imagined.

It was a blunder that could get her killed. "No! Wait." The lieutenant stopped as ordered, his finger hovering over the buttons. "I-I was told that you shouldn't use the sat-phones for this. Th-They're bugged. I mean, the other side can hear what you're saying."

"No shit," Axelrod snapped. "But I think it's something they're going to find out about anyway, so who cares."

"The governor does," Courtney answered. "He cares."

"He doesn't know shit if he thinks surrendering will do us any good," a colonel said, speaking both to the general and to Courtney. "What does he know about the military? And why send a—no offense—but why send a girl? Look at her, all dressed up...and that car?" He shook his head in disbelief and raised a hand to the window.

Right outside the bar, in full view, was the stolen Corvette. A man in a bloody jean jacket had been laid on the ground next to it. He was stiff and staring blankly up at the sky. As she watched, a fly crawled out of his mouth.

"I'm sorry," the colonel went on, "but you look like an idiot driving a Corvette through the middle of a war. This isn't the fucking prom or a trip to the mall. You're driving a target with wheels. Did you ever think about that?"

Courtney turned away embarrassed, her cheeks going so hot that she was sure they matched the color of the Corvette. Everyone in the room was staring at her. She could feel their eyes burning into her, condemning her, making her feel small and stupid. She didn't think she'd be able to turn around again and confront them.

Then her eyes fell on what was pinned over the bar: a massive map of the New England states. There were pins stabbed into it. One was in Webster, another in Woonsocket, another in Ashley Falls and Stockbridge. There were some in Connecticut as well: Danbury, Torrington, Hartford...she knew all these places. In a manner of speaking, she had been to each and taken part in the fighting of each, sometimes in a pivotal manner.

It was more than any of the people in the room could say.

"We don't need to be so harsh," the general said, his voice, low and gravelly. "This isn't the young lady's fault. I'll straighten out the governor and we'll carry on as though..."

By his tone of voice, she could tell that the general had slipped into a "Father Knows Best" role. His dark eyes had seemed almost kindly, reminding her vaguely of General Collins. Of course, Collins hadn't needed to "act" fatherly. It hadn't been an act with him.

Thinking that Collins would not have wanted her to back down, Courtney spun, slowly, saying, "You'll do no such thing. Our orders are specific, whether you like them or not, whether you think I'm competent or not, which I am."

By the way Axelrod's eyes turned hard and sharp, Courtney could tell that he certainly did not think she was competent. She'd have to change his perception quickly if she was going to have any chance at changing his mind. She pointed at the Corvette. "That is the perfect camouflaged vehicle. Two miles from here I ran into an Apache. It had me dead to rights and could have ripped me up, but it didn't. Tell me, Colonel, if I had been in a Humvee would it have let me go?"

The colonel who had tried to embarrass her, said nothing, however the major who had blocked the entrance was now standing beside her; he snorted out a, "No."

"And since you seem to have a problem with my, uh, attire," Courtney said, continuing, "would it have been better if I had showed up here in an army uniform?" Again, the major snorted. Courtney gave him a smile and said, "Exactly. You would have scoffed at me. You would have said I was 'playing' soldier."

To his credit, the colonel gave a half-shrug. Courtney read the move as: *You're right, but I'm not going to admit it out loud.*

"As for the governor," Courtney went on, "Clarren knows what he needs to of the situation." She went to the map and pointed to a little spot on the map sixty miles north of New York City. "This is where everything started. The Walton facility of R&K Pharmaceuticals. Four days ago, at eight in the morning, the first of the IPs were infected. Local police, state troopers and the CDC were called in to contain the problem."

She touched another spot on the map, north of the first. "This is Poughkeepsie, New York. Cases of the disease began turning up there in the late afternoon and by midnight, it became obvious that the quarantine around the city had failed. Governor Stimpson called up the 42nd Infantry Division soon after. Because of presidential..."

Courtney struggled to find the right word and the major suggested: "Weakness? Interference?"

"Let's say both," she said, giving him a smile. "Because of presidential weakness and interference, the situation was not nipped in the bud as it could have been and containment was, once again, lost. The line fell numerous times until, at eleven that night, the remnants of the 42nd was surrounded on this hill, just east of the Connecticut border. And…and at exactly 12:06 a.m. General Collins was shot in the head at point blank range."

Axelrod and Courtney locked eyes. "You can't know that for certain," he said.

"Actually, I can because I was there and he asked me personally to shoot him. You see, he was a true warrior. He fought until he was dragged down and he fought even after he was infected." Murmuring stopped her. Some believed her, some didn't. So far, she hadn't lied but she would need to in order to tie things up and end this stupid war.

Taking a steadying breath, she began her lie: "Governor Clarren asked me to assess the situation. I was there during that fight. I took over the general's communications unit and coordinated Apache gunship strikes, air assault reinforcements and Coast Guard flights that kept the battlefield illuminated. If you wish to use that sat-phone, dial up the Joint Base at Otis. The number is 011-880-508-672-1518. Ask for Lieutenant Commander Holt. Tell him Courtney Shaw says hi."

As much as she wanted to use a fake name, no one had ever heard of Eva Mansetti. The officer with the phone was given a nod by General Axelrod and in a couple of minutes, Courtney's alibi was proved to be, at least partially, true.

"And that brings us to yesterday," she said as soon as the lieutenant hung up. "I was with General Frazer outside of Hartford as he drew up his defensive lines and I was in Hartford City Hall with Mayor Perez when it was finally overrun. If you wish to verify, I have a FBI number you can call. We were trying to set up an extraction for the lead scientist who had created the Com-cell. Governor Clarren and I think she was…is our best hope in creating a cure for the disease. The number you want is 011-8…"

"That's not necessary," Axelrod said. He was quiet, struggling with indecision. The woman seemed sincere,

223

that wasn't the problem. "Everything you've just said points to why we have to resist. So far, the only line that has held is ours. It doesn't make sense that the governor wants to just throw that away."

It made a lot of sense to Courtney. There were other maps around the room and they showed a dozen major battles being fought along the state's border. On the edge of the maps, where the ocean was depicted in blue, were more pins. These were naval forces, all of which were currently enemies of the Commonwealth of Massachusetts.

"You are surrounded on all sides," Courtney told him. She went to the map and pointed to the long, jagged shoreline. "And not just by the zombies. The Navy has a Marine Expeditionary Force; it can land anywhere, and you don't have anything that can stop it. And even if you did, the Air Force has knocked out eighty percent of the bridges in the state." It was a number she had pulled out of thin air. "Think about that. Eighty percent."

"Eighty?" the general asked in astonishment. "We knew it was bad, but eighty percent? Why would the president do that?"

That was a good question—almost too good of a question. Courtney's ability to lie had to be based in some sort of reality. "We don't know if he's really in charge of his own faculties, and, and, uh, there has been talk of him resorting to a nuclear option."

She knew the idea wasn't out of the realm of possibility when it came to this president and just threw it out there. Unfortunately, she followed it up with, "It's why we don't dare use the sat-phone. Not until we've managed to get the majority of refugees across the border."

"That doesn't make any sense," the general said.

"I know," Courtney said, thinking furiously and not coming up with anything that would make sense of something that didn't make sense. It felt like she had backed herself into a wall.

The major, who had been standing next to her, looked just as confused, but he offered a thought, "Maybe it has to look as though they won. That way the president isn't 'cheated' out of his victory. It's sort of like playing checkers with a toddler. If you want the game to end, you can't just quit, you have to find a way to lose that's not obvious."

Axelrod looked far from happy. He didn't like to lose, either. "But nukes? Nukes are fucking cheating," he grumbled.

Chapter 18

1– 4:21 p.m.
—Webster, Massachusetts

The fight to open a hole in the Connecticut/ Massachusetts border had started aggressively enough with a two-pronged attack. On paper, it looked like a sure thing: one regiment of the 101st would pound north through the town of Webster, while an air assault force would be dropped in at the highway junction in Auburn and then head south, linking up in the town of Oxford, which was an equal distance for both.

The 2nd Battalion of the 327th was tasked with punching through the line just south of Webster. Instead of punching through, they got bogged down in a slugfest as the weekend warriors from Springfield and the preppies from Cape Cod rushed with suicidal courage into the fight. The 2nd never even cracked the first of the defensive lines.

This left Sergeant Ross and the 1st Battalion of the 327th stranded in enemy territory where they were mauled so badly by counterattacks that it essentially ceased to exist as a command structure. At four that afternoon, the 1st battalion had only three officers still alive. One officer had been targeted by so many snipers, for so long, that he was now little more than a twitching, life-sized doll that had to be pulled from cover to cover, where he would immediately roll into a ball.

Sergeant Ross was one of only seven NCOs still on his feet. A part of him understood what the catatonic officer was feeling. The first time he felt the air swish across his skin as a bullet missed his eye, but not his eyelash, he had laughed in a panicky way. Next, he felt a tug on his blouse and thought that one of his soldiers had tried to get his attention when it was really a thirty-thirty round the size of his index finger tearing a hole in the fabric of his shirt. He had cursed and grew angry thinking that someone was trying to kill him on a personal level.

Now, whenever he paused to reload or bark orders, he would subconsciously rub his arms and chest, feeling for holes and blood. One of his troops had asked him if he was cold and Ross didn't have an idea what the guy was talking about.

The 1st Battalion had suffered so many casualties that when they were reinforced with soldiers scrounged from every unit at hand, plus some untrained civilians, many of whom actually thought that they were being choppered to safety, the battalion wasn't exactly a mob, but it was very close.

Sergeant Ross was put in charge of the heavy weapons company. His first act was to throw out every heavy weapon they possessed, except for a single M240 machine gun. It made sense since the mortars platoon had no mortars left, and there weren't any targets for the anti-aircraft squad. The M2 .50 cal was too heavy to lug about when speed was needed, and there wasn't enough ammo for the SAWs.

"Everyman is a rifleman," he said to the grumblers. There wasn't a lot of grumbling as they headed south. The men were too busy fighting for their lives as they went from house to house, or crawled through fields, or charged through forests under what seemed like endless sniper fire.

The 1st Battalion was being subjected to a modern-day version of Lexington and Concorde. Just like the Redcoats from two and half centuries before, they found that getting into Massachusetts was far easier than getting out again.

They were swarmed by soft civilians. Men, women and teens, speaking in their God-awful accents, were still streaming down from Gloucester, Manchester by the Sea, and Marblehead. They were not infantry by any measure: they couldn't stand up to a charge of any size, they couldn't maneuver and they lacked cohesion. *They* were the mob. However, they could shoot their rifles reasonably well and, as the afternoon wore on, through endless practice, or so it seemed, their aim got progressively better.

Although it couldn't have been true, they seemed to have unlimited ammo, while at the same time, Ross was screaming at his company to save their bullets. He couldn't exactly say: "Don't shoot until you see the whites of their eyes," because the militiamen would not allow them to get that close.

Their march south, what had begun with a triumphant charge by Ross and the bloody remnants of his original company, had started with nearly twelve-hundred soldiers and civilians in an even mix. 1st Battalion was half that size now with the civilians taking shocking losses.

Ross, who had been fortunate enough to be anchoring the battalion's right wing, which was bordered by the marsh-filled French River, was able to see what was happening in the neighboring company. The civilians would clump together, charge without preparation or covering fire, shoot from the same spot over and over again. And, oddest of all, they had a bizarre desire to "see" what was going on. He didn't know how many times he saw some idiot standing up and squinting around, just asking to be shot.

This amateur behavior was as ugly as it was unnecessary. To keep his own company from being as decimated, Ross conducted an on-going class in the art of combat as they moved south. "Stay low! Lower! Act as a unit. Three firing, three moving. Spread out, you morons!"

It made him a target and Ross spent as much time crawling through the mud or under sticky bushes, or crabbed up against parked cars, as he did leading or teaching his men. Still, two hours into the attack, his was the most intact unit. On one level, this was good. On another, it was horrible.

"Captain Spencer needs you," a private from the Headquarter's platoon yelled from across a pretty little street where the lilacs were in bloom and the houses had rose bushes set in their window boxes and the snipers had a perfect lane to shoot down. The runner wasn't going to chance crossing the street when he could just as easily yell and tell the entire world exactly what was happening.

Ross thought it wouldn't have been a waste of a bullet to shoot him. "I'll be right there," he said, wishing he had a bullet to spare. Crossing the street took three minutes. Two minutes and fifty-five seconds of which he spent sitting against a white painted fence that came to waist height.

He didn't look to see if there were any bad guys, because he knew that there were plenty of bad guys. After the long pause, Ross jumped up and ran across the street as if the entire state militia was gunning for him. Twenty-three bullets zinged in his wake as he dove behind a wrecked Peugeot, breathing in gasps.

The Peugeot suffered some more, while Ross gave himself a quick checkup. Once his subconscious was assured that he had no extra holes in his skin, Ross slowly crawled the remaining two hundred yards to the command post, and didn't give a rat's ass who was waiting for him. The CP was located in a savings and loan, and for the first time that day Ross actually felt safe.

He spotted a decorative bowl filled with *Dum Dums* and before he reported to the C.O. he filled his cargo pockets with the candy.

"What the hell are you doing, Ross?" Captain Darren Spencer of Charlie Company demanded. As the highest ranking officer, he was the acting battalion commander. Ross didn't know it, but he was fourth in line for the job.

"Just picking up some supplies, sir. They're for my guys, you know, a treat for doing such a good job. Some of them have been doing…"

Spencer held up a hand and Ross stopped talking, noticing for the first time just how hairy the captain's hands were. Thick, black arm hair crept down out of his sleeve and down across the back of his hand. Ross wondered if the same hair carpeted his entire body.

"I'm sure they are doing great," Spencer said. "How many effectives do you have?"

It wasn't as easy a question as it might have seemed. Ross hadn't done a count in half an hour. He could have lost twenty men in that time. Even if he hadn't, some of the civilians were so ineffective that he couldn't exactly count them. "I'd say about seventy-five, sir, give or take."

The captain rubbed his hairy hands together. "Great, we're going to need you to pop this open again for us." He spread out a map and pointed to a light green patch. "The assault led by Charlie Co hit a wall in this graveyard. I thought we'd be able to outshoot anyone trying to hold it but those fuckers turned those, what do you call them, tombs?"

"Mausoleums?"

He snapped his hairy fingers. "Mausoleums, right. They turned them into fucking pillboxes. Each overlapping the next. It's a fucking nightmare. I sent Delta to relieve them, but you see this forest? It's not a forest anymore. It's a fucking, what do you call it? It's a fucking solar farm. Or it was. We had a couple Warthogs fly by to help out and they turned that fucking place into a fucking mess. There's glass everywhere. I mean everywhere. Everyone's all cut up." As proof, he held up his left hand, where there was a bandage on his palm.

Ross was in a weird mental spot. He was safe in a brick-walled bank with a pocketful of *Dum Dums* and all he could think was that Captain Spencer was probably just using the bandage to cover up his hairy palms. He had to grit his teeth to keep from laughing at the idea.

Spencer sobered him up by saying, "Here's what we need from you." He tapped a forested area, west of the town. Ross felt his stomach drop.

The air assault force had battled to a point just a mile north of Webster. Their right flank was on the French River and their left was on the main highway, I-395. For the most part, the battlefield consisted of quaint little homes and baseball fields where little leaguers had once jousted with ball and bat.

Now, the captain wanted Ross's company to attack across the French River. It wasn't the biggest river, *only* thirty or forty yards wide with heavy forest on the other side—the perfect place to hide half the Massachusetts National Guard. All it would take is one guy with a machine gun to kill half of his company.

"Um," Ross said and then paused. "How, uh, how deep is that river?"

"Probably not very," was Captain Spencer's casual reply. "It'll be okay. I asked for some air support. We should have three or four F-16s coming in about ten minutes."

Ross's mouth came open. "Ten minutes? Ten minutes? Why the hell are they coming in ten minutes…sir?" He was on the edge of insubordination and it was hard for him to care since he was going to be dead in ten minutes.

Spencer put his face right into Ross's so that they were nose to nose. "Because the fucking zombies are this close to breaking through!" he screamed, holding his thumb and finger an inch apart. "And what the fuck do you think will happen then? Huh? We all die, that's what. So, get your fucking men ready to jump off the second those fast movers swing by."

"Yes, sir," Ross said, quietly.

He turned to leave, but Spencer stopped him. The captain had three smoke grenades in his hands. "Let them go in ten and, uh, I'm sorry." He wasn't sorry about screaming in Ross's face; that came with the uniform. He was sorry for what he was asking Ross to do.

Ross didn't have time for apologies. He raced out of the bank and ran down the middle of the street, listening to the whine of bullets as they skipped off the pavement at his feet or just behind him. The cars all along the street had their windows shot out as he passed. All of this formed a backdrop. His mind was somewhere else.

Under the best of conditions, a river crossing, mid-battle was fraught with complications. So many things had to be considered: where were the suppressing teams going to be set up? How many men would go in the initial wave? Would they establish a toe-hold or would they try to drive inland? Who was coordinating with the artillery? Where was the JTAC? Sleeping again instead of directing the close air support like he was supposed to? Did they have the supplies for an assault? Did they have supplies for a sustained assault once across? And how would they be resupplied once over? Would engineers set up pontoons or would a bridge be seized down river?

All of this breezed in and out of Ross's head without gaining any traction. None of that mattered. He had no artillery and the only forward air control he had were the three smoke grenades. There were hardly any supplies and they would find none on the other side except for what they stripped from the dead.

The only real question that Ross was thinking about was: Could everyone swim?

"Fuck," he said, when he got back to his little neck of the woods. One of his platoon leaders tried to ask him what was going on, but Ross didn't have time. He pushed through the underbrush until he got to the river's edge. At this particular stretch, there was a built-up mound of earth of about four feet in height on which sat a set of train tracks.

"That's good," he whispered. The mound would provide cover. It would mean some sort of surprise.

That surprise would get them ten yards into the water. The river was thirty-five yards across, meaning the final twenty-five yards would be made under fire. Twenty-five yards was nothing when one was in swimming trunks. It was a little more difficult when fully clothed. With a rifle in one hand, a helmet, boots and armored vest, it was a challenge that would take at least two minutes,

"Fuck," he said again and then walked back into the woods. "Gather everyone up," he said to the platoon leader. "Everyone. I need…" He heard a new rumble in the air and realized that he had forgotten to check his watch when Captain Spencer had told him the air strikes would be in ten minutes. He checked it now. "Shit. It's been three minutes, maybe four. We'll go with four and that means we have six minutes left."

"Six minutes to what, Sarge?" one of his soldiers asked. "You don't look so good."

Ross touched his face with a dirty hand. "It's, um, nothing. I need you to drop everything. Keep your helmet, your rifle and all the ammo. Everything else goes in a pile. Let's go!"

When his company was gathered and stripped down to the bare minimum, he divided them into three groups. "In three minutes, I'm taking group one across the river. Groups two and three will provide suppression." As he spoke the men swore and groaned. He ignored them. "The moment we're across, group two will go. Then group three. We will spread out and establish a firm beachhead." He checked his watch once more. He had two minutes…or one, or three; he really didn't know.

"Let's go," he growled. A few of the men in group one glanced around, but when a specialist followed after Ross, they all fell in line. He had chosen thirty for the first group. He spaced them five feet apart, giving the men on the ends one of the smoke bombs and when he guessed the time was right, he pulled the pin on his and tossed it over the embankment.

Blue smoke plumed upward and almost immediately drew rifle fire from across the river. The other two grenades were tossed next and, as his company huddled, every one of them looked up, waiting…waiting…waiting.

When the two F-16s streaked past at tree-top level with a roar of engines so vast that it threatened to split Ross's head. He stuffed his fingers in his ears. Many others did as well, but those who didn't were deafened as the cluster bombs opened up and rained death on the land across the water.

The river was not so wide that the explosions didn't affect the Heavy Weapons Company. The air was sucked out of their lungs and then, seconds later, it rushed back at them only it came back superheated and in a violent, angry wave, like the storm of an angry god. The world shook and the water frothed.

Ross felt his body lift from the ground before he was slammed back down. His head rang from the explosions and only one thought was able to muddle through: *We have to go, now!* before the enemy recovered. He stood on wobbling legs as he screamed for his men to get up.

"Now! Now! Into the water!" He was the first into the river and he was the first to discover that the bed of it was mud. It grabbed his boot and held him. It was a fight to free that first foot. Then he was slogging through waist-deep water that quickly turned to chest-deep water, and then the water was over his head and he was struggling to stay afloat as a machine gun started to rattle on the other side.

The river danced and leapt as bullets skipped across its surface. The little, evil splashes were everywhere, there were so many that it felt like it was raining death. Ross figured that if he got hit, he wouldn't even feel it. It would be bang-dead, that quickly. Only just then, the specialist who had been first to come after him had his left ear shot off.

"Shit! Oh, shit!" the specialist screeched, trying to swim and clutch his ear at the same time. He lost his rifle and then lost the top of his head as a second bullet struck him quarter on, just above the temple.

Ross moaned as if he'd been shot. There was nothing he could do for the specialist or the others who were wounded. There was really nothing he could do for himself, either. He could only swim with his clothes sticking to him, and his boots weighing him down like little anchors, and the M4 banging his helmet with every spastic stroke.

Gasping, his face screwed up in fear, his left foot suddenly hit something sturdy beneath him. It was a log with branches jutting up to his left. He'd actually been trying to avoid the branches, but now he saw he could use them to get across faster. He kicked with his legs and dragged himself from branch to branch until he felt the mud under his boots.

He could have stood—if he wished to die. Instead, he slithered forward like a pollywog and went up onto the bank.

Eagerly, he unslung his rifle and looked for a target, however there was so much underbrush that, at first, he couldn't see anything but green and more green. He could hear just fine. There were seven or eight people shooting at his men. While in the water, he would have thought it was a hundred.

Still, their aim had been dreadfully accurate and he needed to silence them. He crawled through the bog and the brush until he caught a glimpse of movement. It was a man in a ghillie suit. Had he stayed still, he would have been invisible—now he was obvious and Ross killed him with one burst.

Before he could congratulate himself, what looked like a living bush turned and fired at him. It was another person in a ghillie suit. He had a deer rifle and his first shot missed by an inch. He jacked back the bolt, but before he could ram it home, Ross shot him, as well.

Then more of his men were on the bank and squirming up. "Cross! Everyone cross!" Ross yelled over the sound of the firefight.

Someone ran and Ross took a shot and thought that he had been on target as the person fell, however the person was up again in a flash, running and jumping, acting strangely. *He's panicking*, Ross thought. He was sure that his company was on the verge of another breakthrough and so he jumped up as well. He didn't get far as he was confronted with an alien appearing landscape of marshes, bomb craters, fire, smoke and body parts flung here and there.

"Don't stop!" he screamed and plunged into this dreadful new world. The battle for him was a fight against the environment as much as it was against the militia. He crawled from a downed tree trunk, to a newly formed pit which was filling with a mixture of blood and mud. He fired his rifle at anything that was remotely human and with each passing minute, he looked less human himself.

Ross was slicked head to toe in bog shit, but he kept going, leading his men, knowing that there would soon be farms and fields, knowing that his was a just cause, knowing that even if he died, he would have done his duty. They had forced the river. In no time, the rest of the company would be across and then the battalion would follow.

They were winning.

It was the last thought that went through his head before Ross low-crawled through a bush and slid down an embankment. When he looked up, he was surrounded by at least thirty men…and women…and children, all with guns pointing at him. Behind the guns were the harsh, angry faces of simple Americans, defending their lives and their lands.

He had no wish to hurt them, and even less of a wish to die at their hands, but that didn't seem likely. He was an exhausted, sitting target, and he wasn't even sure how much ammo he had left, or if his M4 was empty.

"I…was… doing my…duty," he rasped out.

"Uh-huh," one of the older men said. "And we were doing ours." He sighed, wearily and scratched in his mud-caked hair. "Man, I hate to do this."

Here it comes, Ross thought. They were about to shoot him; he was so exhausted that he almost didn't care. Had they been Russians or the Red Chinese, he would have tried to get one or two of them before he died, but they were Americans, for crying out loud. He slumped, turning to look at a sparkle of shining brass from a spent shell casing.

"Do what you got to do," he told them.

"Alright," the man said in low voice. "We surrender."

2—Webster, Massachusetts

The word went out quickly: *Surrender in place. Do not give up your weapons. Maintain the lines at all costs.* It was an odd set of directives and Courtney Shaw feared that there would be bad blood between the army and the Massachusetts National Guard, however the threat of the coming zombies was great enough to overcome most of the friction. Company by company the shooting stopped and the two sides came together with more confusion than animosity.

Courtney also feared what would happen to her when it was discovered the part she had played in the surrender of an army that was still full of fight. She had to get out of there as fast as she could. "Okay, I should be getting back to Boston," she told General Axelrod. "I'm sure you got this from here."

"Wrong," he snapped. "Sorry, but you're going to miss your afternoon tea and scones. I need someone in authority who speaks for the governor. Someone who isn't one of them egg-headed, intellectual pussies out of Cambridge. Wait, did you go to Harvard?"

She had a year and a half of community college under her belt; a far cry from Harvard. "No, uh, I went to, uh, Boston College," she lied.

"Oh, good school. My third son went there."

Courtney would have to take the general's word for it that it was a good school. It had been the first college that had popped into her head, probably because she had just mentioned Boston. The only thing she knew about Boston College was that Doug Flutie had gone there. Her father had been a big Flutie fan; thought he was an absolute wizard with a football.

"Small world," Courtney replied and then tried to change the conversation back. "Look, I can't speak for the governor on everything. I-I don't have that authority."

"Then fake it," Axelrod ordered. "We have some tough shit to work out very quickly, and I don't have time to waste waiting on Clarren to send out someone else. Besides, you seem to have had more experience with the infected than most...unless you weren't telling the truth before."

"I know too much about them," she assured the general.

That seemed to please him and he took her by the arm. "We'll take your car, those Air Force pukes might not have gotten the word. Do you mind if I drive? That baby is a classic." She nodded, hoping that he wouldn't ask too many questions about the Corvette, because she didn't have any answers. He grinned but it didn't last more than a second as he bawled, "Lipcomb! Get the maps. Stevens, bring the sat-phone and get the damned door for the lady."

A lieutenant colonel rushed to hold the door open for Courtney and before she knew it she was in the Corvette with the general, while a handful of senior officers followed at a discreet distance in a hummer.

"We're going to need to set up an internment camp," Axelrod said, taking a turn, looping away from the main battlefield around Webster. "Those Connecticut fucks aren't going to like it, but that's on them. They could have defended their border, but instead they chose to hole-up in their cities. Morons. So, where do you think? Up by Quabbin Reservoir?"

She didn't know where that was; she started to give him a shrug, but his glare stopped her. If she didn't know where it was, that meant it wasn't close. "No, it's too far."

Axelrod snorted. "It's just a little over twenty miles. What's far about that? Hell, if they can walk across Connecticut, then they can walk to Quabbin. It'll be perfect, the peninsula that sticks out into the middle of the reservoir should hold them."

"It's not how far the walk is," Courtney said, contradicting herself. "It's that there will be leakers. They're not going to want to go to an internment camp and they're going to run at the first opportunity."

"And they'll be shot at the first opportunity," Axelrod replied. "Speaking of which, we're going to need to set up execution squads. When you talk to Clarren use a different term. Maybe something like: *contaminated individual suppression team*. Or use whatever you want, just don't have the word execution in the name." Courtney nodded, hating the very idea but understanding the need. She was glad that she wouldn't have anything to do with the execution squad, other than finding a way not to be one of their victims, that is.

"I'll, uh, uh think of something," she spat out, doing her best not to choke on the words.

"We'll also need some way to detect the infected individuals before they become a threat. You said you were with the scientist who made this thing? Can you get a hold of her?"

At first Courtney wanted to lie about that as well; there was some danger in talking to Thuy with the general around, but at the same time, thousands of lives could be saved if Thuy could come up with a way of spotting the infected before they became dangerous or contagious.

"I would, but the radios don't seem to work."

Axelrod grunted. "Tell me about it. I didn't know we were so far along with E.W." Courtney gave him a look and he explained, "Electronic warfare. Jamming radios, electromagnetic interference, that sort of thing. The Russians have a device called a Borisoglebsk-2. From what I heard, it's a bitch, but we must have something even better."

Courtney leaned over and turned on the police scanner and tried: "Deck 1 this is Dispatch 6, come in."

A few seconds passed and she was about to repeat herself when Thuy came over the radio: "Ms. Shaw?" Thuy's voice was cool, the two words clipped as if she were a diplomat who was practiced at masking her true intention. Courtney breathed a quick sigh of relief. That Thuy answered on that particular frequency and to those call signs meant Deckard had, against enormous odds, somehow found her.

"Yes, I'm here with General Axelrod of the Massachusetts National Guard," Courtney said, speaking very quickly, her nerves running high. A slip of either her tongue or Thuy's would be disastrous. "As I told you earlier, the governor was keen to see the war end and I think we are close to that goal."

"That is good," Thuy answered, still cool, but now she was guarded.

"It is," Courtney agreed. "We are going to get the two of you out of there, that's a promise the governor will keep, but I have a question for you while we set that up."

Courtney paused to let that sink in. When Thuy didn't reply, Courtney asked, "Is there a way to detect the infected individuals before they become a threat?" As Courtney knew she would, Thuy didn't answer until she had an answer. After thirty seconds, Axelrod grew impatient and muttered something about *useless eggheads*.

Eventually, Thuy spoke, "Without access to a lab or instruments of any sorts, the best I can suggest is to try using flashlights."

Axelrod took the mic from Courtney's hand and demanded, "Did you say flashlights?" He'd been to a seminar once on the power of "Eastern Medicine" which had been three wasted hours. When he had walked out of the conference room he had worn the very same look of skepticism as he was wearing just then.

"Yes, sir. The infected are highly photosensitive," Thuy explained. "In the early stages, they may be in denial and although they will be aware of their headaches, they may lie. I doubt very much that they will be able to hide the effect a sharp light will have on their eyes. I know it's not much, but it's something. If we can speed up the evacuation process, I'm sure I could come up with a better method of detection."

The general sat back for a moment, driving without really seeing the pleasant April scenery or the unpleasant sight of tanks and trucks that had been blown to pieces. He didn't even see the Humvee behind him flashing its lights.

"She's the real deal?" Axelrod asked Courtney.

"If her work hadn't been sabotaged, we'd both be at the parade in her honor. She developed a cure for cancer. Is that real enough?"

Axelrod raised an eyebrow. "Cancer? Really? That's real enough for me. Tell her that once we get done kissing Platnik's ass, I'll scrounge up a helicopter."

Excitedly, Courtney relayed the information and asked, "Where are you? Please, tell me somewhere close and safe."

"Not really. We're heading back to that place where we picked up the balloon last night. If we hadn't gotten in touch with you, we were going to try to float across."

"Stay put," Courtney told her. "We'll get you out as soon as we can. Whatever you do, don't try to get out by balloon."

Axelrod laughed. "They were going to get out by hot air balloon? I thought you said she was smart. That's dum…" The beeping of the Humvee's horn cut him off. "What the fuck?"

He considered stopping only they had swung full around the town and were at the defensive lines where Massachusetts guardsman and soldiers from the 101st were slowly coming together. And he could see the Screaming Eagle banner flying a little ways down the bombed-out road.

General Platnik would be there and he would be insufferable. He would act as though he had won some great victory when it had really been the Air Force and the dogged determination of the air assault force which had been shockingly tough to stop.

Suddenly, General Axelrod was glad he was riding in the Corvette. He drove slowly along the road and around the craters and the dead bodies and when he stopped at the furthest point in the lines that the 101st had gotten, he gunned the engine while it was in neutral, making it roar in fury.

He then stepped out and stood staring as Platnik made his way towards him. As Axelrod waited, the lieutenant colonel who had been in the trailing Humvee came hurrying forward and whispered into the general's ear.

Courtney watched with a sinking feeling in her stomach—Axelrod knew what she had done.

There had been a chain of events that started with Sergeant Ross, who had been first to find out that the Massachusetts National Guard was surrendering. He told Captain Spencer, who had told a major on Platnik's staff. That major had sprinted to where Platnik stood pissing against the trunk of a dead oak. With his dick hanging out,

241

Platnik had barked orders to move everyone to Webster as fast as they could. He had then called General Phillips, commander of the 7th Army who had called his boss, General Heider.

Heider had been sweating bullets all day as the President strayed between megalomania and utter depression. At least once an hour, the President would say: "Why can't I use the nukes? I'm the boss. I'm the man."

Upon hearing the news of the surrender, the President had jumped up with both fists in the air and screamed: "I am the man!" He had then called the governor of Massachusetts to gloat.

"We have not surrendered," Governor Clarren said to the President. He then cupped the phone to his chest and hissed, "Get me Axelrod, now!"

Eight minutes later, the lieutenant colonel was whispering in Axelrod's ear and one minute after that, the general ordered him to kill Courtney Shaw. When the lieutenant colonel could only splutter, an out of control Axelrod screamed, "Pull her out of that damned car and shoot her in the head. Now!"

He was loud enough for Courtney to have heard. In a childlike manner, she reached over and locked the Corvette's doors. It was a useless gesture and the quarter of an inch glass broke with one swing from the butt of the lieutenant colonel's pistol.

Chapter 19

1– 5:21 p.m.
—Brunswick, Maryland

Special Agent Katherine Pennock was finding out the hard way that there was an official "by the book" formula when it came to a zombie apocalypse. In truth, the apocalypse envisioned was an "Out of Control, Mutating Virus." As the saying went, it was close enough for government work.

During the last few days, things had been moving far too rapidly for anyone to put the guidelines to the "Out of Control, Mutating Virus," scenario into play, but with the capture of Anna and Eng, the FBI returned to form. After all, the joke around Quantico was that it wasn't the Federal Bureau of Investigation, it was the Federal *Bureaucracy* of Investigation.

Hundreds of agents who had been groping blindly throughout Maryland or stuck waiting in Baltimore for a ride were now racing to Brunswick, running like children after the ice cream truck. The worst, by order of rank, were the Senior Special Agents, followed by the Supervisory Special Agents, the Assistant Special Agents-in-Charge, who were so high-ranked that they were acronymed "ASACs," and the Special Agents-in-Charge, the "SACs."

They came by helicopter, Humvee and personal car. One even commandeered a fishing boat—Assistant Special Agent-in-Charge, Ron Tupa, his Humvee having broken down fifty miles north of Brunswick in Hagerstown, Maryland took possession of a fishing boat belonging to an old man who only gave the name of "Red." Tupa sat in the front, miserable and drenched by the rain, while Red sat happily in his yellow slicker and matching trousers as he drove the boat down the Potomac, illegally setting out six trolling lines and catching far above his legal limit of three different types of fish.

These agents descended like flies and immediately started to bicker and issue contradicting orders. Things grew simultaneously stagnant and more confused when two separate Executive Assistant Directors showed up, one bringing his own news crew on a separate chopper, and both claiming jurisdiction over the scene.

Special Agent Katherine Pennock found that the only way to restore order was to declare everything within a hundred yards of the barn to be a quarantine zone. Stuck in this zone were Anna and Eng, Warrant Officer Swan, PFC Jennifer Jackson and Swan's Blackhawk.

While the brass bickered, chatted, smoked cigarettes and drank black coffee in the driving rain, Katherine tried to interrogate her prisoners. She had them handcuffed separately, their arms looped around the steel girders that held the aluminum structure up. Eng remained steadfastly mute, while Anna built lie upon lie until she had fabricated a story of innocence, persecution and personal courage that would have made a great daytime movie on the Lifetime network.

"And can you offer any corroborating evidence?" Katherine asked her. "Any eyewitnesses?" Anna had looked to Eng, who rolled his eyes and spat out a "Pffft!"

"Okay, back to the cure," Katherine said. "You need to start talking if you're going to have any credibility."

Anna and Eng shared a look. They clearly hated each other, but in this they were unified. "As we explained," Eng stated, "because of the racist and sexist persecution we've been through from the very beginning, we demand full immunity from prosecution before we go forward, and we want that signed by the President."

Jennifer Jackson, her long, brown hair molded into an odd duck's ass from wearing her helmet so long, and her uniform sticking to her from the rain and Mark Rowden's blood, rolled her own eyes. "Puh-lease! I have a better idea, how 'bout we start breaking their fingers? I have a wrench out in the 'Hawk that weighs like ten pounds. It'll do the trick."

"Mind your place, woman," Eng said, dismissing her. "I reiterate tha…"

Jackson was up in a flash. "Mind my place! My place! Fuck you. My place used to be in New Castle, Delaware but because of you I might not ever be able to go back. You fucked it all up!"

Eng gazed at her. At best, his expression could be described as bland, although bored was probably closer. "How do you Americans put it? It sucks to be you. As I was saying…"

"I'm getting my wrench," Jackson said, walking out of the barn with Joe Swan following after.

Eng muttered something that sounded like, "hysterical women," and gazed placidly at Katherine. The FBI agent folded her hands in her lap and stared back, a little smile on her face. "It looks like we have two options," she said, "the wrench or the letter. Or, perhaps, it's the wrench *and* the letter. I do have two of you, after all."

Anna Holloway set her chin just so and said, "You wouldn't dare. The fate of the country rests on this cure and we are the only ones who can create it. Eng worked with Dr. Lee and I worked with Dr. Riggs. Our knowledge of the Com-cell only overlaps in certain areas. To do this right, you need both of us and all our fingers."

Katherine wiped the smug look from her face, saying, "You're probably right. A scientist needs her fingers, but you don't need your toes, however." She stood tall over Anna, thinking that it would be so easy to kick the woman in the face. She deserved it, there was no question about that. "I am going to get the truth about what really happened in the Walton Facility and if you don't think I'll use the big-ass wrench to get it, you're mistaken."

While Anna went pale and subconsciously pulled in her toes, Eng only made that annoying sound again, "Pffft."

The sound of yet another Blackhawk landing interrupted Katherine just as she was about to call for Jennifer Jackson and her wrench. She went to the open bay doors of the barn and saw more men in dark suits and blue surgical masks coming toward the yellow tape that marked the edge of the quarantined area.

She was sure she looked a mess, but could do little besides running both hands through her hair to slick it back. Katherine didn't go straight towards the men. She detoured to "her" Blackhawk where Swan and Jackson were sitting in the cabin, next to the body of Sergeant Rowden.

Katherine gave them a little wave, saying to Joe Swan: "I need you to watch the prisoners. Don't talk to them at all and especially don't threaten them. It'll be best if we let Anna stew by herself for a while, so move her to the other end of the barn."

Jennifer, who held a huge wrench in her hands, looked disappointed. Katherine patted her shoulder. "You're doing great. Keep that fire going, you might need it still." Katherine was glad to see Jennifer's grim smile. She turned and began to make her way towards the men in the suits, one of whom stood beneath a huge golf umbrella that was being held by another agent. "Shit," Katherine whispered as she recognized the man beneath the umbrella despite the blue mask covering his face.

It was *The* Deputy Director of the FBI, Matthew Bradbury. The Director was a political position and could be held by a congressman or a governor, or some Joe from off the street if he could get the votes in the Senate. The Deputy Director position was different, altogether. It's the highest position attainable within the FBI without being appointed by the President.

Every Executive Assistant Director of every branch within the FBI works for the Deputy, as does every SAC appointed to every investigation. Within the FBI, the Deputy was "The Man," which was literal as there had never been a woman Deputy Director or Director, for that matter.

"Hello, sir," Katherine said, dipping her head slightly and feeling immediately foolish for doing so. As powerful as he was, he was a man, not a king and a head dip was not far from a bow in her book. She forced her eyes to lock onto his.

"So, you managed to snatch up both one and two on the Hit Parade," Bradbury said. "Very impressive, Katherine."

She was taken aback that not only did he know her name, he had used it as if they were old friends. She knew his name, but there was no way she was going to call him Matt or even Matthew, except by invitation, and even then, she figured it would feel awkward.

"Thank you, sir."

"Very impressive indeed and couldn't have come at a better time. You saw the President. The man's on the edge of, well, we'll just leave it at that. I wish you weren't stuck behind this tape. I was hoping that you would give the briefing on the capture."

Katherine had been hoping for that as well. Earlier that day, she had been disgusted at the idea of being the pretty girl who "massaged" the information being given to the President. This was different. This had been an actual accomplishment that had gone a long way to making the country safe again. As things went, someone was going to get credit and reap the rewards, it should be her.

"That would have been nice," she said, hoping her disappointment didn't show. "Maybe next time."

"Maybe," he agreed, touching the tape. He wore latex gloves and after touching the tape, he looked at his finger, as if he'd be able to see the Com-cells. "They mentioned a cure. What do you think? Are they jerking us around?"

It was a strange question to Katherine, because it didn't matter. The world was desperate for a cure and would do anything and pay any amount to get it. "I'd say it's fifty-fifty. They want a Presidential pardon for all crimes real or imagined, and they want it before they say a thing."

"That was to be expected. Tell them we want the locations of all the people they infected on Long Island, first. Tell them it'll be tit for tat. They give us the zombies, we give them the pardon. They give us the cure, and only then, do we let them go." There was something in his eyes that suggested the second part of that was a big fat lie.

She didn't care. Anna and Eng didn't even deserve an unmarked grave as far as she was concerned. They should be strung up and the family of all the people who died should be allowed to come by with a switch and give them three whacks. It would be a slow, horrible death, and that was just fine with Katherine.

"I'll tell them," she said. He gave her a nod and turned. Before he could get too far, she asked, "Are we winning?" She had hoped that the question would come out in a somewhat breezy manner, as if she were just curious and nothing more, but she heard the soft fear in her voice the same as he did.

Instead of answering, Bradbury jerked his head at the umbrella carrying agent to leave. When they were alone, he said, "It's hard to know what's what for certain. The 101st was able to get across the border. We had a big win there, but other than that, I don't know. General Phillips is doing everything he can, but he's got cities burning and cities overrun with zombies, and he's battling militias in Massachusetts, Delaware and even here in Maryland. Despite all that, he is still telling the President he's got everything under control. And I thank God that he is."

Despite the rain soaking them, Katherine lowered her voice and asked, "Are the use of nuclear weapons off the table, then?"

"For now. What you did here was more important than I think we will ever know. But we have to keep on top of this." He snuck a quick look behind him, before adding, "It may be that you *have to* find a cure." He looked intently into her eyes and asked, "Do you understand me?"

Bradbury was asking her to lie to a President who, by all accounts was slipping into paranoia…a man who had already condoned torture and summary executions. If she got caught lying to the President, there was a strong possibility that the penalty would be a lot stiffer than just losing her job or spending time in a federal penitentiary, she could face a firing squad.

2—5:46 p.m.
Wilmington Delaware,

The stratosphere between 1,000 feet and 2,500 feet above the northern suburbs of Wilmington was crowded with aircraft going in every direction. Turning long slow circles were two E-2D advanced Hawkeyes, while shooting across the city, one after another, were five F-18 Super Hornets setting up bombing runs. There were also four Apache gunships coming back from a mission, light on everything. They were heading to the Wilmington Airport to meet up with a flight of Blackhawks carrying ammo, which were, even then, crossing west to east.

Lastly, six General Atomics MQ-1 Predators, UAVs—unmanned aerial vehicles—buzzed about, their operators sitting safely in comfy chairs hundreds of miles away.

The Predators were divided up evenly between the Air Force, who needed to keep a constant eye on the shape of the battle, and The Department of Homeland Security, who needed to please the President. The big man was far from pleased. He knew he had been lied to. The evidence was right there on the screen.

"Someone pull up Google Earth," he demanded, thumping the gleaming table. "I want to verify this myself."

He didn't even fully trust Homeland Security. They wore uniforms, after all. To him they fairly stank of the military. Someone, *another* man in uniform, brought up Google Earth on one of the screens.

"You can zoom in and out using the mou…"

"I know how to work a damned computer," the President snapped. He centered the screen just south of Philadelphia, where the battle wasn't supposed to be happening, and zoomed in, closer and closer, getting more and more red in the face. He was on the "map" view and he wanted the "other one."

"The satellite view is that box right there," the same officer who had just been snapped at said. "Just click on it."

When the view changed, the President grinned like a madman and began comparing the Google Earth shot to the feeds generated by the Predators. "Yep. Look right there, that building is the same in both pictures." He squinted in at the screen. "It's the Monroe Refinery and look how close it is to the Delaware border. Son of a bitch! You see that, Marty, he lied."

Marty Aleman rubbed his temples. They were in the Situation Room, once again. It seemed to Marty Aleman that they practically lived in the damned place. He yawned behind a hand. "I see the top of the circular buildings, sure. They look the same, I guess. Maybe there were extenuating circum…"

"Extenuating circumstances!" the President yelled. "He told us three hours ago that Philadelphia would hold, and look." He poked the screen with a manicured nail. "The place is a ghost town, or a zombie town, or whatever. There's nothing alive there. When does he land?"

"Soon," Marty said, climbing to his feet, stretching, grimacing as his soft muscles pulled tight. "I'll go clear the lawn so that he can come straight here."

"Good," the President said, his right knee bouncing up and down. "And go snoop out Heider. He's going to have to find me a replacement general."

Only through years of practice, was Marty able to keep his face frozen in its normal bland, but pleasant expression. He didn't trust his mouth and so only nodded. There was no way he was going to fire General Phillips. Phillips was holding the war effort together almost singlehandedly.

He was a whirlwind of energy, moving units here and there, shifting supplies as needed and frequently before the need arose. In the last twenty-four hours, he had barely slept and yet he appeared to be just hitting his stride. It wasn't Phillips' fault that the men and women on the lines, the majority of them civilians, couldn't withstand the assaults when they went on and on, hour after hour.

When Marty left to forewarn both Phillips and Heider, the President stared back down at the map. "Can we make this interactive? I want to see where the units are and what their strength is. You know with bars. Like a bar graph?"

"Uh, sir?" It was the same officer who had helped earlier. He spoke reluctantly. "This is Google Earth. I can't manipulate that program. We can place markers on the other program or on stills."

"I don't like the other program. It's too cluttered. There's too many symbols on it. That's the problem with you military types, you have to have all the bells and whistles. It's why your fucking toilet seats cost seven hundred dollars."

The officer, trying to keep his face as neutral as possible, replied with a simple, "Yes sir."

Although the Situation Room could hold twenty people with ease, the President had made life so unbearable that there were only six people around the table; everyone else had found something better to do than to listen to the man whine or be berated. Presently, other than the frequent "hmmms," from the President as he studied the maps, the room was anxiously quiet. Everyone was waiting for the proverbial "other shoe" to drop. They'd been dropping all day.

When General Phillips arrived, the President's first words were: "Why the fuck do your toilet seats cost seven hundred dollars?"

Phillips stopped in the doorway, his tall lean frame bent from weariness. Before answering, he eased himself into one of the soft, leather-bound chairs. He glanced up at the feeds and frowned. He knew about the extra Predator UAVs. Their presence had sapped four precious minutes of his day. Minutes were like gold to him and he didn't have one to spare on useless Predators and even more useless questions.

But this was the President and there were still a handful of people who thought that he still mattered. "If I answer your question, sir, it'll take a minute and during that time somewhere in the neighborhood of a hundred people will die. Perhaps we should deal with a more pertinent question."

"Are you going to dodge all my questions?" the President asked. "Or just the ones you find inconvenient, like why the fuck didn't you tell me that Philadelphia was about to be lost?"

"I didn't tell you because I didn't know. From what I understand, someone hit the breaking point and ran. It started a chain reaction and," he shrugged, gestured at the monitor and said, "that's the consequence. It wasn't foreseeable except to say that the same thing could happen anywhere along the line and at any time."

This hardly appeased the President. "So, you're saying that shit happens and it's not your fault?"

That was surprisingly succinct. "Yeah, pretty much."

"You're fired," the President said, softly. He enjoyed the way the words rolled off his tongue. Out of habit, he added the usual boilerplate, "We have lost confidence in your ability to lead the troops. I understand that circumstances may not…"

Phillips interrupted. "You know, everyone talks crap about how you are nothing but Marty's butt-puppet. I kind of wish his hand was up your backside right this moment." The President glared but said nothing. "If it was, you'd just sit there calmly when I told you that, no, I'm not fired."

"You are, too!"

"Have you chosen my replacement? No? You're just going to let the 7th Army sway in the wind until you find someone you can push around and then blame when everything falls to shit? That'll take some time, a day at the least and by that time you'll have zombies at the White House gates."

"Oh, don't flatter yourself. I could find someone in ten minutes. All you military guys are the same. You're all power hungry."

Phillips laughed. It was genuine, but he was too tired to carry on for long. When the laughter was down to a few chuckles, he pulled out his Sat-phone and dialed General Platnik, putting him on speaker phone. "Hey Milt, sorry to bother you, but I may be stepping down as C.O. of the 7th. Would you like the job? You would have to start pretty much right away."

"Are you fucking kidding me? Tell that moron to fuck off. While I got you on the phone, when can we get those big birds up here? The Vipers and the Hornets can only do so much and we got grey meat like you wouldn't believe."

"I'll see what I can do, thanks." He hung up and dialed another number. "Let's see what Ed Stolberg says. You remember him, he's the guy who took over for General Collins of the 42nd. He's got a salty tongue on him especially since his command has essentially been destroyed."

The President held up a hand. "Just stop. These guys won't be right for the job anyway. They lack the proper temperament. What we need right at this moment in history is a true leader."

Phillips almost started laughing again. "I take it you mean yourself?" In answer, the President sat upright. The two men stared at each other until Phillips flat out said, "That is insane. It's so insane that maybe we should be having this conversation in private. Maybe in a doctor's office, on a couch. You could wear one of those sharp, white coats with the wraparound sleeves."

Just then, General Heider came in, took one look at the President and asked, "Did he fire you?" Phillips shrugged and Heider said, "Yeah, he does that. I think I've been fired twice so far. I wouldn't worry about it too much. I can't find anyone to replace you."

"The two of you shut up right this instant!" the President shouted. "His job is not that hard. If Platnik needs something other than the Hornets and Vapors, then he'll get it. Simple. And here, look." He pointed at the Google Earth map. "If we've lost Philadelphia we should fall back to this line." On the map was a line, what appeared to him like the curve of a shield, surrounding the northern part of Wilmington.

Heider and Phillips shared a look. The line was nothing but the imaginary arc created by the state border between Delaware and Pennsylvania. It would be worse than useless for Phillips to drag his soldiers from prepared positions and send them to stand in empty fields. He was about to say so when Heider nodded suddenly and said, "We can do that. It'll take time and I'm going to need General Phillips's help. He knows the dispositions of his men better than I do."

Phillips felt like he had been knocked on the head by a board. He was wondering how on God's green earth Heider could be saying this, when his old friend tipped him the smallest wink.

A lot of bad things could be said of General Heider, and a lot of bad things were, but no one had ever called him a fool. Ten minutes earlier, Marty had found him snoozing against a potted plant in a West Wing corridor. "We have a problem with the President," Marty had said.

"No shit," Heider responded, without opening his eyes. "We've *had* a problem with the President. Are you just figuring that out?"

"I think it's worse, now. He's not listening to me. He…he could be getting dangerous."

If Marty was finally admitting this out loud, then Heider knew they were in desperate trouble. He leaned his head back and snorted loudly, sucking back the phlegm that had been coming on for the last day or so. He spat into the potted plant and stood. "He should be happy. We got those two terrorists, the 101st is safe…for the moment, and we saved New York, like he wanted. Things aren't great but we might be getting a handle on it."

Marty was staring at the potted plant with a queer look on his face. Slowly, he dragged his eyes away from the dripping snot and answered. "He doesn't think we saved New York. To him Manhattan is New York City and the rest is just, I don't know, suburbs, I guess. As for the rest…

he's taking the credit. 'We' didn't capture Anna and Eng, he did."

"What? Does he think he caught them?" Heider was shocked, outraged, and a bit hopeful. One of the easiest ways to remove a sitting president was to prove mental instability.

"No, he just thinks that they were captured because *he* ordered them to be captured. And the 101st was able to compel the surrender of the Massachusetts National Guard because *he* wanted it to happen. If we're not careful, he's going to try to assume direct command."

Heider and Marty had not always seen eye to eye, but just then, minutes before Phillips had landed they locked eyes and came to an agreement. "You'll help me?" Heider asked.

"Yes." The treasonous word came whispering out of Marty's mouth just as soft and gentle as a night breeze. "We have to make him think he's in charge. Can you get those feeds he's watching to loop?" Heider knew a man who could and nodded with a grin. Marty shook his head, fear making his stomach twist. "No, be careful. The President is getting paranoid. If you don't act just like you've been acting, he'll suspect."

"So, you're saying, be a dick?"

That's exactly what Marty was saying. It's why Heider had been so flippant about Phillips's firing when he had walked into the Situation Room, feeling the perspiration collecting down the middle of his back.

"You will have to postpone Phillips's 'firing', of course," Heider said.

His use of air quotes around the word firing caused the President's eyes to flash. "For now, and as long as he does exactly what I say. I won't put up with anymore crap. He either kisses my ass or I kick his." Phillips sat like a furious stone statue until Heider gave him a warning look.

"Of course," Phillips managed to spit out. "What are your first orders?" He had to actively bite his tongue which wanted to add: *Mein Fuhrer*.

255

"I want every man, woman and child standing firm on that line," the President said as Heider slumped a little in relief. "That arc will be where we make our stand. The zombies will go no further!" The President had stood when he said this. Now, he looked around. "Where's Marty? I'm going to want to repeat that on T.V."

Heider did his best to shrug in pure innocent ignorance. "Probably taking a dump," he said, and nudged Phillips, flashing him a quick grin, hoping to play up the idea that they were just two military men flush with testosterone and vulgarity.

It seemed to work as the President's lips bent in disgust. "Right. While we wait, I want to be brought up to date on all of these units," the President said, slipping around the table and getting in close to one of the monitors. "I need to know what you two know. What's their supply situation? What are their casualties like, if they even have any? Like what's this EX over these companies? I know the E means engineers. What's the X? And why are there so many of them, and why aren't they on the front lines?"

Heider and Phillips shared a look. "They're auxiliary teams. They're small. I wouldn't worry about them."

"Don't worry?" the President asked, a green glint in his eye. "What are you keeping from me?"

3—5:55 p.m.
Boothwyn, Pennsylvania

Sergeant Brent Garvey, the leader of the 13th EX Squad, readjusted his mask, and checked the seal by putting his gloved hands over the filter holes and sucking in a breath. He barely got a mouthful of air, which was good. Next, he pulled the hood over his head and velcroed it down. The jacket, a ridiculous yellow rain slicker, had been the closest thing to a bio-suit he could find.

"Tape me," he grunted to the man standing by the door. The two of them, menacing figures despite the canary yellow slickers, stood in someone's first floor apartment. A single mom had lived there, judging by the fifty or so pictures of a woman and a little girl that hung, magnetized to the refrigerator. The place stank of bleach. With the rain outside bringing on an early evening, the apartment was dim, lit mostly by their two flashlights sitting on the counter.

The man by the door, a sick-to-his-stomach private, had sweat trickling down the interior of his jacket. His insides were jello, and it took a lot to kneel in front of Garvey. He had a roll of grey duct tape that he used on Garvey's ankles and wrists, not to bind them, but to seal them up.

When he was done, Garvey wrapped him in the same manner and then to the private's shock, Garvey held out the gun. "You need to practice. That last one was pathetic."

"I-I-I'd p-prefer not to," the private said.

"You told me you had a mom," Garvey said, thrusting the .38 into the private's hand. "You told me you had a mom and that you loved her and would do anything to protect her. Was that a lie?"

Confused by the question, the private shook his head and then nodded, quickly. "It wasn't a lie. I-I-I just can't do this. These people weren't hurting anyone. Th-they're innocent."

The .38 was a small gun, and when they used it on one of *them*, it usually put a single hole in the skull without blasting through and making a diseased mess everywhere. Sergeant Garvey's 9 mm Beretta seemed much larger as he pointed it at the private's stomach. "Do you know what the penalty is for disobeying an order during wartime?" he asked.

The private shook his head, his eyes looking like glass marbles behind the lenses of his rubber goggles.

"Let this be a hint," Garvey said, showing him the Beretta. In truth, summary executions hadn't been carried out by the US Army against one of their own since the Civil War. So far that day, Garvey had killed twelve soldiers and thirty-seven civilians, all without a trial. He wouldn't kill the private, however. The Beretta was only a threat. Killing the boy would be murder and so far, Garvey hadn't murdered any *person*.

Once someone became infected, they were no longer a human being. They became something else.

No, if the boy couldn't do the job, he'd be sent to the front lines, where the possibility of getting killed was ten times as likely, and that was a shame.

"Tell me right now," Garvey said. "Are you going to be a standup guy, or what?" Reluctantly, the private nodded.

Garvey gave his shoulder a manly squeeze. "Good, good. Okay, you have four of them to do. Don't fuck around. One slug in the back of the head. Shoot 'em and move on to the next. If a shot's not clean, take a second, but don't waste the ammo. Make your shots count."

The private didn't reply, he only stood staring at the pistol in his gloved hands. "I need a yes or no, here," Garvey demanded. "Can you do this?"

"Yeah."

That was all Garvey needed. He took the boy by the arm and marched him out into the grey, wet evening. The sound of the rain on his plastic hood was very loud. Still, he could hear both the sound of battle four blocks to the north of them and the screaming across the street at the elementary school, which was festooned with yellow police tape and placards with the skull and crossbones, the universal sign for poison.

The screaming came from a young woman who was probably just barely old enough to buy a drink. Along with fourteen others, she was being offloaded from the back of a five-ton. Soldiers lined them up against a wall and went through a light check.

A couple of them were obviously infected, their eyes very dark, but the girl and two others seemed normal enough. Garvey paused and watched as the flashlights were beamed into their eyes—they all flinched. He cursed under his breath and strode to the door to the gym and hammered on it.

"It's Sergeant Garvey. It's time." It was the top of the hour, killing time. The door was opened by a man in ancient MOPP gear, the sort that hadn't been used since the eighties. His protective outfit was puffy and faded almost to grey, except the arms of it, which were a pale, near white color from the bleach.

The gym had been cordoned off with sheets into a hundred little cubicles, forty of which were empty save for the smell—once again bleach. With his mask on, Garvey couldn't smell the bleach, but even just imagining it sent a spike into his head.

The headache wasn't new. It had been coming on for a while now and was the reason he was insisting that the private learn to stomach the killings. Garvey had a squirmy fear in him that it wouldn't be long before someone would have to put a bullet in his brain, and when that happened he didn't want whoever was doing the killing to screw it up.

He marched past the empty, bleach-smelling cubicles to the first that held a live creature. Normally, when presented with both a flashlight and a gun, they feared the beam more than the gun. This *thing* proved true to form. It turned and tried to push the light away with a hand.

"What was your mother's maiden name?" Garvey asked it.

"M-My mother's maiden name?" it repeated. Garvey did not answer. The advanced photosensitivity, which had been suggested by Dr. Lee as a diagnostic tool, had come through. This was definitely a thing. That really hadn't been in question, but the uppity-ups had demanded a three-check process: on the line, off the truck and just before termination.

The question concerning the maiden name had only been a distraction. The private should have used that moment to fire the pistol. It had been the perfect set-up: the thing had been turned away and was too worried about trying to answer the question correctly to care about the little pistol in the private's hand.

259

However, he did not shoot. He had seen Garvey do this enough to have known what to do. Garvey grabbed him and pulled him closer, hissing, "Do it!"

The thing turned its black eyes into the light. The hate radiating from them was obvious now. It should have been enough for the private.

"It's you or him," Garvey said, holding the Beretta high enough so that it couldn't be missed. The private choked back a sob.

"Don't do it," the thing growled, trying to sit up. Its shackled hands like claws were stretched out at the private. There was so little of the man left within the monster that Garvey had no idea what more the private needed in order to pull the trigger. The .38 came up, but the hand that held it shook. The barrel twitched all over the place. Its black bore seeming to hypnotize the thing with the black eyes. It watched it, matching the twitch.

Garvey knew what was going to happen even before the private finally pulled the trigger. The hand jerked the shot, the barrel rose and the bullet plowed a divot across the top of the thing's head. It fell back with a scream of rage.

"Plug it again, you idiot!" Garvey raged, as the private only stood there, his eyes huge behind the goggled lenses.

The private fired twice more. The first poked a bloodless hole in the thing's cheek beneath its left eye, the second went through the eye itself, shutting it forever. It crumpled back, its black-gummed mouth gaping open.

"Okay, that wasn't bad for a first ti…" Garvey began, however just then the private started to gag violently, working the contents of his stomach up the back of his throat. He was about to puke and reached for his mask. "No! Get outside!"

He didn't make it, but it was close. Twenty feet from the doors he lifted the mask slightly and vomited over and over. He left a trail all the way out the door. "Asshole," Garvey muttered. The private was going to get off easy. He would end up in quarantine for eight hours, while Garvey would have to keep up the killings, unless the headache got worse and it already was.

Sitting on the hardwood floor, still hot to the touch, was the .38. He picked it up and checked the load. Three shots left. He would have to be perfect. The next cubicle held a woman with wild eyes and tattoos up the sides of her throat—Chinese characters. She was the kind of girl Garvey would have humped and dumped the week before.

"Please, don't," she whispered. "I didn't do anything wrong."

"I'm just checking your eyes again," Garvey said. "The other guy next door was infected and dangerous. I'm pretty sure you're okay." He flicked the flashlight on and felt a quick stab of pain. "Oh, shit," he whispered to himself.

The woman didn't hear. She was straining to keep her eyes open and fixed, staring straight ahead. Reluctantly, Garvey shined the light more fully into her face.

She started to shake, her mouth pulled into a grimace. She was panting with the effort to appear normal. She was one of them. "What's your mother's maiden name?" he asked her.

"Ringwald," she answered quickly. After what she had heard from the next cubicle, she was ready with the answer. "Like Molly Ringwald, but her name was Beth. Why?"

"I don't know," Garvey answered, suddenly completely undone. His head was thumping and the light felt like shards of glass in his eyes. He could no longer deny it, he and this woman were the same. They were both demons now and they both deserved the death that was coming to them. He could picture his body being thrown on the funeral pyre next to hers.

"My mom's last name was Jensen, but I don't think it matters anymore." He flicked off the light and put the pistol in the pocket of his yellow slicker. With a long sigh, he pulled off the protective mask.

The woman stared at his face in wonder. "You're a man? I couldn't tell. I couldn't tell what, or…or who, or… wait, does this mean you're not going to kill me?"

"I don't think so," he told her. "I think I just want to sit for a while and not think about any of this. Do you mind if I sit with you?"

The fear faded from her dark eyes and what replaced it was an image of the disease. She was sick and would turn into a demon soon. He would kill her before she became dangerous, but for now he just wanted a few minutes of peace and she did as well. When he put out a hand, she took it, and together, they sat in the darkened gymnasium listening to the rattle of battle and, every once in a while, the thrum of jets. Their last minutes weren't perfect, but they weren't alone, and they weren't afraid.

Chapter 20

1– 6:13 p.m.
—Webster, Massachusetts

Here it was two hours later and Courtney Shaw was still picking glass out of her hair and clothing. The Corvette's window had disintegrated, covering her in tiny cubes and flakes and shards of glass. She had screamed as she was pulled out of the car and had begged for mercy as she was thrust to her knees in front of a thousand battle weary soldiers.

In her spotless pantsuit and with her clean hair spun up in a perfectly tight bun, Courtney seemed completely out of place, and no one knew what to think of her or the sudden anger from the generals.

General Platnik was outraged that Axelrod was choosing that moment to conduct an execution. It wasn't just insulting, Platnik assumed that Axelrod was trying to undermine him as he transitioned from enemy to leader of the Massachusetts National Guard.

In a god-like voice that rang over the battlefield, Platnik had ordered Courtney's release, but General Axelrod, furious at having been betrayed by her, refused. He stood, one hand on his service pistol, his bald head gleaming even as the sun started to dip in the west.

Guns, which had been pointed down or slung on shoulders, were suddenly pointing everywhere. A minute before, the Civil War had ended, but it seemed about ready to flare up again when one of the weary citizen-soldiers who had taken up his rifle to defend his state came forward, cursing.

"What the fuck?" he asked, part in fury, part in pure amazement over what he was seeing. "What the holy fuck do you guys think you're doing?" His name was Andy Liebling and he had been fighting the zombies for so many hours that when guns were turned on him, they didn't scare him in the least.

Despite having absolutely zero rank, Andy went right up the lieutenant colonel, shoved his gun away and stood, shielding Courtney. "I don't care what she did, this is not happening." He refused to move no matter who screamed at him. Others joined him in protecting her and gradually, Axelrod's temper subsided.

"Arrest her then," he said to the lieutenant colonel. "She'll get what's coming to her. Chances are she'll get eaten alive in jail." He knew in his heart that she had fucked them.

Her hands were cuffed in front of her and she was led away under guard to a little hill overlooking the border. No one talked to her and no one looked at her. For the next two hours, she watched the largest foot race in history. The zombies were coming and anyone who didn't get through the lines in time would be turned away.

What was left of the 101st, jogging in company-sized formations, came through first. After so much heavy fighting, they were hoping for some sort of a break, only Platnik didn't trust the nervous-looking militiamen and he had them take up front line positions.

After them came the masses of civilians. There were over a million of them and there was no way to tell if any of them were infected and there was no time to find out. In a tremendous mob that stretched across both north and south bound lanes of I-395, the median between, both shoulders, and the forest for a mile on either side, they surged forward, running, jogging, and limping at their fastest possible speed. They ran like the very dead were after them.

Dr. Lee's idea of using lights to spot early cases of the disease was put into place about an hour into the influx. Someone set up spotlights at head height and beamed them into the crowd. They were sharply bright, and the people were warned to stare straight ahead and not to grimace or close their eyes. A few people were pulled out of line. They were tested again and some returned, while others were dragged out into the forest and shot.

Behind the civilians came the rear guard, a stout group of a thousand or so men and women, who had put their lives on the line so the rest could escape. They were hard pressed and Courtney could see the flashes of battle through the distant trees. Their leader broke off and ran up the empty highway to where ditches were dug deep and the mounds of earth and rock resembled battlements with barbed wire strung out in triple lines.

"Clear a way for us to get in!" he screamed.

The men on the walls would not look at the man and they pretended not to have heard. Five minutes earlier, there had been yet another loud argument between the generals. Like titans they had nearly come to blows over the fate of the rear guard.

General Axelrod steadfastly refused to allow them through the lines, saying that the possibility of them being infected was too great.

General Platnik, although he claimed to be in charge and had the rank to make that claim, was in a weak position with tensions running sky high between the two armies. He was forced to tell the desperate man that he and his men would have to "make a run for it."

"Pardon my French, sir," the officer, a filthy, exhausted major said, "but where the fuck should we run to exactly?"

Normally, Platnik would have torn into the man for having the temerity to talk to him in such a manner, but this was a special case. "For now, go southwest on Route 197 and then south on Route 171. The recon photos show the way is pretty clear for about ten miles. After that, I'll let you know. I'm going to try to set you up with some transport to a place called Block Island, it's right off the coast." Platnik guessed the chances of them making it all the way across the state of Connecticut to be about one in ten, and the chance of getting a ride even less than that.

But he had to give his men hope.

It was all he could give them.

The major hurried back to his men and soon the sound of battle dwindled to nothing as the rear guard ran away.

Most of the men on the wall wished they could run as well. The rumors were that in about thirty minutes the wall would likely be the most dangerous place on the planet. According to the recon photos, there was a veritable typhoon of zombies making their way from the massacre at Woonsocket.

In the CP, Platnik and Axelrod stared at the photos in silence. They looked up briefly into each other's eyes, saw the fear there and then looked away again.

"What's the estimate?" Platnik asked his S2.

"Two and a half million," the intelligence officer replied in a dry, soft voice, as if he were a doctor and he was telling Platnik that he had terminal cancer. "Maybe more, maybe less, but not much less."

"It could be worse," Platnik said. The fact was that he counted himself lucky. To Milt Platnik, it was obvious why General Axelrod had resisted as strenuously as he had: he had been hoping that the coming zombie horde would dash itself to pieces on the 101st and its one million refugees. He had been hoping to use their deaths as a buffer to save Massachusetts.

It would have been temporary, at best. The undead had not been appeased or sated in any way after tearing through the trapped civilians just south of Woonsocket. The people there had fought and died in a heroic last stand that had done little to slow down the hellish army.

The Massachusetts border guard just north of the doomed city, having fought off the civilians in a cruel, selfish, and absolutely necessary battle, were almost out of ammunition and could not have been able to stop the horde had it not been for an engineering student named Autumn Dempsey.

With people already fleeing around her, Autumn stood over a map, not looking for a place to run to for safety; no, if the border fell, there would be no safety anywhere. That was just a fact. She was looking at the watershed around Woonsocket, which was dominated by the Blackstone River.

Most people would have thought "dominated" to be a strange word to use in conjunction with the Blackstone River. It was little more than a deep stream with an average width of only twenty-five feet. But if one could take a step back and see how the Blackstone had looked historically, then the word made more sense.

Autumn saw that the Blackstone of the present would never stop so many zombies, however the Blackstone of a hundred years ago could. What was more, she saw how she could make the past into a present-day reality. Frantically, she ran to the command post, where a private standing guard outside the tent held up a hand. "You're going need to stop. No one gets in without permission."

Under one arm was the rolled-up map. "This is my permission," she said, tapping it and marching right past the soldier before he could even think to stop her. There were three men and three women in the tent discussing how they were going to retreat, and to where, and what sort of chance they had of making it.

"You're not going to retreat," she told them, walking brazenly into their midst and laying down the map. She was a bit of a pixie, barely five feet tall and weighing a hundred pounds soaking wet. She was used to tall people gazing down at her as the six of them were. "You're going to blow up these three dams and you're going to turn the Blackstone into the Mississippi." She pointed out the millions of gallons of water being held back by the dams. "It shouldn't be that hard."

The colonel in charge of that particular section of the defensive line ignored his own chain of command and called the Air Force, the same Air Force that had been making bombing runs against his men.

The dams were demolished each in turn. The first two were blasted into rubble by four F-15 Strike Eagles, each carrying a 5,000 pound GBU-28s. The guided bunker busters could penetrate twenty feet of reinforced concrete. Two bombs per dam was a bit of overkill, but nothing compared to what took out the larger of the three dams.

Forty-five minutes after the F-15s roared by, shaking the earth with their engines and their bombs, a B-2 bomber streaked overhead at fifteen thousand feet. Four minutes earlier it had released a 30,000 pound GBU-57A, what was affectionately called *Big Blu*.

Big Blu was the largest non-nuclear ordinance in the Air Force inventory. When it took out the Harris Pond dam, turning it into just so much dust, the tremor created by the explosion could be felt twelve miles away and the black cloud that loomed hundreds of feet in the air over the hole in the earth where the dam had been, looked so much like a nuclear mushroom cloud that a new panic swept the war-torn state.

As Autumn predicted, the Blackstone flooded its banks, becoming a raging torrent that turned aside the zombie army, giving the people of Massachusetts a much needed breather. It was a short lived reprieve. The zombies went west, heading back the way they had come, drawn by the sound of the battle between the 101st and the Massachusetts National Guard.

From her vantage on the hill, Courtney Shaw could see them coming. At first, it looked like a far off grey haze was slowly creeping across the landscape. Then, as they got closer, it looked like a wriggling mass of insects. At half a mile, there was no mistaking the horde climbing over each other to get at the soldiers and civilians. The sight of them made her want to run.

"Hey, weren't they going to find me a jail?" she asked the guard. He was watching the undead carpeting the earth with a slack jaw. "I think they talked about Boston, or maybe the Philippines, ha-ha."

"Shut up," he said, without looking in her direction.

Her hands were beginning to shake, making the metal cuffs clink. She didn't notice. She was too preoccupied with the horde. There were so many of them that many of the smaller trees were simply disappearing beneath them. Somehow, the trees were being engulfed.

"I-I think we should get out of here. I-I mean, you should lock me up far away or uncuff me. At least uncuff me."

The two soldiers turned long enough from the mesmerizing image to glare at her. There was hate in their eyes. For some reason they blamed her for this. She opened her mouth, but whether she was going to profess her innocence, or apologize, she really didn't know, and she wasn't given the chance.

One of the soldiers grabbed her by the collar of the black suit jacket she wore and threw her down to her knees. "Shut the fuck up," he snarled into her ear. "No one cares about you or what you want."

"I bet the general has forgotten all about her," the other said, with a quick look around and his hand on the butt of his pistol. "And no one cares, like you said."

Courtney looked at each soldier in turn and saw that they were on the brink of killing her. She held up her cuffed hands, pleading with them this time: "Don't. Just don't. I'm not worth a bullet. I can't hurt anyone."

The soldiers locked eyes again and the first shrugged. "We could just chain her hands around the tree. You heard what Axelrod said: chances are she'll be eaten alive. I think it would be justice if we chai…"

A roar from the east startled the three of them as a flight of F-18 Super Hornets whipped by. The roar was followed by a rippling explosion. Fire and smoke obliterated the view. More jets screeched overhead. The soldiers tracked the grey streaks and had their breath stolen when more explosions shook the air.

Far higher flew a string of monstrous birds with tremendous wingspans and belly-loads of bombs, and those bellies were massive. When they opened up and the wind howled and the automated belts began to trundle the thousand-pound bombs forward, the two soldiers gaped. The altitude fuses set the bombs off a hundred feet above the ground to maximize the destruction. Each exploded above the zombies like a small supernova, shocking the senses.

269

The dullest among the people on the wall could only stare, dumbfounded as a searing light struck them like a physical force and even from a quarter of a mile away, the heat from the bombs washed over the soldiers. That inferno was carried on a crazy, chaotic wind from hell. It stank of death and sulphur. The two soldiers on the hill, along with almost everyone else, cowered before it.

"Holy shit!" one of the soldiers cried, covering his face and pushing his hands over his ears. His head rang from the concussive explosions that went on and on. Seven hundred of the huge bombs were dropped, enough to transform the highway and the green forest surrounding it into a nightmare of fire and black clouds and boiling black blood.

Then the ten B-52 Stratofortresses rumbled away, heading west toward the setting sun, unheard by anyone on the ground. The people, and for just a minute or so, they were only simple people, not captains or soldiers or ex-mechanics or any of that, stood, curious to see if the world had changed.

Their ears rang and many felt their insides shake involuntarily. Some grinned oddly, unable to think properly, stunned by the fantastic power that had fallen from the heavens. And some of the soldiers cheered, some stood gazing at the smoke and the flames, laughing foolishly, others thanked God in loud voices thinking that, just like in the movies, the cavalry had arrived to save the day and that the explosions were only the start, and that the war was basically over.

Then the smoke and the dust began to clear and the true extent of the damage was seen. "Holy shit," one soldier kept repeating. The destruction had been cataclysmic. In the span of two minutes, everything had changed. The highway was gone; its signs were gone; its guard rails were gone; the stripe down the middle was gone. There were only craters and charred body parts. The same was true of the forest. It had morphed. Gone were the thick and lushly green trees. In their place were thousands of spindly trunks, their branches either blasted away or burning, filling the air with ash.

"Holy shit," the soldier said, for a third time. He wasn't the only one in awe. Many people uttered those same words. The only ones unimpressed by the destruction were the zombies. Tens of thousands had been killed. The rest, an uncountable hungry, yearning mass stumbled over burning bodies as if the bombing had never happened.

The grey wave came on and on. The smiles on the soldiers' faces, and the cheering, and all the rest faded away.

On the hill, one soldier said to the other, "We should chain her properly and get down there. They're going to need us."

"They're going to need more than…what the fuck?" The two soldiers had turned only to find that Courtney had decided not to stay and get chained to a tree with an unstoppable zombie army bearing down on them. The moment that first Super Hornet had shot past, she had made a run for it.

With her hands cuffed in front of her, she had raced down the back side of the hill and through a short stand of trees. Then the B-52s started dropping their loads and the ground rippled. She was thrown from her feet, only to jump up again a second later. She ran and wasn't the only one. Many were running and they were all faster than Courtney, who not only had her hands cuffed, but was also trying to go cross-country at a sprint in fancy dress shoes.

Certain that she would break an ankle, she forced herself to slow down just as she came to a road. It was the same one that looped around the city of Webster. "I can go right into town or left into nowhere." The road to the left went west. She could lose herself in the west. "West, then north," she amended, remembering her Canadian plan.

In her mind, she saw herself, tired and faintly dirty, crossing into Canada, and being greeted by friendly Mounties. The imaginary Courtney did not have handcuffs on; the real one did. She wouldn't get far in them and she wouldn't get far on foot. Reluctantly, she turned to the right as the last of the bombs went off. By then her mind had adapted to the noise and instead of terrifying her as the first few had, it was more like background thunder during a rainstorm.

"I need a cruiser," she said, for what felt like the tenth time that day. Even before she got into Webster, which was a scarce half mile away, she knew there'd be no chance of finding an abandoned cruiser or any car for that matter. The same was true of scooters, bikes, mopeds or any form of wheeled transportation.

She arrived to find that she had been correct; all the vehicles had been taken. All the beds had been taken as well, and all the food and water. There was barely any room to walk in the town. Two hours before it had been a ghost town and now there were people everywhere. Everywhere. Everywhere. They were lying flat out on the front yards of homes or curled in balls sleeping in the bushes. Tens of thousands sat on porches and thousands more occupied the swings in playgrounds. There were so many on the curbs lining the streets that they reminded Courtney of an infinite number of magpies with dirty feet.

In a way, Webster was similar to New Orleans after the flood, only instead of water sitting in stagnant pools, it was people, everywhere. Courtney went through them, fear running high within her. Although the people looked exhausted, she knew they could turn dangerous in a second. The thought was vindicated a moment later when a huge sound erupted ahead of her.

It was a unified scream of terror, as if an entire stadium filled with people screamed at once. The flurry of gunshots which followed the sound was weak in comparison.

"Y'all better git outta the way," a voice spoke into her ear.

"Huh?" she asked, her mind very confused. The words the man had spoken had run together in such a thick accent that she was still trying to unravel their meaning, while in that same fraction of a second, she realized that she knew that voice. There couldn't be more than two people in all of Massachusetts who had that hillbilly twang particular to Izard County, Arkansas. It was John Burke, looking, if it were possible, skinnier, dirtier and seedier than ever.

Despite his wasted appearance, he took her by the arm with a grip of iron and pulled her out of the street as a new scream erupted. This one was louder and closer. It rolled at them and as it did, a horrible wave of humanity rolled along with it.

Twenty thousand people were simply running and screaming. Maybe they knew why, maybe not. The people around Courtney and John certainly didn't know why. They just upped and ran.

John pulled Courtney to an elm with a dual trunk, put his back to it, and held her against his chest as the river of people flowed past. John stank of three-day old sweat. It was bitter in her nostrils, but not completely so. There was also a minty aroma to him that was a puzzle to her until he turned his head and spat a stream of brown fluid, hitting a young boy as he ran past.

Although Courtney grimaced, she said nothing and, in truth, felt nothing. A normal reaction would have been disgust, however the time for "normal" was long gone. She had seen too much to be overly bothered by a little Wintergreen Skoal spittle, especially since John had kept her from being trampled to death.

"So, what sorts a trouble y'all been gettin' into?" he asked. He grabbed the cuffs and gave them a little shake.

"The usual," she answered.

He laughed in disbelief at her curt answer. Her fancy clothes and the way she was dolled up told him that she was up to something that he wanted to be a part of. Probably escaping. The handcuffs told him she had screwed up somewhere and that was alright with him. She needed his help.

"Iffin' you come clean, I'll get y'all outta them cuffs."

She had given him the abbreviated answer more out of weariness than as an attempt at dodging the question. "Okay, sure. I was trying to get the Massachusetts National

Guard to surrender before the zombies killed us all. It worked, too."

"And the cuffs?"

"I guess not everyone was happy about it," she answered. Actually, it seemed as though nobody was happy. The wave of stampeding people had petered out and everyone went back to their places. Some fell asleep in seconds. One young woman, only steps away from Courtney, had fled her home in Newtown, Connecticut the day before. She had walked eighty miles in the last thirty hours. Her blisters had blisters and she was bleeding through two pairs of socks. She wasn't going any further; somewhere along the way she had lost the will.

John took a long time to consider not just Courtney's words, but also Courtney herself. He was a little surprised she had made it this far. She had seemed soft to him. A good communicator, sure, but not a good fighter or survivor. "What about Dr. Lee? You seen her?"

"Still trapped in the Zone." She lifted her wrists. "Well? You promised."

"Yeah, I guess I did."

He gave a quick look around, not at the people, but at the houses. They were "yuppie" houses and John had to spit out more Skoal juice just looking at them. "Rich fucks," he mumbled. Yuppies were infamous in John's mind for being useless fucks. Still, they had nice tools. He started towards the nearest, knowing that every house on the block would have all sorts of tools. They'd be Craftsman from Sears and they'd look practically brand new, even if they were years old.

He just knew that, for the most part, the hammers hadn't been used for much other than to hang a few pictures on the walls and the screwdrivers' only function was to open the battery compartment on the TV remote.

The first house he came to was a human hive with people crowded in everywhere, even lying on the floor. He had to step carefully to keep from tripping on any. It wasn't easy. The night had not yet come and the sun was still up, and yet there was so much ash and smoke in the air that it seemed later than it was. The bombs had started a hundred fires that burned out of control.

It made everything dark, especially the two-car garage. There were people here as well. Although most were lolling in a stupor, four men were scrounging, looking for food or weapons. They gave John hard looks as he shouldered them aside to pick over the tools. One of them started to get riled. John told him, "You betta' git, 'fore I make you cry like a pussy." John wasn't the biggest of men, but he had a mean streak in him. It showed in his eyes.

They backed away. John spat a brown wad at their feet before turning to the tools. He chose a claw hammer and a hacksaw. He then smiled at the group that he had singlehandedly intimidated, showing the tobacco in his yellow teeth. "It's all yours, ladies."

Courtney followed John out of the house, thinking that although John was clearly unsuited for the real world, with its rules and its insistence on personal hygiene, he seemed ready-made for a world where zombies roamed the land and where only the fittest or the smartest or the meanest survived. Courtney didn't think she was any of these. The best she could say about herself was that she was a pretty good liar, something that would have offended her the week before.

"Aw-right," John said, as they came back out into the gloomed-over evening and went back to the elm. "Let's see dem chains." He had the hacksaw in his hands.

"I thought you were going to pick the lock," Courtney said, pulling her wrists back.

"Y'all thought wrong," was all he said.

With no other choice, she laid her hands out on a low branch and he commenced to saw. Back and forth the saw went in a blur. John coughed and sweated and cursed through fifteen minutes of sawing before the blade cut through the short chain.

"Now, y'all got matchin' bracelets." He chuckled, coughed some more and then asked, "Soooo, now what? You gotta plan?"

She didn't. Or rather her original Canadian plan was out the window. She wasn't going to walk to Canada and she wasn't going to remain a part of this huddled mass of humanity. They were calm now, too tired to be aggressive, but what would happen in the morning when they were hungry and thirsty? What would happen if there were infected individuals among them?

There was danger in Webster and she knew for sure that the army was making plans to deal with it. So, where did that leave her? She couldn't run and she couldn't stay with the herd, and she was wanted by at least half the soldiers defending the line.

But what about the other half? She had saved the 101st, shouldn't that merit getting her something? The honest answer was no. In the middle of battle, it would get her a pat on the head and a boot in the ass. If she wanted the army's protection, she needed to be an asset to them. She needed them to *want* to keep her alive.

Her one skill: *Advanced Lying* wouldn't cut it. "Maybe I don't have to lie," she said to herself. She had at least one very valuable truth on her side. She knew who had the cure.

"Let's go," she said to John and then shocked him as she set off towards the sound of battle.

"Hey, slow down. I think y'alls goin' the wrong way."

Courtney kept marching, her new bracelets jingling. "No. As long as the line holds, the safest place to be is with the army. They need us. They need our knowledge of the Com-cells and where Dr. Lee is." John walked next to her, shaking his head in disbelief. Finally, she said, "We have the cure, John. Dr. Lee can make one. That's got to be worth a helicopter ride somewhere safe, don't you think?"

"That's the least they could do, iffin you ask me." He started dreaming of a soft bed and a belly full of food, but then the image of his daughter, Jaimee Lynn cut through all of that and he told himself that, one way or the other, this was the right direction. Jaimee Lynn was somewhere in Connecticut and she was likely still alive since she was mostly immune to the disease.

That had to be worth something to the army, he thought to himself. *And he was all the way immune and that had to be worth even more.*

With much more determination, he marched to the southern edge of town where the sound of fighting took on a magnified quality so that the air fairly hummed and vibrated.

General Platnik's command post was much closer to the border than Axelrod's had been. He was set up in a bakery that had a fine view of the battle. Not that anyone had a moment to spare to look up.

He was running a skeleton crew, having sent everyone who wasn't absolutely essential to the front lines. That included the usual MPs attached to divisional HQs. The situation was too desperate and his need for live bodies on the line was too great.

Platnik didn't think he would miss them and then in breezed the woman who General Axelrod had ordered to be executed. With her was some scraggily piece of trash with a hammer tucked into a belt loop. They paused in confusion when the bell above the door let out its merry sound.

"I don't have time for this," he told her, before she could introduce herself. He pointed to his S2. "Get them out of here."

The intelligence officer was a big man, but he wasn't going to use his fists, not when he had his pistol. He pulled it and pointed it, his finger within the guard. He wasn't playing around. "Turn and leave, or I will shoot."

"Wait!" Courtney said, putting a hand out to both the S2 and General Platnik. "You need us."

"Yes, I need you to get out," Platnik said. "We're busy." He had just inherited a force ten times the size of the 101st, spread out over nearly two hundred miles. He was currently running three different battles. He had Axelrod running six others, all on the west side of the state. None were more important than the one taking place a quarter mile away. It was epic and nothing this lady could say could take precedence over it.

"I have the cure!" she practically screamed.

Other than that, Platnik thought. "How? Who are you?"

So much for not lying. "My name is Courtney Shaw. I, uh, worked with R&K Pharmaceuticals at the Walton facility. It is where the disease broke out to begin with. We were developing a cure for cancer, only it was sabotaged…"

"Oh, shut up," someone snapped. All heads turned to see a major advancing around the bakery's counter. Courtney recognized him immediately. He had been the same major who had tried to keep Courtney from seeing General Axelrod back in the bowling alley.

For once, Courtney was speechless, her lies lodged in her throat. She hadn't expected to see one of the officers from the Massachusetts guard in Platnik's command post.

"She's no researcher," the major said, walking right up to her. "She's a liar. She told General Axelrod that she was with Governor Clarren's office, but that wasn't true. They never heard of her. She also lied about being on the front lines with General Collins and she lied about having connections with the FBI and about being in Hartford yesterday."

"It's true," another officer said. "She was spinning bullshit."

Platnik had a hundred balls in the air and really didn't need this—but a cure! "Tell me about this cure and make it quick. You say you have it? Where?"

"Back in Walton," she answered. "The cure is back in the hospital. I need a helicopter just for a few hours. We need to pick…"

"No," he said, suddenly. "I can't help you. I don't have a single helicopter left and if I did, I don't have any fuel. And besides, Walton burned down. There's no cure there. Now get out or I will have you arrested."

Courtney wanted to argue her case some more. How could he throw away a chance at a cure? How could he listen to men who had been his enemies only a few hours before? It didn't make sense that…

The major broke in on her thoughts saying, "She should be arrested right now. General Axelrod had her detained, under guard. This guy must have helped her escape."

John Burke had heard enough. In this new apocalyptic world, "detained" was the short time between being arrested and being shot in the back of the head. He grabbed Courtney's hand and ran from the bakery. The highway was to the right and the woods to the left. He chose the left, while she chose an altogether different route.

Courtney ran straight for the parking lot where there were three Humvees, two Volvos and a racy red Corvette.

"Good idear," John said, heading for one of the Humvees. She raced for the Corvette. "Don't be stupid," he hissed. "That ain't prolly got no keys in it."

She was betting her life that it did. The Corvette had been backed into the parking space with exact precision; only a military man would do that. And she knew that in war time situations soldiers left the keys in the cars so there wouldn't be any confusion searching for them in the event of an emergency.

This was definitely an emergency. Two officers were running at them from the bakery, both holding pistols. "Get in!" she shouted, jumping in and reaching for the ignition. The keys were right there, as was the police scanner, which was the real reason she had wanted the Corvette. She didn't wait for John to shut his door before she peeled out of the parking lot.

Chapter 21

1– 7:28 p.m.
—Hartford, Connecticut

She hadn't wanted to go back to where it all started, all the way back to the lonely hospital. She had wanted to get through the battle and be with everyone else, only the fighting had been too fierce and, in her mind, she was just a little girl, easily hurt, easily broken, easily killed.

In reality, she wasn't easily killed. And if she was ever hurt, she healed quickly. And she wasn't exactly little anymore, either. Unlike her father, Jaimee Lynn Burke had grown in the last couple of days. She had eaten very well. There had been so many soft, fat, mouth breathers who had screamed while she fed that she couldn't remember them all. She just remembered the taste of the blood. She had practically swum in it and she had drunk so much blood that her belly would swell as if she were pregnant.

The idea of being pregnant appealed to the girl. Babies were the tastiest of all and she would happily eat any baby that came from her. The thought made her hungry, then again, she was always, always hungry.

Ever since losing Dr. Lee's scent the night before, Jaimee Lynn had followed the sound of battle and the smell of blood. Her bare feet stepped on rocks and sticks and glass, so that she left a trail of black feet-shaped splotches as she headed north to the Massachusetts border; it was where all the people were.

She couldn't get to them, however.

Although she was far from the big battle at Webster, the border was guarded by deep ditches and rolls of sharp wire. In the sky, brilliant lights floated down on little parachutes, and there were loud planes with fire coming from them.

There were also angry men and women with guns. The smell of their tasty blood was wonderful, however the smell of the guns was not. The guns gave off a rich stink whenever the people shot at the strange, black-eyed monsters that swarmed to kill them. Jaimee didn't like the guns. She knew what they could do to her, still she wasn't exactly afraid of them since she could no longer comprehend fear, at least not as it pertained to herself.

Other than the guns and the wires and the ditches keeping her from feeding, there were also explosions which bothered Jaimee Lynn more than anything. When they went off close by, her mind would go utterly blank and she would be frozen for half a minute or more as her brain "rebooted," and she was able to think once again.

Like a stalking jackal, she had gone up and down the lines, looking for a way past all the violence so that she could feed. At one point, she had almost given in to her hunger and had charged with the rest of the zombies. She would have been mowed down, as they were, but a mortar round had gone off nearby. She was thrown from her feet with what felt like needles etching all along her right side and arm. The pain was nothing, not even a nuisance, but she was wet and that meant bleeding. She had a notion that bleeding was bad. She tried to lift an arm to see the wound, only her arm refused to budge. She tried to sit up and her body just laid there.

For half a minute, she found herself staring up at the night sky as tracers zipped overhead and rock and dirt rained down on her. She had a vague notion of being hit here and there by fragments from nearby blasts, but they barely registered.

Smoke from a grass fire rolled down to cover her and the flames came very close before her brain "clicked" and she was able to feel her feet and toes again. Sitting up, she gazed around in disappointment. The defensive line held firm.

There were pieces and parts of monsters everywhere, and there were more fires and thick smoke sowing confusion among the few hundred that were still alive. Those with working legs got up and went every which way. Jaimee Lynn needed them to head back toward the line of humans and she tried to shove them in that direction, but they were stupid and did not understand.

If she had her pack of feral children with her, she could have figured out something to get at all that wonderful blood, but somewhere along the way she had lost them, only she couldn't remember where. In an attempt to find them, she began retracing her steps, which was a fine plan, except she couldn't remember exactly where she had been.

She found a road and started walking and eventually, she saw a sign for Hartford and that sparked a memory of ambushing a woman. It was a wonderful memory, so wonderful in fact that it was almost like a dream. She remembered that the woman had been so full of blood that it had spurted out of her when Jaimee Lynn had chomped into her throat. It was like biting into a ripe tomato. The memory spurred her on and Jaimee walked like a little naked drunk all the way to Hartford.

She didn't notice her nudity or the layers of old blood caking her body. Her entire focus was on her destination and the hope of finally sating her hunger.

When dawn of the fourth day broke, she walked into the city of Hartford and the hope died in her. The city was alive with flies and rats and crows feasting on the remains of thousands of bodies. There were also packs of dogs roaming around—these shied away from Jaimee. And there were cats that hissed at her. But there was almost nothing else alive. To her, the few zombies still dragging themselves around, didn't count as being alive. Most of the ones that remained were missing at least a leg, but usually it was both legs and an arm, and an eye and a nose.

She walked past them as if they weren't even there.

Jaimee Lynn was halfway through the city, when she heard a scream, high and piercing. Her stomach rumbled and she began scurrying towards the sound. Seconds later, the scream came again, exactly like the first.

"Oh, fer shit's sake," she whispered, repeating something her daddy had said on many occasions. For some reason when she said it, it made her feel strange and wrong. "Fer goodness sake, then," she amended and that seemed okay to say.

It didn't make her much happier about the screams, however. The screams had been too much alike to be from a person. They had been made by a zombie-child, one who was hunting.

There were six of the little beasts. Jaimee Lynn found them trying their best to hide. The scream had been the bait for a trap; they were hoping that some Good Samaritan would come by to investigate the scream, at which point they would jump out and eat him. Their hiding spots, under cars or behind trees, were pathetic.

"This was a stoopid plan," she said, berating them, her hands on her skinny hips. She lined them up so she could appraise them. Three of the six looked as though they had been mauled by bears and were missing huge chunks of themselves. One girl didn't have a belly. She had been eaten clear to her spine.

"Look at y'all. Y'alls all gross an all. Who's gonna wanna rescue you? No one, that's who. I shoulda done the screamin' iffin anyone should." Five of the kid zombies just stood there like lumps, but the sixth pointed a finger at Jaimee Lynn.

"Wut?" Jaimee Lynn asked. In answer, the zombie, a straggly thing in bloody rags of flesh and denim, jabbed its finger a second time at Jaimee Lynn. She looked down at herself and saw the black and red blood that covered her. And she saw there was a piece of wood poking right out of her side as if she had a tree growing inside of her that was trying to get out.

"Huh," she said, pulling the stick out and flinging it aside. "I's scarier than a striped haint. Maybe even look like one, too. Ya know wut? It might could be that screamin' ain't gonna work, no how."

She couldn't imagine anyone wanting to come to the rescue of the seven of them. Then again, as far as she knew, no one had tried. "Maybe they ain't no one around here. Maybe they all runned away." As she stared about her at the city, she decided that it was possibly the ugliest place she had ever been. No one would want to stay here if they could leave.

"We should git, too," she told her new pack. They nodded, except for one that made a glugging sound. Jaimee Lynn ignored it and him. She set them lurching west. A few hours later, they fed on a man in some dinky town she had never heard of. He had been hiding in a laundromat and had been diligent about putting down bleach to keep from being infected. The bleach had also masked his scent and for the last few days he hadn't been bothered by the roaming zombies. Unfortunately, the town's water pump had broken and he could no longer use his toilet. He took to urinating in a bucket he kept in the back alley. The urine was concentrated and pungent; Jaimee Lynn had caught the scent from a block away.

She went right to the alley, saw the bucket and the reinforced steel door and in seconds, a plan hatched in her cunning mind. It was simple, she knocked on the door. "Excuse me?" she said in her best "Yankee" accent. "Hello. My name is Jaimee. I have food...a can of food."

She could smell the man on the other side of the door. She could smell his blood and his fear. Her body tensed in excitement as he hesitated, neither answering nor moving away. He wanted to open the door, Jaimee Lynn knew it. "What's y'alls name?" she asked, forgetting her fake accent in her hunger.

"Casey," he said, through the door. "Is there anyone with you?" She told him that there wasn't and he breathed a sigh of relief. When the door came open, Jaimee Lynn launched herself at Casey Rienhold, a florist with a pockmarked face and nervous little fingers. There was blood in the beds of his nails where he had bitten them down to the quick.

She bit them down to nothing but nubs before she burrowed into his stomach. The others joined in and ate Casey in an orgy of pain. Casey lived for a very long time, but eventually he stopped screaming when what was left of his blood and meat turned cold.

Jaimee Lynn stood and ran the back of a bloody hand across her bloody lips. She was a vile little demon. The old blood of her past victims was crusted and cracking. It had dried black, but now she glistened red with Casey's fresh blood. She fairly shone with it in an unholy way.

"We're done," she said to the other kid zombies, and gave one of them a kick in the ear. He was bigger than her, however she was smarter, more present, and he simply stood, sucking gristle from his teeth, waiting for her to think for him.

At the moment, she really wasn't thinking of much. She was comfortably full, but not in the stuporous way she got when she was full to the gills. When she got that full, the evil contents of her belly would slosh around and when she'd burp, bubbles of blood and little chunks of whatnot would come up her throat. When she got that full, she was seized with a need for sleep.

No, just then she was contentedly full. She didn't need sleep or even to feed, though she wouldn't have been able to stop herself if a tasty morsel walked by. For her the moment was perfect and the only thing that would make it more so was if her daddy were there.

He was about the only thing Jaimee Lynn could remember from the past. She had a mommy, but she was a blur. And she'd been in school, only when she thought about that, all she could picture were delicate little calves and big tasty eyes.

It bothered her that she couldn't remember. It made her think that there was something wrong in her head. Well, she knew there was something wrong with the world, just looking around told her that. And she knew there was something wrong with all the people. What made her nervous was that there might be something wrong with her. She couldn't put a finger on it, but she had the feeling that she had changed in some way.

Her daddy would know what to do, of that she was so certain that she marshaled her little pack and started walking west once more, heading to the last place she had seen him alive: the Walton facility.

Although the President had signed the pardon with his usual flourish and it had been delivered personally by the Attorney General of the United States, who had marched off a marine helicopter in a head-to-toe, blue bio-suit, it wasn't good enough for Anna and Eng.

Anna gave the pardon a long read before asking the Attorney General, "What's to stop them from shooting us in the head when all this is over? They could rip up this piece of paper, take us out back and put two in our heads and burn our bodies and there wouldn't be anything we could do."

"But, we wouldn't do that," the Attorney General replied, trying his best to appear sincere and reassuring from behind the face-plate of the bio-suit.

"I would," Eng said.

Ann nodded in agreement. "Yeah, me too."

"But…but we're the good guys," the Attorney General stammered. "We wouldn't do that." The two terrorists had laughed at this and then issued new demands. They wanted a video tape of the President signing the pardon and they wanted a copy sent to the Chinese, Russian, Iranian, and North Korean embassies. Of course, the copying and the deliveries had to be video-taped, as well.

Special Agent Katherine Pennock had not watched any of this bullshit. She had entrusted PFC Jennifer Jackson with guarding the prisoners, something the soldier was only too happy to do, lugging the M240 over to the barn and sitting behind it with a "please do something stupid so I can blow you back to hell," look on her face.

With that taken care of, Katherine had found a spot deep in the belly of the Blackhawk to sleep. The lulling patter of rain combined with her sheer exhaustion sent her into dreamland in seconds. She slept hard, as if her body knew that a lot more was going to be asked of her.

The pilot of the Blackhawk, Joe Swan woke her. "There's a big shot FBI guy asking about you." Feeling woolly-headed, she sat up and the first thing she could comprehend was that it had become dark out. She told Swan this and he chuckled. "That's what happens when the sun goes bye-bye. Come on, get up."

Still feeling slow, Katherine climbed out of the chopper. The rain helped to clear her head and she was basically fully functioning by the time she made it to the edge of the taped off quarantine zone where John Alexander, Assistant Director for National Security was waiting for her, standing warm and dry under an umbrella.

As he wasn't exactly crowding the tape, she couldn't share the umbrella. "Any sign of infection?" he asked. She shook her head, but he didn't get any closer. "Good, I'm glad to hear it. Look, we're going to be sending you into the Zone. You'll be accompanying the two perps to Walton. The President thinks you can handle it. He mentioned you personally."

Katherine felt a momentary stab of fear in her belly, but then her ballooning ego swept it aside. "The President? That's, that's awesome," she gushed. Yes, she thought he was a man who was far out of his depth, but he was still the *President*. "What size team will I be leading?" Before Alexander could answer, she went on, speaking out loud, "At least twenty agents for security, and another three, no, make that four agents from Cyber Command. I want some people who know their way around computers. If Eng thinks he's going to…"

Alexander held up a hand. "It's going to be just you. Well, not just you. There'll be the pilot and the lady gunner, too. You should be able to handle Anna and Eng."

"What?" Katherine asked, completely baffled. She brought a wet hand up to wipe the rain from her eyes. If she wasn't so cold and miserable, she would have thought she was still dreaming. "Me? And those two? Plus Anna and Eng? Y-You know Swan is a pilot. He hasn't moved ten feet from his chopper, not even to take a leak. He pees on the damned wheels!"

She swung an arm back to indicate the black machine. It looked like some sort of lurking beast. Joe Swan was sitting in the cabin door eating a sandwich. For Katherine, this only made her point for her. But she wasn't done.

"And the girl? Sir, she's just a girl. She's nice and all, but she's not trained for what you're asking of her."

"But you are."

"Damn right I am, but that doesn't make a bit of difference. Is…is the President not taking this seriously?"

Alexander took a deep breath before taking one small step closer to the yellow tape. "He is taking it very seriously, however, he also has his concerns. He's afraid of what you might bring out of the Zone. He's worried that too many people going in might mean there's more of a chance that someone comes out infected. And he's worried that Eng might have something worse hiding in the lab. Some sort of super-infection, I don't know. Let's just say that he's…he's conflicted."

Katherine's eyes flared wide. "He's a chickenshit is what he is." Without realizing it, she had strode forward and now the tape was tight across her breasts. Alexander stepped back, a hand slipping into his coat. Katherine rolled her eyes and said, "Please, don't you start. It's unwarranted aggression that's a symptom of the disease. This? This is very warranted. We are looking at finding a possible cure or a vaccination. Doesn't he understand that? Do any of you?"

"Of course we do. There will be precautions taken. We've had a UAV overhead for some time and the zombie numbers are not bad. They are…they are *manageable*. Your Blackhawk will be fully fueled and fully armed. You and the girl, what's her name? Jackson? You'll both be given whatever weapons you want. You'll all have bio-suits and lights and the whole works."

"What I need are three Blackhawks and thirty agents," Katherine shot back. "I'll take thirty soldiers if I can't get the agents. I'll even settle for twenty-five."

He smiled, sadly. "I'm sorry, but this isn't a negotiation. The President will be watching everything."

She turned from him and gazed past Swan as he munched away on his sandwich. Three people to fight off who knew how many zombies *and* to control two of the most dangerous people she had ever met? It was ridiculous and stupid—and at the same time it was a career move.

"The President will be watching?" she asked, him. "Then I'll need to be taken seriously. I'll be going in as a *Special Agent in Charge*." Alexander opened his mouth, but she put up a finger. "And not on a temporary basis, either."

"That's a jump of four pay grades."

Of course, she knew that. "And that's not open to negotiations, either," she informed him.

He took in a very long breath, as though a ten-minute lecture was about to spew out of his mouth. Eventually, he let it out in one long word, "Fiiine," as if he were talking to a child instead of his newest Special Agent in Charge.

"Good. I'm going to need tactical body armor for the five of us. Something very light weight, that includes arm, elbow, and wrist gear. I need the good masks, not that army crap. Latex gloves, flashlights, radios, and flash-bangs. Also, weaponry… what do you think? Daewoos?"

"Automatic shotguns?" His look was one of disgust. "They'll make a mess. Maybe you should go with M4 and try to be precise."

How precise could she afford to be, she wondered. The hospital was half burnt to the ground. It would be dark and dangerous, and there would be no telling what she would find there. Shotguns were perfect in that environment. "I want the Daewoos."

"I can't guarantee them."

She didn't like the way he had said that. "What can you guarantee?"

He shrugged. "A week in isolation…if you survive."

Chapter 22

1– 8:12 p.m.
—Taconic Hills Central High School

It was dark and quiet in the high school as Ryan Deckard eased the truck past. His foot hovered over the gas, ready to gun it out of there at the first sign of trouble and the early night air practically shimmered with trouble. Next to him, Thuy seemed small and delicate, huddled in a heavy Carhartt duck coat; it was thick, tough and warm, yet she shivered.

If asked, she would readily admit to being afraid. She had been running on luck for so long that common sense and the basic mathematics of statistics told her that it wouldn't last. A coin could only come up heads so many times in a row, and when it hit tails…

"There had been a boy here, earlier," she warned, as she watched for the least movement in the windows of the school. This was their fourth shot at finding a secure field to launch from and it hadn't started auspiciously. Two miles back, they had slipped through a horde four or five thousand strong. They had swarmed the truck and it had been close.

"I killed that kid," Deckard said, wishing he could reach out and touch her leg to reassure her, but he needed both hands on the wheel. "And if there's another kid, I'll kill him, too. Try to relax. One more roll of the dice and we'll be safe."

Another gambling metaphor. Thuy didn't like it. In fact, she hated it. They weren't supposed to need luck. She was smart…no, she was a genius. How was it that a genius was one of the last people still in the Zone? How on earth was it possible that she hadn't been able to think of a way to get them out of there?

For the last few hours, as they waited on Courtney to figure something out from the safe side of the border, Thuy had racked her brains for an idea and had come up with absolutely nothing, or nothing they could possibly use. They didn't have the time or equipment to tunnel under the border. And swimming up the few rivers that flowed through the zone was far too dangerous as they were undoubtedly contaminated with the Com-cells. Tanks, homemade or otherwise, might be able to punch a hole through a road block, but there were deep ditches along the entire border, and in some cases, there were moats to contend with.

This left flight as their only option and since they didn't have access to a plane that left one very poor choice. The truck they were driving in was loaded with silk and wicker and had a colorful decal on the door with the words: *Ray & Pearl's Hot Air Balloon Rides—Open Sundays!* written in a rounded rainbow font beneath.

It was with a feeling of ominous deja vu that they had gone back to Ray and Pearl's. They had stood with the setting sun painting the edges of the barn and the fields golden. For a moment everything seemed peaceful, but then there came long, long shadows, stretched out from the feet of so many zombies. Both of them wanted to turn back, only they didn't have anywhere to turn back to, so they took the smallest of the hot air balloons. It wasn't easy. Deckard worked alone, hauling the new balloon and all the fixings onto the truck and as he did, his heart was racing in fear for Thuy, who had run out of the barn on foot with nothing but a small butane torch to hold off the undead.

There had been so many zombies at the farm; thousands of them. It seemed to her that they were somehow multiplying. It wasn't possible and yet, she had been forced to set a thirty acre field on fire to distract them.

She still smelled like smoke and wished she could roll the window down to air herself out. She couldn't, however. *They* would be able to get at her too easily if she did. In the dark, her shaking hand wasn't obvious, as she picked up the mic and tried to contact Courtney once more. "Dispatch 6, this is Deck 1, please tell us the good news."

Forty miles away, sitting in a church belfry to get better range out of her radio, Courtney Shaw glanced down at her scanner, reluctant to pick it up. She didn't have good news. She might have escaped a jail sentence or a quick and tidy execution, however she was far from safe. The specter of death still loomed, and not just along the southern Massachusetts border where the fight had been raging hour after bloody hour and the smell was enough to make one dizzy and the corpses were piling up in hideous mounds.

Worse than all that, her radio was alight with frantic calls for help within the border itself. The virus was on the move. Flying in the face of the doomsayers, there were only sporadic and short-lived outbreaks of the disease within the now teeming city of Webster. The refugees had put survival over every other consideration. Anyone showing the first hint of the virus was butchered on the spot and their flesh put to the torch, sometimes in a literal sense if combustibles were not available.

The more dangerous outbreaks occurred in the west, where there weren't execution squads or people ready with axes to kill their fellow man if they looked at them cross-eyed.

Out in the western part of the state, the land was forest or farm and was generally empty year round. Most of the people who had lived out there had either fled east in terror two days before, or had gone to the New York border to fight. The line was thinly manned and there wasn't a second one, so when some poor soul wandered away from the fight with a headache building into a migraine and their temper turning violent, there wasn't anyone to notice, let alone to corral them up.

The infected had hidden from the sun in some dusty old root cellar or in a garage beneath the rusting Ford Mustang their son had bought years before with the promise that they would fix it up, but never had. One black-eyed young woman had gone to her trailer home and with nowhere to hide from the hateful light, she had crawled between her mattress and box spring, like a piece of bacon in a BLT.

Sunset seemed to summon these creatures from their holes and now Courtney watched them from her perch as they hunted.

"Dispatch 6, come in, please." Thuy sounded nervous and that in turn made Courtney nervous.

"This is Dispatch 6, over."

"What's the plan, Dispatch 6? We are ready to kick it off at any time."

The church Courtney and John Burke sat in was located in the town of Becket, a nothing of a burg that just happened to be equidistant from Pittsfield, Springfield and the empty fields in the very southwest corner of the state. She was monitoring every battle within two-hundred miles. Her plan was to take advantage of any breakthrough by the zombies and try to slip Thuy and Deckard in before the new lines could solidify.

The problem, if it really was a problem, was that the lines were holding. The men were breaking but the lines were holding and all she had managed to do was put herself smack dab in the middle of zombie central. She could see two of them wandering around on the street below her. There had been others, twenty or thirty.

John was sitting on a little ledge, spitting nasty brown fluid down on the ground between his knees. His clawed hammer was still in the loop of his jeans. In his hand was an aluminum bat; he was tapping the barrel in the palm of his hands. Other than the growing puddle of spit, he hadn't been the least bit productive.

Courtney had to give Thuy an answer, but the best she could come up with was, "Hold in place, Deck 1," she said.

"We can't hold," Thuy answered in a tight whisper. "We're getting low on fuel and ammo. We need to move. We're going to implement plan A. You know, the same plan from yesterday?"

Courtney knew. She would never forget that balloon ride, or the crash. On impulse, she glanced up at the sky, where the rumble of jets was constant. "Listen Deck 1. Can you hear that?" She paused with the radio send button held down. "They're up there all the time." It made no sense, but now she was whispering as well. "They'll see you. They have radar. It won't matter if it's night."

"I understand the mechanics of radar, Dispatch 6," Thuy said. "But we are surrounded. They are everywhere. Is there a way to see if there is a lane through which we might travel? Or to create one since we are at the mercy of the elements?"

"I'll see what I can do. Please stay put until I get back to you. Out." She turned to John, who only shrugged and spat again, using the collar of his shirt to wipe his chin. "You're a great help," she grumbled.

"Wut? Dr. Lee is what supposed to be the genius. Let her think sometin' up. I'm more of a man of action, you know."

Courtney had seen him be both a man of action and a man who could run off when things got too hot. "I'm going to need you. Just in what way, I don't know." She had to think of something. She had to think of something. She had to think of some… "Damn it! This is impossible."

"Nuffin's impossible," John told her.

She ground her teeth to keep from cursing at him. Though in truth, he was right. It was possible to clear a lane in the skies for a balloon. She'd just have to either get or fake proper authority. "And I've done that before." She couldn't do it from the belfry and she sure as hell couldn't do it with the scanner. Its range wasn't good enough.

"If I'm going to do this, I'll need a sat-phone or someplace with a big enough radio transmitter."

"Like a radio station?" John asked.

Courtney was about to roll her eyes, when it struck her that it wasn't a bad idea. A commercial radio station had more than enough power for what she needed. "Let's go." She grabbed the scanner and headed down the narrow stairs, first to the balcony and then to main floor. She hadn't been a religious person before, but she was fast becoming one and sketched a quick sign of the cross while facing the altar.

John did the same, only left handed, since he had the bat in his right. He followed her out to the Corvette and made a noise in his throat as she went to the driver's side. He didn't think it was right that a woman should drive when a man was around, especially when the car was as nice as this one was. Back in the day, he would have given his left nut to own a Corvette.

"How you gonna tune the station?" he asked, when they were both seated.

"Don't know."

"They ain't gonna have no knobs like on a normal radio. It's gonna be all digital and shit."

"Yeah," Courtney answered, worry suddenly coming over her. She sped out of Becket on an easterly course, dodging the zombies, her headlights picking them out easily, now she began to slow.

"You know wut else?" he asked, giving Courtney a sheepish look. "Them digital things, they all get them red lights an all. And you know we ain't got no power. You know, we ain't got no 'lectricty."

Her foot came all the way off the pedal and the Corvette's speed began to drop. John was right. The power had been off for two days now. The only people with any power was the military. "And the government," she reminded herself, an overused plan starting to click within her. "And aren't I with the government?"

"No," John told her.

"We're going to pretend, one more time," she said, flicking on the dome light. It was weak and very yellow, making John look jaundiced. Courtney didn't look much better, which meant they would have to make another stop. She found a little soda-shop, pharmacy combo and walked in, stepping on broken glass. The place had been partially looted, though it was mostly just the food and the schedule 1 narcotics that had been taken.

John was pissed. "Fuckin' junkies. My cancer's eatin' me up and those dumb shits just lookin' to get high. Fuck. Fuck, fuck, fuck. There's sometin' wrong with people. Maybe this whole zombie mess is God's way of clearin' out the riff-raff. What do you think?"

Courtney, who was facing a mirror with a small flashlight clamped between her teeth as she tried to re-tame the wild, bushy creature that sat atop her head, could only shrug.

"Well, I think it is," John said. "This world's got too many useless folks just draggin' ass through life. Not me. You know I used to work two jobs so I could care fer me an' Jaimee Lynn? Yeah, I did. And she appreciated it, too. Jaimee Lynn knew her manners. She was gonna be sometin' I knowed it."

Although she had finished forcing her hair back into its bun, Courtney kept the flashlight between her lips. Jaimee Lynn was possibly the most horrific monster in a world full of monsters. But John didn't know that and there was no sense hurting him with the truth.

John leaned up against the open, and very empty, register staring at Courtney in a tired way. "I knowed it," he whispered again, and then bent to look for better painkillers than the Tylenol he'd been dry swallowing for the last few hours. He found a loaded 12-gauge shotgun instead. "Ha!" With a flourish, he tossed away the hammer, scaring Courtney.

"Sorry 'bout that, but lookit what I found." He showed her the walnut-stocked gun. "Ain't she a beaut? This here is a thousand dollah gun."

"Boys and their guns. Just don't hurt yourself with it."

"Hurt myself?" He seemed outraged at the idea. "I been huntin' since I could walk! Hurt myself? That's the most pre-posterous idear…oh, I see. You's just funnin' with me."

She had been making a little joke, however it was his reaction which was really funny. Even his hair had looked shocked and indignant. She laughed at him and felt better for it. Once more, she was going to put her head in the lion's mouth and the stress of it had built lines of tension all across her body. The laughter was a release she had desperately needed.

"Yeah, I was just funning. Come on." They went back to the car, where she paused for a moment, thinking. "I'm going to be the assistant to the governor and you're going to be a guy I'm using as a bodyguard. Don't do any talking…"

"Can't I be, like an undercover cop? You know, like a narco cop and I saved you from these rampagin' zombies?"

"If anyone asks, sure, but until then zip your lip. The more either of us talks, the more likely we'll blow our cover. We'll tell them the balloon was a, uh, scheme cooked up by the governor to observe the lines."

John climbed into the Corvette and laughed, "That sounds exactly like them gov-mint boys. Ain't none of them got a lick of sense." That mentality was exactly what she was counting on.

From her stint working communications for General Collins and the 42nd, she knew there was an air national guard base in Westfield which was only a few miles away. With the jets taking off and landing every other minute, she didn't need a map to get there.

Her first test came at the gate to the Westfield-Barnes Regional Airport. The checkpoint was quiet and dark, and at first, she thought that it was abandoned, however there was a squad of security police lurking in the shadows. When she told them she was with the governor's office, they demanded identification, something she hadn't given a moment's worth of thought about.

"Identification? Now? With zombies running around *inside* the border?" Her voice had risen as though what they were asking was completely beyond the pale. "Are you serious?"

There was one thing she knew about men, which was that they didn't like it when women got upset or loud. They never failed to ask, "Could you calm down, please?"

It was almost always a mistake. "Calm down? Wow. I'm going to need to talk to your supervisor. Calm down… calm down my ass." A few of the security police cast nervous glances back down the road and just like that, she knew what angle she was going to play. "How's this for calming down?" She laid on the Corvette's horn, blaring it into the night.

"What the hell?" one of the guards cried.

"Stop!" another hissed. "What the fuck do you think you're doing?"

"This bitch is crazy!" whispered a third.

They were all talking at once. Some pointed their guns and some held up their hands, palm out. She took her hand off the horn and leaned her head slightly out the window. "Your supervisor, please."

A captain was called. Courtney didn't bother to introduce herself to the sharp-dressed man in Air Force blues when he arrived. She started right in. "There are zombies inside the border. Did you know that?" He started to answer but she spoke over him. "Of course you did. The governor is alarmed about the situation and he's sent me to try to find out the extent of the problem, what the army plans to do about it, and why he wasn't informed."

The captain's lips had become two tight pink lines as he waited for Courtney to stop. When she finished speaking, he said, "Governor Clarren's office was informed. Everyone was informed. What was your name, again?"

A moment of indecision doomed any chance at a lie. "Courtney Shaw. Unfortunately, I lost my ID when I lost my ride. A few miles back, we were unexpectedly attacked…" John took that moment to clear his throat. Her smile dimmed, but by sheer will she was able to keep it from turning into a grimace. "And this young man was able to save me. I believe he was a police officer."

"Is that right?" the captain asked, with a raised eyebrow.

"Yes, it is right. I'm going to need to talk to your commanding officer and inspect the security arrangements, not just for the base, but for the entire western sector. You have drone coverage, I assume?"

The captain snorted, "Wouldn't that be something someone from the governor's office would know?"

Courtney was momentarily taken back, but she recovered in a blink, saying, "I know there's drone coverage. They're everywhere. I meant: do you have access to the drone coverage?"

"That was a quick recovery," he said, laughing, suddenly. The laugh was out of place and sent a cold wave sweeping down her body. He leaned over and opened her door. "You are such a good liar that if I hadn't known better I might have been fooled. Oh, by the way, we know who you are. So, if you'll follow me we can get this over with."

Just like that, John was disarmed and the two of them were professionally frisked. They were then cuffed and now Courtney had two rings of metal on each wrist. She asked for the one useless pair to be taken off, however the captain thought they made a statement and kept them on.

"We'll take your car," the captain told them. "Or should I say, we'll take General Axelrod's car?"

"Shit," Courtney muttered. "Is he here?"

A shit-eating grin was the only answer she received. She knew that he was there, regardless. It was her sort of luck. With a trail vehicle filled with troops behind them, the captain purred the Corvette through the airport and to a well-lit hanger. He escorted his two prisoners inside to where General Axelrod had set up the western command post. Although there were thirty other officers with him, mostly older men in camouflage. Axelrod stood out mainly because of his gleaming bald head, and because he was the only one who bothered to give them a second look.

The captain presented the two and then stood aside, likely so as not to get anything on his uniform when the general vented his anger, which seemed volcanic and on the verge of exploding.

"I don't understand you at all, Ms. Shaw," Axelrod said. "Do you think the people in the military are buffoons? That we're all idiots? I know many people your age have no concept of duty and honor. They have no idea how soldiers fight to preserve your freedoms day in and day out. I'm guessing you're one of these 'protest without a clue' types. Is that right? Is that why you keep turning up like a bad penny?"

Had it been another day, she would have been intimidated by his bluster, but she had seen too much and faced too much real fear to be afraid of one old man. "No, I deeply respect the military, even when they make mistakes."

He lifted his chin and scratched beneath it with one hand. The way his face jutted and his jowls stretched beneath made him appear lizard-like. "You expect me to believe that? After all your lies, you expect me to believe the most blatant of them all? You expect me to believe anything from a criminal?"

Although she had broken many, many laws in the last few days, she didn't think of herself as a criminal.

"You can call me a criminal if you want, but you'd be the only one," she said, glaring up at him. "If anything, I'm a hero. I saved all those refugees. And I saved the 101st Airborne Division. Me! I did that. And I saved your state, too, by the way. I think you're just starting to see that and you don't know what to think about it."

Axelrod tried to keep up his glare, but he was old and tired. He hadn't had a nap in three days; he missed his bed and his wife. War was a young man's game and he was just too tired to deal with this. Whatever the woman's excuses were didn't matter. She had endangered the lives of five million people by her "heroic" actions, and there would be repercussions.

"Only time will tell if you saved anything at all," he said, his voice turning soft. He sighed. "I was wrong to order your execution without a trial. I rescind that order. But you have broken laws. You'll be held indefinitely while you await trial. Your friend can go."

The captain came forward to unlock the cuffs on John's wrists. The hick from Izard County only stared at

Courtney, waiting for her think of something, but she was only standing there. He needed her to do more. "What about Dr. Lee?" he asked. "Y'all supposed to be hepin' her, remember?"

"I'd forget this Dr. Lee person if I were you," Axelrod said. "No one else is getting across the border, and that's final."

"Does it even matter anymore?" Courtney asked. "Your state is…I wouldn't call it overrun, but I must have seen two hundred zombies driving over here from Becket. There's got to be ten times that many wandering around. How are you going to get them all before they really do take over?"

Axelrod had no fucking idea. His forces were stretched too thin and the outcomes of the battles were too close to even think about trying to put together a state-wide zombie hunt in the middle of the night. Platnik knew the situation and was just as clueless. He had kicked it up to Lieutenant General Phillips, who had hissed into the radio: "No matter what, do not mention this in anything official. *Anything*."

The writing was on the wall and the threat of nukes was still on the table. Axelrod couldn't blame the President. Nothing was going right. "That's no longer any of your concern, Miss."

"What if I told you that Dr. Lee could fix your problem?" Courtney cried, as she was being dragged away. "Remember the lights? Remember how she told you about their photo-sensitivity? She can help you with this, too."

On his own volition, the captain ceased yanking on Courtney's arm. The general pointed at him, but it was a confused, half-hearted gesture. Dr. Lee's advice had been extremely useful. Axelrod had sent the idea up the chain of command and now lights were being used everywhere to ferret out potential zombies before they could become a threat.

"How could she possibly help with this?" he asked. "And even if she could, I can't spare the fuel to go searching for her."

"She has a hot air balloon," Courtney told him, hope flaring up in her. "All she needs is permission to cross into Massachusetts airspace. Please, give her five minutes. If she can help you, then let her come over if not…well, she'll have to figure things out on her own." *Because I'll be in jail*, she thought.

It showed just how screwed they were that Axelrod called for a radio and had Courtney uncuffed. With an audience of thirty, she tuned the radio and asked in as controlled a voice as she could manage: "Deck 1 this is Dispatch 6, over?"

Seconds later, Deckard answered in a low tone. "This is Deck 1. Please, tell me you have some good news because we are in a world of hurt over here. We have them all over the fence and we haven't even started inflating the balloon yet. Thuy says they can smell us so she is cooking up something."

"I need to talk to her, Deckard. It's important."

The way she said: *It's important* had Deckard staring nervously at the mic. There was a finality to the word and all he could think was that Courtney hadn't been able to come through. Deep down where his guts were churning and his heart raced, he really hadn't expected anything else; they had asked her to do something that was, on the face of it, impossible.

He was leaning into the truck, sweating despite the cool night, the M4 across his back wedged against the seat, his mask pulled down, dangling at his neck. "I'll get her," Deckard whispered into the mic. Although the word "important" was still lingering, he didn't rush over to Thuy. She had been hoping for a miracle. She had been counting on it. And now she'd be crushed.

Thuy was crouched in the grass, forty yards away, mixing ammonia and bleach in a bucket. There were eight other buckets arranged in an arc that was very close to becoming a circle. The air shimmered and stank with what she had called chloramine vapor. "Don't breathe it directly in," she had warned, a few minutes earlier.

"No shit," he had replied, with a smile that was phony and a wink that was forced. He had been thinking that skulking around in the dark and trying to hide their scent with a deadly gas was all well and good, but what were they going to do when it came time to light the burner? It would light the night and the zombies would come by the thousands, gas or no gas.

Only now it seemed they wouldn't have to worry about the light. "Thuy!" he hissed, "It's Courtney. It's important."

Behind her mask, Thuy's brows came down. She didn't like the word "important" either, but unlike Deckard, she didn't immediately fear the worst. She guessed, correctly that there would be stipulations or obstacles to their escape plan, otherwise Courtney would have just told Deckard that they would have to think of something else.

"This is Dr. Lee," she stated bluntly, into the radio.

Courtney was momentarily taken aback by the lack of radio procedure, but the pause wasn't a long one. "Um, this is Dispatch 6. We are a go on the plan, with one little change. The military is requesting assistance before they allow you to cross."

"What the hell?" Deckard seethed.

Unruffled, Thuy waved him to be quiet, before saying, "I'm always prepared to help our fine military. What can I do for them?"

"We have an issue on this side of the border," Courtney said. "People are turning, if you understand me, and with the battles going on and the need to man the lines fully, we have a containment issue."

Thuy's mouth fell open. "What are you...what are you saying? Are there zombies inside the border of Massachusetts?"

"Yes. Not a lot. A few hundred. Maybe a thousand at the most. The commanding officer is asking for your help in-in-in, uh taking care of them."

Deckard and Thuy shared an incredulous look. "He wants me to help, militarily?" Thuy asked. "Is that what they need?"

"Roger that."

"I doubt this is something I can accomplish from here, however I will assist in any way I can once we're on the other side."

General Axelrod shook his head defiantly at Courtney. She relayed the reply. "No. Sorry, but you're going to have to help from there if you want any assistance. They're not cooperating." This earned Courtney a glare from all thirty officers.

Forty miles away, Deckard hissed through gritted teeth, "Mother fucker! This is ridiculous. This is absurd. How on earth do they think you can help them from here and even if you could, I don't see why you should. If there are zombies in Massachusetts, why would we want to go there? We should try..."

Thuy took his hand, calming him in an instant. "A few thousand zombies are better to deal with that a few million," she said, guessing that the real number was being understated since they were using an open frequency. She keyed the mic and asked, "What sort of assets are available?"

Axelrod glanced over to his operations officer, who shook his head and answered, "Not much. General Phillips hinted that we could have the use of a few Delta teams and maybe a ranger company. It's nothing when you consider they'd have to clear out roughly four hundred square miles in one night. It's not possible."

"What about hunting the zombies from the air?" someone asked. "It'd be safe and reduce the chance that anyone else would get infected."

"We don't have the fuel," the Air Force liaison said. "We can *either* hunt the beasts or continue to make bombing runs. Not both."

Axelrod didn't have time for his men to sit around, spitting out what-if scenarios. There were battles still raging and his staff was the glue holding everything together. "We have an expert," he said. "We'll give her a chance and then we'll get back to work. Tell her what she has to work with."

When Courtney explained the few assets, Thuy was actually puzzled. Military jargon wasn't something she understood and she thought that when Courtney said 'Deltas' she was talking about some sort of fraternity. She knew what a ranger company was, however. "How many men are we talking about?" she asked.

"Somewhere between a hundred and fifty and two hundred," Courtney said. "But that's sort of a dead end. There's too much land for them to cover."

"And they're good fighters?" Thuy asked. "Even the Deltas? They'll have guns as well?"

In the hanger, someone groaned at the question. Courtney felt her cheeks going pink with embarrassment. "Yes, they're all very good fighters and they'll all have guns, but we need a new idea. Maybe a chemical that we can spray by plane. You know like a crop duster? Is there anything like that which could kill the zombies?"

"If there were, they'd kill the normal people, as well," Thuy said. "No, we're going to use the soldiers and it'll be okay. Don't worry."

2–8:58 p.m.
The Situation Room, White House

The President rubbed his hands together. They were winning. Finally, they were winning. The lines had stabilized. "And now we roll them back. Right Marty?"

Marty's smile was strained, but the President didn't notice. "Yes, sir. That's the plan."

"We start right here." The President pointed a buffed fingernail at Manhattan. "You see why? No? Well, I'll tell you. With the 3rd Infantry Division we can split the Zone square in two! We keep our left flank on the Hudson and go straight up to Albany. From there, we'll clear out Connecticut and Rhode Island. Then we'll wheel around and drive them out of Jersey and Pennsylvania! I suspect this will all be over in a month."

He was delusional. It was true that everyone was lying to him about the true state of things—the maps and video footage he was seeing had been doctored—but even taking that into account, he was out of his gourd. There was no way the war would be over in a month, and there was no way any of the generals would march their men deep into the Zone where they could be surrounded and attacked from all sides.

But Marty only said, "Yes, sir." The President couldn't be trusted with the truth and everyone thought he was nuts, however the Attorney General, who knew even less about warfare than the President, did not consider him mentally unfit. This meant that they couldn't strip him of his power, all they could do was continue to lie to him. They were playing a very dangerous game and Marty felt like shitting himself.

"Where the hell is Heider?" the President asked, finally turning away from the maps he'd been staring at. "He keeps disappearing, not that I care, but isn't he supposed to be here, you know, to be kept in the loop? I guess I should be happy that at least *he's* here." He indicated the Secretary of Defense who was sleeping, slumped on the desk with his head in his crooked arms.

"Heider is dealing with logistics," Marty said, just as he'd been told to do. Logistics was something the President didn't understand and steadfastly refused to learn. He thought it was all "mumbo jumbo."

General Heider was really in the West Wing, doing his actual job, and things weren't nearly as hunky-dory as the President supposed.

In Massachusetts, the 101st had been driven from their lines south of Webster by sheer weight, while in the center part of the state huge tracts of land were practically overrun by zombies that had seemingly come out of thin air. In western Pennsylvania where civilians were doing the brunt of the fighting, it was a grind of constant battle, but they were at least being reinforced as people from as far away as Colorado were racing in to help.

The battle for southern Pennsylvania had officially ended an hour before and it had ended with a loss. Philadelphia had fallen as had its suburbs and in the confused retreat a combined civilian-soldier regiment holding a valley west of Wilmington had been left unsupported for too long and eventually it had crumbled.

This left the hard-fought positions around Wilmington untenable and now the battle for southern Pennsylvania had become the battle for Maryland, west of the Chesapeake Bay. Everything east of it was considered lost. Only a few thousand men and women were left to fight the zombies surging into Delaware, and they fought only delaying actions so that all of the Delmarva Peninsula could be evacuated.

Despite all this, the 7th Army was in a difficult situation, not an impossible one.

Of course, none of this could be even hinted at to the President. He was becoming scary. Marty had caught him whispering to himself about *The Ultimate Solution*.

But now the President was on the high side of his new bipolar personality. "You know what we should do, Marty? We should tour the front lines. What better way is there to instill fighting spirit in the men than a visit by their commanding officer? And we can bring some of the press along. It'll give them something positive to talk about for a change."

He gave Marty a close look, searching his face. "It's odd that you didn't think about this. It's what I pay you for, after all."

"I guess I'm just tired," Marty answered. "Sorry."

"It has been a long few days," the President said with more grace than he'd shown in two days. "Why don't you get this set up and then go lie down? We'll need all the major players: ABC, CBS, hell even invite those dicks over at Fox. And make sure we have Marine Corps 1.

We'll probably need a fleet of them. Talk to Heider about that."

Marty actually bowed as he backed to the door. "Yes sir, I will. I'll get it all ready to go. It'll take some time but…but you can count on me." The moment he was out the door, Marty took off running for the West Wing. He was out of breath by the time he found Heider sitting in a cramped office with dozens of men and women in uniform surrounding him. "I need your help! *He* is talking about a tour of the front lines."

Heider was quick to jump up and hurry from the room, dragging Marty along with him. "You have got to stall him."

"For how long?"

The general shrugged weakly. "A few days? If the 3rd ID can finally get their butts in gear, we might be able to push the zombies back."

"And if they can't and he finds out that we've been lying to him?" Marty asked, licking his lips. "It'll be treason. He'll arrest us, I know it. He might even have us killed." It wasn't out of the realm of possibility.

"He won't find out as long as we keep him in the White House. Make that your main priority. No matter what, keep him from touring anything."

This was easier said than done. When Marty got back to the Situation Room, he found the President talking to a reporter from the New York Times. "Of course you can have a window seat, Bob. I'll have Marty set that up. Hey, here he is. What did Heider say? When can we go?"

"He's…he's, uh, he said soon."

Chapter 23

1– 9:36 p.m.
—The Walton Facility, New York

Joe Swan circled the grounds three times, flying the Blackhawk like a noob. With his right hand damp on the cyclic, and his shoulders tensed, and his nerves frayed, it was no wonder.

There were zombies below and they weren't in any way "manageable." They seemed numberless, faceless, fearless. Jennifer Jackson, in the window right behind him, was working the M240 in short bursts. He could feel each pull of the trigger like a little tremor beneath his buttocks.

Jennifer had a thousand rounds and after ten minutes, she had to wonder if it was going to be enough. There were just so many of the monsters. That's how she saw them: monsters. Black-eyed, splintered-toothed, clawed monsters. This was her first time seeing them so close and it was no lie that her stomach was sour and her heart was racing.

She began to curse under her breath every time she fired the machine gun. Heads burst like balloons and arms flailed and black blood flowed—and still they kept coming. She was just wondering what they would do if it turned out there were more monsters than bullets, when the missiles started flying.

"Who's shooting those?" she asked, into her helmet mic. Leaning over the blistering hot gun, she stuck her head out the window and stared around looking for another helicopter or a jet, afraid that they could be targeted by accident.

Swan brought the bird up, thinking the same thing. "There are three UAVs out there. At least one is armed."

"Great," she muttered. She'd seen the "cockpit" of an unmanned aerial vehicle; with its little monitors and the comfy chairs, it had looked like an elaborate gaming console. It hadn't inspired confidence.

The missiles kept blazing out of the night and the Blackhawk wasn't blotted out of the sky. Eventually, they were cleared to land and Swan picked out a spot outside the grounds where the land wasn't filled with debris and bodies. "Oh, boy," he whispered as he shut down the engine.

His stomach was filled with butterflies and, as steady as he was in the air, he felt the shakes coming on. "Okay, let's do this," he said, unstrapping from the chair. Action was the surest way to combat fear. It was something he had learned in flight school which had been, until this very moment, the scariest thing he had ever experienced. This was a hundred times worse.

He was more than a little embarrassed by his fear when he climbed into the back and saw how cool the FBI woman was acting. Behind her mask, PFC Jackson had a sheen of sweat around her huge round eyes, Anna Holloway was practically panting, and Lieutenant Eng kept fiddling with his mask, afraid that it was leaking. But Special Agent Katherine Pennock acted as if this was nothing but a training mission and that those weren't pieces of bodies scattered everywhere, and the M4 in her hand would shoot paintballs instead of 5.56mm rounds.

"Seal check," she ordered. When that was done, she looked the four of them over from head to toe. They weren't in MOPP or bio-suits. She felt that the Mission Oriented Protective Posture gear was too bulky and that the bio-suits were too thin. They wore black tactical gear, armored vests that covered their necks, shoulders and chests. They also had thick gloves, as well as elbow and forearm pads. Katherine felt like a football player in her gear.

The outfits weren't close to being virus resistant, but they didn't need to be. According to Anna and Eng, as well as the most up to date literature, the Com-cells could not hurt you just by landing on exposed skin. It needed a route into the body such as a cut or through the lungs. The masks would keep their lungs safe and, just in case any blood was sprayed, they had six gallons of bleach on board the Blackhawk and each carried a small spray bottle of it.

For weapons, they had M4s which was a bit of a disappointment to Katherine. She had wanted the stopping power and close-in accuracy of automatic shotguns, only none had been available on such short notice. Her disappointment was nothing compared to Anna and Eng's, who were going in, not just unarmed, but also in chains.

They had raised a stink and made demands and threatened not to go, to which Katherine had calmly said, "You're going. Even if I have to throw you out of the helicopter myself, you're going." More for her sake than for theirs, she allowed them each to carry a light riot shield along with their other armor.

"I have point," she said. "Jackson will follow me, then Anna, then Eng. Snow has our six." She gave the pilot a long look, perhaps seeing the fear in him, perhaps not. He couldn't tell. "Keep your head on a swivel. I know it's cliche, but in this case, you have to."

Swan understood, perfectly. Although their masks were state of the art, they still muffled the ears, making it hard to hear, and they compressed vision so that little in their periphery could be seen without turning the head. As the man in back, he would have to either walk backwards or keep his head going continuously back and forth as they moved.

"Got it," he said, but quietly, and she had to ask him to repeat himself. "I got it," he practically shouted. "Let's do this."

She nodded, and with a deep breath, she moved out, walking in a crouch, with her M4 held up to her chin.

The gates of the facility were open and bent. Days before, a car had come through them at high speed and now they hung askew, making an irritating metallic grind of a noise as the light wind pushed them gently back and forth. Eng stuck a rock beneath the bottom of it to stop the noise.

The silence was almost worse. The group paused thirty feet into the journey to listen, but there was nothing to hear. Katherine supposed that should have been better, only it wasn't. It felt as though they were standing under not just one big rock hanging from the side of a cliff, but an entire avalanche worth of them. The silence was a lie.

Going on tip-toe seemed like the best plan, but Katherine wouldn't give in to the temptation. It would show fear and she didn't think it would take all that much more fear before Anna went rabbit and took off, chains or no chains. The blonde had a frantic grip on her riot shield and she was breathing so fast that her mask was fogging up.

"Relax," Katherine told her. "I don't think there's anything left alive out here. It's what's up there that should scare you." She pointed at the looming hospital. It was a charred and partially collapsed monument to greed and evil. The Com-cells had been an inspired idea to save mankind from the cruelties of fate, however mankind had proved they weren't worthy, changing what was perfect and turning it hideous.

"Then what do you call that?" Anna pointed at a *thing*. In the dark, it didn't look human and barely seemed to be a zombie. It was the upper part of a body, just the torso, a single arm and a head that was held on by a few tendons, the threads of its spinal column and maybe an artery or two.

It stared at them with one unblinking eye. It stared as it dragged itself along by its single arm. "I'm going to puke," Jennifer Jackson whispered, wagging her head side to side as she stared back into the eye.

"Ignore it," Katherine said, taking the soldier by the arm and pulling her on into the war-torn grounds. "It can't hurt you, so put it out of your mind." She stepped around the creature and then went straight for the front doors of the main hospital, hoping to get in, find what they needed, and get out again before anything whatsoever could happen.

The doors were closed and perhaps locked, not that it mattered. The glass walls all along the front of the building had been shattered days before by the explosion Anna had cooked up in her attempt to simultaneously escape the building and destroy any evidence that she'd anything to do with the zombies.

As they slipped inside, the shards of glass crunched underfoot making Katherine's skin crawl. It sounded like something with a hundred teeth was alive beneath the tile. Alive and chewing on bone.

There was carpet further on and she hurried to it, only to be brought up short; there were big splotches of dried blood all over the floor. Each of the splotches showed where someone had died, only there weren't any bodies. For some reason, seeing the splotches made Eng snort in an unpleasant way. Jackson turned and glared at him, but he only smiled.

"You're fucked up," Jennifer said. "You did all this and you have the gall to smile?"

He said something in Mandarin, leaned his riot shield against his legs, and then lifted his arms and gazed around as if in satisfaction at the destruction he had wrought.

The lobby, at one point, had been open and expansive, beautifully decorated to give the feeling of not just opulence, but also warmth, which was a very difficult note to hit. Now it was like a cave sketched from a nightmare. Where once the colors of gold and opal were exquisitely and impossibly matched, there were now only shades of black. The walls had been warped from the heat of the fire and where the ceiling hadn't fallen in, it looked as though it was threatening to do so. It sounded like it as well. The building groaned above them.

"This is a waste of time," Swan said. "Nothing could have survived the fire. Nothing useful at least. We should get the hell out of here."

Eng snorted again, this time derisively. "Your fear is making you weak and it's making you stupid. The labs were constructed with containment in mind. A BSL-3 lab may very well survive a fire." Swan looked unconvinced.

"We're here either way, Swan," Katherine said. "We might as well check things out. Where are the stairs?" The bank of elevators was obvious, however with all the soot and the charring and the black splashes of blood on every door, it was hard to tell what anything else was, exactly.

"Around the corner," Anna said, hollow-voiced. A stunned look had replaced the fear. It was hard for her to believe this was the same building, but it was even harder to believe that she had been the one who destroyed it. She had liked the Walton facility. It had been pretty. And they had done important work there. Yes, she had been a corporate spy, but that didn't mean she had wanted the Com-cells to fail.

Katherine was ready to move, but Anna grabbed her arm. "I didn't want any of this to happen," she said, looking Katherine in the eye. "I was being set up and, and there was this guy...Von Braun. He was a zombie, but he could think as long as he was on drugs. Did they tell you that can happen? It's opiates. Opiates calm them enough for them to think, only their thoughts are always...rancid. It was Von Braun who did all this. It was him. I-I just lit the fire to try to contain the rest of the zombies. You believe me, right?"

"I believe the evidence," Katherine told her. "But then again, you have your pardon so it doesn't matter what I believe."

"It matters to me. I'm not the bad guy here."

Katherine saw that Anna clearly believed this. Katherine did not, however. "And what about the people you turned into zombies on Long Island? What are your flimsy justifications for those deaths?"

Anna drew in a breath to answer, but couldn't find the right combination of words that would allow her to talk her way out of those criminal acts. "I don't need to justify myself," she finally said. "You weren't there. You don't know what it was like. And besides, like you said, I have my pardon."

"I suppose now would be a good time to remind you that the pardon is contingent upon you finding the cure. No cure, no pardon."

The two women stared hard at each other before Anna smiled, showing a dimple in her cheek. "Well, we really aren't far. Up a few flights and that's it."

If only they were that lucky. The main stairwell in the central part of the building was the darkest place Katherine had ever been in. The darkness was so thick that when she turned on the under-barrel tactical light, the beam seemed to get swallowed up after only a few feet. She went slowly, crouched behind her weapon, fully expecting to be attacked.

They went up in a single file and found that the set of stairs were uninhabited by zombies, at least as far as the second floor. Then they came to a strange jumble of desks and chairs and lamps, and all sorts of trash. It packed the stairwell, leaving them no room to get by.

"We were trapped in the upper floors, and we didn't have any weapons," Anna explained. "We used this stuff as a barricade. There might be a way around, though. There are other stairs."

In order to find them, all they had to do was manage the obstacle course that was the second floor and third floors. The gas-fed explosion had been located on the third floor and that was where the fire was the hottest and the damage the greatest. Eventually, most of the third floor had collapsed and had fallen into the second floor.

They came out of the stairwell and Katherine stood, gaping about at the alien landscape. The fire and the collapse had turned the simple layout of hospital rooms and nurse's stations into nothing that Katherine had ever seen before.

There were very few walls and nothing that resembled a hall, a corridor, or even a floor. Everything around them was black and misshapen. Shining their flashlights only seemed to make things appear even stranger. In front of them were what seemed like spears jutting up aggressively, and to the side were mounds of metal that had been melted into bizarre shapes. Across their path were twists of copper pipes that were so intricately twisted that they were simply beyond reason or explanation.

Katherine waited for Anna or Eng to give her some guidance, however both were turning in little circles, dumbfounded. "Where to?" Katherine asked. After a final turn, Eng jerked his riot shield to their left.

She led the way through the treacherous terrain, sometimes falling, sometimes stepping on things that seemed stable, but were, in reality little traps. At one point or another, each of them found themselves hip deep in the refuse, unable to free themselves.

With their hands cuffed and the bulky shields getting in the way, this occurred more to Anna and Eng than to the others. It was a slow truck to get to the north stairwell. Here, Katherine had the team pause to rest. As they did, they sprayed each other with the bleach solution.

She had wanted to give them five minutes, however three minutes into the break there were a series of explosions in the front of the building. Jennifer Jackson and Joe Swan were the first to leap up; Eng was the last.

"On your damned feet!" Swan ordered, grabbing the Chinese man by his armored vest and hauling him up. "That sounded like it came from the helicopter. Like they were shooting at it."

He wanted to head back down, as did Anna. Katherine overruled them. "We're going up! If someone is shooting missiles at the helicopter, we're screwed. It's too big of a target to miss. We just have to hope that they're not. Come on." She pushed up the stairs, thrusting aside computers, desks, lab equipment, and all sorts of trash until she came to the fourth floor where the door was hanging by a single hinge and looked ready to fall on the first person who touched it.

There were more explosions and Swan was so anxious that he wanted to kick the door aside. The chopper was his baby, after all. There was a connection between man and machine that non-pilots could never understand. With steadfast calm, Katherine made him return to his position at the back of the team before she stepped past the door and onto the fourth floor.

It was much more intact compared to the second floor. Only a few walls had crumbled and only in a dozen or so places had there been localized cave-ins from the floor above. The fire damage wasn't nearly as bad, either. When the third floor had collapsed into the second, it had smothered the worst of the fires.

"Follow me and keep buttoned up," Katherine said. With her M4 raised, she went down the shadow-struck hallway, shining her light back and forth, pausing at intersecting halls or at doors. She didn't have to go far onto the floor before spying a room with a front facing window.

They all hurried to it and stared down at the Blackhawk. It was surrounded by the dead. Hundreds of them. Some were climbing into it, others were climbing under, but most were just milling around it, perhaps attracted by the fading smell of humans.

As they watched, three more missiles streaked in and exploded in great balls of fire and smoke and flying body parts. The Blackhawk rocked on its wheels but suffered no visible damage. Whoever was operating the UAV was doing their best to kill the beasts without hitting the team's one method of escape.

"Stop! Damn it!" Swan screamed, pounding on the glass. He knew better than anyone that the Hellfire missile was extremely accurate, hitting within five meters of its target over 96% of the time. But all it took was one bent fin, one loose nut, one minor miscalculation and his baby would be scrap.

Katherine was about to berate the warrant officer for being loud, but the one outburst was all he had in him. As she watched, Swan put his forehead on the glass and closed his eyes.

Swan wouldn't have seen the zombie that attacked him even if his eyes had been open. Something huge and dead-of-night black came up from behind him and with the building so dark, it was, for all intents and purposes, invisible. It was on Swan before anyone even knew it was there.

It tried to tear out Swan's throat, but its teeth broke on the armored collar. Then it tried to twist Swan's head off. Swan, even taken by surprise, was not an easy kill. He threw his weight backwards, smashing into the beast and then swung around with his M4, knocking the rifle into the thing's shoulder, giving himself just enough room to fire the gun three times, stitching holes in its chest, its throat and finally into its left eye.

"Holy fuck!" he cried as the sounds of the gunshot echoed throughout the building. "What the ever-loving fuck was…"

Katherine shushed him and the five of them froze in place, listening as the building slowly came alive. There were more zombies lurking in the burned-out shadows and one was a very hungry nine-year-old. Jaimee Lynn Burke grinned upwards. She had the stairwells covered—her dinner was trapped.

2—9:51 p.m.
Monterey, Massachusetts

As always, Specialist Philip Strassle felt queasy before a jump. He never admitted it and never would, not even under torture. He was an Army Ranger after all, and Army Rangers were not afraid of jumping out of airplanes… perfectly good, perfectly sound airplanes.

It just didn't happen.

And that's why he wore the fake grin and it was why he hoped nobody would notice the sweat trickling from beneath his helmet. Fighting rag-heads in the 'Stan, was something he could handle. Mowing down Zs hadn't been a problem so far.

But jumping out of planes? Big problem.

"One minute!" the jump master bellowed, over the endless roar of the engines and the rushing of the wind. In one minute Strassle would be on the ground, fighting for his life, and he'd be a happy soldier once again.

"Please bless me, Lord," he whispered to himself. During every jump, Strassle was the most religious man in the world; after the jumps was another story. Not that he was a bad guy, he was just a guy who liked his beer and his women, even on Sunday mornings.

The minute passed in a heart-racing blur; the light above the door went green and the stick was moving forward, shuffling under the weight of their gear—then he was out the door, his body tight and tucked, his hands gripping his reserve.

Although, technically, it was a combat jump, they were jumping at fifteen-hundred feet and a reserve shoot made sense. Specialist Strassle fell to the end of his tether-line and his chute deployed with a strenuous jerk, snapping him back, just as it was supposed to. As he did with every jump, he practically moaned, "Oh, thank God," as he looked up at the canopy of his parachute and saw that the silk was wide and round, the lines were straight and nothing was fouled up.

Once assured that a quick death had been avoided, he released the tether holding his ruck and his weapon, and the two dropped to dangle fifteen feet below him. Now, all he had to worry about was the landing. Normally, he was just a bit nervous as the ground rushed up at him. Had this been a practice jump and he got hurt, he would simply call over a medic and get an ambulance ride off the DZ, perhaps even giving a little wave to his squad mates, knowing they'd be rucking it half the night while he was, hopefully, chatting up a nurse.

But there were no ambulances on this DZ and if he sprained an ankle, well he didn't want to think about that, not here, not surrounded as they were about to be by countless zombies.

And as far as drop zones went, this was barely one in Strassle's opinion. He had dropped on ten mile long DZs, and one mile long DZs, but this particular patch of ground was not much larger than a football field. The aerial photos made it look like an open field, green and pleasant. He hoped it was a field of lettuce or spinach, or something equally soft, but when he hit with all the grace of a two hundred pound bag of cement being thrown from a second floor window, he discovered that there was nothing soft at all about this field.

He had no idea what sort of hell-plants he had landed in, he only knew that they were constructed of thorns and thistles and every manner of barb.

"What the fuck?" he hissed, pulling a branch of something evil away from his face.

Thirty feet away was a billow of green silk and from the center of it came: "Fuuuuck! Who is that? Is that you Strassle? Y'all stole my fuckin' air." By that he meant that Strassle had slipped beneath him during the descent. It was a paratrooper's equivalent of having the carpet pulled out from under them, though about a thousand times more dangerous.

Strassle sat up, disconnecting his rig. "Don't fucking blame me. I can't see who's above me. You know that." Strassle felt for the tether hooked to the belt of the rig and followed it to his ruck and M4. In a second, the ruck was on his back and the M4 was switched to fire.

"Can you walk?" he asked, PFC Chuck Murray. He knew Murray's voice. He had the deep, deep twang only found in the hollers of West Virginia.

"I kin walk," Murray grumbled. "You knew I went out ahind you. Y'all coulda slipped right."

"And you could have slipped in any fucking direction you wanted," Strassle shot back. "Are you up? We got to move out." They trained to up and move after hitting dirt, and getting to the rally point as quickly as possible, not that it would take very long. The DZ was so small that Strassle could see the rally point: a silver-topped silo sitting due west.

The two soldiers moved out and were quickly joined by twelve others, marching with their rifles at the ready and their nerves keyed up. They kept close to each other, each man straining to see into the dark, expecting an attack to happen at any moment.

No attack came, and Strassle whispered another prayer of thanks. Their night was going to be bad enough without it starting off prematurely. From the rally point, the group marched a quarter mile into "town." The town of Monterey consisted of four little businesses, a library, a post office, the town clerk's office, the fire department, and fifteen or so homes.

They stopped in front of the post office. It was here that they were supposed to put into motion their small part of Dr. Lee's plan.

"I don't like it," someone said. "It's too small."

"And too, I don't know, cramped?" Strassle added. "Where are our fields of fire?"

"But it's brick," Murray said, reaching out a fist and thumping the wall. "Ain't no Zs gonna get in."

"Zs aren't going to get in through the walls of any of these buildings," Strassle shot back. "It's the doors and windows that we have to worry about."

Lieutenant King, the ranking officer, didn't like the building, either. It felt like a trap ready to slam shut on them. "Yeah, it's fubar. We'll set up over there." Across the street and half a block over was a two-story house. Unlike the post office, the house had lots of windows. Too many windows in some of the rangers' mumbled opinions. They'd be vulnerable.

"Quit your bitching!" King snapped. "We all knew this could go one way or the other. At least with the house we'll be able to dish it out, and we have a second floor to retreat to if needed." In the dark, someone repeated the words: "if needed," with a snort. It was a foregone conclusion that retreat was definitely going to be needed.

King led them across the street to the house, which was as empty as the rest of the town. It was locked up tight as well, which wasn't much of a problem. They wanted the doors intact, but the windows were another story. They went in through a living room window and right away King began assigning spots.

Strassle and Murray were given primo spots, or so they thought. Strassle had a family room window to cover.

Its only view was of the side of the detached garage, while Murray had the laundry room window.

"I got my field of fire all set," Murray said, dropping his ruck and fishing out his extra magazines. They each carried twelve, thirty-round magazines, two MREs, two quarts of water, surgical masks, latex gloves, bleach and the "special equipment" that was key to Dr. Lee's plan. What he carried wasn't all that special in his opinion. "I got me some batteries," he called out, his voice carrying in the dark house. He had jumped in twenty pounds of D batteries. "Who needs 'em?"

"I need eight of them," Strassle said, setting up the machine that he had leapt out of the plane with. When the wires were run to the different parts of the house and all was ready, he stacked his own magazines on the window sill and then, as quietly as he could, tapped out the glass.

King went around the house, handing out LED flashlights and checking every position. He stopped next to Strassle and clapped him on the shoulder. "Once Bannon's off the roof, we'll be good to go. You ready?"

"I was born ready, LT."

"That's what I want to hear. Look, when the shit goes down, I want to hear a lot of chatter. If things get too hot, I want to know about it before the situation gets out of hand." Strassle said he would and King clapped him on the shoulder a second time. He then pointed at the machine. "What's in it?"

Strassle grinned. "A surprise."

Minutes later, Sergeant Bannon came off the roof with a small gadget in his hands. He called out: "Strassle, do you want to start, or should I?"

"I'll go," Strassle answered and then looked down at the controls. Although the machine was somewhat archaic, the controls were obvious. He pressed the "go" button and waited, listening as it spooled up and then jerked as the machine blared: *At first, I was afraid, I was petrified…* Gloria Gaynor's soulful voice blasted out of the speakers of the boom box Strassle had jumped in. The thing was the size of a small suitcase.

"What?" Murray yelled, over the music blaring from the speakers they had set up around the house. "What the ever-lovin' fuck is that?"

Strassle was about to answer when Bannon hit his remote and the house was suddenly lit up by spinning blue and white lights. "It's a party!" Strassle hollered. "Everyone disco!" He started dancing, and was joined by half the team, who all sang along with Gloria as she belted out *I will survive*:

Kept thinking I could never live without you by my side
But then I spent so many nights thinking how you did me wrong
And I grew strong
And I learned how to get along
And so, you're back
From outer space...

Murray shook his head. "Outer space? What the fuck kind of lyrics is that? You know what woulda been better than this disco shit? Some Garth. I mean we're goin' inta battle and this is what y'all pick? That's some dumb-ass shit."

Strassle didn't think it was bad at all. The woman was singing about surviving after all. And the next song of the "Sick Seventies" CD was *Eye of the Tiger* and who didn't love that song? He was just thinking about fast-forwarding the CD when someone yelled out.

"I got movement!"

In a flash, the dancers went to their windows. Since Strassle's view was so limited, he slid to the next room which looked out on the street and sure enough, lit by the swirling strobes, were dark, straggly figures heading towards them. "Shit," he whispered.

Dr. Lee's plan to rid the interior of the state of zombies had been simple: if the military lacked the resources to go hunt the beasts, then the beasts would have to hunt them. There were fourteen teams of rangers scattered around the western part of the state and they were all set up with similar equipment.

Strassle was still staring when King came up behind him. "Back to your post. You'll get all the action you can handle in a few minutes." He wasn't wrong. The lights and the music brought every zombie within miles right to them. "Masks on! Masks on!" King yelled over Gloria. "Wait until they get close! Don't fire until you see the blacks of their eyes."

The first rifle went off seconds later. After that it was a mad free for all. Guns were going off all over the house drowning out the music. At first, Strassle had nothing to shoot at and so he reached over to crank the CD player to its maximum. When he looked up again, there was a ragged, limping, human-shaped demon coming from around the side of the garage.

True to his training, Strassle plugged the beast between the eyes at ten paces. More followed after this first one, thousands more. They started to pile up in mounds, especially along the front of the house, where the windows took up most of the east-facing wall.

Someone started to panic as the zombies attacked not just the windows, but also the walls and the doors of the house. "There's too many! There's too many!" he cried as the house shook. King raced to calm the man down.

Who's going to calm me down? Strassle wondered, as a hole appeared in the wall three feet from the window. At first it was small, barely large enough for the grey fingers to reach in and tear at the dry wall. It didn't take long before it was big enough to fit a head.

One of the creatures ripped the flesh from its own face pushing its head into the hole. Strassle calmly pivoted and fired, killing the thing. It slumped there, the head still in the hole.

Seconds later, King was back. "Hey, I want to…" The sight of the dead zombie in the wall stopped him. "What the fuck, Strassle? It looks like you mounted that head. Like it was a big game trophy or something."

"Yeah, it's pretty gnarly. Did you need anything? You had that: *I'm about to give you a fucked-up order* sort of look."

"Oh, right. You need to change the music. Who is this? The Bee Gees? They suck balls, okay? No one likes them, not even the fucking Zs."

He was correct. *How Deep is Your Love* was not an anthem that lent itself to battling the undead. Strassle fired his M4 twice more, changed out his magazine and then went to the next song which was something equally slow and mushy. He kept going until he hit pay-dirt with some Styxx.

Then he went back to firing his gun. The range was almost point blank now. He had built up a drift of corpses in front of the window which he couldn't shoot past. His only option was to wait for them to fall on this side before shooting them. It wasn't long before the dead were mounded up at the level of the sill and the creatures that were still moving could sliver inside.

He had no choice except to back up, further and further, dragging his ruck along with him. A new hole appeared next to the head and it wasn't long before it was big enough for some disgusting thing to stick its head into the opening. Strassle shot it, but failed to kill it, or even to slow it down. The bullet hit the zombie just below the nose.

"Shit," Strassle said and fired again, hitting the thing in the lower part of the forehead, which, unbelievably, still didn't kill it. A bad spin had sent the bullet blasting into the creature's sinuses, where it lodged, doing zero harm. Strassle went to fire again, but his magazine was empty.

Automatically, he went through the simple steps to replace it and, as he did, he counted the empty mags he had tossed to the side. Including the latest, there were seven. "Shit," he cursed once more, wondering how on earth he had already fired over two hundred rounds. For a moment, he felt hot panic well up inside of him, but then the zombie he had already shot twice tore open the wall. Because of the studs, it wasn't a wide hole; not quite two feet. Still, it was big enough for the monster to try to push into the room.

325

Strassle walked up to it and shot it from three inches away. It fell in the opening as another tried to crawl over it. He shot that one as well.

Time seemed to fall away as he methodically fired until there were six more holes in the wall and he had gone through two more magazines. "I'm getting low on ammo!"

"Who isn't," Lieutenant King said, handing over only a single magazine. "We're retreating upstairs before these stupid fucks pull the house down with us still inside."

The retreat was slow and deliberate so that no one was left behind. There were two stairs and the duty of guarding the smaller back stair fell to Strassle and Murray. They did not position themselves at the top. They stood three risers from the bottom and took turns firing. Gradually they were forced back and up, and up, and up, until the stairs were simply clogged with the monsters and nothing could come up and nothing could go down. The same had happened with the main stairs and now they were trapped.

"I got fifty-two rounds left," Murray said, thumbing bullets into his palm. "How many y'all got?" Strassle told him forty-three and Murray gave him five from his stash. "That 'bout makes us even."

The two friends shared a long look before Strassle asked, "What do think? Will the LT let us just chill in here?"

Murray shook his head. "There ain't no chance." He was right. Their mission was one of extermination, not survival.

"We're going out over the porch," King said. "And we'll keep moving until either they're dead or we're dead." He was a brave man and led the way out a second floor window. One ranger hesitated and he was pushed back. Strassle was the fifth man through the window and watched as the LT dropped to the ground. He was attacked immediately.

"To the ground!" King cried, firing his M4 all around. "Don't get trapped up there!" Another man hesitated and Strassle took his place, dropping to his stomach, letting his feet dangle for a moment and then dropping almost on top of a zombie. They were both surprised, but Strassle recovered quicker and shot it from such close range that black blood rained down on him.

Strassle fired three more times and then looked around. He saw that the LT was swarmed and there were zombies attacking the legs of some of the dangling rangers, and more of the beasts charging from the house. Strassle ran to King and blasted away the zombies who had brought him down, he then stuck out a hand to help him up and when the LT gripped his, Strassle knew something was wrong. King had two fingers bitten from his left hand.

"Are you…" Strassle began, then stopped as he saw the extent of King's injuries. His armor and helmet had saved his vital organs, but it looked as though a rabid pitbull had gotten to his face. It took Strassle a few moments to realize that King was going to die.

Before he could think of anything to say, King shouted, "To me! Face out, face out!"

Only nine of them made it to the LT and two of them had also been bitten. Of the others, some were being torn apart by the zombies and some were still stranded on the roof. King led a charge against the swarming zombies in a desperate attempt, not to save the fallen soldiers but to put them out of their misery.

One man was still strong enough to fight. One man was screaming mad. One was blind, his eyes ripped from their sockets. King shot these last two without comment. There was no time to even say: sorry. He took their ammo as the battle raged around him.

Strassle started out fighting next to Murray, however the battle was utter chaos. Half the time he was shooting the zombies that were within arm's reach. The other half the time, they were even closer than that. He was covered in black blood and his shoulder ached from the constant thump of his M4.

Oddly, his greatest fear during this part of the fight was of tripping. One of his fellow rangers had fallen a minute before and had died under a pile of undead. They had tried to help him, but the zombies came on in wave after wave and they were forced to retreat with the sound of the man's screams in their ears.

Ten minutes later, Strassle ran dry—his chest rig was empty, his bolt was back and the port was open on his M4. "I need ammo!" He looked for Murray, however his friend had disappeared. There were only four of them left.

"Murray!" Strassle cried looking back the way they had come. They were now nearly two hundred yards from the house that they had tried to defend. Although it had collapsed into a jumble of wood and dead bodies, the Disco lights still pulsed. They were no longer festive. They showed only piles and heaps of corpses strewn everywhere.

Strassle was shocked to see that there were now only a few dozen zombies left alive. With the lights blinking, they were killed one after another and when the last went down, the little group was stunned to find that they had only six bullets left between them.

Breathing in harsh gasps, King radioed a message of their "victory." He then turned and dropped to his knees. "Someone do it…please. Make it quick."

Another of them was swaying, standing in a pool of his own blood. He knelt as well, saying, "We did it right. We did the job right, now let's finish it right. Riggs, you, too."

"It's not even a scratch," Riggs said, showing them a red line on the back of his right hand.

Strassle pointed at the jagged, bleeding tear in the flesh beneath his jaw. "You don't feel that?"

"Feel what…oh, no," he said, touching the real scratches. He looked at Strassle in horror and looked to be on the verge of running away— Strassle would have shot him in the back if he had. Slowly Riggs took control of himself and knelt as well. "We're heroes, right?" he asked.

"Yeah," Strassle whispered and raised his M4. "We're heroes."

Chapter 24

Courtney Shaw sat with her bushy hair freed from the bun, listening to the reports coming in from the different ranger and Delta teams. They'd all had contact with zombies and the numbers that were being reported within the border of the state was staggering.

Staggering but, manageable. Thuy's plan had worked. The creatures were coming out of the woodwork, and were being destroyed as soon as they showed their vile faces.

"You'll let them through, now?" Courtney asked, speaking loudly enough that her voice echoed in the hanger and every one of General Axelrod's staff heard. Axelrod himself scowled. "Thuy did what you asked, General, now I trust that you'll come through for her."

"Of course," he said. "I made a promise. We will get this done, but it's going to take time to set things up with the Air Force and the line companies."

"So, as soon as that's taken care of, I can contact them?" Courtney asked. He started to nod and she reached for her radio. "Good, because I already have everything set up." She had known right off the bat that Thuy's idea would work. For the last four days, it had been the conventional wisdom to hide from the beasts, to not make a sound or they'd hear and come after you. Thuy had used that to her advantage.

Axelrod's bald head began to turn red. "You did what?" he asked in a low, menacing voice.

Courtney guessed that he was trying to scare her but since she was already under arrest with a charge of treason hanging over her head, what more could they really do to her? "I saved you and your men valuable time. You're welcome, by the way." She had her own map in front of her and put her finger on a little dot. "This is Taconic

329

High, where Thuy and Deckard are. I've alerted all the company commanders from Mount Everett to Stockbridge. As well, I've contacted the operations officers here and at Pittsfield not to shoot at any 'observational' balloons for the next two hours."

"You know they won't be allowed to just land anywhere. They are possibly contaminated."

"I already thought about that," Courtney said. She pointed at John Burke, who was sitting against the wall, wiggling a pinky back and forth in his ear. "John is immune to the disease. He's going to track the balloon and once they set down, he will drive them to a quarantine area being set up for the rangers."

The general was staring at John as if seeing him for the first time. "He's immune? How? And who has verified this?"

Despite the pinky in his ear, John had heard the entire conversation. "I was in the o-riginal test group out at Walton and they shot my ass full of them Com-cells, but they didn't hurt me none. Ever-body else turnt into them zombies, but not me. Dr. Lee can vouch for me iffin you don't believe me."

Axelrod gave John a searching look, then abruptly shrugged his wide shoulders. "It sounds as though you have this mission under control. Carry on."

This was all Courtney needed. "Deck 1, this is Dispatch 6, we are good to go. You have flight clearance. Light your fires, Deck 1."

In the middle of the football field at Taconic High, Thuy and Deckard were crouched down in the truck's cab, their eyes just at the level of the windows. When she heard the message, Thuy felt like crying. She bit it back and whispered into the radio, "Roger that, Dispatch 6. Hopefully we'll be airborne in a few minutes. Wish us luck."

"Good luck, Dr. Lee."

Thuy started to unplug the radio, but Deckard took her hands in his and kissed her palms. "It'll all be over in four minutes," he told her. "Then we'll be safe."

She didn't know if she believed it, but she believed that Deckard would do almost anything to keep her safe, and that was enough. "Don't leave without me this time," she said, meaning for it to be a joke, but her voice was too high and shaky for it to be anything except a desperate plea.

"I couldn't even if I wanted to," he told her. "Are you ready?" She took a deep breath but swallowed her response. "It's your plan, Thuy and that means it's going to work. We just have to carry it out, starting with you driving away."

Just like last night, she thought.

"No, not like last night," he said, reading her mind, perfectly. "This is a better plan, by far." This time the balloon was anchored, it couldn't just float away on its own, and their distractions were more intense, and they had worked out the steps to inflating the balloon so that it would take minimal supervision.

The plan was as good as she could make it, and yet the setting for it was in a world filled with zombies. Their numbers, their speed, their naked aggression were impossible to control by two people for more than a minute or two, and they would need four.

"We had better do this before I really chicken out," she said. Her chest was beginning to thrum and the fear was going to her arms, and soon it would be in her hands where Deckard would be able to see. "Kiss me," she demanded, moving closer. There was little romance in the kiss. She was too afraid for romance.

"It'll be fine," he said, giving her an easy smile. "Now, let's get our masks on and do this." He reached out, pushed aside her long black hair and pulled her mask into place. His was sitting on the top of his head like a blue yarmulke. He snapped it across his face, took the radio and slid from the truck. "Why is it I always want to tell you I love you right before we split up?" he asked, after shutting the door.

"Because you want to torture me, I think. Maybe this time you should wait to tell me. Maybe you can wait for four minutes when everything will be perfect and we're flying off to safety."

Above his mask, his eyes crinkled. "I'll just have to settle for thinking it." He patted the side of the truck and then backed away, disappearing into the dark.

"Love you," she whispered and then turned on the truck. It seemed very loud. "But that's okay," she said to herself. "It's supposed to be loud." She was the bait to draw the zombies away and to that end she flicked on her high-beams and stuck the truck in gear.

Thuy tore out of there, ripping divots in the dirt, the horn blaring a long, ugly note as she leaned on it. Once out of the stadium, she bounced the truck over a curb and into the parking lot where she and Deckard had dumped a pile of broken down cardboard boxes that they had swiped from a recycle bin outside of the high school. They had soaked the pile with varnish from the wood shop and when Thuy set a lighter to the pile, it went up with a whoosh of flames that rose higher than the top of the truck.

She climbed back into the cab just as the first of the zombies arrived. There were hundreds more lurching along behind it. They were so fast that Thuy found herself staring in shock. If Deckard's M4 hadn't gone off, she probably would have been surrounded and killed before the plan had really gotten underway.

"Oh, my goodness," she said, frantically. "It's too soon. It's too soon." She gunned the truck, plowing through the undead and heading for the baseball diamond at the north side of the stadium where they had left more cardboard. As she drove, she kept her head cranked sideways trying to see Deckard, but all she saw were the backs of the bleachers.

"It was just one gunshot," she told herself. "It was prob…" The truck hit the curb at the far end of the lot with such force that she bounced in her seat, hitting her head on the roof of the cab. "Damn!" The truck slewed right as her eyes went in and out of focus. Thankfully, she was in the wide open grassy portion of the baseball field and there wasn't anything to hit, except for more zombies, that is.

Swerving left and right, she raced to the infield to an empty patch of dirt to what Deckard had called "second base." Apparently, it was a sports term, though what it signified, she didn't know and hadn't cared enough to ask. There had been too many zombies lurking in the dark to risk asking any questions.

Now, they weren't just lurking, they were charging in a shambling run, converging on the pile of cardboard in the middle of the infield. She knew she had to get out, light the cardboard on fire and jump back in the truck. Such a simple plan but now complicated by all those horrible creatures. She was terrified. Her system flooded with adrenalin, and she forgot to put the car in park.

It was rolling away before she was even out of it, and with a shriek she jumped back in and nearly broke the gear shifter slamming it into place. Now, it was a race to light the fire before the beasts were on her. It was a race she won in a disgusting fashion. The first zombie came at her from the opposite side of the cardboard pile, which was just shooting up into a roaring bonfire. The beast fell straight into it and, as Thuy watched, the thing's hair burst into flame and its lips blackened and shriveled. There was a furious hissing sound as its flesh bubbled into blisters and then popped.

Thuy had never thought of herself as squeamish, though in truth squeamishness was measured on a scale with small spiders on one end, dirty diapers somewhere in the middle and a maggot-infested corpse at the far end. What she was witnessing was off any possible scale as the creature kept crawling towards her as it burned alive.

"That's not right," Thuy said, backing to the truck and then scrambling inside and locking the doors behind her. She had another bonfire to light, only she was suddenly fumble-fingered, her hands not remembering on their own how to drive. Accidentally, she rammed the gear into neutral and jumped in fear when the engine screamed without surging ahead.

Her brain was just beginning to realize the problem when something hit the side of the truck next to her left

333

knee. She didn't need to roll down her window and look out to know it was the zombie that had been in the fire. An awful black smoke was running right up the side of the door.

The engine was still screaming and she was probably screaming as well when she yanked the gear shifter into drive. The truck shot ahead and her grip on the wheel had nothing to do with steering; she was just holding on as it plowed through the zombies. One went under the wheels and it felt like it caused the truck to leap into the air. Thuy hit her head on the roof for the second time and the pain was similar to having a two-ton hammer swat her.

"Son of a bitch!" she cursed and hauled the truck around so that once again she was racing through the outfield, heading back the way she had come on a parallel course. Another thump and she was in the parking lot, turning circles. There were zombies everywhere, going in all sorts of directions…all except towards the football field, which was exactly what she was hoping for.

The balloon was filling. When she got to the far end of the parking lot she could see it clearly, looking like a cloud had fallen from the night sky and was sagging into nothing on the grass. As she raced back and forth, the balloon grew and grew until it slowly lumbered up from its reclining position and lifted into the air. She made two more wide circles and then raced the truck towards the balloon.

It was time! She and Deckard would get away and they would be safe. She slowed the truck as she neared the balloon but did not stop it. Her mistake with the gears earlier had given her an idea. To add to the confusion among the zombies, she leapt from the truck as it was still moving and watched as it coasted along, brightly lit. She then turned and crawled to the basket and climbed in.

Deckard was nowhere in sight.

"Don't panic," she told herself, "he's probably just drawing some of them away." Even as she said this, there was a gunshot from out in the dark. For reasons she couldn't name, she found the gunshot reassuring. She was hoping to hear more or perhaps the sound of his running feet, returning to her.

Instead, she heard nothing but the moans and growls of zombies, and she slunk down even further into the basket. With the burner going just seven feet above her head, everything in a wide circle around her was perfectly visible, including four zombies that seemed to be heading in her direction.

The first one walked past, going for the truck. The second paused, staring at the balloon. The third and fourth headed right for the basket. The basket was just under four feet tall; it offered zero protection and Thuy's only options were to get out and run around or get the balloon out of reach.

The basket was anchored to the ground by two twenty-foot long ropes, each attached to hundred pound bags of sand, but they were short-hitched, meaning that the majority of the rope was looped and tied off. With two quick yanks, she undid the hitches and the balloon lifted from the ground—very slowly.

Her expectation was that the balloon would leap into the sky. It didn't, and she found herself face to face with a zombie. The thing tried to grab her and she could only shrink back as its claws swung inches from her nose. It was a huge beast with long arms and if the balloon hadn't been rising it would have scratched her at a minimum.

As it reached out for her, the basket ran up under its armpits and lifted its arms away from Thuy, who had kicked back as far as she could. The zombie screamed in anger and clawed and beat the basket as it went up and up and…and stopped. Thuy glanced over the side and saw that the monster had hooked one of its claws into the bottom of the basket and was hauling furiously down on it.

Her one chance to get away was to run the burner full bore. With enough hot air, the balloon could lift the monster and the sandbags. But she would lose Deckard, and she wasn't going to lose him no matter what.

She was still trying to figure out a solution when the basket was jolted. Something else had grabbed hold. She

335

could see its fingers curled over the edge of the wicker. Quick as a cat, she grabbed the radio in both hands and bashed the fingers only to hear a man cry out: "Stop! Thuy it's me!"

A moment later, Deckard's grinning face appeared as he pulled himself up and over the side. The basket swayed alarmingly as she rushed into him. She meant for a longer hug, but the floor tilted at a thirty degree angle and she backed away, grabbing the sides.

He laughed easily at her fear, in fact, he was liable to laugh at the stars or his toes just then. Deckard was almost ecstatic. "Hold on, there's going to be a jerk in a moment." He unslung his M4 and, as Thuy plugged her ears, he shot the zombie hanging from the basket in the top of the head.

They did indeed jerk and then jerked again when they got to the ends of the anchor ropes, which he cut away. Then they were sailing higher and higher, going straight up. He laughed again and she laughed with him, right up until she remembered the radio.

"Dispatch 6, this is Deck 1, we have lift off!" she crowed into the mic. "Tell me, Courtney, do you have us on radar, yet?" Thuy was sure that they were still too low for ground based radar, but one of the E-3s probably could pick them up at any minute.

Courtney came on seconds later. "That's affirmative, Deck 1," she answered. "How could we miss you? There's a great big blob just sitting on the screen." She was quiet for a few minutes and when she came back on, she sounded worried. "Can you give me a weather check?"

"It's as clear as a bell," Thuy said. "Why? Are we expecting storms?"

Before Courtney could answer, Deckard cursed and pointed over the side of the balloon. At first Thuy didn't see the problem. They were probably four hundred feet in the air and down below them was the stadium and the school and the fires and the…

"We haven't moved!" she cried, fumbling for the radio. "Courtney, are you there? We haven't moved at all. We're just sitting here. Can you check in with the Air

Force's weather personnel to see if there are any east bearing thermals higher up?"

Courtney said that she would check but that it could be a few minutes. As they waited, Deckard and Thuy stood on opposite sides of the basket gazing at each other in silence. He was the first to break it, knowing exactly what she was doing her best not to ask. "We have about an hour up here. I only grabbed the one tank. I'm sorry, but there were so many zombies coming for us and I didn't think we'd need more."

"Don't blame yourself. You couldn't…"

Courtney interrupted her, coming across the radio saying, "Don't try to go any higher. There's a backing wind at about a thousand feet. It'll push you west. Your best bet is to hold in place. The forecast is for the wind to pick up here in the next few hours. How much fuel do you have?"

"Not enough," Thuy answered.

2—10:22 p.m.

—Westfield-Barnes Regional Airport, Massachusetts

Courtney stared across the radio and towards the hangar doors, which shook every time a jet blazed down the runway with blue flames shooting out behind. "We're going to need to rescue them," she said to General Axelrod. "I know what you're going to say…"

"That the answer is no?" he asked. "It's not that hard of a guess when we've already had this discussion. I have my orders."

"She's come through for you twice already!" Courtney cried, slamming her fist down. "What more do you need? A cure? If she could get you a cure, would you let her out?" Before he could answer, she grabbed the mic and hit the send switch. "Deck 1, I'm working on an extraction for you, but we might need some promises concerning a cure or maybe a vaccination for the zombie virus."

Axelrod shook his head, the overhead lights glinting from his shining dome. "*Promise me you have a cure and I'll let you out?*" he asked in amazement. "What kind of bullshit is that? How on earth am I supposed to believe anything she says?"

Just as he finished the question, Thuy came back on, asking, "Ms. Shaw are you saying that a rescue is contingent upon me having or being able to create a cure or vaccination?"

Although the general shook his head, Courtney quickly said, "Yes. The general here is stubborn, but I know I can find someone who'll agree with me that you and your research is vital."

Thuy was slow to reply. She had dropped down into the bottom of the basket again and was leaning against the lone propane tank. "I don't wish to deceive anyone. My knowledge *might* prove vital and it might not. First, I should note that a vaccination isn't possible, at least not in the traditional sense. The Com-cells are not viral in origin. Secondly, I don't know exactly how the Com-cells were sabotaged, which makes finding a remedy problematic. I can't guarantee a cure, Ms. Shaw."

Courtney's shoulders slumped and the mic in her hand suddenly felt heavy; she dropped it onto the table. "So, do you believe that?" she asked Axelrod.

"I do," he said. "It's too bad I can't reward such an honest answer."

"Someone will, General," Courtney said, picking the mic up again. "She said that a cure was 'problematic' she didn't say it was impossible. I'll find someone above you who'll make this happen, and if she dies in the meantime, who do you think they'll blame?"

Axelrod opened up his laptop, saying, "No one's going to say, shit. There is already a team going after a cure in someplace called Walton. We received a flash message from the White House about an hour ago."

He showed her the message and she gasped. "This says the team is being led by two scientists who once worked at the facility. They're talking about the people who sabotaged the project in the first place!" She grabbed the mic and practically yelled into it, "Thuy, there's a team heading back to Walton. Anna and Eng are on it. Supposedly they're looking for a cure."

"They won't find one," Thuy answered. "There are some of the original Com-cells, but they're not a cure. They are molecule specific for cancerous tumors. Not to mention they've been unrefrigerated for days now. Their fusarium levels have to be kept at a specific level."

"Ask her why?" Axelrod demanded.

Courtney did and Thuy answered, "The test subjects that were given Com-cells with higher levels of mycotoxins all developed symptoms that were similar to rabies, including the extremes of hyper-aggression. If Anna and Eng try to pass these Com-cells off as a cure, which I fully believe they will, we're going to have a new problem on our hands. We could have a new outbreak occur somewhere where we least expect it."

Axelrod cursed long and slow, "Fuuuuck," letting the word draw out. He then thumped the table and yelled, "Captain Durr! Find out what's going on with the mission into Walton. Dixon, see what sort of info you can dig up on…what's their names?"

"Anna Holloway and Shuang Eng," Courtney said.

The two wouldn't find out much. Almost seventy miles away, Anna was begging Special Agent Katherine Pennock to: "Please, please, please unlock us." She held out her manacled hands. "We got the cure for you and we've been pardoned. It doesn't make any sense to try to run away or do anything untoward. We just want to be able to defend ourselves."

"You want to defend yourself? Then pick up your damned shield and get back in the corner. I don't need you to…" A lurking figure to the right caught her attention and she put a finger to her lips. The five of them tensed, hoping the creature would turn away as the last two had.

This one kept coming and now the five slunk low in the cubicle they were hiding in.

There was a good chance that if they stayed quiet and still, it would miss them in the dark. It did not. Although its face was mostly eaten away, its sense of smell was still intact and it turned towards them.

"Son of a bitch!" Katherine hissed, pushing Anna back and lifting her mop and planting the sponged end of it squarely in the thing's chest. Jennifer had a mop as well and she too thrust hers at the beast. Straining with all their might, the two of them were able to hold the creature back and keep its attention as Joe Swan went around the side.

He held a length of iron pipe, as long as his leg, and swung it Babe Ruth style at the creature's shredded up face. The blow was jarring, stinging Swan's hands and yet, the creature didn't fall. It took two more whacks with the pipe before it dropped and one heavy blow to the crown of its head to kill it.

"I hate this," he snarled. "Killing them like this is…is disgusting. It's not human." It was barbaric, alright, however they didn't have a choice. After they had retrieved the Com-cells, they had fought for an hour against the zombies which seemed to crawl out of the destroyed building like cockroaches. It took half their ammo just to fight their way down to the second floor, where things got crazy. Without real walls, the zombies came from every direction, even from beneath the rubble that made up the floor.

Eventually their ammo began to run dangerously low and Eng had finally drawled, "You're just attracting more of them with the guns. Maybe you should think of something else."

They didn't have much in the way of options and had settled on this mop-mop-pipe routine. That and a bunch of sneaking around. It had worked, and they were alive. What's more, they had managed to elude the majority of the zombies, and found an intact window at the end of the building that faced out towards the front entrance and the helicopter beyond it.

The grounds were destroyed. The heavy metal gate around the property was a twisted wreck and there were gaping holes everywhere from the bombings. But the helicopter was sitting pretty as can be all by itself.

"Here's the plan," Swan said, "you guys make a distraction in the lobby and then retreat here. While you're doing that, I'll sneak out to the bird and get it going. It'll only take a minute or two so once you see the blades going, shoot out the window and make a run for it."

The plan seemed perfect, only they hadn't taken Jaimee Lynn Burke into consideration. She had heard the guns going off and had been afraid. She didn't like guns. They could hurt her. And she didn't like bombs for the same reason. Then the bombs and the guns had stopped, but where were the screams and where were the people?

They were hiding, but she knew they'd come out soon and in her cunning mind, she saw where they'd go. She and her pack had crept to the big black machine and hid, waiting for that exact moment when the pilot would come. He'd jump in his seat and start messing with all the gizmos and dials and all the rest. He wouldn't see little Jaimee Lynn, who was still black as night.

And he didn't.

Swan counted to thirty after Katherine and Jennifer started shooting and then he ran, bent at the waist, making for the helicopter. None of the beasts saw him and with his protective mask clouding up, he didn't see the littlest ones until it was too late. He had just started the engines going and the blades whirling when something came from behind him, launching itself at his neck.

Jaimee Lynn's teeth sunk into the armored collar. "Fuck!" Swan cried in alarm. He was unhurt, but frightened beyond the measure of his opponent. With the mask and the cramped conditions, he assumed that it was a full-sided zombie and he panicked, opening the door of the cockpit and falling to the ground.

He had left both the pipe and his M4 leaning against the side of the bird and as he reached for the gun, Jaimee Lynn leapt out of the Blackhawk. The armor had been a nasty surprise, but then she saw the hand reaching for the gun and went for that. Before Swan knew it, she had his trigger finger between her teeth and was biting down with all her might. He punched her twice with his left hand and when she fell back, she did so with his finger still in her mouth.

"Fuck!" he screamed, again, his shocked mind split between the horrific pain and his need to turn the gun on the beast and kill it before it did something really bad to him. In his shock, he didn't realize that he was infected or that his finger had been bitten off. He tried to grab the gun, but his bleeding hand wasn't cooperating. His grip was wrong and it was only when he looked down that he saw his finger was gone completely.

He was still staring, his mind reeling, when Jaimee Lynn thrust the gun aside and went for the man's underbelly, discovering to her utter fury that he was armored there as well. Recovering himself a little, Swan used the M4 to bash her aside, but two more of the zombie children were on him, trying to tear him open with their teeth.

Swan wasted two full seconds forcing his middle finger into the trigger guard only to find that they were too close to get the gun pointed properly. Luckily for him, the little zombies were just discovering that his armor made him impervious.

To Jaimee Lynn, he was like a turtle in its shell. It was aggravating and, more out of fury, she snatched up the pipe Swan had set aside and brought it crashing down on his head. It bounced right off his Kevlar helmet. Although she was only nine and not the biggest of nine-year-olds, she had an unholy strength about her. Still, it wasn't enough to even scratch the helmet. But it was enough to stun Swan for all of a second, giving her time to hit him again, and again, and again.

By the fourth hit, Swan seemed to lose the ability to control his body and he fell back, staring up at the whipping blades of the helicopter as Jamie Lynn dove in at his exposed neck.

3—10:41 p.m.

The Situation Room

The President watched Swan's death on a live feed, with his lip curled and his jaw set. "So much for a cure," he said. He hadn't believed there was one anyway. In fact, he didn't know what to believe about anything. How could he with all the lies flying around him?

"Should I recall the drone?" one of the officers from Homeland Security asked. There were three of these officers. Supposedly they were loyal to him. Supposedly. Only time would tell and it was almost time to discover where everyone really stood.

"Yes. Send it to Wilmington. I'd like to give those other drone operators a rest. They've been flying for hours, right Marty?"

Marty Aleman felt his politician's smile freeze in place. "They switch out the operators, sir. I'm sure they're doing fine."

"Is that right?" the President asked, staring so hard at his Chief of Staff that Marty was afraid to move a muscle. Somehow the President had changed. That morning, he hadn't been able to answer the simplest question from a fawning press, now he was his own man, and it was terrifying.

Being his own man didn't make him a good man or even a smart man. He was directing phantom armies in a battle that had already moved on, and Marty didn't need a background in military sciences to know that the President was worse than an amateur. He was an inept amateur with God-like powers and an ultra-inflated view of himself.

And now he suspected the truth that he'd been lied to over and over again. He hadn't said it yet, but Marty knew, and it made him want to get down on his knees and beg for forgiveness. The President had never been a forgiving man, however. Even when he was Marty's puppet, he had carried grudges over the smallest of slights—of course back then, the penalty for angering the President had been being sat near the bathrooms at state dinners.

Now, he had real power and there were real consequences. Marty began to squirm under the President's stare.

"So, when do I get to tour the lines?" the President asked. It had been almost two hours since he had come up with the idea and he had heard three different excuses: not enough pilots, not enough fuel, not enough advanced notice for the pool reporters.

It had been this last excuse that tipped off the President. The White House correspondents had been begging for any scrap of news. Hell, they mobbed him anytime he went to take a leak. "I went by the press room and they all tell me they're ready. In fact, they've been ready for ages."

"Th-the Marines are…need more time to-to-to get the fuel for the helicopters. R-Remember, you wanted five of them?"

"I remember. Let's go talk to Heider about that." Without waiting, the President breezed right past Marty and into the waiting elevator. Feeling like a whipped child, Marty hurried after. Once in the elevator, the two stood in brittle silence. It felt like the air had the structure of thin glass and any word would shatter it as well as any sense of sanity Marty had left.

That sanity was strained to the breaking point when the elevator doors opened and Marty saw that the lobby was filled with people. Among the dozens of Secret Service Agents, there were a smattering of congressmen, and reporters with their cameras running.

"Mister President! Mister President!" they shouted, jostling each other, stepping on each other's toes, and talking over each other: "What's the big news? Are we winning? Has a cure been found?"

The President finally saw them as Marty always had: as dogs begging for scraps—and he was their master. He raised his arms for silence. "I have some very grave news. There has been a coup attempt against me." He paused to allow the gasps so as to increase the tension, just as Marty would have suggested. "Yes, treason has been committed by some of my closest advisors, including…" He pointed at Marty Aleman.

Marty froze, his eyes huge, his mouth unhinged and open. He knew he had to do or say something to fix this, only how could he when they were on live television. He was without his usual scripted remarks and rehearsed looks. He didn't have his talking points memorized and he didn't have his carefully researched rebuttals that he always loved to snap out of thin air.

The best Marty could do was shake his head and say, "I n-never…"

"Careful Marty," the President said, his face grim. "Everything you say will be used against you in your trial. You might be forgiven for lying to me, but I can't forgive you for lying to the American people."

"Trial?" Marty said, going light in the head. He could hear his pulse: *whah-whah-whah* racing in his ears.

The President nodded sadly, wisely, like a father who was being forced by an unruly child into doing his duty in not sparing the rod. "Yes, a trial. You…" He pointed at a Secret Service Agent. "Arrest this man on charges of treason."

The agent hesitated and shifted his eyes to his superior. They had known that "things" were being kept from the President. For the good of the country, they had been told —and they had believed it. They knew him almost as well as Marty Aleman. They knew what a weak, self-absorbed and useless man he was.

But he was also the President and they were sworn to protect him. The agent in charge nodded, reluctantly. Marty was dropped to his knees, frisked and handcuffed, all with the cameras rolling.

Feeling the moment, the President went to stand over Marty. "Give me the names of your co-conspirators and I will *try* to be lenient with you."

345

Marty Aleman was undone. No lie in the world could get him out of this. He could only try to mitigate and manage the fallout. "Carlton Francis, the Secretary of Defense. General Heider, the Chairman of the Joint Chiefs of Staff. George Cook, the Secretary of Homeland Security." He knew the President suspected them already.

The press gasped, as one, while the President shook his head, his eyes closed as though hearing the names pained him, though secretly he was glad. He hadn't wanted to torture Marty, but he would have to get those names. "And what about General Phillips?" the President asked.

Phillips was in up to his neck, but Marty knew that out of all of them, he was the most vital. The outcome of the war teetered on the knife's edge. It was still winnable, but only if a real leader was in charge. General Phillips was that leader, and he was irreplaceable.

"No, not General Phillips. He was just following orders."

"Like a good little Nazi?" the President demanded, in a voice that echoed like thunder in the near silent building.

In spite of his predicament, Marty appreciated the question and the way it was delivered with righteous indignation. It was a party staple to castigate opponents as Nazis, but in this case, it wouldn't work.

"No sir. He was following orders like a good *American* soldier. Heider told him to report only to himself, but didn't tell him why. General Phillips had no clue about any of this."

The President stared hard into Marty's eyes, a sneer twisting his lips. "Maybe, maybe. Or maybe he's the real leader of the coup? Doesn't he command the army? The actual army? The army that should have won this a long time ago? I see what is going on. He let this drag out to undermine me. You all did. But you didn't just undermine me, you also undermined this great country and I won't stand for it a second longer."

He suddenly turned and walked a few feet away, snapping his fingers at the lead Secret Services agent. "Have Phillips arrested," the President said to the officer in a whisper. "Him and his staff. And Platnik. And Axelrod. And whoever is supposed to be running the 3rd ID. They're all in on this."

The moment felt like something out of *The Godfather*. It was a "cleaning house" sort of moment in the President's mind, while in actuality he had just cut the head off of his military and like most things, decapitation generally leads to death.

Chapter 25

1– 11:01 p.m.
—Taconic High School, New York

The call had come in fifteen minutes before. "Rod, it's Platnik. The President has gone fucked in the head. He's conducting a purge, and we both made the list, so you'd better figure shit out before they come to arrest you."

General Axelrod hadn't been all that surprised. It had been a wonder that it hadn't happened sooner. "How long do we have?"

"Not long. He's moving on us really fucking quickly."

"Thanks…and uh, good luck."

If history was any indicator, they would both need all the luck they could get. Generals were often scapegoats when the shit hit the fan and they frequently were forced to eat a bullet or have their necks stretched.

Axelrod sat there in the hangar for all of ten seconds feeling a strange sensation of relief. Yes, he would be arrested and he would be sent to some far off jail and there was a chance he would die, but on the plus side he'd get some sleep and this mess would be someone else's problem. The idea held some appeal.

"But who would take over?" he asked, under his breath. "And how long would they last before they were purged as well? And how many people would die as a result?"

So much for relaxing. He stood and clapped his large hands together three times to get everyone's attention. "We are going mobile folks. Take only the essentials. Robert, I'm going to need two of your Blackhawks," he said, deciding on the spot to rescue Dr. Lee. Before, she had been an unnecessary risk, now she and her cure was a bargaining chip.

Robert Middleton, his aviation operations officer, shook his head. "I have one right now, but the second might be thirty minutes, maybe more. The birds of 101st are dry and stranded."

"Shit,"Axelrod mumbled, looking over his staff. Some would have to stay and risk getting arrested. He picked out seven of his staff, men of proven valor and ability. He added Courtney Shaw. As big a pain as Courtney had been, she was an absolute communications wizard, and would be valuable once they took their show on the road.

There was one more slot on the helicopter and, with a shrug, he chose John Burke. He was immune to the disease and there was no telling when that would come in handy.

"We are going, now!" he told them. "Arm yourselves. We're going to make a stop in Indian country." John and Courtney shared a look of hope as Axelrod's staff, a group of senior officers, most of whom were pushing fifty, scrambled for their weapons and their gear and followed him out to the flight line where a Blackhawk was spooling up.

Courtney hauled a scanner in one hand and a blocky sat-phone in the other. As soon as they were on board, she yelled into the radio: "We're coming. Where are you?"

Thuy and Deckard's balloon had run out of fuel twenty minutes before. They were south of the high school and were slowly dropping down into a forest. Among the trees were countless undead, staring up at the expanse of white silk with vacant eyes.

"Please hurry!" Thuy whispered into the radio, just as the basket was scraping the tips of the trees. "We're south of the school. When we hit, we're going to try to make it to a field that's west of it." She flicked off the radio quickly since it would do nothing but attract more zombies.

"You ready?" Deckard asked, as the basket shook beneath them and threatened to pitch onto its side.

Thuy sunk as low as she could. She was terrified of falling, terrified of getting stabbed in the face by a branch, and terrified of getting eaten alive by one of her creations. She only nodded, afraid to say a word. Then they hit for real. She was thrown forward into Deckard. He grabbed

349

her with one hand and grabbed the side of the basket with the other just as it rolled and they were tossed to the other side.

There was a great deal of snapping and smacking and thrashing before a branch impaled the basket, ripping up from the bottom like a spear. The branch then cracked in half and once more the two were on their sides as the basket went over, further and further.

"Grab onto the ropes!" Deckard cried when it became obvious that the basket was going to tip completely over. Thuy didn't so much as grab the ropes which were spilling all over the place, as she fell into them. For a moment, she felt like a fly caught in a web, then she was falling, as the forest echoed with the high scream of tearing silk.

She dropped through the green canopy, the ropes spinning and searing along her arms and back, her body twisting uncontrollably until she landed on the soft earth with a heavy thud and a most unladylike: "Ooof!" The wind was driven from her body and as she lay there desperately trying to suck in a breath, Deckard descended from the heights, sliding easily down a rope, making it look effortless.

He came down to one knee, pulled the M4 from across his shoulders, and asked in a whisper, "Are you okay? Can you walk?"

Since she couldn't breathe, she couldn't talk. Thuy nodded her head and before she could blink, Deckard had lifted her to her feet and was pulling her along, hurrying through the forest as best as he could. It was too dark to go faster than a quick stumble and Thuy, still struggling to catch her breath, seemed to trip over every root and fallen branch.

Almost at once, the zombies were upon them, appearing like phantoms out of the dark. Deckard was running now, somehow keeping the two of them just ahead of the swarming beasts. They only made it fifty yards when the shadows in front of them birthed more of the nightmare creatures.

Deckard lifted the M4 and fire seemed to leap from the muzzle. Five shots and then the two were running again. They didn't get far before they were cut off by a second wave. There were hundreds of them, too many to fight and too many to try to run through.

"The trees!" he cried. "Quick, get up in them."

Thuy hadn't climbed a tree since she was eleven and these trees were thick and the branches were high. She scraped at the bark, trying to get some purchase as Deckard started firing again with a noise like thunder. The rifle was so loud that she didn't hear the Blackhawk suddenly appear over them.

It shot flares from its sides, lighting up the forest and mesmerizing both the undead and Thuy, who thought that dozens of repelling soldiers would be following the flares.

Deckard knew better than to expect an assault team to try to drop down through such a thick canopy. The flares were meant as both a distraction and as a way to light his path. With so much light, he was able to actually sprint. Thanks to the sneakers she had taken from the lost and found, Thuy was able to keep up for once.

They darted around the zombies and the trees until the flares went dim. Then the zombies came alive again and chased the two out of the forest. With a thousand zombies behind them, they ran for the Blackhawk that was settling down in the field.

Thuy should have been thankful, but all she could think was: *why on earth did they land so far away*. She was flagging badly and gasping for breath when the door gunner on the Blackhawk started firing, walking his rounds from left to right. Deckard didn't flinch as the tracers came uncomfortably close. In his mind, the closer the better when the other option was being dragged down by a horde of zombies.

Then the two of them were in the chopper, being pulled aboard by a helmeted crew member. For a few moments, Thuy knelt on her hands and knees, her heart racing and her nerves tingling with a sudden surge of happiness—she had made it! She was alive and free and safe. Happiness surged wildly through her. She wanted to kiss the deck of the helicopter, but knew that it would look weird.

Sitting up she yelled, "Thank you!" above the roar of the engines as they lifted off. "Thanks so…" She faltered upon seeing the other passengers, who were, for the most part, shockingly old. In her mind, rescue work and fighting were a young man's game. Then her eyes fell on Courtney Shaw and she rushed over to her and embraced her tightly. Thuy tried to thank her, however the noise was too great. One of the older men took off his headset and gave it to Thuy.

"Dr. Lee, this is General Axelrod," Thuy heard Courtney say through the soft foam headset. Courtney pointed to the oldest of the soldiers. He had two black stars on his collar and dark eyes that were sizing her up. Thuy stuck out her hand, which was swallowed up in the general's big paw.

"It's nice to meet you," she said. "And thanks for the ride. We'll need to get to the Walton facility as fast as possible."

He gave her a queer look. "We're not going to Walton." He didn't really know where they were going, but they certainly weren't going to be leapfrogging around the Quarantine Zone at the whim of a civilian. "Why would we go there anyway? You said there was no cure."

"I said that there wasn't a cure yet," Thuy explained, "but I'm convinced that the possibility for one lies in Walton. Anna and Eng will go for the ruined Com-cells. I know it. More than likely they'll doctor the results of any demonstration by using high doses of opiates and then blame any later issues on a mutating gene."

"Why don't they just replicate your work?" Axelrod asked.

Thuy laughed. "Because they can't. Neither of them is actually a Ph.D. and I'm sure I'm the only one on any of the teams who has memorized every single data point within this study. In case you're wondering, yes, you should be impressed."

Across the helicopter, Deckard snorted. When Axelrod glared at him, Deckard said, "If finding a cure is a priority, then you should trust her."

"Unfortunately, right at the moment, a cure is low on my priority list. It ranks behind winning the war and not being arrested." The general took a few minutes to explain the situation.

Thuy listened with her steepled fingers touching her full lips, her eyes staring down across the tips of her nails, which were ragged and ripped. In her concentration, she didn't notice them. When he finished speaking, all eyes turned to Thuy, who sat there, gently nodding her head. She had come to a conclusion on how to proceed. "We'll go to Walton. There are thousands of pre-receptored Com-cells in the BSL-4 labs. I'm going to need them."

Axelrod started to speak, however Thuy held up a single finger. "From there we'll go to the R&K Research Center in Stoney Point. It's about twenty miles north of New York City and it has everything you need, sir. One of the founders of R&K, Stephan Kipling, insisted on security. It's basically a fortress, sir. It has a generator, secure communications, and biosuits. You should be able to run your war from there and I'll be able to work on a cure."

"In the middle of the fucking zone?" Axelrod demanded.

"I think so," Deckard said, seeing the idea as the perfect balance between safety, danger, and productivity. "It's the last place anyone would look. You can run the battle through junior officers. If the President finds out, do you really think he will send soldiers into the Zone to arrest you guys? I doubt it."

"And there aren't any zombies there?" Axelrod asked.

That was a question Thuy couldn't answer. The R&K Research Center had been constructed with security in mind and yet, she knew that far more secure locations had been overcome by the zombies. She shrugged. "I'm sure there are some, but no more than anywhere else. I don't see what you have to lose."

"How about my life?" He sat back and gazed at Thuy like a poker player looking for tells in an opponent who had just gone all in. Thuy stared back, calmly, without emotion. He was the first to blink. "Fine," he said. "Let's do it. Someone tell the pilot to head to Walton."

Courtney Shaw held up a hand. "I sorta already did a minute ago. Since I knew you were so smart and all, General, I figured that you would appreciate the time I saved you." She gave him a weak smile and he glared it into a grimace. "We can talk about that later, right? Hey, I see Walton. There's the helicopter. Are they about to take off? Is that a body next to it?"

"Why is there a fire on top of the building?" the general asked. "That looks like a beacon. Do you think the FBI is calling for help?"

Thuy gazed down on what had once been her pride and joy, the place where she had discovered the cure for cancer. It had once been beautiful but was now ugly, burnt, black and tortured. "The FBI didn't light that fire," Thuy told him. "*Something* else did."

2—11:26 p.m.
The Walton Facility

Inside the facility Special Agent Katherine Pennock was horribly, dreadfully alone and had never been more afraid in her life.

Earlier, on their way up to the fourth floor, as the team crept through the building, she had been nervous, but when she saw zombies crawling out from under the ruined floors, and out of dark crevices, her nervousness quickly became fear. Later, witnessing Joe Swan being swarmed and eaten pushed her blood pressure sky high and increased her fear tenfold.

"Back inside!" she hissed to the others. They raced into the admin section, where she was forced to shoot three hulking creatures that had torn aside the cubicles to get at them. The last one took three bullets to the head before it went down, almost at her feet.

"That was close," she said, turning to the others. "We can't stay…" Her foot came down on something soft and she jumped. Katherine had stepped on PFC Jennifer Jackson. The soldier was lying face down on the floor. There was no sign of Anna or Eng, or of Jackson's rifle.

In a flash, she saw her predicament: She was in a building filled with zombies, there were two terrorists on the loose who would think nothing about murdering her, and she had no way to escape the Zone. It was right then that her fear began to boil into terror.

"Jennifer? Jennifer?" Katherine whispered, giving the woman's shoulder a little shake without eliciting the slightest response. She then slid her fingers beneath the woman's mask, feeling for a pulse. She was still alive. There was blood leaking from the back of her head and Katherine guessed that Eng had hit her with the edge of his shield just below the lip of her helmet.

"Please wake up, Jennifer," Katherine practically begged, slapping her lightly on the cheek and shaking her again. There were more zombies coming. They had heard her shooting and now they were stumbling through the refuse.

Katherine stood so that her eyes just cleared the top edge of the cubicle. She counted eight shadowy creatures coming for her. She wanted to run away, but she knew that they would eat Jennifer if she did, so Katherine dragged the soldier to the nearest room that had an intact door. It was a storeroom and there was a corpse in it.

"Hey!" she hissed at it. The body certainly looked very dead, but she was no expert. With her M4 pointed at it, she gave it a kick. It didn't budge. This was all the time she had for corpse testing and she slid Jennifer inside and shut the door.

"Now what?" Katherine asked herself. She had no idea. She couldn't stay in the storeroom; the zombies would sniff her out and break down the door. And she couldn't fly a helicopter… "But maybe Jennifer can." It was possible. Jennifer wasn't an expert or even licensed, but she had been around Blackhawks for the last few years. "Maybe she had picked up enough to fly a little."

Katherine was grasping at a very thin, very brittle and very short straw, but it was all she had.

She tried once more to wake Jennifer before she heard the snuffling of a zombie coming closer. She came up with a plan on the spot. She would distract the zombies, find Eng, get the Com-cells that he had volunteered to cart around in his backpack, and get back. Hopefully, by that time Jennifer would have regained consciousness.

With a deep, hot breath, she threw open the door, bashing aside a zombie that had been sniffing the cracks. There were more of them all around her. She fired the M4 three times and then kicked the storeroom door closed. A scabby hand grabbed her armored shoulder but she shook it off and ran, ducking through the billing room and into the patient reception area, which was windowless and pitch black.

Her shin struck a desk with a rocket of pain. Stifling a grunt, she felt along the desk until her hand hit nothing but the empty, black air. She hurried on, stumbling like one of the things that were chasing after her, when the door opened behind her.

At first, she thought that one of the brain-dead beasts had accidentally hit the handle but then, just as she slunk low, she heard a little voice: "She here? She here, Jammee?"

"Hush. I cun smell her good."

The voices had been croaky and evil, but also small. They were the voices of children—child zombies. The same ones that had eaten Joe Swan. The thought sent a wave of goosebumps across her flesh and she ducked lower until she was practically lying on the floor.

Katherine began to crawl away as the patter of little feet came closer. There were more than just two of them. The pack was in the room, sniffing and poking about. Katherine was just about shitting herself when she saw a gleam of dull light. There was another door!

She scuttled across the floor to the door. Without hesitation, she threw it open and ran out of the room and found herself in a corridor with doors leading from it at regular intervals. Afraid that she would be seen if she didn't pick one of the closer ones, she took the third door and closed it behind her just as the pack spilled out into the hall.

"Where she, Jammee?"

Jaimee Lynn walked into the corridor, naked as ever, blood dripping down from her slick jaw. "She's hidin' I reckon. You hidin' missus? I like it when y'all hide. Because, it's more funner. I's gonna find youuuu! And I's gonna eat youuuu!" She screamed this and the words echoed throughout the silent building.

A floor above them, Anna and Eng heard her scream. Anna cringed behind her riot shield, while Eng felt a queer, quivering sensation slip through his bones. When he had been locked away in the trooper's station, he had heard stories about the little ones with their little rat-teeth and their cunning little minds. He had only half believed it then.

He believed it completely now, but he told himself that he wasn't afraid. "They're after the FBI agent and that is why I left her alive," he said.

Not a minute before, Anna had dared to question him on the subject, hinting that he had been afraid of her. *You should have killed the fed*, she had insisted. *She's the one with the keys to the cuffs.*

Eng hadn't been exactly afraid. He preferred the term 'cautious.' Katherine had proven to be no slouch with a gun. Besides, there was another set of handcuff keys in the building. They just had to get to them while the zombies were busy hunting down the agent.

"We must hurry," he hissed and picked his way through the mess, heading for the north stairwell. It wasn't empty. They heard the zombie coming down towards them. It fell frequently, making all sorts of ruckus. Eng hoped that it would be a 'partial' in other words, a zombie that was already mostly dead. He wasn't so lucky.

It was a female, but a big one and fully formed. Having no other choice, he shot it and the sound of the M4 in the confined space was like a canon. Everyone and everything in the building heard it. The zombie fell at Eng's feet and he stepped lightly over it as if it were nothing more than a blob of gum that he didn't want to step in.

Anna held the beam of her light on it longer, afraid that despite the gaping hole in the side of its head, it would come alive and get her. "Jesus," she whispered and then ran up after Eng. It wasn't easy to run with cuffed hands, one holding the unwieldy shield and the other the flashlight. But he wasn't waiting for her or for anyone. He had the Com-cells in his pack, a gun in his hands, and soon he would have the keys to his cuffs.

Four days earlier, there had been an infected police officer with a battering ram who had nearly made it onto the fourth floor. Eng remembered it very well. That man had died a real death and Eng was betting his life that his body was still in the stairwell.

And it was. Grinning behind his mask, Eng pulled the blackened keys from the corpse and handed them to Anna. "Unlock me," he ordered.

She pushed the keys back towards him and held out her own hands. "Unlock me, first. You'll still have your gun, don't worry."

"I'm not worried," he said, taking the keys and unlocking her hands. "I could kill you without the gun."

He was right. He could kill her with ease and at the same time, she knew she could reach out and yank his mask off; she was sure her gloved hands were just covered in Com-cells. She unlocked him saying, "Just tell me how we get out of here alive. Can you fly that helicopter?"

"No," he said, dashing her hopes. They left the stairwell and went to the window that overlooked the helicopter, which was still spinning its blades. They could see zombies flocking in and at first, he didn't understand why they were heading towards the hospital.

Anna went to the window and looked up. "There's a fire on the roof. I can see the flames. But who would do that? It's only attracting more zombies. No! It was those awful little ones! They did it."

Eng didn't want to believe it was possible. It was one thing to retain rudimentary speech and to perhaps open simple doors, but this was a level far beyond that. If the fire had been set on purpose it meant…"We're trapped," Eng whispered.

Jaimee Lynn had indeed sent two of her pack to make fire. The big monsters were slow and dumb, but they were also necessary. She needed them to eat all the bullets in the soldier's guns so that she could eat the soldiers just like she had eaten Joe Swan. Her craving for his blood had been more than just desire. After her long trek across Connecticut, she had been weak and dizzy. Now, she was strong, full of malignant energy.

It pulsed through her, and when she put her hand on the wall of the first floor corridor, she could almost feel the building as a living thing. She could feel the air around her as its breath and the walls as its bones. And, along those bones, ran a current that she alone could feel.

From behind the third door on the right along that first floor corridor, she felt Special Agent Katherine Pennock trembling in the corner as she pointed a gun at the door. And Jaimee Lynn could feel Anna and Eng's panic sifting down from above. She could even feel the warmth of PFC Jennifer Jackson lying unconscious in the storage room.

Jaimee Lynn could eat her at any time, only right then she was in the mood to hunt. She loved the taste and feel of the blood when it was filled with adrenaline. It was hotter and richer and made her stronger.

The little zombie would eat Jennifer Jackson, that was certain, but she wanted to taste the fear in Katherine Pennock first. She started tapping on the walls, knowing that Katherine's fear would amp with every knock. She had only tapped three times, coming closer and closer, when she heard General Axelrod's helicopter. This changed her plans, but not by much. A grin creased the drying blood on her face as she said, "More meat."

3—11:40 p.m.

The Walton Facility

Deckard looked down at the facility and just like Thuy, thought of it as *his* building. It had been his responsibility to protect and he had failed in that responsibility. This was a second chance for him and, unlike Thuy, he wasn't afraid to go back inside.

He could see her fear and it was understandable. She was small, weak, delicate, and what was being asked of her was preposterous.

There were only four of them going into the building. Himself, Thuy, John Burke and one of the crewmen of the Blackhawk. Axelrod wasn't even allowing Courtney to go in, though she hadn't fought all that strenuously for the chance to be eaten alive.

"There are millions of people counting on this group of people," Axelrod said, gesturing to his staff, all of whom were trying to run their perspective commands from the cramped cabin of a moving Blackhawk.

"And there are hundreds of millions of people counting on a cure," Deckard shot back.

Axelrod lifted a hand, suggesting with it: *what can you do?* "You have your job to do and I have mine. So, let's get cracking."

Thuy had not counted on the facility being so overrun with zombies. She figured there would be a couple of dozen and that Deckard and most of the soldiers would accompany her. They'd be in and out in no time. This was much, much different. Clearly the first team had met with some sort of disaster.

They could see a body next to the grounded Blackhawk. It was the only sign of the first team—and if a team under the auspices of the White House could be obliterated, how on earth could four people win out?

An M4 was thrust into her hands. Deckard held out a magazine for her. She took it and fit it up into the bottom of the gun, gave it a little smack to make sure it was seated properly and then pressed the little button that sent the bolt home, loading the weapon.

"Piece of cake," she said, with a sour grin.

"It won't be," Conan Westemeyer, the crew member who was going with them said. "We have to get in and out of there in twenty minutes. The pilot says he doesn't have the fuel to hang around any longer."

Thuy felt her stomach drop, and even Deckard looked shocked. John Burke was unfazed. He squinted out of the Blackhawk's open door. "We is gonna do this just fine, don't y'all worry none 'bout that. We'll get them what not-cells and once we get safe, y'alls gonna fix me up with a real cure, right Dr. Lee?"

She owed the world a cure. "I'll do what I can, though some things will…"

The Blackhawk's M240 began barking as the chopper slowly descended across from the first helicopter, whose blades were still spinning. There were plenty of targets for the machine gun and the carnage was sickening. Thuy couldn't watch. When she turned away, Courtney grabbed her hand and mouthed over the storm of noise: *Be safe!* Thuy nodded, her stomach whirling with butterflies.

She thought that she should've been more prepared for battle. After all, she'd been in near constant danger for days now. But here she was, trembling and feeling as though she were about to be sick. Thuy fought the nausea, not wanting to add the embarrassment of puking on top of everything else.

"Deep breaths," she told herself. "Deep breaths and you're going to be fine…Oh, shit!" The Blackhawk thumped to the pavement and she fell to the side, only to be caught by Deckard, who yelled something into her ear. "What?" she yelled back. He had already turned away, pulling her out of the helicopter.

The moment she dropped onto the ground, the Blackhawk shot up again, its blades sounding like they were slapping the air, its gun going nonstop.

"Stay right on my ass!" Deckard yelled to her. He led the way, hurrying forward, his M4 pointed straight ahead. Westemeyer was three steps back and to the right, while John was three back and to the left. Thuy came last, mindful of only three things: it would be bad to accidentally shoot Deckard in the back, there were hundreds and hundreds of zombies rushing right for them, and her completely filled bladder felt as though it were about to burst.

Fearlessly, Deckard walked through the destroyed front gates and although he had his finger on the trigger, he didn't fire. Their ride had not gone far. It hovered sixty feet up and about fifty to their right, a perfect angle for the door gunner who was spraying fire and lead from his M240 like it was a hose, sweeping back the undead and creating a gruesome lane for the four of them to hurry through.

Thuy had been a bridesmaid at a wedding once. She had walked on rose petals wearing dainty, pink sandals. Here, she walked through a flowing river of black blood and body parts. Had she not been so frightened, she would have been too sickened to move. Her fear kept her going and the helicopter kept them safe right up until they entered the building. Then they were on their own.

Outside it had been dark, inside it was an entirely different sort of dark. Thuy could only think of it as "nightmare" dark. She fumbled for a flashlight and flicked it on.

"Fuck!" John screamed without warning, and began shooting as hideous beasts with diseased humanoid faces and wide, gaping mouths lunged out of the dark. The lobby became lit by flashes from the guns, but it wasn't enough.

"The light! I need the light!" Westemeyer yelled. Thuy swung the beam to the right and watched him blast three zombies into pieces. He was firing an M249, a light machine gun that was usually called a SAW. On the helicopter, it had appeared to Thuy to be heavy and cumbersome. Now it was a blessing.

Wherever Westemeyer pointed the SAW, the undead were hurled back and Deckard had the good sense to drop into a crouch and pull John Burke down with him. Westemeyer fired over their heads, killing everything that moved, and Thuy felt a strange elation at the death.

But it didn't last. The SAW jammed, and try as he might, he was unable to clear it. Deckard took Thuy's as yet fired M4 and handed it to him. "We'll find you something," he said to Thuy. "For now, take this and keep us covered." He gave her his flashlight so that she had one in each hand. To Thuy, the flashlights were one step up from being naked.

She shone them back and forth as Deckard led them through the carnage and to the central stairwell, stopping as dozens of undead poured from the open door. Jaimee Lynn had propped open all the stairwell doors and now the beasts could go anywhere they pleased in the building.

"Not this way," Deckard said and then ran down a hallway with Thuy and the others struggling to catch up. They went through the admin section, keeping low and heading for the north stairwell. They were just passing a maze of cubicles, when a slight voice called out: "Help me."

Deckard stopped so suddenly that Thuy rammed into his back. "Over there," he whispered, pointing. "What is that?"

Thuy shone one of her lights. They saw a soldier with long dark hair spilling from her helmet, kneeling against a chair, her head bowed. She looked as if she was using the chair to get up.

"Are you okay?" Deckard asked, as he hurried up to her. She didn't answer or move. She looked stuck in that simple position. "Hey, are you..." He touched her shoulder and she fell over. "What the fuck?" he hissed, jumping back. In the light of the beam, they saw Jennifer Jackson's

363

corpse, her throat had been torn out. It barely bled. Jaimee Lynn had sucked her dry.

"What the fuck!" Westemeyer cried. "Wait, if she's dead then who called to us?" In answer, there was a childish giggle from their right and a door opened. Thuy spun the light in time to see a flood of undead spewing from the open door.

Deckard shot the first two, dropping them and causing a pile up. "Let's go!" he bellowed and raced on, just as more doors opened. The first door to open was to their left and the four of them shied away from it just as another door on their right burst open.

In a flash, diseased hands were clawing at them. Westemeyer screamed a curse as something with shocking strength caught hold of his chest rig and pulled him off balance. He turned and fired a long burst, but the M4 was torn from his hands. In the semi-dark, which was lit only by gun flashes and the chaotic beams from Thuy's flashlight, he came face to face with what looked like a single horrific monster. It seemed as though it had a hundred arms and a hundred mouths. "Fuck!" he screamed at the top of his lungs as he was yanked forward into the creature and was swallowed beneath it.

Thuy saw the writhing mass and tried to dodge around it, but a long grey arm reached out and grabbed her ankle, tripping her and sending her sprawling.

Deckard had been spinning and shooting in every direction; now he charged, but his magazine was empty and the gun was useless. He used his heavy boots to stomp Thuy free.

Then she was up and running and he was running right beside her. With the dark and zombies coming at them from every direction, she had no idea where they were exactly or where they were going. She only knew that as they raced around the first floor of the building, they ran from one mob of the undead to the next. And it couldn't last. Their bullets would run out, their energy would run out and, lastly their blood would run out of them.

Thuy was gasping for breath when she heard a new voice, "This way!" The voice was high and piercing, and all three of them stopped in their tracks, fearing another trap, but then a flashlight flicked on and they saw what they thought was another soldier.

It was Special Agent Katherine Pennock decked out in body armor and carrying an M4. "Get over here, damn it!" This was no monster playing tricks and the three of them charged through the open door and then threw their weight against it.

They eyed Katherine, dubiously, none of them able to hide their disappointment—Katherine was alone and small and not terribly well armed.

"Turn off the lights, Dr. Lee," Katherine commanded.

Hearing her name made Thuy jump and before she turned off the lights, she shot one into Katherine's face. "How do you know me?" Thuy asked.

Katherine pushed the light away. "You're on the FBI's most wanted list. Currently you're number one, but you won't be for long. Anna and Eng escaped. They knocked out a soldier who was with me and I'm pretty sure they went upstairs, though why, I don't know. They have the Com-cells already, so it doesn't make sense."

"My, that's a lot to take in," Thuy said, trying to recover her wits. "I-I'm afraid we found a dead soldier over by the admin section. It was a woman with dark hair and she was freshly dead. And perhaps the reason why Anna and Eng went upstairs is that they realized their mistake. The Com-cells are ruined. Likely, they're after the same things we are."

"Your notes?" Katherine asked.

Thuy shook her head. "No. We are after the different structures that make up the Com-cells. You might call them building blocks in much the same way amino acids build proteins. I'm hoping to reconfigure these structures so as to produce a new…"

"We don't have time for this, Thuy," Deckard said. "We need to get upstairs, get the shit and go. But we'll never get up there without a distraction. Any volunteers?"

Being a distraction sounded like a death sentence and John snorted at the idea. Katherine had a real mask and actual armor, but still found herself looking down at her boots. Deckard figured that he would have to do it and had asked the question without any real hope that someone would say, *yes*, thus it was a surprise when Thuy raised her hand.

"I'll do it," she said. When Deckard gave her a sharp look, she added, "Trust me. I was somewhat turned around back there and panicked, but I'm better now…at least a little. Come on. Follow me."

To everyone's amazement, she opened the door to the hall and strode out, flicking on both flashlights.

"Damn it, Thuy!" Deckard cried, following after her. He was barely out the door before the first of the zombies were upon them, moaning in hunger and reaching with their long arms. Thuy hadn't run away as she should have, instead she illuminated the beasts with her lights, giving Deckard a fine opportunity to kill the first four in front of them.

John and Katherine joined in, killing a dozen, but also attracting so many that they filled the hallway.

"Now!" Thuy cried, waving her lights. "Run!"

Katherine ran with the others, thinking that Thuy's reputation as a genius did not seem well founded. In fact, she seemed a little crazy as she sped ahead to where the hall branched and then just stood there swinging one flashlight in circles as if she were at a one-woman rave.

Thuy pushed Deckard away from her, saying, "To the left!"

Without questioning what appeared to be a break from reality, Deckard moved to the hall on their left where the darkness was very deep. But what good was darkness when the creatures could sniff them out? John followed just as obediently and Katherine could only succumb to the same sort of peer pressure that made Jonestown such a vacation site. They stood against the wall fifteen feet from where Thuy was still swinging the light in circles.

With the monsters rushing down on her, she waited until the last second before sliding the still lit flashlight far down to the right, where it skittered and bounced sending out beams in every direction. It was the only light source and the zombies didn't question whether or not there was still a human attached to it. They rushed after it while Thuy eased over to the others.

"That was fucked up," John muttered.

Thuy shushed him and proceeded to lead the group to the north stairs. Once they were behind the door, and somewhat safe, she felt a strange euphoric rush from being so close to death. She felt like giggling, but stifled it and forced herself to revert to form.

"We should spray ourselves down and change out our masks and gloves," she said, her voice higher than normal. The fighting had been so close and so intense that they all agreed. The process went quickly, but not quickly enough. Thuy was just starting to get her first latex glove on when she saw a glow of light at the bottom of the stairwell door. She sucked in her breath and leaned back into Deckard, pointing at the light.

Katherine, who had her mask dangling around her neck, grabbed her M4 and pointed it at the door, whispering, "There's one that can still talk and think. It's…it's evil."

Deckard put a finger to his lips and started backing up the stairs. He had his gun pointed at the door as well and nearly pulled the trigger when Jaimee Lynn sang out, "Doctor Leeeee. I cun smell you, Dr. Lee. An' I cun smell that man, an' that woman, an'…an' I cun smell…"

Before he had almost flinched off a random shot. Now, he shot on purpose: *BAM!* The gun going off in the enclosed space almost deafened them. "Get upstairs, quick!" He was not afraid of Jaimee Lynn. But he knew her. He knew the sound of her voice and he was afraid what John Burke would do when he found out that it was his little girl with a bloated stomach full of blood and mad, black eyes.

367

He fired twice more and then ran with the others. Thuy had led the way with John next to her, but she was out of shape and he was dying of lung cancer. Katherine passed them. At the third floor landing, she shot and killed two of the beasts that had been lurking in the dark. This was a reminder to put her mask on, which made breathing twice as hard, and the next two flights had her lungs billowing as she fought for air.

She paused at the top as that horrible child's voice called up from the dark depths of the stairwell. "Daidy? Is that y'all, daidy?"

Deckard yelled, "Go!" and then turned and shot down the small opening that went from the top of the stairwell all the way to the bottom. There wasn't anything to shoot at, he was just trying to drown out the sound of her voice.

Thuy started pushing John Burke up the stairs. She was gasping and afraid, while he was lightheaded and dazed.

It was just dawning on Katherine what the evil child was saying. She was asking for her daddy. She was asking for John Burke. Katherine had read his file as well and vaguely remembered that he had a daughter. It was no wonder that Deckard was trying to get them up the stairs as fast as possible.

But they couldn't rush it. Even with the seconds ticking past and hundreds of zombies boiling up from the depths of the building, she knew that Anna and Eng were somewhere in the building and they were as deadly as adders. Katherine kicked open the door to the fourth floor and immediately saw Anna Holloway. She was twenty feet away, framed against a window. Although it was dark, Katherine knew that it was her.

"Freeze!" Katherine ordered and stepped out from the stairwell, and that was when she felt the barrel of a gun jab her in the back of the neck.

"No, you freeze," Eng whispered, as he grabbed the back of her armored vest and yanked her away from the door.

Katherine had not checked her six as she had been taught, and was paying the price. She raised her hands, lifting the gun, hoping to be able to spin into her enemy and smash him across the face when he least expected it, however Eng kicked her in the back of the knees and dropped her.

"What are you doing?" Eng hissed to Anna, who was still standing in the doorway with her hands up. "Get over here."

The next twenty seconds were complete confusion. Anna ran past the stairwell door just as Thuy and John Burke stepped onto the floor. Thuy only had a flashlight and John was spinning, both mentally and physically. He gaped at Anna but then saw Eng crouched behind Katherine and nearly choked. Eng had his gun pointed in such a way as to be able to shoot either Katherine or himself with just a twitch.

"Hey, Eng, I didn't do nuffin' to you." He raised his hands and Anna darted forward to grab his gun.

As she did, Thuy turned in a circle, not knowing which way to turn. Everything was happening so fast. "Deckard!" she cried. "Don't come in…"

Eng pointed his gun at her. "Yes, we don't want him to come in. Shut the door and sit down against it. You hear that, Deckard? She's going to be a doorstop, either dead or alive. It's your choice."

Deckard froze just on the threshold of the doorway. Through the crack, he could make out Eng crouched down behind the woman they had just met. In between her and the door were John and Thuy. Eng could kill all three in a blink—but he wouldn't. He would shoot to wound knowing that the zombies would stop to feast and he'd be able to get away.

It was exactly what he was planning to do with Deckard. He'd be trapped in the stairwell, alone with hundreds of zombies, and the only light he'd have was the flashlight carried by Jaimee Lynn Burke. A shiver went up Deckard's back, because he was stuck.

He had no choice except to reach out and shut the door. It didn't shut easily and screeched like an old woman and then banged closed with a thunderous noise that marked not just the end of the day but the end of his life as well.

The sound rolled down the stairs and for a moment the zombies paused and in the silence, a hideous voice whispered from out of the darkness, "Who is that? Is that the man? I smell y'all, mister. I smell y'all's blood."

Chapter 26

1– Midnight and Beyond
—The Walton Facility

"That's Jaimee Lynn," John Burke said, his face queered up. "That's my daughter." The voice echoing up the stairwell was madness itself. It was impossibly evil, so how was it Jaimee Lynn's? He had no idea, but he aimed to find out. "I gotta see my baby," he declared, reaching for the door handle.

"Touch that door and I'll put a bullet in your guts," Eng said, with such cold menace that John's hand froze inches from the door. "Is that how you want to meet her again? Bleeding and trying to hold in your intestines? I don't think so. You heard her. She's getting very hungry."

"But, she's my baby girl," John said, his hand opening and closing only a fingernail's distance from the handle. "She wouldn't hurt me and maybe she can't. I'm immune to that zombie stuff." He puffed up a bit as Anna and Eng shared a quick look. "Y'all thought you'd do me like the others an' shot me up with that zombie juice, but I didn't get sick."

Eng grunted out a laugh and asked, "Are you also immune to bullets? No? Then get away from the door. The only reason that any of you are still alive is that I need you to help me escape. That's your sole purpose, now. If you keep me alive, maybe I'll keep you alive. Any questions?"

"No, we get it," Thuy said, quickly, not challenging the obvious lie. He wasn't going to let any of them live. Only a fool would believe otherwise and there was no time to argue. "You'll hurt us if we don't cooperate." *And Deckard will die if we don't leave as quickly as possible*, she thought to herself. Only once they were gone would he be able to escape from the stairwell.

"Exactly," Eng said, his dark eyes at squints as he smiled behind his clear mask. "Now, please get against the wall while Anna frisks you." Thuy was the quickest to comply and her hands were on the door when Deckard fired his first shot. The vibrations of it went right into her palms and into her arms and then down into her soul. She couldn't help the whimpering sound that slipped out of her.

"Afraid for your boyfriend?" Eng asked. "That's sweet. Would you like to join him? You know I don't really need you, Thuy, I have a pardon. All I have to do is bring them the Com-cells and I'm home free. Sure, I may not have the cure for the zombie disease, but I'll be the man who cured cancer. They're going to give me a fucking medal."

Her eyes blazed as she looked back at him. The fury in her was so great that she almost launched herself at him. But, that was what he wanted. His right arm was tense, ready to slap her square across the face, something he'd been dying to do for months. She forced her anger to drain away, leaving her with that infuriating calm that he hated.

"A medal?" she asked with a raised eyebrow. "I highly doubt that since, as any actual scientist would know, the Com-cells have gone bad. They've been left unrefrigerated for days. I know you don't have a Ph.D. Eng, but even a high school science teacher knows what happens to fungal agents when they assume room temperature. They multiply. The Com-cells are more than useless. They'll likely turn any subject rabid."

His dark eyes opened a touch wider as he realized that she was right.

"I could help you," she said suddenly, seeing a better chance to save Deckard. "We have all the base molecules and the prepared stem-cells here in the lab. If you let Deckard back up, I'll make a new batch of Com-cells for you. You'll be the man who cured cancer and maybe we can find a cure for the zombie disease, as well. Think about that. Think about what a hero you'd be, then."

It didn't take more than two seconds for Eng to discard the idea. Its major flaw was that he would have to trust her. He didn't trust anyone. He didn't even trust his own partner in crime, Anna.

"The answer is no," Eng said. "But, thanks for the heads up about the Com-cells and the idea about starting from scratch. Anna and I can probably figure it out without your help. Right Anna?"

Deckard fired his M4 again, causing Anna to jump. Anna had quickly frisked the three, taking Katherine's service piece along with the M4s. Presently she stood off to the side, feeling as though she was losing it a little. Here they were on the fourth floor of the Walton Facility, right where everything had started. She hadn't wanted to be a part of any of this. She had wanted to make an easy ten million and go live the life of the rich and famous. And now, Eng wanted her help in recreating the Com-cell, the chemical make-up of which was so complicated that it could fill two entire blackboards?

Eng was crazy to think it was possible. She had been nothing but a research assistant with a full sweater and he had been more spy than scientist, and yet their pardon was contingent on finding a cure. She nodded and said, "Yeah, we could do that. I'll go get the stuff."

"Don't forget the organelles, they're in the white topped tubes," Eng yelled after her. "And the receptor cells are in the green ones." He turned to Thuy and asked, "What was the alkaline content of the receptor solution?"

"I thought you didn't need my help," she answered. In reply to his swift glare, she shrugged and added, "We are on a time limit, by the way. Our helicopter has about seven minutes of fuel left, and they will leave us." He cursed at this while she fought to maintain her composure. Seven minutes to save Deckard and escape the building. It couldn't be done.

In the stairwell, Deckard began firing faster and faster, the tempo painfully urgent. "Please, God," Thuy whispered. "Please, help us." She needed a miracle, but the closest she got was Anna sprinting out of the BSL-4 labs with a full pack on her back.

"Let's go!" Eng ordered. He felt the time getting away from them as well and jabbed John in the side with his rifle and pointed to the south stairs. John hesitated, so

Anna pushed Thuy in front and she was followed by Katherine Pennock.

Despite everything happening so quickly, Katherine tried to keep her head. She stayed on the balls of her feet and looked for any chance to go after Anna's rifle. With her broken fingers, Anna carried the M4 loosely and with a quick enough move, Katherine could snatch it from her. The problem was Eng, who looked ready to gun down anyone who made the slightest twitch.

John was third in line, dragging his feet, his mind in a whirl. A part of him didn't want to leave the building. Ever since his wife had died, Jaimee Lynn had been his entire world. He had lived for her—and now he was being told to abandon her in a building filled with zombies? It didn't make sense, and it didn't make sense that his little girl was craving blood. It made him sick to his stomach to think about it.

He almost felt like puking and, with every bullet Deckard fired, John's stomach ached worse. He kept wondering: was that the bullet that killed her, or was it that one, or that one?

Eng pushed them on, hissing for them to hurry, but when they got to the stairwell, John hesitated once more. There were burnt bodies here, and piles of refuse, and the smell was enough to make him gag. "I can't," he whispered.

Furious over the slightest delay, Eng bashed him on the back with the butt of his rifle, sending him flying down the stairs, knocking aside both Katherine and Thuy and landing among the trash.

Except where he was bleeding, John was covered head to toe in soot. Next to his hand was a four-foot length of pipe. He grabbed it and staggered to his feet, furious and ready to kill.

"Turn around and get walking or else," Eng said, his clear mask not hiding his sneer. He raised the M4 and sighted it on John's slight paunch.

Somewhere off to their left, Deckard's gun was firing nonstop, and the sound was enough to drain the fight out of John. He turned and trudged down the stairs, the pipe still in his hands. They all knew he would need it when they got to the bottom. Despite his promise of keeping everyone alive, Eng would sacrifice him to get through the main floor. He would sacrifice Thuy and Katherine as well, if that's what it took. And, if they happened to still be alive when they left the building, he would probably simply murder them both anyway.

And try as she might, Thuy could not think of a way to change her fate. She almost wished for a zombie attack. Not a big one, just one big enough to distract Anna and Eng, so she could do *something*, though what that something was, she didn't have a clue.

Her brain felt like mush and she hadn't figured out even the beginnings of a plan by the time they got to the main floor, which was almost clear of zombies. The vast majority of them were two floors up going after Deckard, who was fighting for his life against terrific odds.

Here, there were maybe a dozen or so, and they were widely spaced and slow to perceive the little group.

Thuy would have attempted to run past them, but Eng was cruel. "Go on, John. This is your one chance. Kill them all and you get to live."

John's eyes were full of hate. "Fucking Chinaman," he spat.

"Go," Eng said. With the gun pointed at him, John didn't have a choice. He hefted the pipe and started walking towards the first of the zombies, fully prepared to crush in its head, only just then Eng called out softly, "By the way, you aren't really immune. Anna thought she was stealing the actual cure for cancer when she switched your vial of Com-cells for distilled water. So, be careful that you don't get any blood on you."

This stopped John in his tracks. He was suddenly breathing like he had run a mile. "Y'alls lyin' right? Y'all just makin' that shit up to mess with me, right?"

Anna shook her head. "Sorry, no. I-I don't know why I did it...it was just...you better look out." She pointed past

John to where one of the zombies was bearing down on him with its diseased claws out and ready to infect him.

"Oh shit," John whispered and swung the pipe, but without conviction. His strength seemed to have drained from him, and the pipe merely left a groove in the thing's cheek. He tried again, only he swung while backing away, and this strike did even less damage, and now a second zombie had joined the first.

"Fight, John!" Thuy shouted. "You can still make it to the…"

Eng slapped her hard enough to drop her to the floor. "Keep talking and you'll join him," he hissed, before he reached down, grabbed her and yanked her up. Her face felt like it was on fire and her head swam from the blow. Eng thrust her in front of him. "Let's go. Move! Come on."

They left John swinging the pipe back and forth as more and more of the zombies attacked. For a moment, Thuy was envious of him, thinking that at least he had a fighting chance, while she was being led to the slaughter. The envious moment did not last long. They had just walked out into the night when John let out a terrified, wailing scream.

At best, he had been bitten; at worst, he was being dragged down under the weight of the pack. Thuy stumbled in fright and grief, wanting to go back for him. Eng hauled her on, hurrying through the battle-scarred grounds of the facility towards the sound of the helicopters on the other side of the fence. They could hear the rotors and the engines, but the actual choppers were unseen.

"This is good enough," Eng said, when they were in the parking lot. There were a few badly misshapen "partial" zombies dragging themselves at the group, but they posed no real threat. Eng was the real threat. There was only one reason to stop so close to the helicopters, he needed to tie up loose ends. Knowing this, Katherine and Thuy shared a look, each seeing the fear in the other.

"You don't have to do this, Mister Eng," Katherine said, speaking quickly. "You could let us go right here. Or, better yet, you could turn yourself in. There are drones above us and their cameras are rolling. They'll see if you shoot us and your pardon only covers prior criminal acts. If you kill us, you'll go to jail."

Eng glanced up and, had he been perhaps two feet closer, Katherine might have gone for his gun. The glance was very quick and when he looked back at Katherine, it was with a twisted smile. "Would it be murder if I killed an infected person?" he asked. "I don't think so, not in these times. All I have to say is that you were tragically infected while fighting off a mob of zombies. Heck, I'll even make you a hero. I'll say that you asked to be killed to keep the rest of America pure."

His logic, evil as it was, could not be disputed. "Fuck you, Eng," Katherine hissed between clenched teeth as he pointed the M4 at her face.

Not wanting to get sprayed with blood, even clean blood, Anna stepped to the side so that she was standing next to Thuy. In spite of everything she had done to survive, Anna was somewhat in shock that an execution was going to happen right in front her. "Oh shit," she whispered, the gun in her hand all but forgotten.

"Fuck you?" Eng asked. "Those are your last words? How American of you." His finger touched the trigger and that was when a distant gunshot rang out. Eng lurched forward as the bullet struck him in the back, blasting through the pack he wore, going through both sides of the aluminum case that held the Com-cells and then burying itself in his Kevlar armor.

It was a lot like being punched and nothing like being killed.

2—The Walton Facility

Deckard paused at the top of the stairs, his mind racing down every possible avenue still left open to him. There weren't many and in seconds he saw that he had only one chance at saving Thuy and it wasn't in a gun battle with

Eng, who not only wore body armor but who would also use Thuy as a human shield.

And despite what Thuy had in mind, Deckard couldn't simply wait until the little group left the fourth floor and then rush up the stairs and chase after them. Even if the zombies didn't tear him apart while he waited, there was too much crap and clutter all over the place. He'd make too much noise and Eng would hear him coming from a mile away and set up an ambush.

No, the only way to kill Eng was to get in front of him, set up an ambush of his own, and take him out with a headshot. There were only four or five hundred "problems" in the way of making that plan a reality, and each of those problems wanted to tear him apart and drink his blood.

"If I'm going to die, I might as well take a few of these bastards with me," Deckard said, and charged down into the zombies, firing his rifle with deadly precision. There were only a few of the beasts on the first set of stairs, but when he got to the next, he saw that the stairwell was flooded with them. They were like a wave of giant grey maggots undulating and writhing, crawling all over themselves in an effort to get up the stairs.

Jaimee Lynn was in among the roaring throng. She was too short to get a good bead on, though in truth, Deckard probably wouldn't have killed her even if he had a perfect shot. Her flashlight was the only source of light. Without it, he would be killed in seconds. With it, he could only hope for a few minutes. It was simple mathematics: he had seven or eight magazines left and he would need at least fifty in order to kill his way to the first floor.

He figured he would have to settle on getting to the second floor, but he didn't come close. The beasts were too many and too wild. They surged upwards at him as he strode down to meet them, firing his gun, raking it back and forth. In the enclosed area, he could hardly miss.

Deckard could shoot faster than they could climb and it wasn't long before he was walking on the backs of the dead, gritting his teeth and cursing in a long, low rumble.

The corpses underfoot threw off his aim and the fight became a slog of black blood and flying lead.

He battled to the third-floor landing and, after rattling off an entire magazine, he squeezed through the door and tried to hold it closed with his body as he attempted to make sense of what was in front of him. There was no true third floor left. Although there were a few walls left standing, the great majority of it had fallen through to the second level. He was standing over a crater. It was the last thing he had expected.

"I'm so fucked," he whispered.

Below him, among the charred ruins, were dozens of zombies. They rushed over to stare up at him. Their mindless rage was horrifying. They didn't care who he was or what he stood for. All they cared about was destroying him completely.

"Ya'll trapped yor-sef, didn't ya, mister?" Jaimee Lynn asked from behind the door. "That there door don't go nowheres."

She wasn't wrong and his hope of sprinting to the next set of stairs and getting in front of Eng was dashed.

This left him with two terrible options. He could scramble along what was left of the wall to a point about thirty yards to his left where the fire had burned through to the fourth floor. If he could climb up there, he had about a fifty-fifty chance of escaping, maybe down the outside of the building, or perhaps, by using a less zombie-filled stairwell. He'd be able to escape, however Thuy would be doomed.

The other option was to tightrope across the top of the remains of the walls. If he could get to the other side of the building, he would find himself looking down on the front parking lot, and perhaps, if the timing was right, he would have a clear shot at Eng.

The major flaw in this plan was that the hunks of walls did not stretch all the way across the building. He would be able to get about halfway before he'd be forced to leap down among the zombies and the piles of burnt crap. From there, he'd have to cheat death long enough to get to the

379

front-facing part of the building, where one wall had fallen onto another, creating a little slope. It would be a very temporary refuge from the beasts and he could only pray that Eng would cross his sights during that time.

Although he figured he had only a five percent chance of living through this second scenario, he took it without hesitation. It was his only chance at rescuing Thuy and perhaps of saving the world.

Deckard, slung his rifle, took a deep breath and let go of the door which, immediately burst open. Zombies came pouring out like champagne from a bottle, most falling to the second floor, landing in an ever-growing pile. In seconds, the pile reached nearly to the ledge.

Those that didn't fall right away gaped as Deckard crossed along a two-foot wide section of flooring that hugged the intact outer wall of the building. The zombies charged after him, but each fell, while he made it to a little shelf that protruded from the wall. He had hoped it would be stable. It wasn't. As soon as he took one step on the remains of the scorched carpet, he could feel everything beneath him begin to crumble.

With a cry, he took two steps and threw himself across an open space, aiming for a length of standing wall. He didn't quite make it and fell onto it chest first, with his boots scrambling along the face wall, while below him the zombies reached out to pull him down. One of his boots inadvertently caught on the head of a zombie and he was able to push himself up using it as leverage.

"Git him!" Jaimee Lynn screamed. She had fallen into the pile with the rest and had only just managed to scramble out from beneath it. Her cry of "Git him" had been a useless waste of breath since the zombies were already doing everything they could to get him. What wasn't useless was the shining flashlight she held on him. It pushed back the gloom of the shadows just enough so he could see where to put his feet as he tiptoed along the five-inch wide path.

Then he ran out of wall. There had to be three-hundred zombies on the second floor by then. Most were still extricating themselves from the massive pile beneath the stairwell door, however there was a swarm of them below him climbing the mounds and heaps, trying to get at him.

There were more of the undead on the left side of the wall than on the right and so he took his rifle and blazed away at those on the right, chopping them down, creating the smallest hole in the crowd to leap into.

He was already reloading as he dropped onto a desk and was firing again within a second: *Bam! Bam! Bam!* He unleashed the full thirty rounds, which gave him barely enough room to dash through. He charged for the sloping wall while black hands tore at his shirt and legs. Something caught him by the ankle and he fell, banging against a jutting machine that was huge and black—it was one of the cafeteria ovens. Having fallen through from the floor above, it was propped up on its side and there was a gap beneath it.

Deckard crawled under the oven, forcing himself along what was little more than a jagged tunnel that tore at his clothes and his flesh. He had no idea if the tunnel even had an exit, but he pushed on, thrusting two-by-fours and drywall out of the way.

Behind him zombies crawled after, scrabbling for his boots. He managed to stay ahead of the closest and when he emerged from the beneath the oven, he found that he had a clear shot at the sloping wall. Without hesitation, he raced for it and at the last second saw there was a huge crack in it running in a diagonal. All he could think was: *I hope it's fucking solid.*

He was halfway up when his right foot went through the wall up to his knee. "Shit! Shit!" he hissed, as he tried to pull his leg up, however the angle was strange and for a panicked moment he was stuck. When he looked back his heart quailed at what he saw. The bloodthirsty monsters, hundreds of them, were piling up around the wall. It was a sea of undead, tearing at each other, tearing at the wall and tearing at anything they could grasp, to get at him.

Never in his life had Deckard's nerve failed him as it did right then—in his heart, he knew he was going to die.

"Shit," he said again, this time quietly. Reloading his M4 with his last magazine, he aimed the gun at the edge of the hole that had gobbled up his lower leg and fired three times. There was a sharp pain in the side of his knee, but he ignored it and used the butt of the M4 to make the hole bigger.

His leg was bleeding, but then again so were his face and hands. He had to be infected. Strangely, this realization calmed him. His fight was over. His days of running for his life were through. He could be done with all of this.

"But not just yet," he said. Reaching up, he jabbed his fingers in the diagonal crack and pulled himself up, leaving a red smear behind. A second later, one of the zombies ran its black tongue over it. Deckard didn't see. He had reached the top of the wall where it had stove in a window, and from there he saw four shadows standing in the parking lot.

He brought up his rifle and sighted on the group, but which was which and who was who? It was midnight and very dark. At a hundred yards, the shadows were mere blobs. Any of them could be Eng. Any of them could be Thuy.

Something grabbed his right boot and yanked him just as one of the blobs lifted something slim and black—it had to be a gun and the person holding it had to be Eng.

Deckard kicked his foot, but the beast had too good of a hold and the next thing he knew, his foot was in the zombie's mouth, and even though his boot was thick leather, there was a crushing pain. And now his other leg was grabbed around the calf and there was searing pain in his ankle.

He tried to fight back, but more and more hands were dragging him down into the pile. "Fuck! No!" he seethed, going wild long enough to get one elbow up on the top of the wall. Bringing the M4 to his cheek, he aimed, however the zombies had him and dragged him down. He yelled in fury and strained with all his might to hold himself rigid and there was one split second where he had the M4 at arm's length and his eye stared straight down the barrel from the back sight to the front—and Eng was his target. A mere blob.

Deckard pulled the trigger and never in his life was his aim more true. And it never would be again.

The 5.56 mm bullet rifled through the air and through Eng's pack and into his Kevlar vest. He was thrown forward by the force of the blow and fell into Katherine, who was only just reacting. She went for his weapon knowing this was her one chance. In the dark, the struggle was awkward, uncertain and desperate. They wrestled for the gun, rolling around along the broken pavement, and although the two were equally well trained and similar in speed, gradually Eng's greater strength became the deciding factor.

He yanked the gun from her hands and stood over her ready to shoot, only right then they could hear one of the Blackhawk's engines spooling up, running faster. "I'll kill this one, you kill Thuy," Eng said to Anna. "Or maybe do her in the guts. That's what she deserve…" Eng had glanced back and, when he saw Anna's M4 pointed at him, his words dried up.

Anna fired three times into his chest and this time the Kevlar didn't stop the bullets. He fell back, staring at the sky with wide, shocked eyes. Anna then swung the gun around and pointed it at Thuy, who was so shocked by the shooting that she couldn't breathe.

"I'm not a bad guy," Anna said. "Do you believe me?" Thuy was looking at a mass-murderer, she didn't know what to say. "Tell me you believe me!" Anna ordered, her hand squeezing down on the trigger almost to the firing point.

"I-I believe you," Thuy said.

Suddenly the bore of the gun dropped away and Anna smiled behind her mask. "Good, because I want to be friends. I want the two of us to save the world. We should get going."

Thuy's legs were jello and her mind was empty, save for a single question that replayed itself over and over:

Where's Deckard? Where's Deckard? She stared at the facility, not realizing that she was being dragged to the helicopter by a beaming Anna Holloway. Behind them, Katherine ran to catch up, not knowing what the hell had just happened, but just knowing she was lucky to be alive.

A crew member tried to hoist Thuy in, but she stopped him and despite Axelrod yelling for her to get in the chopper, she looked back at the building one last time, hoping and praying that Deckard would suddenly come running out, waving an arm and smiling that serious smile of his. But he did not come out. The building and the things within it had swallowed him up.

Epilogue

The President leaned back in his three-thousand dollar, black leather swivel chair and gazed at the maps. He was in charge now. He was the Commander in Chief! He had broken the back of the coup and now he was the one making the decisions.

There had been a moment where he thought his nerve would fail him, that without Marty Aleman he wouldn't know what to say or do. The moment had passed quickly as he gave his first command: "Because the military can't be trusted, from now on each unit from the company level on up will have political officers assigned to them. All decisions must first go through the political officers."

His new group of advisors, chosen exclusively from his own party, had given him the highest praise for the command. Puffed up almost to the point of strutting, he had next demanded that all new operations and troop movements be put on hold until the political officers were in place. It seemed logical since there was no way to know where the next rebellion would take place.

This order led to outrage among the remaining generals, which in turn had led to a new round of arrests.

On the Pennsylvania front, General Thomas Merriweather, the commander of the 28th Infantry Division, who was in the process of moving two infantry regiments and a militia regiment from the quiet northern part of the line to the heavily engaged southern part of the line near Philadelphia, ignored the order and was scheduled to be arrested.

Knowing that the troop movements were vital to maintaining the line, Merriweather resisted the arrest order and he and most of his staff were killed in a drone strike ordered by the President.

The new commander, a general pulled from behind a desk in the Pentagon, chose the sanctity of his own life over that of his men. The three regiments were stopped in place and as a result, Lancaster was overrun and all of eastern Pennsylvania to the Susquehanna River was lost. Both General Phillips and General Merriweather were blamed for the thousands who died.

"Our soldiers were heroes," the President said when describing the event to the White House pool reporters. He proved he didn't need Marty Aleman when he shed a tear on cue. "They lived as heroes and they died as heroes." Actually, they died in the dark, abandoned by their government and surrounded by teaming hordes that ripped them to pieces in a bloody orgy of death—but that didn't sound as good as the speech he had prepared.

Once his midnight presser was complete, the President slid into his expensive chair in the Situation Room, ordered a cup of black coffee and a club sandwich, without the crusts, and sat back to ponder the war map…the real war map, not the bullshit map that Heider and Phillips and all the others had tried to pass off to keep him in the dark.

The real war map showed the real danger, and the real danger wasn't in losing eastern Pennsylvania, which, as far as he knew, held nothing of actual value outside his voting bloc in Philadelphia. And it wasn't in Massachusetts where he was certain the entire notion of rebellion originated, as King George the Third undoubtedly could attest to.

No, the real danger to the country was only forty-five miles away from the White House itself. Already the northern reaches of Maryland were being hit by the zombies, and there wasn't much holding them back besides a few measly rivers.

"How many men do we have on this stretch of the Susquehanna?" He pointed to a length of the river that cut across northern Maryland.

It took the junior officer ten minutes to hunt down the answer. "About three thousand. I know it doesn't seem like a lot, but the river is almost four-hundred yards across at that point."

"I don't care if it is ten miles across. Do you know many of those…those zombies are on the other side?" The junior officer swallowed with a clicking sound and shook his head. "Then find out!" the President ordered.

Another ten minutes went by before he could answer, "Two to three hundred thousand, sir."

The President had just taken a bite of his club sandwich. He chewed and then wiped his hands on his napkin before saying, "That's my point. It's a hundred to one odds. That's unacceptable. Don't you agree?" The junior officer swallowed again and then nodded. "Exactly," the President said, "and here's what we're going to do about it: we're going to bomb the living daylights out of them."

"Yes, sir."

"I want every bomber. I want every fighter and every missile and every UAV bombing the fuck out of those zombies. Is that clear? No exceptions."

It was an easy order to give while sitting in the climate controlled Situation Room on a three-thousand dollar, black leather chair, while eating a crustless club sandwich and sipping coffee.

Sergeant Troy Ross of the 101st Airborne Division found the repercussions much harder to deal with. He'd been awake for the last forty-eight hours and fighting for his life for thirty-seven of those hours. In the face of an army of undead that dwarfed the remains of his division, he and his worn-out men had already retreated three times since sundown.

They were dragging from the strain of the endless battle. They were so low on ammunition that they had to wait to shoot until the dead were practically on top of them. They were without reinforcements unless they considered the skinny farm boys with their deer rifles and their fourteen bullets, as reinforcements. And, they had nothing to eat for hours until a bunch of old grandmas appeared carrying big pots full of soup or stew. Occasionally, these same old women dared the battlefield with backpacks full of apples or pears or tortilla chips. The men and women on the line ate whatever was offered and they were thankful.

It was obvious to Ross that the line couldn't hold without airpower and when the President took it away, a fifty mile stretch disintegrated. In minutes, Sergeant Ross was no longer a company commander. He wasn't even a platoon leader. He was just one man standing in the breach so the rest could flee and find whatever shelter they could.

When the President heard about the debacle, he said to the junior officer, "That's what they get for rebelling against the President of the United States of America. Maybe the other states will fall in line and finally respect my authority. Isn't that right?"

"Yes sir," the junior officer answered, in a hollow whisper.

Right at that moment, the President was the ultimate master of life and death, and he knew it. He had finally achieved greatness!

"Yes," he said, with a beaming smile. "It is right and that's because I am right." It was as simple as that in his mind.

Half a world away, Truong Mai was an abject representative of humanity. There wasn't much left to him. The radiation from the nuclear bombs had taken all of his toes and three of the fingers on his right hand. His left arm had been sloughing off bit by bit and it was now only a stump. He had one eye left, no ears, lips or nose. He was a walking horror to look upon, if there had been anyone to see him. He had walked twenty miles and hadn't seen a soul.

The countryside of China was vast and seemingly empty. The people had fled into the interior, most on foot. They had walked all night with whatever possessions they could carry. Some had televisions on their backs, some had family heirlooms. Most had luggage. They had been weighed down and after twenty miles, they couldn't go any further.

There were five million refugees strung out in a wide arc surrounding the blast zone—and Truong walked square into the middle of that arc. People were everywhere, mostly sleeping, but a few were cooking over smoky little fires. They thought they were safe, after all, the government had declared victory. A new holiday was being created and parades were being planned.

Not one of the peasants cared about such things. All they cared about was what they were going to eat that night, where they were going to live and what had happened to Uncle Qe or Cousin Soun? Parades were for capital people, not for peasants in the provinces.

Truong had his pick of victims, but he wasn't choosey. He fell on the first person he came to, a middle-aged man with a bowl haircut, swollen feet and a saggy belly that was painfully empty. He had been sleeping in the shade of a willow with twenty others and they all came awake when he suddenly screamed.

His scream was out of revulsion and not pain. Truong's few remaining teeth had fallen from his rotted gums the moment he had bitten down. They had barely broken the skin, only a tiny scratch—but that was all it took for everything to start all over again.

The End

**
Author's Note

Thank you so much for reading The Apocalypse Crusade, Day 4. I sincerely hope that you enjoyed it. If so, I would greatly appreciate it if you would, please, take the time to write a kind review on Amazon and your Facebook page.

Peter Meredith

PS If you are interested in autographed copies of my books, souvenir posters of the covers, Apocalypse T-shirts

and other awesome swag, please visit my website at
https://www.petemeredith1.com

Yes, there will be a Crusade Day 5, but while you are waiting, you're probably wondering what to read in the meantime. You could go with my *Undead World* novels that have over 2,000- five star reviews. A lot of people seem to like them. Or you might try my new series: *The Gods of the Undead*, but be forewarned: there is an obscene amount of blood spilled and skin flayed and love lost and all sorts of sadness. On the other hand there are also heroes and heroines, bravery and sacrifice. And there's adventure that spans the world as two people fight the undead from New York to darkest Africa.

As many stories do, it starts small with just one man.

The Edge of Hell

Gods of the Undead, A Post-Apocalyptic Epic

Prologue
Alex Wilson

Officer Alex Wilson had to pull his cruiser over. He didn't need to, he had to. It didn't matter that he was in the middle of a southbound lane on the FDR Drive. He had to see and he had to hear for himself what was happening.

He pulled over and cut the siren. He left the lights on, whipping around, cutting the night in blinding red and blue. At first, all he heard was the insane babble of the dispatchers—in three years on the force, he had never once heard fear in their voices. Normally, they spoke in lackluster tones that suggested they were bored to tears with their jobs.

Now, they were screaming into their mikes, ordering units from all over the city to converge on the bridges that spanned the East River, connecting Queens to Manhattan.

"What's happening?" someone demanded over the radio. "Dispatch, say again, what's happening?"

"I don't know...I don't know. I'm not supposed to tell, but...but they're monsters, I think," was the strange reply the unknown officer received.

Alex flicked off the radio and sat still, with his head cocked to one side. Even through the heavy glass, he could hear the pop, pop, pop of gunfire, only it wasn't just: pop, pop, pop. It was a thousand pops going off all at once. Feeling a sudden churn in his guts, he climbed out of the cruiser and the sound of the battle assaulted him. He was a mile away, with a wide river between him and the fire-fight and still the sound was frightfully urgent.

He didn't rush off, however. The churning in his guts intensified, and he slowly climbed back into the cruiser. "Son of a bitch," he whispered, and then stuck the car in gear. Gradually, he built up speed and far too soon for his liking, he was at the Queensboro Bridge and being directed to heel his cruiser in next to a row of forty others.

Even as he pulled in, another cruiser squeezed right up next to him and another pulled up next to that one. He slid out of the car, feeling his stomach twist, going beyond churning; it was a curdling sensation that made him feel sick.

The officer in the next cruiser beat him out, rushing to pop his trunk. "What is it?" he asked, as Alex reluctantly opened the trunk on his cruiser.

Alex couldn't answer at first; the sound of the guns firing was now mingled with screams. So many screams. "I-I don't know," he said, after taking a gulp of air.

"They said monsters," another officer said, a fake little laugh in his voice. It was a high, oddly girlish sound as if someone had a good hold of his balls and was giving them a healthy tweak.

Another officer further down the row of cruisers, was screaming: "Masks! Get your damn masks on! Come on, damn it!"

Masks meant there were germs in the air…zombie germs. The idea that just breathing could turn him into one of them was horrible and Alex dug in his trunk for his protective mask. It came in a pouch that he buckled around his waist. It took three tries to snap in place, and as he struggled with the simple buckle, the sound of the firing came closer and the screams grew ever more urgent and loud. People were dying right on the bridge and yet Alex felt as though he was moving in slow motion. He couldn't seem to get his feet moving despite the urgency in the air.

Some of the officers were pulling on their masks and others were hauling out shotguns or Colt M4s. Alex only had his 9mm Sig Sauer P226 and it felt altogether puny, certainly too puny to use against an army of undead.

He needed something bigger: a machine gun or a grenade launcher. Anything would be better than the pistol. "Hey," he hissed to the officer who had pulled in next to him. "You don't happen to have a…"

Just then, someone turned him around and screamed in his face: "Get to the line! Hurry!"

Alex was pushed and shoved onto the bridge where his fellow officers were lined up. There were forty or fifty of them, all looking green, all sweating and scared. Alex was sure he looked just as terrified. His hands shook as he tried to check on his second magazine. It dropped, clinking on the cement. Frantically, he scrambled for it. He was deathly afraid, but of what exactly, he didn't know. He had no idea what they were facing and yet he was practically pissing himself.

Questions ran up and down the line: "What's going on? What's happening? What are they? Are they really zombies? Really?"

No one knew, but it wasn't long before they found out.

The bridge stretched east toward Queens. Normally, a person could see across the half-mile span without a problem but just then, the far end couldn't be seen. A swirling black cloud engulfed it. And it didn't just hover over it, it advanced against a gentle westerly wind.

Within that unnatural black cloud were creatures masquerading as people. They shambled forward, bringing with them a horrid stench of decay. It was so bad that even the veterans of a hundred murder scenes ripped their masks out of their holders and pulled them on.

Gagging from the stench, Alex held his mask to his face, but didn't put it on. The mask would cloud his vision and he needed to see what he was dealing with. Monsters was what the dispatcher had said. Seconds later, he saw that she had been wrong. These weren't exactly monsters —they were zombies. They could be nothing else.

The creatures stumbling though the swirling darkness had been people at one time, only now they were the living dead. They were corpses somehow imbued with life. They limped along, dragging ropes of intestine and leaving long trails of blood and pus behind them. Their decayed and rotting flesh hung in ribbons off their bleached bones.

They were horrors that had no right to be alive and there were thousands of them.

Someone yelled: "They-they're zombies! Aim for the head!"

Alex was way ahead of him. He had the mask in one hand and the Sig Sauer in the other. He peered down the iron sights, waiting until the leading wave of monsters was within thirty yards. He couldn't miss from that distance.

A captain screamed: "Fire!" The line of officers let loose with a ragged volley, some using handguns, some shotguns and some M4s. Those zombies in the first line were staggered, many falling, causing the wave of undead to slow as it stumbled over them. More shots created more mayhem and the bridge became an obstacle course of black blood and rotting limbs which slowed the attacking monsters even more.

Alex shot his Sig Sauer dry and in the three seconds it took to reload, the zombies were ten yards closer.

Strangely, the thunder of the guns going off all around him and the acrid stench of the spent gunpowder calmed his nerves to a degree.

It didn't last.

A foul creature, grey and stinking of death, pushed itself over the mound of wriggling bodies and came for Alex. He aimed and fired, certain that he had hit the zombie in the head; however, it didn't fall or even slow.

"What the hell?" he whispered, and took aim again. Now, at twenty yards he knew he was a good enough marksman to plug the bitch dead center. He caressed the trigger, a shock that ran up his arm to his shoulder, and he saw the thing's head rock back, bone and brain and unknown crap flying onto the bridge.

Again, it didn't fall. It just kept coming closer and closer, close enough that Alex could see a gaping hole just off center in its forehead.

Alex wasn't the only one just realizing that things were far worse than they realized.

"Oh, my God!" someone screamed. "They're not dying!"

That wasn't possible. In the course of the last two hours, the world had been turned on its head. These were zombies, flesh-eating, brain-chomping, undead zombies and everyone knew that you could kill a zombie with a head-shot. That was supposedly, a fact, and yet the zombies kept coming, seemingly impervious to any bullet. Even the creatures that had collapsed earlier, were fighting their way to their feet.

Movement out of the corner of his eye had Alex turning. Some of the men were running away! Everything was suddenly chaos. A few men ran, a few fired their weapons, a few stood there not knowing what to do.

Alex glanced down at his Sig Sauer for a brief moment, tempted to toss it away and run, but he managed to swallow his fear long enough to empty the gun into the corpse that was now only ten yards away. The 9mm blazed with orange flame as Alex hit the zombie with every round. It jerked with each strike, coming to a standstill almost within reach. Then the two just stared at each other; Alex trying to come to grips with this new reality, and the zombie trying to stand with a body that had been torn to shreds.

An officer standing next to Alex waggled his head side to side, saying: "That ain't possible," while holding his pistol loosely in slack hands.

Another officer, this one a round-bellied sergeant who had been too long at the desk, yelled: "Keep Firing! Keep firing!" He had a shotgun and when he pulled the trigger, the zombie in front of Alex flew back, its head coming off its shoulders. Every time the sergeant squeezed the trigger on the gun, his belly would jiggle and a zombie was blasted back.

Alex watched him with one thought in his head: I'm going to die. There were too many zombies and not enough men with shotguns. He started backing away. With only a pistol, he didn't think he stood a chance. A second later, it rattled on the pavement as he turned to run. The sergeant caught him.

"Stand your ground!" he roared, into Alex's face.

"Give me your gun and I will!" Alex yelled right back. It was suicide to stand there with only a pistol. Already, a dozen officers were screaming with zombies latched onto them, tearing them to pieces with their teeth alone. Those officers with shotguns and M4s were able to hold back the flood of walking corpses, but anyone with only a pistol was already running or dead.

The sergeant hesitated, seeing the truth of the situation around him, but somehow, he found the courage to hold out the shotgun. Alex eagerly snatched it and began blasting the walking dead. The shotgun was like a cannon, it thundered and flashed with every pull of the trigger, throwing body parts into the air.

He fired over and over, his hands growing numb, the corpses piling up in front of him in a mound. When his gun ran dry, he fed shells from the bandolier on the strap, he had twelve shots left—they went in less than a minute. He turned to yell for more ammo, only to realize that he was all alone.

The line of officers had fallen. Some men had run off and some were being fed on by the creatures. The lucky ones had their throats torn out, the unlucky ones were being eaten alive, screaming at the top of their lungs.

Alex spun, desperate to escape; however, before he could take his second step, a grey hand with bloody fingers reached out from the pile of corpses and grabbed his ankle. He went down, the empty shotgun flying from his grasp. He tried to pull away, only the zombie had a grip of iron and a strength that was irresistible.

Slowly, Alex was dragged to the mound of corpses and pulled under, his screams growing more and more muffled until he was buried entirely and the teeth of a dozen zombies tore into him.

Fictional works by Peter Meredith: